HARLEY WAS TROUBLE. . . .

"It's late," he tersely announced. "I'd better get you back to your hotel." He searched the street, spotted an empty cab, and summoned it with sheer willpower. He had to ditch her fast.

He forcibly entrenched himself in his sane, reasonable, gentlemanly self on the ride back to the Millenium. He politely chatted with Harley about Oscar Wilde plays as they rode the hotel elevator to the thirty-seventh floor. He waited until she had inserted her room card key and had safely opened the door.

"Thank you for a lovely evening," he said, shaking her hand.

He had thought that, at least, would be safe.

He had never been more wrong about anything in his life.

Her fingers, as they trembled against his hand, imparted an electrical jolt that fried his brain and sent all the wrong messages throughout his body. He was standing there in the Millenium hallway, raising her hand, watching her eyes widen with shock and hunger as he pressed his mouth to the tender center of her palm.

"Duncan!"

It was a whisper. It was a moan. It fulfilled too many of his fantasies. . . .

ALSO BY MICHELLE MARTIN

Stolen Hearts

AVAILABLE FROM
BANTAM BOOKS

BANTAM BOOKS

New York Toronto

London Sydney

Auckland

STOLEN

MOMENTS

MICHELLE

MARTIN

STOLEN MOMENTS

A Bantam Fanfare Book / December 1997

ISBN 0-553-57649-6

Published simultaneously in the United States and Canada

*Bantam Books are published by Bantam Books, a division of Bantam
Doubleday Dell Publishing Group, Inc. Its trademark, consisting of the words
"Bantam Books" and the portrayal of a rooster, is Registered in U.S. Patent
and Trademark Office and in other countries. Marca Registrada. Bantam
Books, 1540 Broadway, New York, New York 10036.*

PRINTED IN THE UNITED STATES OF AMERICA

OPM 0 9 8 7 6 5 4 3 2 1

Prologue

She could hear herself shaking within the dark blue rain-coat she had borrowed from Annie. Her telltale strawberry blond hair was twisted into a bun and tucked under Annie's hat. Annie's one-size-too-big navy pumps were on her feet. The disguise wouldn't work. Boyd would catch her. He'd stop her.

"I can't do this," she whispered.

But she opened the suite door anyway and stepped between Steve and Rick, her towering bodyguards. All one of them had to do was clamp a massive hand on her shoulder and . . .

Ducking her head a little, she nodded at the two stone-faced men and somehow made it to the elevator. Fingers trembling, she pushed the elevator call button once, twice, three times, and then sent up ardent, silent prayers that Rick and Steve wouldn't see the neon sign radiating around her: *She's getting away! Stop her!*

She heard the elevator coming, the soft clunk as it reached her floor, and surreptitiously looked around. She couldn't believe it—Rick and Steve looked bored. They were buying this!

The elevator doors slid open and she stumbled inside. She pressed the lobby button and, eyes glued to the floor, silently urged the doors to close and close now. They took a moment, then slid shut. The elevator began carrying her down through the Ritz-Carlton. Her fingers fumbled as they opened the top button of the raincoat. She grabbed her gold pendant and hung on for dear life. It had been her good luck charm for nine years. If she'd ever needed it to work, she needed it to work now.

She let herself take a breath and looked up to see her tense reflection in the brass plating of the control panel. This was insane. This couldn't possibly work.

A gentle settling, the doors opened, and she saw Boyd smiling at her.

A hand flew to her mouth to stifle her agonized cry in the same moment she realized the man wasn't Boyd. He was too tall. With a small gasp, she stumbled out into the rectangular hotel lobby, and the stranger stepped into the elevator. She looked frantically around, expecting Boyd to leap out at her from every corner. Two chandeliers cast a warm glow on framed antique tapestries and paintings. There was no one. Legs wobbling, she crossed the marble floor, not daring to even glance at the night desk clerk.

"Good evening, Miss Maguire," said the tall, discreetly muscular doorman as he held the glass front door open for her.

Pull yourself together, she ordered herself. *You're almost free.* She nodded at the doorman. "Evenin'," she said with Annie's faint Irish brogue.

"Would you like a cab?"

"Please."

She hadn't been on her own in nine years. She wasn't about to go walking around Manhattan alone after midnight. She wasn't that crazy, or that brave.

There weren't many cabs out at this hour, but Ritz doormen had special powers. In less than twenty seconds, a yellow taxi pulled to a stop before her at the curb. She stared at it, vibrating with excitement. She was doing it. She was really doing it! The doorman held the car door open for her and she climbed in to the cab's back seat.

"Where to, lady?" the cabbie asked with a pronounced Bronx accent.

"Jane!"

Boyd—flanked by Rick and Steve—was storming out of the Ritz lobby.

"Lock the doors! Lock the doors!" she screamed to the cabbie as she clutched at her door handle.

Boyd's ferocious face was pressed against the door window as he bellowed hateful, ugly words at her. She could feel him pulling on the door handle. He was pulling the door open. He was going to drag her back. He was going to win.

"Drive *now,*" she yelled to the cabbie, "and there's an extra fifty in it for you!"

Tires squealed as the cab shot out into the late night traffic.

CHAPTER ONE

With a song in his heart, Duncan Lang stepped out of the yellow cab at the conservative dark blue awning of the Ritz-Carlton. A doorman in a conservative dark blue uniform held a glass door open for him.

"A pleasure to see you again, Mr. Lang."

"Thanks, Charlie," Duncan said with a grin at the doorman. "You've got a good memory."

"You were always a generous tipper, Mr. Lang."

Duncan chuckled. "Ah, my carefree youth. I'm afraid I'm a working stiff now, Charlie."

"Sorry to hear it, Mr. Lang."

Truth to tell, Duncan had been sorry too . . . until this morning's frantic phone call from Boyd Monroe.

He walked down into the small, rectangular Ritz lobby, liking its intimacy. There was a lot to be said for quiet elegance.

He stepped into the small wood-paneled elevator and rode up to the twenty-third floor, thinking about the first time he had visited the Ritz. It had been summer vacation. He'd been nineteen and riding this very elevator up to the Ritz-Carlton Suite to enjoy a midnight rendezvous with the delightfully demanding Comtesse Pichaud. They had met at one of his mother's boring parties and had . . . hit it off. The last time he'd visited the Ritz was over two years ago, to spend an equally delightful champagne weekend with Charmaine Relker.

As the elevator settled on the twenty-third floor, however, Duncan shoved the adventurous Miss Relker from his thoughts. He was about to embark on the first important job of his so-called career. He wasn't going to blow it by letting his mind wander libidinously through his past. Instead he was going to direct every ounce of concentration on his client. He had a lot to prove. It was time he began.

He stepped out of the elevator and walked up to the white door of the Ritz-Carlton Suite. He knocked three times and waited. Scant seconds passed before the door was jerked open by a glowering man who stood at only five feet seven inches, his body trim and compact, his graying brown hair cut almost to the scalp. He wore cowboy boots, tan slacks, a green shirt, and an innocuous brown sports coat. Most people would have walked right past him in a crowd and never noticed him.

But a life in the fast lane—no matter what his father said—had taught Duncan a thing or two. The gentleman reminded him of a German count he had met once, a control freak *par excellence* who had specified the exact temperature of the wine he wanted at dinner and had screamed at his waiter because the asparagus had not been arranged properly on his plate.

"Who the hell are you?" his client barked.

"I'm Duncan Lang from Colangco International, Mr. Monroe. I hope you haven't been waiting long."

"Duncan . . . ?" Boyd Monroe sputtered. "I don't want *you.* I want *Brandon* Lang. I *expect* Brandon Lang!"

"I'm sorry, Mr. Monroe, but my brother is out of town on another case. I assure you that I—"

Mr. Monroe was turning an unattractive shade of vermilion. "I've heard Brandon Lang is the best and I want the best!"

Duncan had heard this song too many times in his life. "Well, you can't have him," he stated. "Brandon is contractually committed to another client. If you would like to wait for his services, I believe he'll be back in New York sometime next week. Good day, Mr. Monroe." Duncan turned away.

"No, wait!" Monroe yelled, grabbing his arm in a bone-crunching grip.

Duncan hid his smile. His years of experience wooing flighty paramours was paying off once again. "Yes?" he said.

Boyd Monroe glared at him. "I suppose you'll have to do."

"Thank you," Duncan replied, walking into the living room and glancing around. The Ritz had redecorated the suite since he had dallied with Charmaine. The living room was now mauve with white, gold-trimmed antique furniture tastefully arranged around the marble fireplace, but of course there was still the stunning Central Park view. He glanced through the terrace windows at the luxuriant ribbon of green rolling out through the heart of the city. He hadn't really had a chance to enjoy the view on his last visit. Miss Relker had kept him much too busy.

"Sit down and let's get to work," Boyd Monroe ordered. "Jane's been gone nearly nine hours. God knows what's happened to her."

Duncan glanced at his client as he sat down on the sofa. Boyd Monroe was an overgrown bulldog. He would not be pleasant to work with.

Still, it was a job, and a big one. The Princess of Pop didn't disappear every day. He pulled from his inside coat pocket a small notebook and the Mont Blanc pen his mother had given him last Christmas, crossed one leg over the other, and adopted his most professional expression. "You said on the phone that Miss Miller left in a cab just after midnight last night?"

"That's right," Monroe grunted as he sat down in a chair opposite Duncan.

"Did you get the cab number?"

"No."

"Perhaps her bodyguards . . . ?"

"They didn't either."

"Perhaps I could speak to them for a moment?"

"I fired them."

"Of course," Duncan murmured. The bodyguards were probably lucky they hadn't been vivisected. "You mentioned on the phone that Miss Miller wore a disguise to slip past her two bodyguards?"

"It wasn't that elaborate. Just her maid's hat and raincoat. Oh, and her shoes."

"And her maid is . . . ?"

"Annie Maguire. It won't do you any good talking to her. She was in bed with the flu when Jane left."

"Perhaps she spoke with Miss Miller before going to bed, or heard something. I'd—"

"No," Monroe said flatly.

"Strike two," Duncan murmured softly to himself. "It would help me, Mr. Monroe, if you could go over the events of last night."

Boyd Monroe leaned back in his chair, thrust his expensive cowboy boots out before him, and scowled. It was not an attractive sight. "Jane did the last concert of her world tour at Madison Square Garden."

"Did anything happen there to upset her?"

"No."

Duncan had heard that word too many times in his life not to recognize when there was something behind it. "And after the concert?"

"We took the limo back here."

"No end-of-the-tour party? No signing autographs for devoted fans?"

"I don't allow Jane to associate with the minions, and I won't have her signing autographs. She'd be mobbed."

"I see," Duncan murmured. *Minions?* "During the limo ride back to the Ritz, did Miss Miller say anything to indicate that she was planning to leave?"

"Nothing. We just had the same old conversation."

"And that would be . . . ?"

"Whenever we come to New York, she always wants to go window-shopping down Madison Avenue."

"And you said no?"

"Of course I said no!" Monroe barked. "She'd be recognized in two seconds. Besides, there wasn't time. We were going to catch a one o'clock plane back to Los Angeles today. She's supposed to walk into a recording studio tomorrow."

"A tight schedule," Duncan observed.

"She's got to finish out her Sony contract by the end of the year, and she owes them one more album."

"Ah. Did you talk about anything else?"

Monroe shrugged in disgust. "Oh, she's been on a rag lately about changing her music. You've got to understand that I discovered her when she was seventeen and planning to become some sort of rock-and-roll hellion. I soon took care of that idiocy, but the rock-and-roll fantasy still pops up now and again. She's even been balking at signing a new contract with Sony, because she actually thinks she can cut it as a rock singer, that's how little she's grounded in reality."

From the wispy Jane Miller songs he had occasionally heard on the radio, Duncan would have to agree. The lady was not astute about her musical abilities. "Okay. And what happened when Miss Miller got back to this suite last night?"

"The usual. Annie was here and had her bath ready and her supper waiting."

"Did Miss Miller appear in any way unhappy or unlike herself?"

"Oh, she started some stupid argument about her supper."

"Her supper?"

"She'd had Annie send out for a cheeseburger, fries, and shake."

"And you said no," Duncan guessed, beginning to have a pretty good understanding of Jane Miller's manager.

"Of course I said no! I will not have her eating greasy red meat. It's disastrous for her digestion and her complexion. And she doesn't need the calories from the french fries and milk shake."

"I wasn't aware Miss Miller had a weight problem."

"She doesn't, and I intend to make sure she doesn't develop one. I had Annie order a lobster salad from room service."

"And Miss Miller objected?"

Boyd Monroe sighed heavily. "You've got to understand, Lang, that Jane Miller is basically a spoiled and demanding child. She throws a tantrum whenever she doesn't get what she wants. It's my job to make sure she doesn't get anything that will harm her. Conflict is inevitable."

"I see. Did anything else happen?"

Monroe scowled impatiently at him. "Annie placed the room service order and then went to bed. Like I said, she had the flu. I reminded Jane about today's plane and told her she could sleep in as late as she wanted this morning, then I said good night and went down the hall to my own suite."

"What made you suspect that Miss Miller was planning to leave?"

"Nothing," Monroe said in disgust. "About ten minutes later, I realized I'd forgotten to tell her about the press conference I'd scheduled for when we landed at LAX today. So I went back to her suite. It took a minute, but Annie finally answered the door, and that's when we found that Jane was missing. I dragged those two idiot bodyguards down to the lobby to try to catch her. She was getting in a cab. I shouted at her, but she drove off."

"And that's the last time you saw Miss Miller?"

"That's right."

"Did she leave any sort of a note?"

Monroe pulled a badly crumpled piece of Ritz stationery from his pocket and handed it to Duncan. It was all Duncan could do not to smile. Jane Miller's testy manager had obviously wadded the note up and hurled it against an unforgiving wall when he'd found that his bird had flown. He had probably even stomped on it a few times.

The handwriting surprised Duncan. It was tight and cramped, not at all the flowery and feminine handwriting he had expected from the renowned Princess of Pop. It was also brief and to the point.

Dear Boyd:
I told you I need a holiday and I'm taking one. I'll be riding the rails around the country for the next two weeks. Then I'll head for L.A. and cut the album. Don't worry.
Harley

"Harley?" Duncan said, handing the note back to Boyd.

"Her full name is Harley Jane Miller. I made her drop the Harley when I became her manager. It didn't convey the right image to the audience I wanted for Jane."

"Ah." Harley Jane Miller called herself Harley; her manager called her Jane. Interesting. Duncan considered his custom-made Loebs shoes for a moment. "Does she have any friends she might go to or who might help her?"

"No. Her work schedule keeps her too busy to do any socializing."

"What about family?"

"There's only her mother in Oklahoma. I called. Barbara hasn't heard from Jane since she left."

"As I understand it, Miss Miller is twenty-six years old and has just completed a three-month world tour. It makes sense that she would want to take a holiday to relax and regroup before going back into the studio to cut a new album."

"We're scheduled for a vacation in the Caribbean in three months," Monroe said flatly. "She knows that."

We? Duncan surreptitiously studied his client. Were Boyd Monroe and Jane Miller an item? He hadn't seen anything about it in the gossip rags, and they would have printed even the faintest wisp of a rumor. He noted the taut way Monroe held himself in his chair. No, from what he'd just heard and seen, Monroe was the overbearing father and Miss Miller the truculent child. Monroe wasn't using sex to hold her. He had staked everything on parental control, and it seemed to have worked, until now.

"What you don't understand, Lang," Monroe continued, "is that Jane Miller may well be twenty-six years old, but she's as innocent and naive as the day she was born. She has no idea how to take care of herself in the real world, therefore she is in danger every minute she's gone, and that's why you have to find her immediately. That means now, Lang. You've got forty-eight hours and then I call in the police."

"I don't foresee any trouble," Duncan said mildly as he stood up. "Colangco International's resources would put James Bond to shame. I'll need a recent photo of Miss Miller to begin. A publicity shot will be fine. There are undoubtedly a few shut-ins who don't know what she looks like."

"With her face plastered across a Times Square billboard?" Monroe demanded in disbelief.

"A photo would be helpful."

Grumbling, Monroe pulled an eight-by-ten glossy from his briefcase. Duncan took the picture and studied it a moment. Jane Miller's famous turquoise blue eyes stared back at him. Strawberry blond hair tumbled down past her shoulders. She looked like what her unpleasant manager said she was: a sweet, innocent, even virginal girl. Monroe was right. She'd never make it in the real world. He'd have to find her fast.

"Do you need anything else?" Mr. Monroe seemed eager to shove Duncan out the door.

"I'd like a moment to look around the suite, if you don't mind."

"You won't find anything."

It must be nice, Duncan thought, to live in such a certain world. "It'll just take a second," he said, standing up.

The living room and dining room were bare of any personal effects. The door to Annie Maguire's room was closed. The Princess of Pop's bedroom held more interest. An acoustic guitar stood in an armchair in the far corner of the room. Current issues of six different newsmagazines were stacked on one bedside table. On the other were four books, all pulled from the current nonfiction bestseller list.

"Miss Miller seems to be an avid reader," Duncan commented.

"I insist on it," Monroe said from the doorway. "She's got to be able to talk knowledgeably at any of the big social functions she has to attend."

"I thought you said she doesn't socialize."

"She doesn't. Those parties and dinners are strictly business."

"I'll just bet they are," Duncan said under his breath. The Princess of Pop's life seemed to be compressed into a cramped gilded cage. He glanced through the dresser drawers and found very simple bras and panties, nothing overtly sensual. He doubted if Monroe would have tolerated sexuality impinging on Miss Miller's sweet image. "Anything missing?"

"Annie says not."

"What about money? How is Miss Miller fixed for cash or credit cards?"

"She doesn't have anything with her. I manage her bank accounts and her credit cards. Nothing is missing."

Duncan doubted if Boyd Monroe had ever let his client even touch one of the credit cards in her name. "What about her passport?"

"In my room safe."

"Driver's license?"

"She doesn't have one."

Duncan turned inquiringly from the bathroom door. "She can't drive?"

"She can. I won't let her. She needs a professional driver in case of any kidnapping or car-jacking attempts."

"Of course," Duncan murmured. Wonderful. Surly *and* paranoid. He walked into the marble bathroom. A quick scan showed shampoo and conditioner, various lotions and bottles of makeup. Interesting. She hadn't taken her makeup. But she had taken her toothbrush. And her brush and comb. The lady was traveling light.

"Well, that should do it," Duncan said, walking out of the bathroom and into the bedroom again. "I assume you've canceled your flight and will be staying at the Ritz for now. I'll contact you at least once a day to let you know how I'm progressing on the case. I don't anticipate any difficulties."

"Just get her back," Monroe said, leading him into the living room, "and get her back fast."

"Guaranteed," Duncan said smoothly. "If you'll just sign this letter of agreement, I'll be on my way."

He handed the standard two-page contract to Mr. Monroe, who read it line for line. The words "anal retentive" sprang to Duncan's mind. Thin lips tightly compressed, his new client finally pulled a gold pen from his jacket pocket and signed on the dotted line. The "Hallelujah Chorus" rang out in Duncan's ears. This was even a bigger case than his brother was working on. His father would love the international publicity. His mother would love the cachet of association with the upper echelons of the music industry. Duncan had never had a better win-win situation in his life. Finally he had a chance to prove that he could play by the Colangco rule book and succeed. His dim future began to brighten.

He tucked the contract back into his pocket, bid his client goodbye, and walked out of the suite. As he stood in the hall waiting for the elevator, his lungs began filling easily with air once again. There was a definite pleasure in leaving Boyd Monroe's company. He hoped Harley Jane Miller was enjoying her freedom while she could. It wouldn't last much longer.

He hopped a cab for the brief ride back to the Colangco headquarters in the thirty-two-story pre–World War II Sentinel Building on Fifth Avenue at East Fifty-fifth Street. Duncan did not object to exercise. He was an exercise enthusiast, but he liked to keep it in its proper place and that did not include his working hours. He stepped from the cab and walked under the Sentinel's famed gold-leaf archway and into the equally ornate lobby. He loved this building. Every morning, he blessed his long-departed grandfather for having the vision—and the bootlegged fortune—to build the Sentinel. Unlike his parents' house, this had always felt like home.

He rode the elevator up to the thirty-first floor and walked through Colangco's glass doors. He began prioritizing his initial investigative activities as he walked silently on deep-pile carpeting down the hall, scarcely noticing that only a third of the offices and cubicles were occupied on this Monday morning. Colangco was an international business and on call twenty-four hours a day, every day of the week, for its clients. His brother Brandon was on a cushy job in Florida. His father was on a job in Denver. That's why the Princess of Pop had fallen into Duncan's lap. He was the only senior company rep in town.

He walked into his office, but Emma Teng, his assistant, was not sitting at her desk in the small, soothingly decorated outer reception area.

"Em?" he called.

"In here," she called from his corner office.

He walked into the sunlight-flooded room: green leather sofa with matching armchairs to his right, round glass conference table and green chairs in front of him, his teak desk with guest chairs and his credenza with his very expensive computer system to his left. Emma Teng, in a powder blue power suit, sat in his executive chair, feverishly working at his keyboard.

"Okay, Em, out of the B-and-D chat room and let's get to work."

"Darn, it was just getting interesting," Emma retorted, grinning as she swiveled his chair around to face him. "You look happy."

"I am ecstatic," Duncan informed her, leaning against his desk. "I've got a challenge for the first time in two years *and* the chance to prove to my family once and for all that they're wrong about me."

"So, it's a good job?" Emma asked.

"Not as complex as I had hoped, but there's enough of interest to keep me awake for the few hours it will take to crack this case."

"Won't that be a welcome change."

Duncan grinned at her. "Emma, you have no idea. What'd you find on our pampered Princess of Pop?"

"Here's my full report," she said, handing him a computer printout.

"Thanks. You can start logging in my notes," he said, tossing her his notebook. "We'll do this by the book, just so Dad knows that *I* know there *is* a book."

"You got it," Emma said.

While she sat in his chair working on his computer, Duncan took a chair at the glass conference table and began making phone calls. All he had to do was trace the cab the impulsive Harley Jane Miller had used the night before, and he was on his way to earning a gold star in the company's month-end report.

He spoke first with the late night Ritz-Carlton doorman who had held the cab door open for Miss Miller the night before, and whom Boyd had vociferously tried to have fired. Fortunately, the doorman was observant. He was able to give Duncan the cab company name and even a partial cab number.

"The poor kid," Emma said, still typing into the computer.

Duncan stopped in mid-dial on his next call. "What's that?"

"Jane Miller," Emma explained, typing from his notes. "Her life does not sound like a barrel of laughs."

"It's tough at the top."

Emma turned around to frown at him. "Haven't you heard that nineties women prefer sensitive, sympathetic guys?"

"I am not insensitive to Ms. Miller's plight. I might even wish her godspeed if it weren't for the fact that our client wants her back and she has about as much street smarts as a blind puppy. Nor am I fond of spoiled brats."

"It's hell out there on the party circuit."

Duncan grinned at Emma. "Tell me about it. It's not that rich bitches are bitchy, it's just that all they want to do is talk about themselves, rather than something interesting, like me."

Emma laughed and turned back to the computer.

Duncan called Colangco's contact at the cab company and soon had the home phone number of the driver who had helped the Princess of Pop escape her ivory tower the night before.

The promise of a hundred-dollar tip went a long way toward loosening the Bronx native's tongue, but still the conversation did not go the way Duncan had expected. He hung up the phone, the middle finger of his right hand tapping frenetically on the glass tabletop.

"You're frowning," Emma said.

"What?" Duncan looked up to see Emma sitting on the front of his desk, calmly regarding him.

"You're frowning," she repeated. "Wasn't the cabbie much help?"

"Enormous help, just not the way I expected. Guess where he took our naive Princess of Pop once he got her away from the Ritz."

"Grand Central?"

"Nope. To one of those Korean-owned all-night drugstores on upper Sixth Avenue. She said pick one, and he did."

"Curious," Emma said, swinging her crossed ankles.

"I thought so."

"Was she sick?"

"The driver said she was tense, but she looked as healthy as a horse when he finally dropped her at the Sheraton Manhattan."

Emma cocked her head. "What happened to her train ride around the country?"

"Exactly," Duncan said. "And there's more. She didn't go into the Sheraton Manhattan. She gave the driver a fifty-dollar tip as promised, so he was naturally interested in insuring her welfare. He watched her cross the street and walk into the New York Sheraton and Towers."

"Curiouser and curiouser."

Duncan pursed his lips. "There are several points of interest for the trained investigative mind."

"Tell me more, Holmes."

Duncan grinned at Emma. "The bit of fluff our client and her manager described to me acted with a certain amount of intelligence to hide her tracks. She did not, in short, act as I expected her to act. That is not merely annoying, it is troubling."

"What interests me is why she went to the pharmacy. She must have known she could get just about every toiletry she needs in any decent hotel room."

"Elementary, my dear Watson. She was bent on disguise.

Everyone knows what Jane Miller looks like. As Mr. Monroe pointed out, her face *is* plastered across a Times Square billboard. It's my guess that that worried her. Monroe is certain she'd be mobbed if she was ever recognized, so she must be certain too. Hair dyes and makeup and even reading glasses awaited her in the pharmacy. She could look like a myopic librarian now for all we know. I think it best that we take no chances and assume, at least for now, that our Princess of Pop—while spoiled—may actually have some intelligence. Here," Duncan said, handing Emma the Jane Miller publicity shot, "you'd better run this through the computer and print out every variation of eye color, hair color, hair length, hairstyle, and makeup you and it can come up with. Oh, and add some eyeglasses, just in case."

"No problem," Emma said, taking the publicity shot.

"When that's done, I want you to go ahead and check the various trains out of New York last night and this morning. Fax the photos and a description to every train you can, not that it will do us much good."

"You think the note she left Monroe was a red herring?"

"Of the ripest," Duncan said, picking up the phone again. "Four more and I'll be able to tie Peter Wimsey."

"You're mixing your fictional detectives, boss."

Duncan smiled at her. "Bless you for being literate."

While Emma ran the Jane Miller Photo Gallery in her office, Duncan reclaimed his desk and his computer and began hacking into the Sheraton's booking system. He found seven people who had checked into the Sheraton between midnight and two the night before. Three women, four men. He was immediately able to eliminate the wife of one of the male guests.

But the other two women were strong possibilities: Janet Miller and H. Smith. His father always said to follow the obvious trail, and certainly Janet Miller was a logical alias. So, with visions of wrapping this case up by the end of the day dancing in his head, Duncan went round to the New York

Sheraton and Towers and waited by the elevators on the eighteenth floor. He waited for three hours. When Miss Miller finally appeared and inserted her card key into her room door, she proved a major disappointment. She was not five feet five inches with strawberry blond hair and turquoise blue eyes. She was in her late forties (and that was being generous), stout, and primarily gray haired. Miss Janet Miller was a bust.

That left H. Smith and unfortunately, according to the computer records, H. Smith had checked out of the Sheraton that morning. The only additional charge to her tab was room service the night before: a cheeseburger, chocolate milk shake, and french fries. Duncan smiled for a moment. Miss Miller demonstrated a certain flair for parental flouting that he could appreciate. He'd once used a parental credit card to replace his Talking Heads collection after his father had methodically destroyed every copy of the group's albums he owned.

Unfortunately, Miss Miller had not been kind enough to leave a forwarding address. The morning desk clerks could not say where she had gone. Still, a doorman was of help. Studying the dozen computer-generated pictures Emma had produced of Harley Jane Miller in various disguises, the doorman finally recognized her, not with long strawberry blond hair, but with short brown hair. The blue eyes were still a dead giveaway.

Duncan had Emma run the name H. Smith through all of the midtown, then downtown, then uptown hotel computers. Nothing popped up. That meant more legwork.

His body might be in peak physical condition and form, but legwork was still anathema to Duncan. He preferred brainwork and computers, but the office was short-staffed on this Monday, it was his job, so it was up to him . . . and his legs.

He went from hotel to hotel for the remainder of that morning and well into the afternoon until he found a doorman who recognized his flown pigeon and was willing to admit it. It seemed Miss Miller not only had brown hair, she now had brown eyes. Somewhere, somehow, she had acquired brown contact lenses. The young doorman had admitted her—sans luggage—into the RIHGA Royal Hotel on West Fifty-fourth Street at ten-thirty that morning. A quick call to Emma, a little computer hacking, and Duncan soon had Miss Miller's newest alias: Grace Smith. She had used cash to pay for a single night's stay.

This raised two questions: where the hell had she gotten the money, and did she intend to change hotels every day? If so, it required an upgrade in his opinion of her from smart to highly intelligent. She seemed to be doing everything she could to make it hard for Boyd Monroe—and him—to find her.

Well, he had been wanting a challenge. He would find her, and no amount of hotel hopping and hair dye would stop him. Further conversation with the RIHGA doorman elicited the information that, immediately after checking into the hotel, Miss Miller had walked right back out of the lobby and into a taxi.

The pampered Princess of Pop was running wild in the Big Bad City.

Card key tucked into her purse, Harley Jane Miller, alias Grace Smith, walked out of the RIHGA lobby. Heart beating a little fast, she looked up and down the street, but Boyd wasn't lurking nearby. It still surprised her, his absence. She nodded at the young, uniformed doorman and he opened the door of the cab parked right in front of her at the curb.

"Where to?" the Pakistani driver asked as she slid onto the back seat.

"It's a clothing store downtown called Canal Jean. It's on Broadway between Broome and Spring streets."

The taxi blasted into the traffic while Harley hung onto

the door handle for dear life. She still wasn't used to the noisy, hurly-burly cab rides that were so different from the quiet, seamless grace of the limousines she'd been traveling in these last nine years. It was staggering, really, how different her life had become in less than twelve hours.

Last night she had sung at Madison Square Garden, the energy from the audience practically lifting her three feet off the stage. Then she had climbed into the back of a white limousine with Boyd and had sat there miserable and scared as the limo started back toward the Ritz-Carlton.

"Just let me take a little time off by myself," she had pleaded after ten minutes of fruitless arguments. "Just two weeks."

"By yourself?" Boyd had said in disbelief. "You wouldn't last two seconds out there on your own."

Well, Boyd, I have, and I will.

Harley huddled down in the back seat as her taxi hurtled around a corner. She had run away from Jane Miller, but what should she run to? The past? It was certainly an option. She had been relatively happy when hard-ass rock and roll had been her life . . . to her mother's despair. Barbara Miller had wanted Olivia Newton-John for a daughter and had ended up with guttural rebellion rock emanating from her garage. Finally years of guilt at letting down her only parent had stuffed Harley into a frilly dress to sing a treacly love ballad that had thrilled her mother, won the regional talent contest, and attracted the intimidating attention of Boyd Monroe, star maker.

The irony was not lost on Harley that it was she who had created the image that was now strangling her. Yes, Boyd had demanded that she cultivate that image, and her mother had backed him all the way, and Harley had been too young and inexperienced to argue them down to the career she wanted, not the one Boyd had ruthlessly planned out for her down to the last millisecond. But still, shouldn't she have fought harder, held out somehow, when he insisted on eradicating her name and the music she loved in favor of a delicate flower he named Jane?

Well, she was fighting now. Yes, she had created the monster, but she had finally escaped it, if only for a little while.

It took twenty minutes of driving through the Manhattan traffic as if the cabbie's life depended on it, before he jerked the taxi to a stop in front of Canal Jean.

"Thanks," Harley said, a little breathless from the death-defying trip. She paid him—overtipped him because his medical insurance would never be enough to cover his certain forthcoming accident—and walked into the store. *Wow.* She felt as if she ought to genuflect or something. There wasn't an inch of lace, or even pastels, to be found anywhere. Everything was black or red or purple or some form of neon. All the clothes she had loved as a teenager and secretly lusted after while she was trapped in Jane Miller's dull sack dresses were here in one store. "Heaven!" she sighed.

She looked around, her gaze passing over boy clerks and girl clerks dressed in black or grunge flannel until she found what she was looking for: a young woman in purple Doc Martens boots, black stockings, jean miniskirt, and black fishnet top. Her hair was a deep purple, her makeup akin to Kabuki. A Technicolor clerk. Perfect.

Harley walked up to her before anyone else could grab her. "Hello, Denise," she said, reading the young woman's name tag. "I'm going to need your help for the next few hours."

The clerk looked her up and down. "This should be fun."

Harley grinned at her. "Count on it." For the last nine years, Boyd had relegated Jane Miller to whites and pastels only. "Let's start with basic black and work our way up," she said.

Harley dashed through the marble entrance into the RIHGA Royal Hotel that evening carrying six different bags of lingerie. She had just enough time to change and grab a quick dinner in the hotel restaurant before she went out to see her very first Broadway show. A well-dressed couple in their mid-thirties stepped off an elevator and she stepped on it, still amazed that a dye job and some contacts left her unrecognizable, and that Boyd still hadn't leapt out of the shadows to drag her back to the Ritz.

She walked into her suite—small living room in forest green and white, a bedroom taken up almost entirely by a king-size bed, and a pale peach marble bathroom—and groaned as she stared at the couch and chairs and her bed piled high with boxes and bags of clothes. She'd have to pack if she wanted to sleep tonight.

But for now, she took a quick shower and then pulled out the black sleeveless minidress she had hung in the mirror-lined closet that afternoon. She found the scandalous black silk panties and bra she had just bought that would make little Miss Jane Miller die of a perpetual blush, and the black cowboy boots. She wouldn't wear any stockings. She was going to be skimpy and sexy and daring tonight no matter how many times she heard Boyd in her head yelling *"No, no, no!"*

She turned slowly in front of the full-length closet mirrors, staring at the brunette in the clinging black dress. It was still a shock to see herself so different from what she had been these last nine years. It set her to thinking scary thoughts about Boyd and Jane Miller and whose life was it anyway?

She turned hurriedly from the mirror, grabbed her new money belt off the bed, and locked it in her room safe. Then she picked up the tiny black purse she had bought to go with the dress, checked to make sure she really had put in the two twenty-dollar bills, in case of emergencies, and her theater ticket, and headed out of her room. The time had come to meet the Great White Way.

She ran into an immediate detour.

She had just opened her room door, when she found a

RIHGA manager in a navy blue suit about to knock on her forehead. He quickly lowered his knuckles.

"Miss Miller?" he inquired.

"Yes," Harley warily replied. She had had to identify herself to the RIHGA management—with strict promises of their secrecy—to get a room under an alias.

"I'm Greg Crandell, one of the RIHGA's day managers. I'm afraid we have something of a problem. A gentleman was asking about you just a few minutes ago."

Boyd. Harley's face felt frozen. "A gentleman? Medium height? Short brown hair? Wears cowboy boots?"

"No. This gentleman more precisely fits the tall, dark, and handsome profile. And he wore English custom-made Loebs shoes."

"And he was asking about *me*?"

"Yes. From what one of our doormen said, the gentleman is apparently following you."

Boyd had hired someone to find her. And he'd succeeded. An image of Boyd as every implacable horror movie monster she'd ever seen iced her lungs. "Does the gentleman have a name?"

"Duncan Lang, of Colangco International."

Harley winced. Trust Boyd to hire the best firm in town. She hadn't been able to pick up a newspaper or magazine these last nine years without reading about some security system Colangco had installed for a celebrity, or some case it had solved. "Where is he now?"

"I believe," said Mr. Crandell, "that he is on his way to the Windows on the World restaurant downtown at the World Trade Center. At least, that's where I had our senior doorman tell him you had just gone."

Harley took the young manager's hand in hers and gave it a heartfelt shake. "Mr. Crandell, you're a peach. I've got to get out of here, fast." She stopped as an absolutely brilliant idea lit up her brain. "And with your help, I think I can pull it off."

•   •   •

It was just after eleven o'clock that night when she walked out of the Richard Rodgers Theatre and turned right onto West Forty-sixth Street. She was actually humming one of the musical's tunes. It had not been great music, but it had been satisfying. Besides, she always loved happy endings. It had felt a little odd, at first, to be sitting all alone in a theater with hundreds of strangers around her, rather than standing on the stage and singing to them. She had scanned row after row looking for Boyd and not finding him. And then the show had made her forget herself, and forget being a stranger amidst strangers. If it hadn't been for the cramped seats, she would have felt entirely comfortable.

"Wow!" She had just walked out onto Broadway. The hotel desk clerk had assured her she could catch a cab here. "Wow!" she said softly again. "It's like Christmas."

Broadway and its sidewalks were packed with people who glowed beneath the colored lights that were everywhere, turning night into day. Electronic billboards with gold and silver and white lights towered up into the sky. Blue and green and red and every other color of lights shone from every Times Square building and marquee. Happiness and beauty enveloped her. Now she understood that old cliché "the city that never sleeps." Who would want to? She felt special just standing here on this warm night watching people who looked as happy as she felt, all of them bedazzled by the lights and the crowds and the fun emanating from every doorway. She couldn't stop smiling. Manhattan was a wonderful place to be.

A cab didn't seem so important anymore. Her cowboy boots would get her back to her hotel. The cheerful crowd all around her made her feel safe. She'd be fine.

With Greg Crandell's help, she'd managed to shake Mr. Duncan Lang off her trail, at least for the time being. The

Manhattan night and her freedom were still hers for the taking.

Strolling on a warm, muggy July night through midtown Manhattan was exhilarating. It was wonderful to breathe in real air and humidity, not air conditioning. It was wonderful to stretch her legs and swing her arms as she walked down a street, a real city street, in the city she had fantasized about visiting since she was eight. On her previous trips to New York, all she had ever seen was her hotel room, the inside of a limousine, and the stage she performed on.

Well, not this trip! Even if it meant sinking the supposedly tall, dark, and handsome Duncan Lang in concrete and dropping him into the Hudson River, she would have her two weeks to explore the city she had loved from afar. Let Colangco International put *that* in its pipe and smoke it!

CHAPTER TWO

*I*t was almost seven o'clock at night when—more than disgruntled by his recent wild-goose chase to the World Trade Center and an entire day spent following his prey from cab to store to cab again, never quite managing to catch up with her—Duncan took a taxi back to the RIHGA, planning to stake out his elusive prey's room till doomsday, if necessary. He'd once waited beside the hotel room door of a plump heiress from Melbourne for thirteen hours. Room service had supplied him with the necessities of life, and she had made his wait more than worthwhile by supplying the remaining necessities of life. He depended on the Princess of Pop to provide a vastly different—but equally satisfying—denouement to this wait as well.

He rode the RIHGA elevator up to the fiftieth floor and knocked on the door of Grace Smith, alias Harley Jane Miller, only to be confronted by a disgruntled Japanese businessman of about sixty in shirtsleeves, crumpled slacks, and black socks.

It was the last thing Duncan had expected. "Excuse me," he said with a slight bow. "Isn't this Miss Grace Smith's room?"

"No," the gentleman frostily replied. "It is my room. Good night."

The door slammed in Duncan's face. This was not unduly perturbing. Many people—at least, many women—had slammed doors in his face. What *was* disturbing was that Harley Jane Miller would not be returning to this room. Maybe Emma had gotten the room number wrong. But Emma never got anything wrong. Ever.

Duncan took the elevator back down to the RIHGA's low-key lobby, sat down in a soft pale green chair, and called his office on his cellular phone.

"Emma?" he said in carefully modulated tones when she answered the phone on the second ring.

"Hey, Sherlock, what's happening?" she said cheerfully. "Case all wrapped up?"

"Not entirely. There is a glitch. A rather important glitch. You seem to have made a mistake."

"A mistake? I don't make mistakes. Ever."

"There is an exception to every rule. Our party, currently known as Grace Smith, no longer claims Room 5007 as her own at the RIHGA. Or perhaps you gave me the wrong room number?"

"Let me check," Emma said in a low, quick voice. He heard the rapid clatter of computer keyboard keys. "Holy moly," she said.

This was not reassuring. "Do I want to hear this?" Duncan inquired.

"She checked out at six-ten this evening, and there's no forwarding address. You don't suppose . . . Could she have spotted you tailing her?"

"Don't be insulting," Duncan said witheringly. "Besides,

I've been one step behind her all day long. If I haven't seen her, she couldn't have seen me."

"Then someone blabbed."

Duncan swore, virulently. "I was hoping she wouldn't know I was on her trail until I had her safely in hand. I must not have been careful enough asking my discreet questions."

"Now, now," Emma said soothingly, "don't take it so hard. These little glitches happen on any case. It's not your fault."

"Dad would not agree," Duncan said bitterly. *"Brandon* doesn't have glitches on *his* jobs. Run another screen of Manhattan hotel reservation systems, Em. Look for variations on Smith and Miller. Throw in Jones for good measure. I should be back in about ten minutes."

"You got it."

Duncan tucked the phone back into his coat pocket, sighing heavily. He'd have to start checking the different taxi companies, looking for a single fare—who now had a lot of luggage—who had cabbed from the RIHGA that evening to somewhere in Manhattan. If the Princess of Pop had even stayed in Manhattan.

She was just perverse enough to take that damned cross-country train trip after all. Feeling aggrieved, Duncan slid a stick of cinnamon gum into his mouth and walked out of the RIHGA. His first big case and he couldn't even find one measly female in his own hometown. He should never have joined the family firm. His father was right. He didn't have the skills or the persistence or the determination to do the job and do it well.

By eight o'clock that night, he and Emma had come up empty and he sent Emma home. He sat in his chair, staring out his office windows at the beautiful nighttime skyline. How the hell was Miss Miller pulling this off? How had the innocent that Boyd Monroe described to him succeeded in eluding a trained investigator for nearly twelve hours?

She might be pampered and spoiled, even bitchy, but a

day on her trail had shown him that the Princess behind the dye job and brown contact lenses was more resourceful than he had originally thought, and that interested him. He began trying to put himself in Harley Jane Miller's shoes. If he was a bird just escaped from a gilded cage, where would he fly?

Tuesday morning, Duncan walked into the office at seven. Emma walked into his office at eight and dumped a stack of newspapers on his desk.

"Have you seen these?" she asked.

He looked up from the report on Harley Jane Miller he was studying and glanced at them. "I saw a few of the louder headlines."

PRINCESS OF POP DISAPPEARS! and JANE MILLER MISSING! and VANISHED! and PRINCESS POPS OUT! were some of the calmer media announcements.

"Was this your idea?"

"Nope. I've always believed in keeping a low profile," Duncan replied, turning a page of the report.

"Then what gives?"

"If there was a bookie at hand—and why isn't there, I'd like to know—I'd lay good odds that our beloved client Mr. Boyd Monroe has been busy. These have his bullish hoof-prints all over them."

"Okay. But why would he want anyone to know that his meal ticket has run away from home?"

Duncan leaned back in his chair and linked his hands behind his head. "Think about it, Em. Instead of one brilliant detective, Boyd Monroe now has hundreds of thousands of fans in this city alone looking for his vanished meal ticket. I knew he was cagey the first minute I laid eyes on him." But there was more to these headlines than managerial machinations. There was a feeling of anxiety, almost desperation to them. Was Boyd that worried that his Princess would be hurt on her holiday?

"Swell," Emma said, "but what does this do to us?"

"I've already brought in a second receptionist to handle

the flood of calls—Mr. Monroe referred all tips to the agency—and I've ordered a case of aspirin."

"You should have been a Boy Scout."

Duncan grinned. "I was expelled when I was twelve for starting up a crap game with some of the other boys during one of those god-awful wilderness adventures. To work, Emma. Find me the hotel of Harley Jane Miller."

"Aye, aye, sir," Emma said, saluting smartly.

Duncan picked up her thorough report on Harley once again. If he could just figure Harley out—figure out what made her tick—he could find her, he was certain of it.

He returned to her gestation years in Sweetcreek, Oklahoma. Now *there* was a hometown. Unlike him, the Princess of Pop had actually begun life as one of the little people. He stared at her senior year picture: short, spiky strawberry blond hair, no smile, direct gaze. She may have been a small-town rocker and he a prep school prisoner, but he knew that defiant look well. He'd been a rebel once himself. But she had ended up conforming, just as he had conformed. And here was the result. Duncan flipped through picture after picture of a meteoric career and found—not the expressive, rebellious face of Miss Miller's girlhood—but mask after mask after mask. He flipped back to the earlier pictures. Yes, BB (Before Boyd), every thought and feeling had been illuminated on her slightly freckled face for all the world to see. Something in Duncan recognized that Harley Miller. He saw a kindred spirit . . . and he was still going to put her back in the gilded cage of her choosing.

All he had to do was find her. Duncan sighed and went through her history once again. Harley Jane Miller had been Sweetcreek's rebel with a cause: rock and roll. Then Boyd had come along and straitjacketed her into a pop persona she had once reviled. He had changed her wardrobe, her hairstyle, slapped on a lot of makeup, changed her name, even changed her voice from alto to soprano, and hired a voice coach to remove the Oklahoma twang from her speech.

Duncan began tapping his desk with his middle finger. Nine years of living a lie could build up a lot of anger, or cunning, or both. He should know. He'd spent a lot of his youth alternately conforming to the mold his parents had cast for him, and rebelling against it. And when he'd rebelled . . .

Duncan sat bolt upright in his chair. "Oh, she wouldn't! She couldn't!" He swung around to his computer and hacked into the RIHGA Royal Hotel's reservation system. He stared at the screen for a moment and then pursed his lips in an appreciative whistle. *She had.*

"Watson," he called, "we've been duped."

"What do you mean, Holmes?" Emma said as she left her desk and leaned against the doorjamb.

"Get this," Duncan said. "Last night when we were trying to find Jane Miller again, you checked the reservation systems of every hotel in Manhattan, but it never occurred to either of us to check the RIHGA. Yes, Grace Smith checked out of the Royal RIHGA at six-ten last night. But what's interesting is that a Miss B. Monroe checked in one minute later."

Emma blinked. "She used Monroe?"

"Yep."

"She changed her name and her room and she didn't go anywhere?"

"Yep."

"Jeez. Private Detective 101 never covered *that* gambit." Emma looked at Duncan queerly. "How in the world did you figure this out?"

"Elementary, my dear Watson. In my youth, I too rebelled against parental control, just as Miss Miller seems to be doing now. On one memorable occasion, I tried to escape an interview with the second of my three prep schools by slipping the parental leash and using my father's name to check into the only local hotel for three blissful days of freedom. If it hadn't been for my known penchant for pizza parlors, I'd probably be hiding out there still. There's no better way of getting back at an authority figure than by using something personal against him, and what's more personal than a name?"

"Brilliant, Holmes."

"Thank you, Watson."

"But how did you guess she'd stayed at the RIHGA?"

"I did not *guess*," Duncan corrected her sternly, "I *deduced*. Were I in Miss Miller's shoes and informed that I'd been run to ground, I would be peeved. I would want a little of my own back. I don't know about you, Em, but I feel downright asinine for not checking the RIHGA's reservation records last night."

"Oh, she's *good*," Emma said admiringly.

"I could like her a lot if my fee didn't depend on her not being quite so clever."

"I suppose she's already checked out of the RIHGA today?"

"Of course she has," Duncan said. "I'm starting the day where she left me last night—one step behind her again. But she made one mistake. Before, this was just a job. But with her room switch last night, she's made this personal. I can hear her chortling, Emma, and I don't like it. I'm going to get her no matter how many dodges she tries. Even if it means throwing out the damn book and winging it, I am going to get her *today*."

"That's the spirit, boss. Never say die. I'll start another computer search through the hotels."

Emma walked back into her office while Duncan stayed right where he was, his middle finger frenetically tapping his desk. There was a good chance Emma wouldn't be able to track the Princess on the computer. Miss Miller's native intelligence seemed to be in full bloom. She knew she was being hunted now, so she'd be even more careful. He would have to figure out what was going on in the Princess of Pop's mind if he was going to find her.

Unfortunately, she was, to quote Yul Brynner's King of Siam, a puzzlement. She'd been making millions—and doing what Monroe told her to do—since she was seventeen. It begged the question: why break out now?

Why make like Audrey Hepburn and take a powder from the trappings of music royalty for one brief moment of freedom? Practically every line in Emma's report had emphasized that, as the Princess of Pop, Jane Miller was personally responsible for the livelihoods of dozens of people, she was contractually responsible to her recording company and her concert dates, she was responsible for ensuring that her millions of fans worldwide were satisfied with her music and secure in her "goodness," and she knew it and had fulfilled those obligations to the letter. Until midnight two nights ago, she had obeyed all the rules that Boyd Monroe had used to imprison her, because to flout them would be to disappoint or even hurt too many other people.

Why break nine years of hard conditioning now? The only thing looming before her was a recording session in Los Angeles, and after eleven Top Ten albums, she could do that in her sleep.

Or could she?

The memory of Harley's acoustic guitar sitting forlornly in a chair in her Ritz suite slammed into Duncan's brain.

Emma's background report had stressed that Harley was a talented and dedicated musician. *But she had left her guitar behind.*

Yes, it might have been difficult smuggling it past her bodyguards, but according to his interviews with the many and varied taxi drivers she had used yesterday, and all the shop clerks she had lavishly tipped, *she had done nothing to replace her guitar.*

And that didn't make sense. That didn't make sense at all. He had had a brief fling with a brilliant concert violinist once and she had gone into panic attacks whenever she wasn't within ten feet of her violin.

But Harley had gone nearly thirty-six hours without any kind of guitar close at hand. Duncan swore softly. This whole case—from her final performance at Madison Square Garden Sunday night, to the guitar she'd left behind, to the wardrobe reversion to her teenage hellion phase, to that recording studio waiting for her in Los Angeles—it had all been about *music*. Harley Jane Miller's music.

What if she was blocked? What if she hadn't been able to come up with new material for that recording session? That might make her just desperate enough to duck out on her responsibilities for the first time in nine years.

She had avoided music stores and anything resembling a guitar all day yesterday, but if Duncan knew his musicians—and he did—she wouldn't be able to hold out much longer. When Mark, his rock-and-roll friend from college, had been blocked, he'd still practiced on his guitar every day.

Making music for a musician—singer or performer—was a physical need, a craving, an addiction.

Miss Miller might think she didn't want or need a guitar on her holiday, but Duncan knew better. She'd be breaking out into a cold sweat any second now.

Emma walked into his office. "I give up. I have not been able to find any alias that would even hint at Jane Miller's presence in any of the hotel computer reservation systems. What now?"

Duncan's eye was caught by Harley's defiant senior yearbook photo. "Run a search for every female rock and roller the computer can come up with—Laverne Baker, Ruth Brown, Betty Everett, Grace Slick, Patti Smith, Linda Ronstadt, Chrissie Hynde—all of them. Then run those names through the hotel reservation systems."

"Sure," Emma said, not looking at all sure.

Duncan, meanwhile, had grabbed a phone book from his desk drawer. To hell with legwork. He'd let his fingers do the walking. He opened up the yellow pages to music stores and began hunting.

"I've got her!" Emma shouted ten minutes later as she ran into his office.

Duncan looked up eagerly. "Where is she?"

"She checked into the New York Hilton and Towers just after nine o'clock this morning as H. Everett. I faxed her picture to one of our contacts there. It's her, all right. How did you know she might use Everett?"

For the first time on this case, Duncan knew a certain amount of triumph. "Look at this face," he commanded, holding up Harley's yearbook photo. "If this is who you used to be, what genre of names would you choose from?"

"Genius, Holmes!"

"Elementary, my dear Watson," Duncan said with the utmost satisfaction.

"So, are you off to the Hilton?"

"Nope. I'm off to Manny's Music on West Forty-eighth Street."

"Why there?"

"Because any musician worth his or her salt has to make a pilgrimage to Manny's, and from everything I've read in your report on the Princess, Manny's would be a magnet she couldn't resist. The game is afoot, Watson. She'll turn up at Manny's, I'm certain of it. And when she does, I'll close this damn case. Even if it isn't by the book, I'm going to prove to Dad once and for all that I *can* do this job."

Wearing her new green terry cloth robe and her equally new slippers, Harley pulled open her room's peach-colored curtains and looked out over the city she had fallen in love with yesterday.

Manhattan felt like the world in microcosm. Life in microcosm. Boyd had kept her hidden away from life for so long, that to be suddenly thrust into the midst of poverty and abundance, the beautiful and the ugly, had been a huge shock to her system. A welcome shock, because with it had come the growing determination not to let fear and reality do what

Boyd had done for so many years: keep her isolated from life
. . . and herself.

Looking down on the vibrant street below her window,
she saw a small crowd of office workers stopping on their way
to work to listen to a trio of street musicians—a violinist, a
cellist, and a clarinetist—playing near the corner. A love for
those musicians surged within her, just as it had last night as
she had walked back to the RIHGA, drawn forward by the
startling sound of bagpipe music. She had dropped one of
her twenty-dollar bills into the piper's open instrument case,
not because he was good—he wasn't—but because he was so
enthralled with his pipes and the bad music he played and
she envied him that.

Two blocks later, she had dropped her last twenty-dollar
bill into the case of a jazz trumpeter who played far better
than the piper, but with an equal love of the music.

She turned from the window, paced the room for a moment, got irritated with herself, and ordered breakfast from
room service. An hour's workout in the Hilton's fitness center had left her famished. The sooner she ate and got out into
the day, the sooner this restlessness would disappear.

She looked around the room. Her pendant, small itinerary
notebook, and brush and comb were lying on her dresser.
Her two large suitcases were sitting by the desk. The king-
size bed took up most of the room, and what was left over
was taken up by an armchair and ottoman, the desk, the
dresser.

But the room looked empty.

She stared at herself in the dresser mirror. She wore a
thick Turkish cotton robe, and she felt naked.

Restlessness worried at her skin.

She understood then. She was alone, not because Boyd
wasn't next door or Annie nearby, but because there wasn't
any music in this room. A part of herself was missing.

There was a knock at her door. She looked through the
peephole and then let in the room service waiter with her

breakfast cart. She paid him and closed the door after him, and even sat down and ate. But every cell was focused on the guitar she had left behind, the music that had died within her, and the emptiness in this room.

She was supposed to check out of the Hilton this morning and into the smaller Mansfield Hotel. But the restlessness had seized her and would not let her go. She grabbed the small notebook with her holiday itinerary and quickly scanned through it. She wasn't like Boyd. She could be flexible. She could move things around.

Maybe all she needed was a quick fix, then she could come back and check out and get on with her day.

She dressed quickly in black high-tops, black jeans, and a sleeveless black T-shirt. She attached the anklet money belt to her ankle, slid her pendant back over her head, and she was ready. Checking the hall in case Boyd was lurking there, she strode out of her room and then walked out of the Hilton, scanning the crowd of people near the main entrance, some arriving, some leaving. No Boyd. No detective. She was still safe.

She smiled as she headed down to Sixth Avenue. She had a date with Manny's Music. She would walk, she would fulfill a teenage dream by visiting the Musicians' Mecca, then she would feel better, and that was that.

She strode down Sixth Avenue to West Forty-eighth Street and discovered almost a full block of music stores, with a tiny park and waterfall separating two of the buildings about half-way down the street. Magic turned up in the oddest places.

Then she saw the sign for Manny's Music. White wrought-iron vines climbed up posts at the door and along the display windows that held trumpets, drums, a sax, an electric guitar, flutes, and clarinets. She felt as if she were coming home.

Smiling, she stepped under the dark green awning, opened the front door, and crashed into a broad chest. Muscular arms went around her to steady her.

"I beg your . . . pardon," she faltered as she stared. He

was about six feet of tanned virility. He had short, black, naturally curly hair and expressive black eyes that were a little wide and a little startled just at present. His broad chest was encased in a plum-colored T-shirt. Tight faded jeans lovingly enveloped long, muscular legs. Brown leather shoes and a forest green jacket completed the ensemble.

Harley's heart began beating wildly in her breast. *"Wow,"* she said, and then realized that she'd said it, and blushed. She couldn't bring herself to look any higher than his chest. His yummy chest. "I-I-I mean, I'm sorry I barreled into you like that."

"No problem," he said. His hands were on her shoulders. She could feel their weight, their strength, their warmth. It had been so long since a man had touched her. She dragged her eyes back up to his. Wow! He blinked and took a sudden step back. "It . . . was entirely my fault. Are you okay?"

"That depends," Harley said, her brain still leaving her completely in the lurch. "Are you any relation to an Oklahoma tornado?"

He had a lovely smile that crinkled the corners of his black eyes. "My mother was a glacier and my daddy was an earthquake. Were you just coming in?"

"Yes. I . . . I thought I'd look around."

"I hope you enjoy yourself," he said, stepping aside and holding the door open for her.

She walked past him, turned to thank him, but he was gone.

Darn. She'd just made a complete ninny of herself in front of the most gorgeous hunk of manhood she'd ever met. So much for feeling better this morning.

Harley turned and found herself in bedlam. The place had just opened, but already it was crammed with people, all colors and kinds of people. Hundreds of black-and-white photographs of all the famous musicians who had come to Manny's crowded every inch of available wall space. Down the narrow aisles she could see every size of amplifier and every imaginable instrument. Manny's packed a lot of music into a very tight rectangular space.

But it was the right wall that held her transfixed. Guitars of every shape, color, size, and style ran the whole length of the store. "Oh . . . my . . . God," she whispered. *Guitar heaven.* Mesmerized, she took the few steps necessary to bring her into contact with nirvana. She reached up. Her fingertips brushed the glossy finish of a Paul Reed Smith. She shivered. Slowly she walked down the wall, gazing rapturously at Martins and Gibsons and Ibanezes. She stopped in front of a turquoise blue six-string Washburn acoustic guitar. It was gorgeous.

A little more than halfway down the room, she faltered to a stop once again. She stood before a small alcove, a three-sided room with electric guitars, dozens of different electric guitars, hanging from the walls and ceiling. Her gaze narrowed, all peripheral vision lost as she stared up at a Fender Stratocaster. A black Fender Stratocaster hanging in a sea of Fender Stratocasters. The most universal of all electric guitars. It could, and did, play anything. The beloved of Buddy Holly, Jimi Hendrix, and Eric Clapton was hanging right before her eyes. She could reach up and touch it, but dared not.

"May I help you?"

Vaguely, Harley was aware that a young man with long red hair combed back from his forehead was standing to her left.

"Are you looking for anything in particular?" he asked.

Harley gazed back up at the Fender. "Can I touch it?"

He smiled. "You can play any guitar in the store."

"Nice girls don't play electric guitar!" her mother had insisted.

"I'd like to try . . . that one," she said in a strangled voice, pointing to the black Stratocaster.

He lifted it down as if it were just an ordinary guitar. He plugged it into a small amp sitting on the floor of the alcove and handed the guitar to her. "Here you go."

She stared at the Stratocaster a moment and then watched herself hold out her hands, taking it from the blurry young man and slowly pulling it against her body. "God!" she whispered. It was slim and light and fit perfectly against her belly and diaphragm, cupping the undersides of her breasts.

She strummed an E chord, and then an A, shuddering a little as the music filled the alcove.

"It's better than sex, isn't it?"

Harley focused her eyes on the shop clerk. He was probably in his mid-twenties. A name tag on his white shirt read "Clark."

"It's even better than double chocolate mousse," she said.

He laughed. "Been playing long?"

"Fourteen years," Harley said, playing chord after chord. "But acoustic, not electric."

"Seems to me like you've found your guitar of choice."

Harley stroked the gleaming black surface of the Fender. "Oh yeah."

She hadn't planned it, she hadn't even imagined it, but ten minutes later she was removing sixteen hundred dollars from her money belt to buy the Stratocaster, complete with carrying case, strap, and guitar picks. She placed a few hundred more down on the light oak counter in the center of the store to buy a Maxi-Mouse amplifier so she could start practicing.

She found herself standing under the green Manny's Music awning, the guitar case in her left hand, the amp in her right. She didn't think about checking out of the Hilton, or about the Bartlett Museum, which she had planned to tour later this afternoon, or about Côte Basque, where she had a dinner reservation, or about the show she had planned to see that night.

Right now, what she wanted more than anything was a place to sit down before she fell down.

Dimly she saw the tiny pocket park with a fountain splashing down a stone wall across the street. Forgetting to look left, let alone right, she crossed the street and entered the narrow oasis. She sat down with a thump on the nearest stone bench and stared at the cascading water opposite her.

A Fender Stratocaster. *She* had just bought a Fender Stratocaster! She set the amp down on the ground and hugged the guitar case with all her might.

She wasn't naked or alone or restless anymore. And she felt *lots* better.

"Hello again, Miss Miller."

Harley's heart stopped. There was a roaring in her ears. Slowly she turned her head and looked up. A man stood beside her bench. It was the hunk from Manny's, and he knew who she was. Staring up into those dark eyes, she knew it was futile for her to even attempt to pretend that she didn't know that he knew who she was. "Are you Duncan Lang, the man who was asking questions about me at the RIHGA yesterday?"

"One and the same."

"Did Boyd send you?"

"Boyd *hired* me. I found you thanks to high technology and brilliant deductive reasoning."

Harley stared up at him. "Can you be bought off?"

His dark eyes crinkled in amusement. " 'Fraid not. Dad would be peeved. Colangco has a sterling reputation for honesty and results. Sorry," he said as he picked up her Maxi-Mouse. "Shall we head back to the Hilton for your things?"

Crud, he knew where she was staying. Harley tried to think, but her brain felt like iced sludge. It was over. She hadn't even had two full days of freedom yet, and it was over.

Her chest ached. "I'm twenty-six, a grown woman, legally independent," she stated. "You can't just haul me back to Boyd like he *owns* me!"

"I can when that's what I'm hired to do."

"But I haven't even had a chance to try out my new guitar," Harley said, hot tears welling in her eyes. She hurriedly pushed them back. "Boyd is not about to let me keep it. He hates electric guitars. He doesn't think they're feminine."

"What?"

"And he won't let me wear black clothes, or red clothes, or anything resembling a bright color. And no jeans. Not even slacks."

"He's got a tight rein on you," Duncan Lang agreed as he sat down beside her.

"He is sucking the life's blood out of me."

"Why do you let him?"

"Boyd is deaf to anyone's 'no' except his own," Harley replied bitterly.

"But as you pointed out, you are twenty-six and legally independent. You don't have to put up with his crap if you don't want to."

"Why do you care?" Harley demanded, glaring up at the treacherous hunk.

"I don't," Duncan Lang stated. "I'm just curious. You did a very good job of hiding yourself among eight million people—"

"*You* found me."

"Ah, well," he said, ducking his head in false modesty, "I'm a trained investigator, after all." His winsome smile must have charmed every female who'd even glanced at him sideways from the time he was sixteen. It made Harley's teeth grate. "My point is that," he continued, "Boyd's opinion not withstanding, you seem fully capable of taking care of yourself. Fire the control freak and get on with your life."

"It's not that easy," Harley said, her arms tightening around the guitar case. "I owe everything to Boyd: my career, my success, my fame, my money. I'd still be a little hick from Oklahoma if it weren't for him. And I'm not so sure I can make it in the industry without him now."

"He *has* run a number on you, hasn't he?"

"Oh yeah," Harley said, staring down at the concrete ground.

"So why did you run away?"

Harley felt her stomach freeze over. Her jaws began to

liquefy. She stared blindly at the fountain. "The music stopped coming," she whispered.

"I thought so," Duncan Lang said.

Harley turned her head and met his sympathetic black gaze. It nearly undid her. Oh God, her music! "It's been two months and not a note, not a lyric." The well she had depended on all of her life had gone dry. There was nothing left to be tapped. She looked up at him, pleading for a stay of execution. "I thought if I could just have a few weeks of fun. A few weeks of not being Jane Miller. A few weeks of just letting go, and maybe it would come back. Maybe I'd be okay again. Then I'd fly to L.A., get back on the treadmill, and make the damn album for Sony."

Harley almost clapped a hand to her mouth. Years ago Boyd had forbidden Jane Miller to swear in public or private.

"A reasonable plan," Lang agreed.

"Then let me go!" Harley said, her hand clutching his arm. "Let me have my two weeks. No one will be hurt. I'll come back and fulfill all of my obligations, I promise."

"Sorry, Princess, that's not part of the plan."

"Who the *hell* do you think you are?" Harley exploded. "You're not God. You have no right to tell me where to go or what to do. I'll fly off to *Brazil* if I feel like it and you can't stop me."

"Oh yes I can," he retorted.

"How?"

"By physical force if necessary."

He looked like he could do it too. "*Oh,* I hate men," Harley seethed. "The arrogance. The stupidity."

"I'm actually pretty intelligent," Duncan Lang retorted, dark eyes glittering. "Don't forget, I found you."

"If you found me, you can lose me."

"No."

"Dammit, Lang—"

"I signed a contract, Princess. I am obligated to fulfill it."

"But not today," Harley pleaded. "You don't have to fulfill it today, or tomorrow, or even a week from tomorrow. Give me back my holiday, Mr. Lang."

"It won't do you any good. Boyd would just fire me—"

"I'll pay you whatever fee your firm wants!"

"—and he'd hire some other private detective who *would* find you like I did and turn you over to Boyd," Lang concluded gently.

Harley felt bloodless. "But at least I'd have a few more days of freedom."

"I'm sorry, Miss Miller, I can't help you. I have a responsibility to my client and to my company, and I've been given something of a deadline."

Harley's gaze locked on his surprisingly sympathetic eyes. "I have never begged for anything in my life, Mr. Lang, but I'm begging you now. Let me at least have until midnight tonight and then you can take me back to Boyd."

"Sorry, Miss Miller. If I return you to Mr. Monroe now, you've got enough time to catch a one o'clock flight to L.A. today so you'll only be one day late to the recording studio."

"What are you talking about? I'm not scheduled to start working again until the middle of next week."

She had surprised him. "Then why is Boyd Monroe so desperate to get you back and get you back fast?" he demanded.

She shrugged, antipathy welling once again. "Beats me. You're the great detective, you figure it out."

He was staring at her Maxi-Mouse. "Why do I get the feeling that there's more going on here than even *you* know about?" he murmured.

At first she was puzzled—what on earth was he talking about?—and then she realized that opportunity was banging on her door. "If you think there's something wrong," she said eagerly, "don't you think you ought to check it out before blithely throwing me back into what could be a lion's den? There are many different kinds of results, Mr. Lang.

Shouldn't you protect your company's sterling reputation by investigating anything that seems off-kilter?"

Knowing dark eyes smiled down at her. "You just want another day of freedom."

"Of course I do!" Harley exploded. "But aren't I also right?"

It occurred to Duncan that she just might be. He realized now that his intuition had been bothering him during his initial interview with Mr. Monroe. Why had Boyd kept him from interviewing Annie Maguire? Why had he lied about who Harley was and what she was capable of doing? Why had he lied about the recording date? Why was he sweating? Could he be hiding something, and could it endanger Harley?

He looked down at her. A gamine with breasts, dressed all in black. He'd known an odd kind of fascination as he'd surreptitiously watched her in Manny's Music. She had a quality . . . like Sleeping Beauty just waking up from a hundred years' sleep and discovering the world anew. Her thoughts and her feelings had been right there on her slightly freckled face for all the world to see. No makeup. No masks. She had looked like she was in nirvana, and Duncan had wanted nothing more from life than to join her.

He'd never felt that kind of immediate attraction to a woman in his life. Oh sure, he'd been drawn to beautiful women, and voluptuous women, and even bewitching women. Harley was none of those things. She was just somehow . . . familiar.

No, wait, stop, Duncan ordered himself. Harley Jane Miller was a job and nothing more. She was Boyd Monroe's meal ticket and Duncan's chance to prove once and for all to his family that he wasn't a lazy, womanizing disaster waiting to happen. He would satisfy his curiosity about Boyd Monroe's ulterior motives and then turn in his report to his father—job completed in only thirty-six hours—and he would finally be accorded at least some of the respect he deserved. He would no longer be a drain on the company's overhead. He would get the more important jobs. He would finally carve his niche in the family firm.

"Okay, Princess, here's the deal," he said with sudden decision. "I'll do a little digging while you make like a tourist or a musician or whatever the hell it is you want to be today. But at midnight I put you back in your pumpkin and return you to Mr. Monroe." Duncan held out his hand. "Deal?"

Faux brown eyes stared up at him a moment. Then Harley Jane Miller's slim fingers slid across his hand, clasping it firmly, disconcerting him with a sudden feeling of connection. "Deal."

CHAPTER THREE

*T*he light changed and Harley started across Sixth Avenue with a clutch of other tourists and two men in suits who actually looked as though they belonged in New York.

She could feel Duncan Lang watching her, his gaze unsettling to her back. And she could still feel his large warm hand enfolding hers as she had promised her holiday away. She wanted to turn around and ask him how he'd done it. How had he enfolded all of her body in his just by clasping her hand?

Why, in the midst of despair, did she still feel the imprint of his heat?

She reached the curb and continued walking down West Forty-eighth Street, wanting to weep. Her holiday. Her poor, dead holiday.

What was she to do? Run away and try to hide? She'd given her word not to and Harley had never broken a promise in her life. Besides, she'd tried that plan and Duncan Lang had found her anyway.

Should she find a bar and get drunk? That had a certain appeal. Numbing out while breaking one of Boyd's taboos in a major way. The rebellion alone would be worth it.

Should she try to cram two weeks of sightseeing into twelve hours? No, there would be no satisfaction in that.

Harley stopped at the corner of West Forty-eighth Street and Fifth Avenue and slowly looked at the people and buildings all around her. She could fulfill one fantasy at least and window-shop. But her heart complained.

She looked down at the guitar case she held in her left hand. A Fender Stratocaster. She had bought a black Fender Stratocaster, and for the next twelve hours—if only for the next twelve hours—it was hers, truly hers. Or rather, it would be truly hers if she and it made some music together.

In that moment, Harley knew that was what she wanted to do most in the world. Weeping and raging, drinking and window-shopping, were nothing compared to the hours of music—other people's music—waiting to be played.

She took a shaky but full breath. There, that felt better. Lots better. Every little gray cell in her brain focused on finding some place safe where she could play her Stratocaster. *Her* Stratocaster. Central Park was too far away. She pulled her map from her purse. There! Bryant Park was just six blocks away, behind the New York Public Library. She started walking down Fifth Avenue, feeling her strength and her confidence return with each step she took.

She turned right on to West Fortieth Street and walked through a black wrought-iron entrance into Bryant Park. It was a surprise. It was big and green and lush, denying the very existence of the shadowed commercial streets that bordered it. To her left stretched two long rows of mature London plane trees shading neatly arranged wooden benches with dark green painted metal arms. In the center of the park was a huge square of green lawn, with a band shell at the far end. To the right she saw another allée of trees and benches.

It was lovely. She walked halfway down a row of benches and sat down. She lifted her Stratocaster reverently from its guitar case, plugged it into the mini-amp, set the sound on its lowest setting, slipped the guitar strap over her neck, and hugged the guitar against her body.

Oh yeah. Much better than chocolate mousse.

She slowly placed her fingers along the frets and then, heart beating fast, she strummed first one chord, and then another, and another. She started breathing again. Here, now, in this park, on this bench, the music she had always longed to play began to transfer from her fingers to her Stratocaster and out into the afternoon air. All the rock-and-roll classics she had loved back home in Sweetcreek. But what was this one? It sounded vaguely familiar, but she couldn't remember the song's title, the artist who had recorded it, anything. Her fingers suddenly froze on the guitar strings.

It was new music. *Her music!*

She wanted to weep. She wanted to scream. She wanted to dance wildly through the park and hug everyone in sight. Her music was back!

Paper! She needed some way to write down her music so it wouldn't be lost. Music sheets, paper bags, anything! She looked wildly around and suddenly saw a discount audio store across the street from the park. Perfect!

Ten minutes later, she was back on her bench, her Stratocaster resting on her thighs, a handheld recorder sitting beside her, music welling from her soul, through her fingers, and into the guitar. There was no time or park or sky while she played. Only a joy so intense, her eyes continually welled with tears. The world only impinged when she accidentally dropped her guitar pick and a young man picked it up and handed it to her.

"Here you go."

She looked around in amazement. There were nearly two dozen people sitting or standing around her. Where had they come from? "Was I playing too loudly?" she asked, badly embarrassed.

"No," said the young man with the rainbow-striped hair who had handed her the pick, "not loudly enough."

The others laughed and smiled and slowly moved away.

Ye gods, she'd had an audience and hadn't even known it! But even worse, it was already dusk. She had promised to meet Duncan Lang at the Hilton at the end of the day. He'd be coming for her soon. In just a few hours, she'd be locked back in her own personal little hell.

With a little help from his old friends at the Ritz-Carlton, Duncan procured a desk clerk uniform for Emma and sent her in undercover to contact Annie Maguire and arrange a rendezvous without Boyd Monroe finding out. There was a lot about Harley Jane Miller, and her holiday, and Mr. Monroe that he did not understand. He wanted some answers. An hour later he stood near the stone ticket booth at the Fifth Avenue and West Sixty-fourth Street entrance to the Central Park Wildlife Center and Zoo. He didn't wait long. A plump woman with graying red hair and large gray eyes strode toward him. She bristled with self-confidence and the air of a mother hen ready to do battle for her chick. It was all a little disconcerting, because Annie Maguire was only Harley's maid, her tenth in nine years.

"Mr. Lang?" she said with a faint Irish brogue.

"Thank you for agreeing to meet me, Miss Maguire," Duncan said, holding out his hand.

She considered it a moment and then shook it. "Anyone who wants to avoid Boyd Monroe interests me."

"You don't like him?" Duncan asked as he led her a few feet away from the ticket booth and they sat down on a wooden bench.

"No."

"But you work for him."

"I work for Harley. There's a difference."

Duncan considered her a moment. She had said Harley, not Jane. Interesting. "You seem unusually protective of a young woman who goes through maids like tissues."

"Boyd fires them, not Harley."

"Just a string of incompetent help, then?"

"No, a string of women who became Harley's friends. Boyd objects to her being close to anyone."

"You seem close and you're still employed," Duncan pointed out.

"That's because Harley and I agreed from the start to play it cool in public. It's worked so far. Boyd hasn't suspected a thing."

So, the Princess was sneaky. Very interesting. Duncan sat back and felt several pieces fall into place in his brain. "Miss Miller has been spending *your* money, hasn't she?"

Annie smiled. "Just a loan. She's good for it."

Duncan smiled back. "More than good for it. Do I understand you right? The escape wasn't as impromptu as it seemed?"

"Yes, and no. I was hired seven months ago. It was just a few weeks after that that Harley started talking about needing to take some of her life back from Boyd. A few months later she was talking about having a holiday, just her, the kid herself, on her own in the big wide world for a little while. Then, about two months ago, her music well dried up and she panicked. I wish you could have seen her, Mr. Lang. You wouldn't be trying to haul her back to Boyd now. All of the light in her soul just started fading away. She plotted a dozen different escapes, figuring out how to evade Boyd, how to pay for her holiday, what she wanted to do."

"Only she didn't do anything."

"You've got to understand," Annie said, leaning toward Duncan, "that Boyd Monroe has spent the last nine years trying to destroy every ounce of self-confidence Harley ever had. He wants her to be completely dependent on him, and that has meant making her afraid of being out in the world alone."

"That's not the woman I met today."

"Really?" Annie said eagerly. "How is she?"

Memory of that brief moment in the doorway of Manny's Music when he had held Harley Jane Miller in his arms warmed Duncan's skin. "Delicious," he almost said, but caught himself just in time.

"Butch and belligerent and in love with her new guitar," he said instead.

"Ah, now that's hopeful."

Duncan began to think so too. "So what made her finally fly the coop?"

"She was teetering on the edge, just about to take the plunge because she had to do something to find her music again," Annie's smile was darkly humorous, "and then Boyd went and pushed her too far."

Duncan loved it when he was right. "The final concert at the Garden?"

"That's right. He wouldn't let her send that audience home satisfied by giving a third encore on the last night of a grueling world tour. He wouldn't let her go to the end-of-the-tour party the band and the roadies were throwing at the Radisson. He wouldn't even let her thank them for all their hard work."

"And then the cheeseburger made her snap."

"You know about that?"

"Enough."

"Well, you're right. The minute Boyd walked out of the suite, she was pacing like a wild animal, scared and determined all at once. It took under five minutes to get her into my coat, hat, and shoes, hand her the three hundred dollars I had on me and my Visa card, and watch her walk out that door."

"You risked losing your job to help her like that?"

"I'd help Harley fly to the moon if that's what it took to escape Boyd Monroe. Besides," Annie said with a grin, "I figured she'd just hire me back."

"Over Boyd's certain objections?"

"You've got to understand, Mr. Lang, that it takes an incredibly strong woman to survive Boyd Monroe for nine long years. I figured a few weeks of freedom would make Harley realize that and give her the courage she needs to take a final stand with the miserable tyrant."

Duncan liked the woman more and more. Smart and loyal, a wonderful combination. The fact that she was so fiercely devoted to the Princess of Pop said a lot for Miss Miller. Annie was nobody's fool, nor was she the type to suffer doormats gladly. "You could be right," he said. "I think a week or two away from Mr. Monroe would have her making *him* dance to *her* tune."

"Is that why you're talking to me instead of collecting your blood money?"

Duncan cringed. For a moment there, they had been getting along so well. "Not at all," he replied. "It's just that Boyd bothers me, and not simply because he has a stranglehold on Harley."

"Aye, I thought you liked her."

"I do not *like* Miss Miller," Duncan testily retorted. "I simply dislike seeing any human being locked in a cage, no matter how golden. My interest in Miss Miller is purely professional."

"Of course it is," Annie said soothingly.

"What I'm really interested in," Duncan grimly continued, "is finding out what's going on in Boyd Monroe's cramped little world. Something's got my antennae up and vibrating all over the place. I don't know what it is, so I'm not entirely eager to throw Miss Miller back into the lion's den, as she calls it, until I know she'll be safe."

"Boyd has never hit her," Annie said, puzzled.

"I didn't think he had. But there's something going on under his surface concern for Harley's well-being and his fear of losing his control over her. I thought you might be able to help me figure it out."

"Why the devil should I?" Annie demanded. "That girl doesn't need a few days of freedom, she needs a lifetime of it, and I won't be the one to help put her back in Boyd's cloister."

The word bothered Duncan, because it was too accurate.

He tried to shake off his discomfort. He had a job to do, no matter who or what Harley Jane Miller was, but the word still chilled his hands. "It could go the other way, you know," he said smoothly. "You might have just the information to prove I shouldn't fulfill my contract. You might be just the one to keep her out of that . . . cloister."

"Where is she now?" Annie demanded mulishly.

"Bryant Park with her new Fender Stratocaster."

"Her what?"

"It's an electric guitar."

Annie's gray eyes widened. "Now that's more like it. She didn't even own an electric guitar before she met Boyd. Her mother said electric guitars weren't feminine."

"Barbara Miller and Boyd Monroe seem to be cut from the same cloth." The same one, actually, that his parents shared.

"Oh, they've got similar ideas about Harley, all right, but Mrs. Miller is basically a weak woman. Harley's taken care of her all of her life. No one would ever call Boyd weak."

"No," Duncan said, "that's not how I would describe him." He stopped a moment. It was a wonder Harley hadn't turned to booze or drugs or even sex to escape the man. But she hadn't. She had simply taken a holiday. She was . . . admirable.

"Look, Annie, I know the guy's a control freak," Duncan hurriedly pushed on, "but is there anything else going on with him? Anything that feels strange or looks odd or some-how doesn't seem to fit his job or his character?"

Annie was silent for a long moment as she considered this. "The only thing I can think of is that sometimes he gets tense about our schedule when there's no reason to be tense."

"Like what?"

"Well, like getting back to Los Angeles, for example. When he returned to the suite after trying and failing to bring Harley back Sunday night, he ranted and raved for a good half hour, not about her being out in the city alone, but about how we'd probably miss the next afternoon's flight to L.A."

"But the recording studio wasn't booked until next week," Duncan said slowly. "Still, he'd scheduled a press conference at LAX."

"Yes, but that's not it," Annie said, frowning in concentra-tion. "He wasn't yelling about Sony or the reporters or any-thing like that. He was yelling about how Harley had screwed up *his* schedule and how he had to be on that flight to L.A., not an earlier flight, and not a later flight, but that one o'clock flight we had tickets for."

"Interesting," Duncan murmured, staring out at the lush trees without really seeing them. Boyd had created a schedule that had nothing to do with Harley and everything to do with reaching Los Angeles on a particular day and at a particular time. He suddenly stood up and held out his hand. "Annie, you've been a tremendous help. Thank you."

"You're welcome," she said in confusion, shaking his hand as she stared up at him. "What does it mean?"

"I haven't the vaguest idea. But I'm going to find out." He started to turn away, and then stopped. "Just out of idle curiosity, what kind of cash advance limit do you have on your Visa?"

"Ten thousand dollars. I told her to use all of it."

"She's doing her best," Duncan said with a grin.

He strode into Emma's office ten minutes later bristling with energy and excitement. "Em," he said by way of hello to his assistant, "I want you to get me a detailed itinerary for every second of Jane Miller's recent world tour."

"Sure. But before—"

"I also want you to get me Harley Jane Miller's complete bank records, and then do the same by Boyd Monroe."

"Okay. But you—"

Duncan strode through the connecting door and into his sunlit office. "Then I want—" He stumbled to a halt. Two inordinately handsome men were sitting at his conference table. He glanced back and saw now how anxious Emma seemed. She mouthed, "I tried to warn you." He nodded and, feeling very much like a truant child being confronted by the principal and the truant officer, walked across his office to the two men. "Hi, Dad. Hi, Brandon. You're both back early."

Brandon Lang was two inches taller than his younger brother. At thirty-two, he had golden blond hair, pale blue eyes, a sleek, well-groomed body draped in a dark blue Armani suit, and a million-dollar smile that had effortlessly opened every door for him his entire life. Their father, Colby Lang, was Brandon's older, slightly thickset twin. He was wearing a pale gray Oxxford suit. He was not smiling.

"What in blue blazes do you mean by taking on the Miller case without my approval?" was how he greeted his younger son.

Duncan's eyes narrowed. "I couldn't reach you and it's just the kind of high-profile case you're always hammering at us to bring to the firm," he coolly replied.

"Precisely," the elder Lang snapped as he rose from his chair and began to pace the office. "You botch up this case and the whole world will know about it. You'll give the firm a black eye. I want you to turn the job over to Brandon. Now."

"No," Duncan said. If the Princess of Pop could take a stand, then so could he.

His father stared at him. "What did you say?"

"I said no. I am not a child, Father, no matter what you

believe. I am fully capable of completing this case to everyone's satisfaction, and I will."

"You haven't got a clue how to run a proper investigation," Colby sneered. "You've worked on this job for a day now and I'll bet you anything you care to name that you don't have an idea where the girl is."

"Then you'd lose," Duncan retorted. "I know exactly where she is."

Colby stared at him a moment. "Then why the hell haven't you brought her in and closed the case?" he demanded.

"Because there are some things that don't add up," Duncan replied, shoving his hands into the back pockets of his jeans. His wardrobe was his one corporate rebellion. After two years even his father had stopped complaining. "I want to pursue a few leads and make sure nothing fishy is going on before I return Miss Miller to our client."

Colby swore, virulently. "I might have known *you* would try to make a mountain out of a molehill. There is nothing going on, Duncan, except a very simple missing-persons case which you claim to have solved. There will be no grandstanding in this company, particularly by *you*. Bring the girl in and bring her in now."

Duncan felt shrink-wrapped. "Oh, I'll bring her in, Father."

"Good," Colby barked, heading for the office door. "I've got a five o'clock meeting. I expect this case closed when I return."

The two brothers stared after their father for a moment. "Do you really know where Jane Miller is?" Brandon asked mildly.

"Of course I do!" Duncan snapped, whirling around to his desk.

"Good work," Brandon said, standing up. "I didn't think you had it in you."

"Imagine my surprise," Duncan said bitterly as he sat down in his green leather chair.

"I'm joking, Brother!"

Duncan flushed. "Sorry, Brandon. I'm the overly sensitive type."

"That must be why you get all the best women," Brandon retorted.

Duncan wryly regarded his older brother standing in front of his desk. "You do all right. How come you're back from Florida so soon?"

"Oh, case successfully closed, on to new adventures. The usual sort of thing."

Duncan chuckled ruefully. "It must be nice where you live. Don't you ever get tired of everything going so smoothly and easily for you?"

Brandon's smile faded for a moment and then made a quick recovery. "It has its benefits."

"Yes—Dad doesn't yell at you every hour on the hour, for one."

"He'll lighten up, Duncan. Just be patient."

"Two years adds up to a lot of patience, Brother."

"Yes, and everyone is impressed. Really, we all are, Duncan."

"Except Mother and Dad. There are times, Brandon, when I've resented your status as Favorite Son."

"And there are times, Brother, when I've resented all the fun you've had while I stayed at home with my nose to the grindstone."

"Really?" said Duncan with interest.

"Really," Brandon replied with his million-dollar smile. "Or at least I've resented all the party invitations you've received from the Beautiful People over the years."

"Sure you have."

Brandon chuckled. "Look, Duncan, I need your help. I've convinced Armand Giscard to use Colangco to protect his collection of diamonds while they're in the country for the Bartlett Museum jewelry exhibit."

That made Duncan sit up. "I thought Baldwin Security was handling that job."

Brandon's smile was smug. "I convinced Giscard that we're the better firm."

"But Colangco doesn't take mob clients, even French ones."

"There is an exception to every rule."

"Publicity?"

Brandon nodded. "This is a very high profile security job, and not because of Giscard's connections. It's not every day that a million dollars' worth of diamonds that once belonged to Catherine the Great go on display at the Bartlett Museum. And it isn't every day that we get to guard them. It took a while, but I finally convinced Dad just before you came in that Americans have no idea that Armand Giscard is one of the kingpins of the French mob. Our clients will hear the name Catherine the Great and that's all they'll care about. The publicity for Colangco will be tremendous.

"Anyway," Brandon continued, "I'm in charge of managing security while the diamonds are in the country, and I've got a problem. Giscard only agreed this morning to hire us, and the diamonds are due to arrive Thursday for the Friday opening. I'm up to my neck on this one. The Bartlett's security system is ten years out of date. I'll be working day and night until the opening to make sure the diamonds are properly protected. I was wondering if you'd be willing to help me out with the transport route. Come up with the security plan we'll need to get the diamonds from Giscard's private jet to the museum, you know the sort of thing."

Duncan was not merely surprised, he was stunned. It was the first important job anyone in the firm had ever voluntarily given him, and it was Brandon playing Santa Claus. Recognition of any kind from his older brother was rare. "Sure," he said, careful to hide his eagerness. "Glad to help out. Have the background material sent to Emma. I'll come up with a plan by tonight."

"Great. Thanks a mill, Duncan," Brandon said with a lazy salute as he strolled from the office.

Duncan folded his arms across his chest with a happy sigh. He'd been right all along. The Princess of Pop was just the push he needed to start carving a niche for himself in the family firm. He glanced at his watch. Three-thirty. His father would be back by seven. Time to grab a late lunch or an early dinner.

He walked out into Emma's office. "Brandon's going to be sending over some information on the Giscard diamond job. When it arrives, have it messengered to my apartment, will you?"

"Sure," Emma said. "Are you really going to bring Jane Miller in before we check out this banking and itinerary information you asked me to get?"

"That's what Dad wants," Duncan replied, walking out into the hall.

It was just after four-thirty when Duncan walked into Bryant Park. He didn't need the tracker he had surreptitiously attached to Harley's mini-amp to find her. He seemed to have developed his own personal Harley radar in the last few hours. She sat cross-legged on a wooden bench beneath well-manicured shade trees, softly playing the new guitar balanced across her thighs, a small black tape recorder sitting beside her, and oblivious to the crowd of people around her. She had kept her word not to run off, then, in spite of her pleas and her arguments for freedom. Interesting.

He should not be here, of course. There were other things—like the transport plan for Armand Giscard's diamonds—that needed his time. But sitting all alone eating a late lunch had given him time to think, and all he had thought about was Harley. He had wanted to see her again (he would not let himself ask why), so he had tracked her to the park. Now he had found her, but he didn't want to disturb that vacuum in space she had created for herself. It seemed too important to her. So he sat down on a park bench two rows away and studied her, wondering why he couldn't seem to take his eyes off her.

She wasn't beautiful or even pretty in the traditional sense, but there was something wonderfully attractive about her, even with the fake brown hair and eyes. He watched her playing her guitar now and envied that guitar. She had beautiful hands—strong and slender and graceful. He wondered how they would feel against his skin. And he liked her expressive, slightly freckled face too. But it was more than that.

There was something within her that radiated out for all the world to see, if the world would only look. His world had been gray for so long, that it took a moment for him to identify that bright aura: it was passion. Passion shimmered in her and around her with a glow that was hypnotic. A passion for freedom. A passion for the music she played, even though Boyd Monroe had spent the last nine years trying to murder that in her.

Duncan had never summoned the energy to hate anyone before, but he began to think that it would be an easy thing to hate Mr. Monroe. Annie Maguire had described nine years of soul murder. It had made him think of his own existence. Was that what he'd been doing these last two years? Murdering his own soul? Did he have his own internal little Boyd Monroe smothering the life out of him?

It had never occurred to him before this, perhaps because he had never really understood what life looked like and felt like before this. He began to understand now. Life was the passion shimmering in Harley, which he lacked. It was intelligence that was startling in its intensity. It was a smattering of freckles across a pert nose and angular cheeks that had always been hidden before by Jane Miller's skillful layers of makeup.

But this wasn't the Princess of Pop he studied, and he suspected it wasn't even the Jane Miller who had been caged for nine years. This was Harley, the Harley that Barbara

Miller despaired of and Boyd Monroe despised and Annie Maguire was so loyal to. A Harley who was beginning to spread her large, cramped wings just when he had been ordered to stuff them back into her gilded cage.

Duncan shuddered a little. What kind of self-respect would he have if he turned her in to Boyd? She didn't deserve imprisonment, she was too much a creature of life. He knew what it was like to live in a small cage. He'd lived in one of his own choosing these last two years. Was escape his only chance for happiness too? But how could it be? Freedom for him had been just as bereft of satisfaction as the Lang family penitentiary.

Duncan had got the idea at an early age that life should be enjoyed, and he had set out to enjoy it with gusto. He had partied his way through high school and college, graduating from both institutions by the skin of his teeth. Rather than stepping onto the narrow path his family had laid out for him straight to a corner office in the prestigious Colangco International security firm, he had fled New York and even the country to partake of wine, women, and song with an exuberance that had made him extremely popular on every inhabited continent.

But after a while, a life of wine, women, and song had begun to pall. All of his relationships with women like Charmaine Relker and la Comtesse Pichaud had been casual—pleasurable, it was true—but short-term and ultimately unsatisfying. At the age of twenty-seven, he had finally taken stock of himself and didn't like what he saw: a man without strong morals or ethics, a man whose life was empty and purposeless, a man who had hundreds of friends and was very much alone.

There had seemed only one way to escape that miasma of the soul: forsake revelry and follow in his brother's footsteps. From his birth, Brandon had been held up to him as the good son, the perfect son, the pedestal to aspire to. Duncan had quite naturally rebelled against that goodness at an early age.

But as a very experienced and world-weary twenty-seven-year-old man, he had decided that perhaps Brandon had had the right idea all along.

So he had crawled over broken Dom Perignon bottles back to his parents, vowed to be good and sober and even celibate if necessary, and asked to be taken into the family firm to prove himself. And he had been taken in, except no one in his family believed his sincere avowals of temperance, obedience, and duty for a second. They had relegated him to the simplest of cases to keep him out of trouble and to avoid staining their company's sterling reputation with his inevitable (as far as they were concerned) mistakes, laziness, and disregard.

This mindless work left him bored out of his mind after one year, and in agony after two. He had tried to stay the course, thinking his sheer persistence would finally prove that he was an able member of the firm. He had even dated all of the trust-fund females his parents had thrown at him as suitable potential mates. But it hadn't worked. Watching Harley now, he felt the absolute failure of these last two years.

There had been no satisfaction, and no happiness. Watching Harley now, he realized that in his entire life he had never tasted even a moment of the sheer happiness she exuded as she softly played her Stratocaster. Not with Charmaine Relker. Not in obediently coming into the office on time every day for two years.

Did the possibility of such happiness even exist for him? He thought about escape again, but where could he go? He couldn't think of a job or a career he'd like. Relationship, commitment, and marriage were not in his vocabulary. What else was there?

Duncan looked again at Harley through the growing shadows in the park. Well, there was this case. It had actually demanded that he use his brain, and it offered a real opportunity to finally prove to his family that he had value. Maybe he could siphon the beginnings of satisfaction from this case.

Maybe he could learn something about happiness by studying it in its native habitat for a little while. Maybe the Princess of Pop really could help him turn his life around.

He smiled as he watched her. She was a gamine with a lovely, slender throat that he very much wanted to feel arched against his lips.

Suddenly the air left his lungs. He had the sensation of major backpedaling, and he was grateful. This was *not* the time to let hormones wreak havoc with his life, and this was not the woman at whom those hormones should be directed. She was an innocent, for Christ's sake, and a professional responsibility!

She was also his long-awaited pardon from this damned barren rock of penitence and obedience to which his family had banished him.

He stood up, slipped a stick of cinnamon gum into his mouth, and walked toward Harley just as she began putting her guitar back into its case. Duncan had deliberately missed his father's arbitrary deadline to turn her in. He'd miss it some more by letting her have this one last night of freedom. He'd given her his word and not even Colby Lang could make him break it. Only at midnight and not before would he take her back to the Ritz-Carlton, close out the case to his father's and Boyd Monroe's satisfaction, and maybe, just maybe, jump-start his life.

CHAPTER FOUR

"*R*eady?"

Harley finished closing her guitar case and looked up. Duncan Lang's black eyes smiled down at her. "Yes," she said, hastily standing up.

She bent over her Maxi-Mouse, focusing all of her attention on the amplifier so she wouldn't have to notice that Duncan Lang really was amazingly, disconcertingly, gorgeous. Then her brain started working again. "Wait a minute," she said, puzzled. "What are you doing here? I thought we were meeting at—" Then she saw the tiny electronic square on the back of the amp. "What's this?" she said, pulling it off. She straightened up and studied it a moment. Then it hit her. "This is a tracker. You bugged me!"

"Well . . ." Duncan said, looking ill at ease.

Righteous fury swelled within her. "I gave you my word I'd meet you at dusk and *you bugged me*?"

"I'm not in the most trusting of professions," he explained, turning his winsome smile on her.

"Get away from me!" she yelled, shoving at his broad chest and making him stumble back a few steps.

"Put yourself in my shoes, Miss Miller—"

"No!"

"I saw a very determined and very desperate young woman," he persisted, "who might very easily have decided that her promise to me had been extracted under duress, making that promise null and void. You could have flown off to Brazil the minute my back was turned."

"You really are the most despicable," Harley seethed, picking up her guitar case, "horrible"—she grabbed the Maxi-Mouse and tape recorder—"detestable man I've ever met!" She began to stalk from the park.

"Actually," he said, trotting up to her side, "I'm a charming, even entertaining, kind of guy once you get to know me."

"I have *no* intention of getting to know you!"

"People have actually been known to cheer when I walk into a party."

"Looking forward to playing pin the tail on the *ass,* no doubt."

"The interviews you've given haven't done you justice," Duncan said admiringly as he followed her toward Sixth Avenue. "You really have got some kind of mouth on you."

Vibrating with fury, Harley stopped stock-still in the middle of the sidewalk, took a deep breath, and screamed. Passersby looked at her curiously, but didn't stop.

"Feel better?" Duncan politely inquired.

"Lots," she growled, starting to walk again. The problem was, venting some of her frustration *had* helped. "Okay, we've checked in, I'm still in New York, your precious case is safe. You can go off and harass some other poor slob now."

"No can do, Princess."

"Why the hell not?" Harley demanded, glaring up at the hunk.

"Because you object to electronic surveillance," he blandly replied.

"So?"

"So, remove the technology and what have you got? The personal touch."

"Oh, for crying out—"

"Besides, I agreed to give you until midnight so I could do a little digging and satisfy my curiosity on a few subjects. One of those subjects happens to be you. How can I dig if you're nowhere around to be dug into?"

"That wasn't part of our deal!"

"It is now."

Harley was feeling a little naked. She didn't have a single bargaining chip to her name. "I suppose I'm stuck with you for the rest of the night."

"That's the general idea."

"Swell," she muttered. Her last few hours of freedom and she had to spend them with a maggot like Duncan Lang.

"What's on the tape recorder?" he asked. "Death threats?"

"New music."

"You're kidding! So soon?"

She looked up at him, nonplussed. He actually seemed happy for her. "I guess I lucked out," she replied. "It's probably because of the guitar."

"Or your new wardrobe, or seeing *The Pinnacle* at the Richard Rodgers last night, or having a cheeseburger whenever you damn well please."

Harley stopped and studied him a moment. "You *have* kept good tabs on me."

"That's why I make the big bucks."

"So why didn't you accost me yesterday?"

"Because you were always one step ahead of me yesterday. You really did a very good job of hiding yourself, Miss Miller. The switch at the RIHGA was nothing short of brilliant."

An odd little pleasure burrowed into her heart. "Thank you. What made you look for me at Manny's?"

"The theme of your escape seemed to be music, you didn't have your guitar with you, and you love rock and roll." He shrugged. "It added up to Manny's."

He had puzzled her again. "Most people wouldn't think so."

"I'm not most people."

"That's an understatement."

He smiled down at her, and Harley realized her first impression of him was right: he really did have the loveliest smile. It drew her in and asked her to share in his amusement. It was also the most amazingly seductive smile, because, for a moment, she almost *did* smile back at him. She caught herself just in time.

"Hungry?" Duncan asked as they reached Sixth Avenue.

Harley's stomach gurgled loud enough for half of New York to hear.

Duncan laughed. "I'll take that as a yes."

"I didn't have lunch," Harley said, hating her blush. "I was distracted."

Duncan took the Maxi-Mouse and the tape recorder from her right hand. "Let's drop this stuff off at your hotel, then, and go have some dinner. My treat."

"And that's supposed to make up for having to spend my last few hours of freedom with *you*?"

"No. But no one should have to face Boyd Monroe on an empty stomach."

He had disconcerted her again. For a moment there, the man who had been sent to clip her wings had felt almost like . . . an ally. At the least, he had a commanding way with taxis. He raised one hand, whistled, and a yellow streak barreled to a stop beside them at the curb. Duncan opened the door for her and then loaded her equipment into the trunk of the cab, handling the Stratocaster as gently as even she could wish. Then he slid onto the back seat beside her, and they charged toward the New York Hilton and Towers.

"That Stratocaster and you seem made for each other," he said.

"Oh yeah." An old familiar heaviness weighed her down again. "Only Boyd won't let me keep it."

"You're twenty-six years old and legally independent. Tell Boyd to lump it."

Startled again, Harley looked up into his face. She saw anger there, and something else she couldn't quite read. "You don't have to take me back tonight."

"Yes I do."

"Why?" Harley cried.

"Because it's my job and because I have something to prove."

"To whom?"

"To everyone," he replied bitterly.

They were silent as the cab swung around in front of the Hilton lobby. Duncan paid the driver, then slid out of the cab and unloaded Harley's equipment from the trunk. "I'll wait for you here," he said, not quite looking at her.

Harley carried her things through the lobby and onto the elevator. She stared up at the mini-TV monitor. CNN was on, reporting on the stock market as the elevator sped upward. There was nothing to distract her from the tension blanketing her and the hunk in tight-fitting jeans waiting for her.

He had put a tracker on her amp, and now he trusted her not to escape through one of the Hilton's many other exits? The man did not make sense.

Even though he waited seventeen floors below, she could still feel his presence as she walked into her room. It actually made her nervous as she looked through her packed closet for something to wear on her last night of freedom. He was dressed casually, so sequins were out. She finally chose a dress she was certain Boyd wouldn't let her keep: a neon pink off-the-shoulder minidress with matching stockings and shoes. She pulled off black and put on pink, slid the slim gold chain holding her pendant back over her head, and then stood in front of the dresser mirror brushing her hair, still surprised at the brunette who stared back at her and how quickly and easily the brush slid through her hair.

Back in Sweetcreek, there had never been enough money for her to get her hair cut every month. It grew fast and she liked it short, so she had learned to cut it herself. That skill hadn't left her. She had chopped off her long strawberry blond hair an hour after she had escaped the Ritz-Carlton and she'd been luxuriating in two-inch-long hair ever since. Boyd would be horrified when he saw her again, and that made Harley smile.

Short hair was something she would *not* give up when she went back to him. She'd find a way to get her hands on a pair of scissors every four weeks, and there was nothing he could do to stop her.

She shoved some money and her room card key into a tiny pink purse and rode the elevator back down to the lobby.

"Whoa."

Harley faltered to a stop just outside the Hilton's main entrance. Duncan Lang was leaning against a cab opposite her and staring at her in open admiration. A blush heated her face. A man hadn't looked at her like that since she was in high school. Unfortunately, she had lost her teenage aplomb long ago. She wasn't quite certain where to look or what to say.

"It is absolutely criminal of Boyd Monroe to hide you in those damn sack dresses he insists you wear," Duncan stated. He opened the cab door. "How do you feel about Italian?" he asked, as if he hadn't just scorched her body with his hot gaze.

"That would be great," Harley said as she ducked into the cab, disconcerted by his sudden shift into cool waters. "Boyd won't let me eat pasta. He says it's fattening."

"No wonder your music dried up," Duncan said, sliding

onto the seat beside her. "You've been denied even the most basic of pleasures. Let's order you every pasta ever made."

For the first time since she had met him, Harley grinned. "I like the way you think, at least sometimes, Mr. Lang."

"Please," he said with a pained expression, "call me Duncan. Mr. Lang sounds like my father, and there's no better way to take the fun out of an evening than to bring *him* into the conversation. I called and made reservations at Torre di Pisa. I hope that's all right."

"It's fine," Harley assured him. *"Travel & Leisure* gave it a good review last month. I had even thought about putting it on my itinerary."

Duncan gave the driver the address and then looked at her. "What itinerary?"

Harley pulled the small notebook from her tiny purse and handed it to him as the cab pulled out. He idly thumbed through the pages, dark eyes beginning to glow with badly suppressed amusement and she couldn't for the life of her figure out why. All she had done was write down what to do in Manhattan and when to do it for every day of the next two weeks. "You are very . . . organized," he said.

"I learned from the best," she said, taking back the notebook and putting it in her purse. "Boyd's maniacal about scheduling. And I wanted to pack as much fun into my holiday as I could."

"I have never equated schedules with fun before."

"Oh, really?" she said, feeling testy. "And what do you do for fun?"

He looked away. "I've forgotten."

Ten minutes later they were sitting across from each other in flowing, curved-back dining chairs opposite the open kitchen of Torre di Pisa on West Forty-fourth Street. Harley was more than a little uncomfortable. The last time she had had dinner alone with a man she had been seventeen. Ed Broderick had taken her to Bubble's Diner for a burger and shake before driving her to the Sweetcreek Drive-In for a movie and some halfway decent necking.

This midtown Italian restaurant with its skewed interior perspectives and bright red clock tower was hardly Bubble's Diner, and Duncan Lang was the farthest thing from being gangly, nineteen, and sunburnt. She got the distinct impression that he had a wealth of experience in the delicate art of necking and other, more advanced, activities. She hurriedly raised her menu to hide the soft blush creeping into her cheeks. Almost twenty-seven and a virgin, seated across from a probable Don Juan. There was no way to balance those scales back into comfort and ease.

"So, why Harley?" he asked.

"Hmm?" she said, lowering her menu in confusion.

"Why did your folks name you Harley?"

"Oh. Daddy named me after his favorite motorcycle. I've always been grateful he didn't call me Hog instead."

Duncan chuckled, adding to her unease. She had just discovered that laughter and sensuality were a lethal combination.

Having struck out with predinner libations, their waiter—in black slacks, white shirt, and burgundy vest—returned to their table and took their orders, keeping his face expressionless as Harley went on and on. If this was the last meal of the condemned, she intended to make the most of it. She wanted to start with the deep-fried artichokes and cardoons with shaved Parmigiano-Reggiano and the exotic field greens salad with lemon-mustard dressing, followed by the mussel soup with toasted croutons and saffron. With Duncan grinning at her and egging her on, she ordered the rigatoni, and the Fettuccine Rusticana, and the chicken and sun-dried tomato ravioli. She even agreed to a bottle of Italian red wine, although she hadn't had a sip of alcohol in nine years. Purity was the hallmark of the Jane Miller image.

"So," Duncan said, leaning back in his chair once their bemused waiter had left, "tell me all about yourself."

"You're the Great Detective," she retorted. "Aren't you supposed to know everything about me already?"

"Oh, I know all the facts," Duncan blithely replied. "They just don't add up to the woman sitting in front of me now."

"Don't they?" Harley said coolly.

"Nope. Tell me some more about your father. I know he split when you were two. Was it hard not having him around?"

"No. It was for the best. He was no account."

"Did you ever see him again?"

The pain of that single meeting awoke in Harley. She hid from Duncan's X-ray eyes by taking a sip of water. "Once," she casually replied. "I was eighteen. My second album had just hit the charts. He came around to see what I could do for him. I refused to give him a dime. I haven't seen him since."

"I wish I could say the same about most of my relatives," Duncan said feelingly.

That chased most of the pain away and made Harley grin. "I haven't heard you say one nice thing about your family. Don't you like them?"

"They don't make it easy," Duncan said with a sigh. "My brother is a paragon, my mother is a social doyenne, and my father treats me like an eight-year-old who should be spanked every day. They are neither loving nor lovable."

"You *have* had it rough," Harley said sincerely. "I mean, that was something I could always count on: my mother loved me. A lot of times she didn't particularly like me, but she did love me."

"Why didn't she like you?"

"Oh, I was just such a huge disappointment to her."

"How could you be?"

"I wasn't the daughter—I wasn't the girl—she wanted me to be."

"She wanted Jane Miller," Duncan said quietly.

Harley looked up from the slice of bread she was buttering

to find warm black eyes regarding her. He *did* understand! "Yes. The irony is, she finally got her."

"It's odd," Duncan said after a long moment of silence. "We both seem to be the black sheep of our respective families."

"Ye gods, what did *you* do? Become a Grateful Dead groupie?"

He shook his head. "Worse. I had this strange belief that life was to be enjoyed and chances were there to be taken. So I took them. I turned my life into one continual party. You don't realize, Princess, that you are sitting with the self-annointed Playboy of the Western World."

"Actually," Harley said modestly, "I'd guessed."

"Did you? How?"

There was that damn blush again. "Woman's intuition. So let me see if I've got this right: while I was slaving away in recording studios and on concert tours, you were doing your level best to have as much fun as humanly possible?"

"Yep. I even thought I'd succeeded"—he was looking at her strangely—"but it seems I was wrong." He grabbed a breadstick and began breaking it into bite-size pieces. "It turns out that even a life of continual pleasure can pall after a while."

"No challenge," Harley said, nodding.

He looked startled. "Exactly. So I returned to the family fold and the family business and I've been doing penance ever since. So you see, you're not the only black sheep at this table."

"But I've been whitewashed," Harley pointed out.

"Have you?"

"Sure. I'm Jane Miller now, remember?" Harley unconsciously clenched her right hand on the table. "There's no one whiter than Jane. Boyd is satisfied. The record-buying public is thrilled. My mother is thrilled." Harley's clenched fist began to throb. "And it's getting harder and harder to hold back the scream that's been building in my throat these last nine years."

"Why don't you just let it out?" Duncan asked quietly. "You made a good start on West Fortieth Street."

"It wasn't supposed to be like this!" Harley said ferociously. "I *never* wanted to be a pop star. Rock and roll was my life. I ate, breathed, and slept it. How in God's name did I become Boyd Monroe's doormat?"

"The man bears a striking resemblance to a bulldozer. That's a pretty hard thing to stand up to when you're a seventeen-year-old green girl from a small town."

Harley blinked back sudden tears. The last thing she expected from the man hired to return her to Boyd was gentleness and understanding.

Their waiter returned and began setting dishes on their table: salad and soup and fried artichokes for Harley, grilled calamari and red onions topped with pesto and a watercress salad for Duncan. The waiter poured dark red wine into their goblets and then headed off to the rest of his customers.

"This looks fantastic," Harley murmured, breathing in the luscious aromas.

"It is," Duncan assured her.

"You've been here before?"

"With a trust-fund female from Long Island. The food made it bearable. Dig in."

They both dug in with gusto.

"You know, I don't think you give yourself enough credit," Duncan said, waving a speared calamari at her. "You're practically Rapunzel, the way Boyd Monroe has kept you locked up in his ivory tower all these years. But you ventured out into the Big Apple all on your lonesome anyway. Most women, especially the whitewashed ones, wouldn't have that kind of pluck."

"I wasn't sure I did either."

"And now?"

Harley slowly stirred her soup. "Now I'm beginning to believe I do."

"But you're not convinced?"

"I think . . . I think it's the real reason I took this holiday in the first place. The Cowardly Lion in search of his courage."

"As the Wizard pointed out," Duncan said, taking another bite of calamari, "the Lion always had courage, he just didn't know it."

"Your point being?"

"That Annie Maguire is right: you are a very strong and courageous woman and even Boyd couldn't kill that in you."

"You spoke to Annie today?" Harley said in surprise.

"Just doin' my job, ma'am."

"What did you find out?"

"I don't know yet. I'll let you know when I do."

That puzzled Harley. But then, a lot of things about this man puzzled her. He was a lot more complex than he appeared on his very attractive surface. "But you're taking me back to Boyd tonight. Isn't that the end of the story?"

"Only for some," he said after a sip of wine. "My curiosity has been piqued. I intend to do some more digging."

"You don't make any sense."

"Tell me about it," Duncan said, starting on his salad. "Your mother thinks you've been kidnapped by white slavers, you know."

Harley choked on her mussel soup. "She would," she gasped. "Mama always figured that a female's life was like a Hitchcock film—danger around every corner. I'd better call her again."

"It's okay. I spoke with her a few hours ago and reassured her that you're hale and hearty with innocence intact. She thought at first that I had kidnapped you, but I was finally able to allay even that fear. Isn't she a little high-strung for a store clerk?"

Harley chuckled as she cut into her salad. "Mama's had a

lifetime of hard knocks. That sort of thing makes some people nervous."

"The last nine years can't have been hard on her. Why is she still working? From everything I've read, you've built her a new home, you buy her a new car every two years, you give her enough money for a family of twelve to live on luxuriously, but there she is, selling hair ribbons and frozen dinners at the Sweetcreek General Store."

Harley shrugged. "She likes to feel useful."

Duncan leaned back in his chair, balancing his wine goblet in one hand. "And how do you like to feel?"

"I don't know anymore," Harley said, staring at her salad. "That's one of the things I hoped to figure out on my holiday. Couldn't I—"

"No."

It sounded cold and final and not at all like a black sheep who believed life was to be enjoyed and chances were there to be taken. Talk about mixed messages. She couldn't figure him out at all.

Harley sighed as her right hand fiddled with her pendant. "You really are the most annoying man."

"So I've been told. Why do you always wear that? It's in every picture I've ever seen of you."

"This?" Harley said, holding up the gold musical note. "It's my good luck charm. I bought it the day I cut my first single. You've got to admit that, careerwise at least, it's worked pretty well. I'd feel jinxed without it."

"I'm amazed Boyd didn't make you wear a cross instead."

"He tried," she wryly informed him.

To her surprise, Duncan spent the rest of the meal keeping their conversation very much away from the personal. He talked about the lunacy of the Rio de Janeiro Mardis Gras. He succinctly summarized a highly colorful scene thrown by an Australian matriarch at the Sydney Opera House that had even stopped Luciano Pavarotti in mid-aria. He described Italian villas he had known and loved.

"I get the feeling you did *not* have a working-class up-bringing," Harley said as their waiter placed a bowl with scoops of hazelnut, vanilla, and chocolate ice cream before her.

"Hardly. I led the usual sheltered life of the young and rich: private school, prep school—I should say *schools*. I was thrown out of three before I graduated," Duncan explained as their waiter placed a duplicate bowl of ice cream before him. "Then on to Harvard, which asked me to leave, and finally Columbia, where I actually managed to earn a degree."

"And that made you a trained investigator," Harley said doubtfully.

"Anyone joining the family firm has to take courses at the Police Academy along with some follow-up college courses in computer science, criminology, and psychology."

"Hence Colangco's sterling reputation?"

"We always hire the best people," Duncan modestly replied. "Eat your gelato."

Harley ate her dessert as she tried to puzzle out the man seated across from her. Youthful rebellion and adult debauchery did not lead to the dedicated detective now demolishing three very delicious scoops of ice cream. He'd said he had something to prove. What was it and to whom?

And why was she spending so much energy thinking about Duncan Lang when in a few short hours he'd be returning her to Boyd Monroe's clutches? She made as little sense as he did. All of the pleasures of the day rolled through her—even the surprising pleasure of Duncan's company—and coalesced into a despair that robbed her of further appetite.

"Finished?"

Harley looked up from her melting ice cream to find Duncan regarding her with veiled black eyes. She hadn't even been through Central Park or seen the Empire State Building. Her music had just started coming back. An hour in Boyd's company and it could disappear forever. "Yeah, I'm finished."

"You've got three hours left before you have to get back into your pumpkin. Where do you want to go now?" he asked, dropping money onto the table to pay for their meal.

"Brazil?" she asked hopefully.

He smiled. "Try again."

"Okay, okay." She thought for a moment. "It's nighttime in Manhattan. Let's hit the clubs."

The Surrealistic Pillow—named after one of rock and roll's classic albums—resided in a three-story dark red brick building and announced itself with a pink neon sign that matched Harley's dress.

"Where are we?" she demanded as she stepped out of the taxi.

"At one of the best clubs in town," Duncan replied.

They walked through a simple wooden door and into a foyer that led down three steps to a horseshoe-shaped level with nearly a hundred small wooden tables and discreet lighting. Five steps below that was a large wooden dance floor, already crowded, with a small stage rising up a few feet at the far end. A six-piece Latino band had everyone moving enthusiastically to its intoxicating combination of rock-and-roll and salsa rhythms. Every age, color, and type of humanity was either dancing or talking at the small tables. Harley was in love.

"How on earth did you find this place?" she demanded.

He smiled down at her. "I live just around the corner."

"You live in *Chelsea?*"

"Yep."

"Why?"

"I like it."

He liked it. The boss's son liked living in unglamorous Chelsea. The man seemed determined to avoid all pigeonholes.

Duncan managed to claim a table on their right. Feeling

practically effervescent, Harley ordered a mineral water and lime from the tattooed waitress and settled back in her chair to soak in everything.

The band's music bore no relation to the material she had dutifully written and performed these last nine years. It thrummed through her veins and heated her cheeks and lightened her heart. She forgot all about Boyd and midnight and the recording studio in Los Angeles.

"Great group," Duncan said as the band started to leave the stage.

"They have real possibilities," Harley agreed.

"They remind me a little of the Miami Sound Machine, with just enough hard-ass rock and roll to give it some edge."

Harley's jaw fell open. "You *like* hard-ass rock and roll?"

"Of course I do," Duncan replied as he leaned back in his chair. "It's primal and sexy and energizing, everything my parents loathe."

Harley laughed. "What albums do they have in their CD collection? Engelbert Humperdinck?"

"Jane Miller."

Harley gasped and then dissolved into laughter, nearly sliding off her chair. "You're awful!"

"That's what *they* always say," he woefully replied. "All right, this looks interesting!"

A multiethnic group, announced as Meat-Grinder, had taken the stage: five young men dressed in black leather pants and boots and nothing else. "They leave nothing to the imagination, do they?" Harley murmured. Their tattoos and pierced earrings were copious. Their music exploded into the club as almost every female in the audience rushed the stage to stand in hyperventilating adoration before the group.

"What do you think?" Duncan asked when Meat-Grinder had finished its first song.

"Hot music, lousy diction," Harley pronounced. "What's the point of writing lyrics if the audience can't understand a word you're singing?"

"Purist," Duncan charged.

Harley grinned at him.

They listened to the music and compared notes on their favorite rock groups, singers, and songs, finding a surprisingly strong similarity in tastes and appreciation. Harley found it invigorating to finally talk about the music and performers she loved with someone who didn't disparage her tastes, like Boyd, or shrink back like her mother when she discussed Grace Slick in a five-minute monologue of superlatives. During the Meat-Grinders' set, Duncan made her forget that to all intents and purposes she was his prisoner. But that didn't last long.

Their conversation was interrupted by the thunderous applause and shrieks and whistles all around them as Meat-Grinder took its final bow and left the stage. The band was replaced by a man in his late forties, perhaps early fifties, with an enormous black waxed mustache. A white sweatshirt covered a small potbelly. His bald head gleamed under the stage lights.

"Ladies and gentlemen," he bellowed into a cordless microphone, "this is your last chance to sign up for our weekly open mike sets tomorrow night. Groups, duos, and solo artists can perform two or more songs as long as they don't add up to more than ten minutes of material. We've still got some time slots left, so if you're interested, come see me over by the bar."

Harley stared at him as he left the stage.

"What are you thinking?" Duncan demanded. *"Harley?"*

"I've always loved rock and roll and I've always wanted to sing it in front of a rock audience."

"Harley—"

"Boyd says I can't, that I'm no good at it. He says no one would want to listen to anything I sing outside of Jane Miller's comfy little niche in the music world."

"Harley—"

"Duncan, I have to know!" she cried. "I have to know if

he's right. I have to know if I've been wanting something these last nine years that I really can't have because I'm not good enough. I have to know if I should just settle for being Jane Miller."

Duncan propped his elbows on the table and rested his head in his hands. "You have no idea what you're asking of me. My father will gleefully boil me in the biggest vat of oil he can find. *Then* he'll fire me. And as for your devoted manager—"

"All I'm asking for is just one more day. What's one day out of a lifetime? It's nothing. It's not even spare change. It can't be an accident that we came here tonight. Fate *must* be pushing me to that open mike performance tomorrow. You don't think a mere human being can stand in the way of fate, do you?"

"Stop it, Harley," Duncan said in a tightly controlled voice. "Just stop it."

"You don't understand what that open mike performance means to me!"

"Yes," he said quietly, dark eyes burrowing deep inside her, "I think I do."

Meeting that gaze was like being pulled into the vortex of a frantic whirlpool. "I'd give *you* twenty-four more hours if you asked me to," she said quietly.

"I know," he said, turning to stare at the stage and the Latino band that began to set up again. For a moment he looked almost haunted.

Oh, what was she doing to the man? "Life is to be enjoyed and chances are there to be taken, Duncan."

He turned back to her. "*Damn* you, Harley Jane Miller."

Her heart was racing. "Is that a yes?"

"Of course it's a yes!" he yelled and then hurriedly lowered his voice. "Walk yourself over to the damn bar and sign yourself up to sing tomorrow night before I change my mind."

"Really?"

He looked right into her. "Really."

Tears filled her eyes. That he should risk his job and things she knew nothing about to help her do this. She had just discovered the antithesis of Boyd Monroe, and he was making the pulse throb in her wrists.

"You're an angel," she said, standing up on shaky legs. "I'm insane, you're insane, and I'll never forget this, Duncan Lang. Never."

She was more than scared as she threaded her way through the club tables, walked up to the dark wooden bar and the bald man with the handlebar mustache sitting on a red leather bar stool, and signed herself up for the nine forty-five slot.

Dazed and more than half blind, she stumbled back to her table, where Duncan was finishing off a double whiskey.

"Am I causing you trouble?" she asked tentatively as she sank back down onto her chair.

"*Untold* amounts of trouble."

"Oh. Sorry."

"Think nothing of it," he said bitterly.

"Why is this case so important to you?" she asked, her hand covering his on the table. It was a shock how good that felt.

He stared at their hands as if suddenly confronted by a bug-eyed creature from outer space. "I took a chance of my own a few years back," he said slowly. "It didn't pan out. I thought I'd found a way to make it work. Looks like I was wrong."

"Even though you'll be turning me over to Boyd after my set tomorrow night?"

"Even though."

She felt as if his eyes were dragging her into that dark whirlpool again. She pulled her hand from his, sat back in her chair, and that seemed to help a bit. "There are probably options you haven't even thought of yet," she said a little breathlessly.

"Perhaps," he said, middle finger tapping frenetically on the table. "For now, though, I get to look forward to the dubious pleasure of babysitting you all day tomorrow."

"What?" Harley sputtered. "You are not going to shadow me all day tomorrow!"

"Oh yes I am."

"Oh no you're not!" Harley retorted.

"Have you noticed that we can't have a single conversation without arguing?"

"I am an honorable woman. I am twenty-six years old," Harley snapped. "I don't need a babysitter. Do whatever it is you do when you aren't harassing me and then you can pick me up after my set tomorrow night."

"I will pick you up tomorrow morning, make sure you don't fly off to Brazil and that none of your fans discover you and claim the reward your devoted manager has offered for your safe return, and then I will bring you here before taking you back to Boyd."

"I did just fine on my own yesterday and today. No one mugged me. No one kidnapped me. No one recognized me. I'll do just fine on my own tomorrow."

"What you fail to understand, Princess, is that by taking this case, I have become responsible for you," Duncan grimly stated. "That means sticking close and making sure you return to Boyd Monroe safe and sound."

Harley mulishly returned his glare. "Well, I hope you like visiting Central Park and the Empire State Building and Chinatown, because that's where *I'll* be tomorrow."

"Whoa, Nellie! Mama didn't raise no tourist."

Harley chuckled, surprised at the sudden emotional shift. "If I'm stuck with you, then *you're* stuck with *my* itinerary."

He stared into her eyes for a moment. "All right, but on one condition," he said slowly.

"What's that?" she managed.

"That you lose the brown contacts."

She felt suddenly weightless and light-headed. "Deal."

Silence for a moment.
"Then I'll try to survive playing tourist tomorrow."

Duncan dropped her off in front of the Hilton just after midnight. She watched as his cab carried him away, then she rode an elevator back up to the seventeenth floor, wondering what it would feel like to spend an entire day with the man. In her room, she slowly began to undress, feeling very different from the prison escapee who had left the Hilton that morning. In only a little more than twelve hours, she had bought her fantasy guitar, reclaimed her music, and survived a night on the town with the Playboy of the Western World.

She gratefully removed the contact lenses, put them in their case, and stared at herself in the bathroom mirror. She was shining, there was no other way to describe it. Not glowing or beaming, but shining. Even her eyes looked different, or maybe it was her mouth. It seemed fuller, softer than she remembered it from this morning.

She walked back into her bedroom and saw the black guitar case lying on her bed. Music from the Manhattan streets and parks and restaurants and her unnamed feelings thrummed in her soul. Sleep could wait.

CHAPTER FIVE

*T*here were five messages from Colby Lang on Duncan's home voice mail, each one more infuriated than the last. There were two messages from Brandon, one warning him about their father's growing wrath and begging him to bring Jane Miller in, and the second reminding him that Brandon needed the transportation plans for the Giscard diamonds on his desk first thing in the morning.

The calls did a good job of deflating what had felt almost like happiness these last several hours in Harley Miller's company. It was probably for the best. He shouldn't let himself be happy in her company. It interfered with important things like his job, and toeing the line, and remembering who he was.

After all, when you came right down to it, the woman was a major headache. She had screwed up his chance to make his father see him for the competent man he was. Jane Miller returned to the fold after thirty-six hours was an impressive accomplishment even Colby Lang couldn't ignore. Jane Miller returned to the fold after seventy-two hours had none of that cachet.

Worse, he had promised both Boyd and his father that he'd have Harley back at the Ritz tonight, and he was not honoring his promise. He had never broken his word to anyone before. He could easily hate Harley for that. She was messing with his honor, with his emotions, with his hormones, and with his plans. There was nothing to like in any of it.

With a weary sigh, Duncan picked up the package of background material on the Giscard diamond job Emma had sent to his apartment and dumped it out onto his round Victorian dining table. Maybe *this* case would help demonstrate his competency and edge him back into his father's good graces. If he came up with something that actually worked, that is.

An hour's review gave him the glimmerings of a plan. Catherine the Great's former diamonds were too important—and their current owner too treacherous—to take this job lightly. But that needn't cancel out creativity. Most transport plans involved armored cars surrounded by security agents and maybe a police escort. It didn't seem like the kind of attention a French mob kingpin would relish. Perhaps the key to this job was to *not* draw attention to the transportation of Armand Giscard's diamonds from his private Lear jet to the Bartlett Museum. Maybe it was time to once again deviate from the book.

By three A.M. he had printed out the completed plan. He left a laundry list of tasks for Emma on her office voice mail and then left a reassuring message on Colby's voice mail, using his crisp, businesslike voice to explain an unexpected side trip taken by the Princess of Pop and his personal guarantee that he would return her to Boyd Monroe the next evening.

Finally he slid into bed and was asleep before fifteen minutes had passed. His energetic alarm clock woke him up three hours later. Groaning, he forced himself out of bed, dressed in his sweats, and hit the streets for his habitual morning jog through Chelsea and Greenwich Village. His parents, of course, had been appalled when he chose to live downtown, not in midtown or uptown, and horrified when he chose a neighborhood that hadn't even been fully gentrified yet.

But Duncan liked the real life of his neighborhood. He liked that none of the mostly brick buildings were more than five stories tall. He liked the black iron gates and the hopeful flower boxes and the fact that there was a dry cleaners, a pet store, and a really good corner deli not half a block from his Chelsea flat. He even liked the other tenants in his three-story building: a lesbian couple from Miami on the second floor and a grizzled World War II vet and his apple dumpling wife of fifty-four years on the first floor.

At seven-thirty, Duncan carried the Giscard transportation plan into Brandon's office, stifling his disappointment when he found his older brother already at his desk. No matter how hard he worked, no matter how hard he tried, Brandon was always there first, doing it better.

Brandon waved him into the office, propping his phone receiver between his left shoulder and ear, while he played with a half-dollar in his right hand, making it appear and disappear, over and over again, as he spoke in fluid French on the phone.

Surmising that his brother was talking with Monsieur Giscard, Duncan sat down in a midnight blue upholstered guest chair in front of Brandon's desk and waited. Brandon made the half-dollar disappear again, winked at Duncan, and continued talking.

Brandon had been hooked by magic from the time he was four. Duncan could remember all the amateur magician kits he had bought with his allowance, the shows he had given for his classmates as he got older, the tricks he had used to impress girls when he had first started dating. Duncan had tried and failed to follow in his footsteps, as he had always failed. Brandon was more graceful, more skilled. Duncan had given up on magic by the time he was ten, but not Brandon.

Duncan had expected his brother to become the next David Copperfield—he had the looks, the flair, the skill, the inventiveness. But Brandon had shocked him by calmly acceding instead to their father's decree that he enter the family firm. It was the first and only time he'd ever seen Brandon give up on something he wanted.

Watching him cheerfully reassuring their nervous French client now, Duncan thought his brother seemed happy enough in his work and his life. He couldn't detect any regrets at being forced to give up a childhood dream. It was yet another arena in which Brandon had succeeded and Duncan had failed, because more and more Duncan *did* regret giving up his own youthful rebellion.

Even in the midst of resenting Harley for messing up his life, he could still see the lesson she was learning about the importance of rebellion and freedom, and he wondered—suddenly—if that lesson was infectious.

Brandon bid Monsieur Giscard adieu, hung up the phone, and smiled at his brother. "You're in early."

"I knew you wanted this," Duncan said, tossing the manila envelope onto the desk, "and I figured it would be wise to get in and get out before Dad comes in."

"Very wise," Brandon wryly agreed. "He's livid, to say the least. How on earth did you lose Jane Miller?"

"I didn't lose her," Duncan said, standing up, eager to get out and get on with the day. "I just made a field decision that the world would not end if the Princess of Pop had another day of freedom."

"Don't be a fool, Duncan. Why risk another official reprimand from Dad? Get the Miller woman back to Monroe and get her back now."

"It's my case, Brother. I'll handle it as I see fit."

"Look, Duncan, Monroe's just the kind of guy to make trouble for us if we don't come through and come through now."

"I'll come through for the company tonight and not before."

Brandon looked as if he would argue further, then stopped himself. "It's your neck."

"And the guillotine's been sharpened. I know," Duncan said wryly. "I'll be fine. Let me know what you think of the transportation plan. It's a bit different from the usual scheme. I'll be out of the office today, but Emma can always reach me if you want me to make any changes."

"I'm sure it's fine," Brandon said smoothly.

"Of course you are."

"No, really, Duncan. I'm grateful for your help. Colangco's name will be in every paper thanks to all the hype Giscard's diamonds are going to get. Our rep's on the line with this one and I'm responsible if anything goes wrong."

"Brandon, stop sweating. Nothing ever goes wrong on your cases."

"Until now," Brandon ruefully retorted. "Have you seen the Bartlett security layout?"

Duncan grinned. "It was in the background material. Pretty archaic. You've got your hands full, Brother."

"That's why I'm so grateful for your help."

"Any time," Duncan replied, heading for the elevator.

Colby Lang arrived at the office punctually at eight every morning he was in town, and Duncan had no intention of enduring a face-to-face confrontation with his father just yet. Instead, he went to breakfast a few safe blocks away from the Sentinel Building. Then, fortified by coffee and a bagel with cream cheese, he pulled out his cellular phone and called Boyd Monroe at the Ritz-Carlton.

It was almost as bad as listening to one of his father's diatribes. After suffering nine minutes of stinging personal abuse, Duncan finally interrupted and provided enough information about Harley's activities to convince Boyd that he really was working on the case and close to netting the Princess of Pop for him once and for all.

Somewhat mollified—at least he wasn't screaming anymore—Boyd issued a few threats and then slammed the phone down with such force that Duncan's ear kept ringing for a good twenty minutes afterward. He began to hope Boyd Monroe *was* up to something. There would be a definite pleasure in hanging him out to dry.

Soothed by a latte, Duncan pulled out his cellular phone once again. His former life in the fast lane, it turned out, had provided him with some surprisingly useful contacts. He placed an international call to an old acquaintance in Monaco. Then he called Carmine Bellini, one of the best-connected bookies in New York. Between them, he would find out if Boyd owed money anywhere in the world. Boyd's illogical concern for his schedule might be connected to the payment of debts, legal or otherwise. It at least seemed a good place to start.

Just after nine o'clock, he called Emma.

"You hear those blood-curdling yells in the background?" she greeted him in a lowered voice. "That's Colby Lang demanding your head on a platter. He's put Brandon on the Miller case. You're on suspension."

"Good. Now you won't have to come up with creative excuses for why I'm not in the office today," Duncan philosophically replied. "Besides, Brandon will be too busy with the Giscard job today and tomorrow to give Harley much attention. But play it safe and don't give him anything more than the bare minimum of information, Emma, and *don't* mention your investigation of Boyd Monroe's bank account, let alone Harley's world tour schedule."

"It's Harley now, is it? What's going on, Sherlock?"

"Nothing lascivious, so don't sound so suspicious." Duncan cringed at the sharp retort and forcibly mellowed his voice. "I just decided that she deserved one more day of freedom."

"I can't argue with you there. I've got her world tour schedule. Monroe didn't give her time to breathe."

"Fax your report over to the New York Hilton and Towers under my name. I'll pick it up in about half an hour. Oh, and just to be safe, go ahead and book Harley a room at the Millenium down on Church Street. I think it's best to move her again this morning just in case Brandon does stumble onto her trail. She'll pay cash as usual. Let's call her . . . Babe Hitchcock."

"You got it. Keep a low profile, Holmes."

"Count on it, Watson." Duncan hung up from Emma and then called Harley. "I hope you're packed," he said by way of hello. "You're moving this morning."

"I *am* packed and I was planning to move to the Mansfield," she replied.

"Uh-uh," Duncan countered. "That fits your pattern of midtown hotels too well. Emma's making a reservation for you under the name Babe Hitchcock at the Millenium downtown."

"Babe? As in Hog?"

"You *are* clever," Duncan said admiringly.

"Put a talking pig in a movie and I'll watch it every time. Who's Emma?"

"My able assistant. She does all the work, I get all the glory. I'll meet you in the Hilton lobby in twenty minutes."

In ten minutes he strode into the lobby of the New York Hilton and Towers and found the appropriate desk clerk to fetch him Emma's fax. He carried it over to the Mirage Lounge near the bank of elevators, sat down amidst marble, brass, bronze, and greenery, and considered Harley's world tour schedule. The illogic of it was amazing for a man of Boyd Monroe's experience.

All of the different countries and cities fell into place neatly enough, but why throw Harley onto a midnight flight just minutes after her Berlin concert had ended, when her next concert (in Paris) wasn't scheduled until three days later? Surely he could have let Harley, the band, and the roadies sleep in the next day and leave for Paris in the afternoon or early evening, or even the day after that. And why do a one-day turnaround in Tokyo when she wasn't scheduled to perform in Sydney until five days later?

Duncan's antennae were quivering like crazy. This schedule reeked of Boyd's hysteria about not getting to L.A. at the right time on the right day this week. Damn! He *was* up to something.

Duncan pulled out his cellular phone and called Emma again.

"Good news!" she greeted him. "Brandon just left a message saying he loved your Giscard transport plan and thanking you for all your hard work. Even Colby signed off on it."

Brandon *loved* his nonconformist plan? "Huzzah," Duncan murmured. "Look, Em, I need some more help on this world tour schedule. Find out if any of it was altered during the actual tour. I'm particularly interested in learning if Boyd did any last-minute scheduling of press conferences, interviews, TV or radio appearances, that sort of thing. If he changed hotels or concert venues, I would be *very* interested."

"What do you think he's up to?"

Duncan slumped down in his chair. "Lord, I wish I knew. Whatever it is, it seems to be tied to Harley's schedule, so that's the thread we follow. Call me if you find anything interesting. And keep digging on those bank records."

"Got it."

Duncan slipped the slim cellular phone back into the inside pocket of his dark blue Zegna sports coat and stood up. He realized—almost with wonder—that he felt nervous and that it had nothing to do with his father's rage or Boyd's scheduling, and everything to do with seeing Harley again.

How in the world had he regressed to the emotional development of a pimply teenager?

"Hi, there."

He turned. His ears began to ring.

A gamine in an emerald green midriff top, khaki shorts, and green sneakers stood before him. She was delectable. It vaguely occurred to Duncan that a trained investigator should not be thinking that the object of his professional search was delectable, but it was a little hard to focus just at present. Big turquoise blue eyes stared up at him. If the wallop they had just imparted to his solar plexus could be packaged, the world would be nuclear free in a year.

"Thanks for losing the contacts," he managed.

"Believe me," she said, a tinge of pink creeping into her slightly freckled cheeks, "it is entirely my pleasure. I have never liked sticking things into my eyes. I've got one of the doormen loading my stuff into a cab. You ready?"

"Of course," Duncan said, blessedly getting his second wind. "Come on. Work before boredom."

"I bet you anything that you'll like playing a tourist today."

"Boyd was right: you *do* live in a fantasy world."

Twenty minutes later Harley's luggage had been redeposited in a guest room at the Millenium Hilton Hotel on Church Street, just across the street from the World Trade Center. The furniture was carved from light maple and wrapped itself around the corners and walls of the room in clean modern European lines. The colors—toast, off-white, pale blue—seemed deliberately chosen to efface everything except the stunning view out the large windows. Harley's thirty-seventh-floor room looked north over the entire city, without a single building to impede the view.

"Not bad," Harley said, staring out the windows.

"Thank you," Duncan said.

"Pity I won't be staying the night."

"Isn't it, though?" he blandly replied.

She stuck her tongue out at him. "Come on," she said, pulling him out of the room, "we've got work to do. *My* work. Central Park first," she announced as she led Duncan to the elevator.

"God help me," Duncan groaned. He followed her out of the cherry wood lobby and into a cab, careful to keep a good five feet between them. Being in a hotel room with Harley had not felt safe. The surprise of that realization had led to some equally disturbing questions, like what the *hell* was wrong with him? She was a pampered and sheltered princess who insisted on having everything her way and messing up his career and his father's blood pressure and his brother's already packed work schedule.

She was also someone he was beginning to like *way* too much for his own comfort and peace of mind. Somehow he had to find a way to fend off the pleasure of her company, and fast.

"We'll start at the Lenox Avenue entrance on Central Park North and work our way south," Harley announced as the cab pulled out.

"You don't seriously intend to walk through *all* of Central Park?" Duncan demanded. "That'll take all day."

"It will?"

"*Yes.* Even half would be more than I can bear."

"Well, you're stuck. I've heard about Central Park all of my life and I *am* going to see as much as I can pack into . . . well . . . half a day." She consulted a map she pulled from her shoulder purse. "We'll start at East Eighty-fifth Street. I want to see the Great Lawn and the Obelisk and Belvedere Castle."

"You're deliberately trying to make me suffer, aren't you?"

"Oh stifle it," she said, frowning at him.

But he didn't. He complained all the way up Sixth Avenue. He grumbled as she led him around and through Belvedere Castle. He groused as she looked for turtles in Turtle Pond.

He lowered himself to bellyaching as she dragged him into the Ramble. The horrible part of it all was that none of it helped him fend off the growing pleasure of Harley's company.

He had never in his life known anyone who burbled, but Harley did. She couldn't say enough about the lushness of the trees and lawns and ivy and flowers. Brazen squirrels and the short tree-to-tree flights of red-winged blackbirds, bluejays, and robins were rapturously enthused over. When she wasn't burbling she was skipping, yes, *skipping* at his side, apparently as an alternative to flinging herself into orbit in a blue sky she couldn't extol enough.

He had never met anyone so adept at enjoying the moment. He could almost hate her for it, because it made him feel how hollow his own life had become.

Brimming over with honest-to-God happiness, she led him across Bow Bridge and then south along the lake, rhapsodizing over the white heron moving in slow jerky steps near the shoreline in search of food.

"They look good," Duncan conceded, "but they're not the most tasty of birds. Now *ducks*—"

"That's it, I've had it!" Harley seethed, taking him completely by surprise as she grabbed fistfuls of his teal blue polo shirt and shoved him back hard against a mature elm. "I am sick to death of your wet blanket routine, Duncan Lang, and it ends right here, do you hear me? You are going to give this glorious day its due. You are going to enjoy the sunshine and the beauty all around you and that's final!"

Duncan couldn't help it. He grinned down into flashing blue eyes. A woman of strong emotions. How wonderful! "Did you know that your freckles become more pronounced when you're angry?"

A strangled scream of frustration gurgled up from her slender throat. "Look, bub," she said, pushing hard on his chest, "I didn't want you to come along today, but you insisted, and I will *not* have you ruining my first and only visit to Central Park. Either you straighten up and fly right or I will drown you in the lake here and now!"

Duncan grinned at her. "You would, wouldn't you?"

"In a hot minute."

Duncan laughed. In all the delightful years of wine, women, and song before he had settled down to being good, Duncan couldn't recall ever meeting anyone who was this much fun. He impulsively caught her hand in his. Startled, he stared at their clasped hands. A perfect fit. A lovely fit. Better than he had let himself remember from last night.

Laughter vanished even as something warm and lovely took its place. Only a fool would resist the pleasure of Harley's company. "I'll be good," he vowed, immersing himself in turquoise blue depths.

"Thanks," she said a little breathlessly. She tugged slightly at his hand, but he wouldn't let her go, couldn't let her go.

She'd won. He felt her happiness stealthily invading his blood and he loved it, because it was life flooding into his parched veins and stirring up psychotropic fantasies of Harley in his arms, Harley's slender throat arched against his lips, Harley curled beside him in the dawn.

He only released her hand when he had to sit down across an entire table from her. After their caloric feast at Torre di Pisa the night before, their early lunch at the Boathouse Cafe was salad and mineral water and Harley forgetting to eat every few minutes as she stared out over the water toward Bethesda Terrace or fed the already well-fed fish who came up beside their waterside table to beg for food.

"I can't tell you what this means to me," she said, staring out at the sunlit water. "I feel like I've been locked up in hotel rooms and concert halls and recording studios for the last nine years and haven't even *glimpsed* the sky or trees or flowers actually growing in the ground. And when I think that all of *this* is in the heart of Gotham City—"

"It's a very nice park," Duncan primly agreed.

She threw a roll at him, hitting him square in the chest.

"To hell with your world-weary-sophisticate routine, Duncan Lang."

"But I *am* world-weary and I *am* sophisticated," he complained, picking the roll off his lap and putting it back on the table.

"You're also human, or had you forgotten?"

"No," Duncan said quietly, looking at the delectable woman seated across the table from him, "I haven't forgotten."

Her eyes dropped first. "I suppose hundreds of love affairs would make anyone world-weary," she conceded.

"Well, there weren't exactly *hundreds,*" Duncan felt compelled to confess, "and love had very little to do with them."

"Have you ever let anyone love you?" she asked, just as if she were asking him if he thought it was going to rain.

"Nope," he replied. "Much too messy. I never wanted to be responsible for leaving a slew of broken hearts in my wake."

"Noble of you," Harley said, nodding. "I gather the idea of love and marriage and a baby carriage has never entered your head."

"Never," Duncan assured her. "I realized long ago that long-term relationship is just not part of my makeup. When I think about actual *commitment,* I practically break out in hives."

"Skittish," Harley said, nodding wisely. "How come?"

"Something in my DNA, I expect."

Harley pursed her full lips. "Genetics, hmm? I suppose you've been conducting field tests for years."

"Research is my life," Duncan calmly replied.

Harley chuckled, an oddly evocative little sound halfway between the rumbling purr of a satiated kitten and a gangster's machine gun. "You're no fun. You don't react to even the most blatant provocation."

"You have no idea how wrong you are," he murmured.

She hurriedly focused her attention on the fish begging for scraps near their table.

After lunch, Duncan was careful not to take her hand again as they walked back out into the park toward Central Park South. He thought he was safe. But he had made one serious miscalculation.

"A merry-go-round!" Harley shrieked when she saw the brick housing of the carousel just off the Sixty-fifth Street Transverse. "Come on!"

"Harley—"

"Duncan, *please*?"

Staring down into pleading turquoise blue eyes, it occurred to him that Harley bore a distinct resemblance to an irresistible force.

"I will never live this down," he muttered and then lost his breath when she shrieked with happiness, threw her arms around him, and hugged him hard, before dashing up to the ticket booth, apparently oblivious to the havoc she had just inflicted on his central nervous system.

She bought them four tickets each, and with each new ride, Duncan found it harder and harder to hide the fact that he'd fallen in love with the traditional carousel music, and the large wooden horses, and Harley's infectious grin. Duncan wryly shook his head at himself. La Comtesse Pichaud would not recognize him. He scarcely recognized himself.

When they finally left the park—Harley insisting that they avoid Central Park South and the Ritz-Carlton because she was convinced Boyd Monroe would be watching—she announced that she intended to go to the top of the Empire State Building next.

"You're kidding," he said. "That's old news. The view from the World Trade Center is much more spectacular."

"I don't care," she retorted. "I *like* old buildings, and the Empire State Building has been famous for decades longer than those inhuman towers. I'll bet you haven't even been to the top of the Empire State Building."

"Of course not. World-weary sophisticates don't go in for that sort of thing." Actually, he hadn't even been *inside* the Empire State Building, clearly something Harley would consider a character flaw.

He found himself standing with her at the top of the Empire State Building just after four o'clock that afternoon gazing out at the vast Manhattan skyline bathed in summer sunshine and loving it. He was happier than he had been in two years. It was completely unexpected. He hadn't thought one person could make such a difference, but Harley had. She might have her life scheduled down to the nanosecond, but she knew how to enjoy that life. It was a gift, he realized, that he valued above all others.

"I know it's crazy," she said, her shoulder bumping against his arm, "but I'm really beginning to feel like I've come home. Like I belong here. I keep thinking about what Moss Hart wrote in his autobiography: 'The only credential the city asked was the boldness to dream.' I used to have bold dreams. I think I'm beginning to have them again. I mean, this city is *inspirational,* isn't it?"

No, he thought, gazing down at her, caught by effervescent turquoise, *you are.*

"I want to come back tonight, after the Surrealistic Pillow, and see the city at night," she declared.

"Okay," Duncan replied. "It's your day and your itinerary."

"But you're still taking me back to Boyd tonight," she said, grim.

"That's the deal."

"You are as tenacious as a half-starved pit bull, you know that?"

"Why thank you!" Duncan said in surprise. "That's the nicest thing anyone's ever said about me."

She stared up at him with an odd expression in her blue eyes. "You mean that, don't you?"

"Sure. Everyone sees the fluff, no one sees the steel."

"You're fluff?"

"I have fluffy aspects," Duncan said with a gentle smile.

"Man, you don't know yourself at all, do you?"

Duncan was saved by the bell. His cellular phone rang. He gratefully pulled it from his coat pocket and answered on the second ring. "Yo, Emma, what's up?"

"There were three changes," she replied, "to Jane Miller's original tour schedule: the flights into both Paris and Sydney were moved up. And here's the biggie: the Cairo concert wasn't on the original schedule."

"What?" Duncan stared down at Harley, his hand covering the phone's mouthpiece. "Cairo wasn't on your original world tour schedule?"

Her expressive face was masked, which worried him. "No," she said. "Boyd added it two days before we left L.A. Why?"

Duncan turned back to the phone. "Anything else, Em?"

"That's it for now. Ciao."

Duncan slipped the phone back into his coat pocket and stared out across the sunlit city. Boyd *had* used Harley's tour schedule for his own purposes. But what were they? And were they potentially threatening to her? "Ready to go?" he asked, still puzzling over the problem.

"Sure," she said, glancing at her wristwatch. "We've got just enough time for the walking tour of Chinatown before dinner at the Rainbow Room and my set at the Surrealistic Pillow."

"You don't want to go to the Rainbow Room," Duncan announced. "Not on your last night of freedom."

"But I've heard that it's wonderful."

"It *is* wonderful, but you can find wonderful upper-crust restaurants all over the world. If you want something truly unique, then you want Goodies."

"Goodies?"

"As in, oldies but."

"Wait a minute," Harley said, frowning in concentration, "I've heard of that."

"Of course you've heard of it. It's one of the most fun things you can do in New York and still be legal. A 1950s retro dance club with great milk shakes and better music. Vintage *rock-and-roll* music, Harley. You want to go?"

A playful smile teased her lush mouth and did terrible things to his belief system. "You mean you're actually asking me, not commanding me?"

"It's your itinerary."

"Sure it is. Okay, I'll nix the Rainbow Room."

"Great!" Duncan said. "If we're going to go to Goodies, then we'll have to drop your Chinatown plans."

"Like hell," she retorted. "It's still the middle of the afternoon. There's plenty of time—"

"Not if we go shopping, and we have to go shopping."

An hour later, Duncan—dressed in a circa-1955 leopard-pattern shirt and tan slacks—and Harley—wearing a 1950s Christian Dior in turquoise blue silk, which molded itself to her torso and then flared out into a full skirt—walked into Goodies. Red doors led them into a red-and-white-tiled foyer. The place was already three-quarters full, noisy, and beaming with good vibes, even though it wasn't quite six o'clock on a weeknight. Big red vinyl overstuffed booths lined three walls. A stage took up the fourth wall. In between were dozens of large tables and soda fountain chairs and a large oak dance floor. Eddie Cochran was lamenting "The Summertime Blues" over the hidden speakers.

Harley turned to Duncan and impulsively clasped his shoulders. "*Thank you* for talking me into coming here."

He stared down into her large, shining blue eyes and forgot everything he'd ever believed about himself. "Come on," he said gruffly, catching her hand in his. He pulled her out to the dance floor and into an exuberant jitterbug that matched everything he was feeling. He segued into an East Coast Swing for "Goody Goody" by Frankie Lymon and the Teenagers. Chubby Checker sent them into the hip-churning twist. The Penguins, Elvis, and the Everly Brothers followed.

Then "I Only Have Eyes for You" by the Flamingos filled the club, and he felt Harley stiffen slightly. She stood a little awkwardly on the dance floor, not quite meeting his gaze.

"Come on," he said softly, his finger brushing under her chin and tilting her head up. "It's all right."

Blue eyes searched his face for a moment, and then a miracle happened. She stepped into his arms for the slow dance, her head sinking onto his chest as if it were the most natural thing in the world, her body moving slowly, easily with his.

He forgot to breathe. Touching Harley, feeling her grow fluid and lyrical in his arms, stirred happiness where it shouldn't exist. Perfect. She was perfect in his arms. And right. And achingly familiar.

Oh sweet Jesus. What was she doing to him?

With a barely suppressed gasp, he took a hurried step backward, throwing her off balance.

"What are you doing?" she demanded, looking aggrieved.

Duncan was looking everywhere but at her. "Sorry. My . . . um . . . My mind wandered. Let's sit down and get something to drink."

His hasty retreat from idiocy got little support as they wended their way through the crowd of dancers to their booth. Her hand in his seemed to fill one of the more demanding holes in his soul and soothe something that had been rough and jagged for too long within him.

He slid onto the red vinyl seat and forced himself to remember reality. She was a job; she was his ticket to a decent career; she was a package to be delivered at midnight tonight.

But reality was a hard thing to hold on to when Harley was sitting across from him, face aglow as she examined a large menu that would make the American Heart Association blanche.

Their beehived waitress came up to them, snapping gum, and took their predinner orders: a root beer float for Harley and a chocolate soda for Duncan.

"You are the most fun I've had in years," Harley informed him once their waitress had decamped.

Reality hit the road. "I was about to say the same thing of you," he said.

A tinge of pink crept across her cheeks. "Oh, come on, now," she said hurriedly. "With all of those Mardi Gras parties and celebrity-packed jaunts to Cannes to compare me with?"

"Well, the fact of the matter is, I haven't been out of New York in two years."

"Why not?"

"I've been trying to be good."

Harley frowned. "Are you telling me that you can't have fun and be good at the same time?"

"Not according to my parents."

"But who's to say your parents know what makes one person good and the other . . . not?"

"They are, of course."

"Yeah, but you're a grown man. Why do you put up with that crap?"

"Why do you?"

That stopped her.

"Chain Boyd up, Harley," he said in a low, urgent voice. "Muzzle him."

"I don't know if I'm strong enough."

"Yes," he said, "you are."

Their waitress returned with their drinks. Harley slowly stirred her root beer float, considering. "Don't you think it's odd?" she said at last.

"What?"

"That we were both unsatisfied with our lives and we both

did something about it: you took a job, I took a holiday. Only neither of them has worked out the way we'd planned."

"Your point being?"

"That we've got the same problem."

"Oh. I thought the point was that we're very alike."

"No, that's different," she said, frowning at him. "And we're not."

"Aren't we?"

"No! I mean, our backgrounds are completely different, our education is completely different, our life experience is completely different—"

"Except for unsatisfying paths, finding the drawbacks to goodness, and being miserable."

"Well, yes," Harley conceded. "But still, our dreams are different—"

"How do you know?" Duncan demanded.

"Well," she said with an uneasy little shrug, "they are. I have dreams of being an independent rock-and-roll singer and you have dreams of being . . . what?"

"I don't know," Duncan said in surprise. "I never realized it before, but I've never really had a dream of being one kind of person or having a particular career."

"But that's awful! Everyone needs a dream."

"Do they?"

"*Yes*. It's practically a requirement for being human."

"Well, if you say so. I suppose . . . Wait a minute! I've got it: I've always dreamed of being happy. Haven't you?"

"Well, yes. But—"

"We also both love hard-ass rock and roll, black leather jackets—"

"How do you know about my—"

"Getting our own way," Duncan ruthlessly continued, "old-fashioned carousels, Italian food, cheeseburgers, chocolate milk shakes, and Goodies."

"What," Harley demanded, "is your point?"

He made his gaze meet hers and felt that wallop strike him

hard once again. He couldn't believe he was going to say this. "We're kindred spirits."

The world was a steady turquoise blue gaze. "Even though you're taking me back to Boyd tonight?"

"Even though."

"Oh." She looked away then.

"Let's order dinner," he said.

Harley glanced at her menu and then hurriedly put it down. "I can't eat."

She was pale. White, actually. Her freckles were more prominent. Her fingers were nervously turning the menu into a keyboard. "You'll need something to help you get through the rest of the night," he said gently.

"If I eat, I will throw up."

"Are you that scared of performing at the Surrealistic Pillow?"

"Oh yeah."

"You're taking a pretty huge risk," Duncan agreed, "singing the music you love in front of a bunch of strangers and not even hiding behind that safe little mask you've built up all these years."

"Yeah," Harley said, staring down at the Formica tabletop.

"But it's no bigger risk than walking away from Boyd and Jane Miller and venturing out into the biggest city in the world late one Sunday night," Duncan added as he settled back against the red vinyl seat.

That brought her eyes up to stare at him. "It isn't?"

"Nope. In fact, I'd say your set at the Surrealistic Pillow tonight will be a helluva lot easier. You know what you're doing when you walk on a stage. You know what you can expect. You had no idea what you were capable of doing or what to expect when you walked out of the Ritz and into your holiday."

"No idea at all," Harley wryly agreed.

"So, have some dinner."

Her eyes widened, and then she smiled with a warmth and a sweetness that pierced his heart. "You're a good man, Duncan Lang."

Duncan felt his ears burning and prayed he wasn't blushing elsewhere. He hid behind his menu. "I can personally recommend the burgers. And the banana splits are to die for."

She didn't eat a lot—just half a cheeseburger and most of a chocolate milk shake—but it was enough to leave her looking steady and almost confident at the end of dinner.

"Do you want to stay here," he asked, "or move on to other city attractions?"

"Neither," she replied. "I'm going back to the Millenium to change and rehearse my set."

"Want a practice audience?"

"No!" she said and then blushed as several people turned to stare at them. "I mean, thanks for offering, but I really need to do this alone. I'll meet you at the Surrealistic Pillow after my set."

Duncan didn't like that plan at all. "It is my professional opinion that you need some judicious hand-holding before you walk out on that stage tonight."

"Thank you, Duncan. You're very sweet, but no. When I left the Ritz-Carlton, I thought I just wanted a holiday. I know now that what I really wanted was to find out if I can make it in the real world on my own. I'm going to get my answer tonight, which means doing it on my own with no outside help or support, even from such a gallant white knight."

"You have the most cockeyed ideas about who I am," Duncan said, shaking his head. "Well, if you want to be a martyr to independence, it's no skin off my nose."

He wasn't feeling even remotely that glib when he sat at a small table at the Surrealistic Pillow two hours later applauding the end of a very good set by an R-and-B duo. His palms were cold and clammy. The same could be said of his stomach. The club was warm, even hot, but his skin was covered in goosebumps. He couldn't recall ever being this nervous before.

He was amazed at himself. He was amazed that he cared so much about what was going to happen to a woman he had known only forty-eight hours.

Maynard Kip, the club's owner, walked up to the single microphone stand on the small wooden stage. The stagelights made his bald head glow. "Ladies and gentlemen," he bellowed into the mike so that the entire club reverberated with his deep voice, "I want you to give it up now for Miss Harley Smith!"

The audience obligingly applauded as Harley walked onto the stage. She wore red high-tops, black leggings, and a belted ruby red satin tunic top. Her black Stratocaster hung from its strap against her belly. She looked a little nervous, but basically steady on her feet. Duncan wanted to bolt from the club.

"Good evenin', folks," she said into the microphone, startling him with a touch of Oklahoma in her voice. "I figured I'd start out with an oldie but a goodie. I hope you love it as much as I do."

She surprised everyone—and shocked Duncan—by breaking into a guitar intro that every rock-and-roll-loving human being on the planet knew. *My God,* he thought, *the chance she's taking!*

Then she began singing "Johnny B. Goode," only she had changed the lyrics to "Janey B. Goode." Duncan felt the hair on his scalp rise up just as it had done the first time he had heard the Beatles sing "She Loves You." She was good! She was better than good. She sang in a strong, infectious alto, so different from Jane Miller's gentle soprano, and played the guitar like Chuck Berry and Eric Clapton combined. She had pulled three-quarters of the house down onto the dance floor before she had finished the first verse.

Duncan was grinning like an idiot. Harley had eschewed Chuck Berry's duckwalk to drop to her knees for the guitar solo. She owned the Surrealistic Pillow and every human being in it. The club was surging with an energy high Duncan had never felt before. When she adjusted the final verse to sing "Her mama told her, 'Honey, you don't need a man, 'cause you will be the leader of a big old band,'" every female in the club screamed herself hoarse.

Two measures into her second song, "Dancin' in the Street," and Harley had 212 devoted slaves who eagerly became her backup group, singing the "dancing in the street" lyric at the top of their lungs.

She gave them great music and pure joy and the audience beamed back love with a force that could have knocked out a Patriot missile. But rather than swallowing it whole and demanding more, like some past and present vampire performers Duncan could name, Harley beamed that love right back at the audience, happier than any human being he had ever seen. He wanted to sit right there and see Harley that happy for the rest of his life.

She concluded her set with a gleeful rendition of the Killer's "Great Balls of Fire"—which made Duncan wonder just how innocent she really was. She bowed to the thunderous applause. Then her blue gaze swept the crowd and stopped unerringly when it reached Duncan. She grinned right at him. "Ain't this a kick in the head?" she said, and he laughed out loud with some of the joy she was radiating as she started to leave the stage.

"No!" the audience bellowed.

"Sorry, gang," Harley said into the mike with an apologetic smile, "but my ten minutes are up."

It only made the audience pound the floor and their tables harder. Maynard Kip stepped up to the microphone. "You're not going anywhere, Harley Smith. Get back here and sing to these people."

The crowd cheered this change in club policy as Harley, looking a bit bemused, walked back to the mike. Then she grinned at the audience. "You folks are terrific," she said into the mike. "I'm gonna buy a bus and take you with me everywhere I go!"

Happier and more satisfied than he'd ever felt, Duncan settled back into his chair to enjoy himself. Harley loved the music and loved performing and she wanted the audience to know it. It was a tremendous gift that she gave them, Duncan decided, and him. Boyd Monroe must have spotted it the first moment he laid eyes on her.

Boyd. He'd have an apoplectic fit if he ever saw Harley perform with such exuberance. It was the antithesis of Jane Miller's decorous, feminine appeal. Unlike the girl Boyd had groomed, Harley was all woman on this stage. Duncan suspected Mr. Monroe was going to have his hands full trying to stuff Harley back into his tiny cage. The question was, would he eventually succeed? Had Harley had enough time away from him to fully reclaim the strength she would need to stand up to him from now on? Or would he bulldoze through the last few days as if they had never happened?

"Okay, now," Harley said at the conclusion of "House of the Rising Sun," the guitar work she had used to replace the song's electric organ raising goosebumps on his skin. "This is going to be my last song, so I might as well take a chance and try out something new I've been working on. It's called 'Nice Girls Don't.' Have a listen."

Duncan leaned forward against the small table. She *was* feeling brave tonight. And with good reason. The song rocked. It was sassy and hot as it ranged over all the advice parents had handed down to their daughters through the years—nice girls don't kiss on the first date, nice girls don't date boys with tattoos, nice girls don't skinny-dip in the local swimming hole, nice girls don't go out on the town by themselves. The chorus was simple and direct.

"Ni-i-i-ce girls don't," Harley sang, then dropped her voice to a sexy growl, "but I do!"

The audience bellowed its approval louder and louder with each chorus.

At the end of the song, she dropped a demure curtsy—wholly belied by her grin—thanked everyone for listening, and walked offstage.

Duncan was out of his chair and heading backstage before the roar of applause had even begun to abate. A side door to the left of the small proscenium led up four steps to the narrow and congested wings. He had to squeeze past a skinny bass guitarist who looked no more than fourteen, an acne-scarred sax player, and a magenta-haired girl holding a pair of drumsticks in her hands, before he found enough room to expand his lungs into an actual breath. Ten feet away, near the back brick wall, stood Harley and Maynard Kip. She was nodding earnestly, eyes shining. Then she saw him.

"Duncan!" she shrieked, hurtling herself into his arms like she'd been shot out of a cannon. "I did it! I did it!"

"I know, I know!" he said hugging her back and finding it hard to let her go. "You were wonderful. Stupendous!"

"My old voice and the songs I love and I still connected with the audience! I can't believe it. All these years . . . Boyd lied to me. Hell, I lied to myself. I *can* make it on my own. I *can* be the performer I always wanted to be. I've never felt like that on stage before," she said, blue eyes glowing up at him as she stood within the circle of his arms. "It was like a continuous jolt from fifty thousand watts of electricity and falling off a cliff like Wile E. Coyote and ten *zillion* Christmases compressed into one excruciating moment. It was the most incredible, wonderful, amazing experience of my life! *Thank you* for giving it to me," she said, hugging him fiercely.

His hand, trembling slightly, sifted through her short brown hair. "You're very welcome."

He felt her sudden awareness that she was in his arms—
and they weren't dancing—in the slight stiffening of her
body. He let her step away as he also rocketed back to earth.
Neither could quite meet the other's eyes.

"We all set, Harley?" Maynard Kip asked as he walked up
to them.

"You bet, Maynard," Harley replied, turning with almost
palpable relief to the bald club owner.

"Then I'll go announce the next group. Try to keep it
down, you two."

Duncan watched Maynard walk off and then turned back
to Harley feeling very grim. "*What* is all set?" he demanded.

She looked wary. "One of the groups Maynard hired for
the Friday-through-Sunday gig next week canceled on him.
I'm filling in."

"*Harley—*"

She took a step back, arms folded defiantly across her
chest. "I have never broken a promise in my life, but I'm
breaking one now. I'm not going back to Boyd tonight, Duncan. Not after that set. It just changed my life, don't you
see?"

"*Harley—*"

She took a deep breath and looked him straight in the eye.
"I am not going back until I've had my full holiday."

"Oh yes you are."

"Oh no I'm not."

"We had an agreement. I have kept my end of the deal—"

"I know. You've been great."

"—and it's time for you to do the same," Duncan grimly
concluded.

"Not tonight. Not tomorrow night. Not until I've had my
fourteen days."

Duncan exploded. He swore at her in English, French,
German, and Italian even as the newest band to take the stage
pounded the club with decibel-stretching music. He accused
her of every crime since Lizzie Borden took ax in hand. He

threatened her with handcuffs and chains. "You will *not* ruin my career single-handedly!" he informed her. "You will not destroy everything I've worked toward these last two years just so you can indulge some selfish little *whim*!"

"*Whim?*" she shrieked. "This is no *whim,* this is my *life* I'm talking about. This is my music and my soul and my freedom!"

"Talk about them on your own time, Princess. Right now," Duncan said, grabbing her wrist, "you are coming with me."

"The hell I am!" she yelled, jerking herself free with surprising strength. "You aren't *God.* You can't just order me about and expect me to obey. I am a living, breathing, thinking, *free* woman and you're not taking me anywhere!"

Both were panting for breath as they glared ferociously at each other.

"Oh, *fuck* this," Duncan said as he grabbed Harley and threw her over his shoulder.

"Put me down!" she shouted, twisting and struggling until she suddenly tumbled free.

He lunged for her again, but she jumped back. "Now wait just a minute," she ordered.

"Sure," he said, grabbing for her.

She scrambled just out of his reach. "Come on, Duncan. Maybe we can compromise."

"Compromise?" he said in utter disbelief. "I have compromised *enough*!"

"But I think I know a way that I can have my holiday and you can protect your career. Really."

"Sure you do."

"No, Duncan," she said, holding up her hands, "think about it a minute. My holiday and your job security are all about Boyd. And the thing is, he *has* been acting strangely lately. You think something's going on, too. I saw your face this afternoon when Emma was telling you about my world tour. Boyd worries you, and not simply because he's a control freak."

"All right, I agree, he's up to something," Duncan said, arms akimbo, "but it could be as little as having a lover in your every port of call. I am not going to ignore my responsibilities—"

"Change your responsibilities."

"What?"

"Work for me, Duncan, not for Boyd. Let me hire you. Let me be your client."

Duncan gazed down into dark blue eyes. "Oh, you *are* wicked," he said.

"Really?" she said eagerly.

He couldn't help it. Duncan gave it up and laughed. *"Really,"* he assured her with a smile.

She gave him a lopsided grin. "Look, I don't want to get you into any more trouble. I really don't. And I think this is the perfect plan to get you *out* of trouble and into Colangco's good graces. I mean, think about it, Duncan. First of all, you did your job. You found me. You got me. Case closed. Now I'm giving you your second big case. If Boyd *is* up to something other than international nooky, and you can prove it, that becomes another major feather in your cap. In the meantime, I think I know just how to talk your father around so he won't have to be hospitalized and you don't have to stay on his blacklist."

"Too late. I've been permanently enshrined."

"Still, I can calm him down *and* provide the firm with another high-profile job."

"Maybe," Duncan murmured, thinking it over. He'd always hated the idea of locking Harley back in Boyd's prison. Now he wouldn't have to. By presenting her to his father, he would prove that he really could get the job done. Now the Giscard case would just be icing on the cake. By taking Harley on as a client, he would have an even better chance to prove himself to his family *and* he would be able to allay his own growing concerns about Boyd Monroe.

He refocused into hopeful blue eyes. Oh yes, this was

definitely a win-win situation. He smiled suddenly. "Boyd has *badly* misjudged you," he pronounced. "Okay, here's the deal: I don't take you back to Boyd, I do take you on as a client, you talk Dad into accepting the switch, you get your holiday, and I get my career-making investigation."

"Deal!"

"There's just one condition."

"What?" Harley demanded suspiciously.

"You talk to Dad tonight. I see no reason to keep him in agony until tomorrow."

"You are a devoted son, Duncan Lang."

"I just don't want him to drop dead before he has a chance to put me back in his will."

CHAPTER SIX

*D*uncan had told her what to expect and he hadn't steered her wrong. Colby and Elise Lang lived in a neo-Federal town house on East Sixty-fourth Street between Fifth Avenue and Madison Avenue. The town houses and mansions up and down the street screamed wealth and prestige and exclusivity. Harley felt like a trespassing hobo. The Langs' immaculate five-story red brick town house with limestone trim was not welcoming. Nor was the austere, hatchet-faced butler who opened the broad front door and surveyed Duncan with forbidding chill before stepping back to admit them both to the house.

Harley found herself engulfed by a huge reception hall complete with towering columns and marble floor. A grand marble staircase rose from the middle of the hall and swept up to the other floors.

"I trust we're not interrupting another one of Mother's

boring dinner parties, Johnson," Duncan said with surprising cheerfulness.

"This is Wednesday night, Master Duncan," the butler stated in a frosty English accent. "If you will be so good as to recall, Wednesday nights are reserved from social activity."

"So they are. Mom and Pop in the parlor?"

"Mr. and Mrs. Lang are in the library," Johnson frostily corrected. "I have just taken them their cognacs."

"We've arrived in the nick of time, Harley," Duncan said, catching her hand and pulling her toward the stairs. "The final sip of cognac precedes beddy-bye time. Be an angel and watch over this for us," he said, handing Harley's guitar case to Johnson. "Don't bother announcing us," he called back to the slightly quivering butler. "We can do the honors ourselves. We'll bypass the elevator," he informed Harley, "to give you the full effect of the ancestral home."

"Gee, thanks," she muttered.

"The basement has a fully equipped billiard room and bar," Duncan announced in a masterful impersonation of a celebrity tour guide as they began to climb the stairs. "The dining rooms—one for family, one for guests, of course—and a formal drawing room are on the second floor. The library and the master bedroom suite are on the third floor. Brandon's and my old rooms are on the fourth floor; the servants' quarters are on the fifth floor."

"What? No swimming pool?"

Duncan grinned at her. "Much too nouveau riche for the Langs."

The wall framing the staircase was lined with originals by Watteau, Boucher, and Fragonard. The third floor landing boasted a Rubens and two delicate Cellini statuettes on ebony stands.

"Your parents like the old masters," Harley observed, silently blessing Boyd for making her study art history.

"They like anything that makes them look like old money. Grandfather built the family fortune on bootlegging during

Prohibition. Security work seemed like a natural offshoot of that—something Dad prefers to forget. Ah, here we are," Duncan announced before a set of imposing neo-Federal wooden doors. "Brace yourself and remember, this was basically your idea, so don't blame me if you have nightmares later."

Harley's fingers slid up to cling to her gold pendant. The man was not reassuring.

Duncan pulled open the doors and led her into a warmly lit paneled library of pale rose and white. Mid-to-late-nineteenth-century masters hung on the walls. The floor was oak parquet. The furniture was neo-Federal. The people seated opposite each other on matching rose brocade chairs were dressed in attire appropriate for a royal reception.

Standing in her red high-tops, it forcibly struck Harley that she and Duncan were badly underdressed.

"Hello, Dad; hello, Mother," Duncan called as he ruthlessly pulled her into the room. "I'm glad we caught you."

Colby Lang glanced up from his book, his blue eyes narrowing with both distaste and anger when he recognized his son, in a leopard-print shirt no less. He surged out of his chair and pointed an incriminating finger. "You!" he said in an awful voice. "You miserable, lying dog! It is only because of your mother's pleas on your behalf that I don't banish you from the company forever."

"Mother always had a soft heart," Duncan said with a sardonic smile.

Harley doubted it. She couldn't find any evidence of softness in the thin, dark-haired woman in the silver Givenchy gown.

"How dare you burst in on us at this hour of night!" Colby Lang continued in the same awful voice.

"Outrageous of me, I know, but I thought you'd both like to meet Jane Miller. Miss Miller, my parents."

Colby was actually struck dumb for a moment. Harley could only admire Duncan's technique.

"How do you do, Mr. Lang," she said, stepping forward and holding out her hand. "I'm so glad to meet you. I am in very great need of your help."

She heard Duncan choke on something that sounded suspiciously like laughter. Still, Colby Lang appreciated the performance.

"Miss Miller!" he said, taking her hand, his composure instantly restored. "This is an *unexpected* pleasure."

Harley winced inwardly. If Duncan and his father had been armed, the body count would already be piling up. "Thank you," she murmured. "Mrs. Lang, you have a lovely home."

"It would be a great deal lovelier without the ragtag nouveau riche element trying to take over our street," Elise Lang retorted. "Imagine having to put up with Ivana Trump as a neighbor!"

Well, so much for small talk.

Elise Lang looked her critically up and down. "I thought you were a blond."

"Strawberry blond," Harley corrected. She sifted one hand through her short brown hair. "This is my disguise. It's actually worked. No one has recognized me, except your son, of course. It's embarrassing how quickly he found me, and after all my efforts to hide my tracks, too."

"Won't you have a seat, Miss Miller?" Elise Lang said as her husband digested this information. It did not seem to sit well.

"Are you telling us that *Duncan* located you?" Colby demanded as Harley sat down on the rose brocade sofa, Duncan walking around to stand behind her.

"Late yesterday morning, and I've been nothing but trouble to him ever since. I'm afraid it's entirely my fault that he didn't return me to Boyd Monroe. In fact, that's why he brought me here tonight. I've got a proposition for you."

As Duncan had predicted, Colby refused point-blank to drop Boyd and take her on as a client. He used a variety of arguments, including all of the moral, ethical, and professional barriers, plus a good ten minutes' more. Harley sat through all of it, trying to look like she really cared.

"I do understand your position," she said when she could finally get a word in edgewise, "but I don't believe you fully comprehend what's at stake here. Boyd Monroe is engaged in something—possibly something illegal, and possibly something dangerous to me. Duncan has basically fulfilled your contract with Boyd by finding me and keeping me safe. He can't take me back to Boyd because I refuse to go and, legally, he can't force me to do so.

"With that case closed," she rolled on before Colby could argue her down, "there's no conflict of interest, so now you can take *me* on as a client. I promise you, Mr. Lang, that Jane Miller has far more photo ops than Boyd Monroe."

Colby closed his mouth. Duncan lightly squeezed her shoulder. She had made a direct hit.

It took Colby a quarter hour to reframe her logic to his taste and convince himself that it was he who had come up with the idea in the first place. He criticized Duncan for not raising the problem of Boyd Monroe sooner, apologized to Harley for his son's negligence, and assured her that Colangco International was just the company to help her and all of her hundreds of friends in the music industry. How, Harley wondered through this deadly monologue, had Duncan survived in this house? His father could squeeze the life out of a nine-hundred-year-old redwood.

"Mr. Monroe will have to be handled delicately," Colby concluded.

"That's why I came to you, Dad," Duncan said, speaking for the first time in half an hour. "This sort of situation is right up your alley. If anyone can allay Monroe's suspicions, convince him that Miss Miller *will* return to the fold after her holiday, and keep him from hiring someone else to find her, it's you."

"I don't foresee any real difficulty," Colby murmured,

considering the matter. "Very well, Miss Miller, Colangco is happy to help you in any way that it can. I'll brief my son Brandon tomorrow morning after he finishes supervising a security job, and he'll get right to work on your case."

"But I don't want Brandon, I want Duncan!" Harley exclaimed, and then blushed. "I mean, Duncan did a good job for Boyd, he's been honest with me, and he's on top of things now. I want him assigned to my case."

Colby would have argued with her, but to tell her, as he clearly longed to do, that Duncan wasn't fit to walk the dog let alone handle her case would be to threaten his company's credibility and his own judgment in hiring Duncan in the first place.

"I will, of course, provide full oversight on this job," was all Colby could say.

"Thank you," Harley said, obeying Duncan's slight tap on her shoulder and standing up. "Well, I don't want to take up any more of your time. It's been a long day for me, and I'm sure Duncan wants to get right to work."

"Emma has already pulled up some background material and left it for me in my office," Duncan said smoothly as he began to lead Harley to the door. "I'll leave a status report on your desk for your review tomorrow morning, Dad."

"Thank you."

"Good night Mrs. Lang, Mr. Lang," Harley said at the double doors, "it was a pleasure meeting you."

"And you, Miss Miller," Elise Lang coolly replied.

Now there's a loving pair, Harley thought as Duncan quietly closed the doors on their escape. No kiss or hug of greeting, or farewell, for their son. Not even a goodbye.

"Come on," he said, sotto voce, "let's get while the going is good."

"How'd we do?" she asked as they started down the stairs.

"Hole in one," Duncan assured her, warmly squeezing the hand he had clasped in his. She realized that there hadn't been a moment of their visit when he hadn't been touching her in some way, physically fending off the arctic chill of his parents and this house. "We should be free from Colangco's interference for a couple of days," he continued.

"And Boyd?"

Duncan grinned. "Consider him neutralized. Once Dad makes his play, Boyd won't know what hit him."

"Your dad's a real piece of work."

"Ain't it the truth."

She glanced at him, so calm, even cheerful, at her side as they walked down the stairs. That he took his parents' coldness and lack of affection in stride spoke volumes. That he felt no compunction to explain them to her said even more. Clearly, this was normal life in the Lang household. What was there to explain?

They reached the large ground floor reception hall. Harley looked around at the Gainsborough on the wall, at the marble beneath her, at the crystal chandelier above, at the beauty that was completely overwhelmed by a cold formality that seemed to have oozed into the very foundation of the building, and its occupants. "You really grew up here?"

"And in a mausoleum in the Hamptons that we laughingly call our summer cottage."

She looked at Duncan, his black curls charmingly rumpled, his 1950s leopard-print shirt and tan slacks completely out of place in this setting. "I don't see it."

"Neither have I," he said, opening the front door. "Let's blow this joint before the walls start closing in on us."

Harley thought about that phrase as they walked up East Sixty-fourth Street to catch a taxi on Fifth Avenue. The walls must have closed in on Duncan every day of his childhood in that house. She understood him so much better now.

Of course he was stubborn and strong and determined. He had to be to have survived that icebox. Colby and Elise Lang were perfect for each other, but the worst possible parents, and all for the same reasons: they were cold, judgmental, harsh, and demanding. And abusive. To withhold affection from a child was abusive. To criticize him with every other sentence was abusive.

No wonder Duncan had broken out in social excess at every conceivable opportunity. He'd been fighting for his life. He'd been searching desperately for human warmth and affection. But had he found it? Harley frowned as a cab pulled up to them at the intersection and she slid across the back seat.

No, Duncan had said life as the Playboy of the Western World had palled. So he couldn't have found the human connection he'd been searching for. Her heart ached at the thought. She'd been locked away from human contact for nine years; he'd been locked away all of his life.

It was no wonder he was skittish about relationships and commitment—he had his parents' example before him and a lifetime of experience that apparently had led him to believe he was incapable of loving and being loved.

What was surprising, what was almost incomprehensible, was that he should have come away from that house and those parents and that lack of everything the human heart needed with gentleness and compassion, whimsy and insight not merely intact, but flourishing. They should have been stomped flatter than roadkill. They should have been hardened into selfishness and cruelty and soul ice.

Yet here he sat, this man who could blaze at her in righteous and perfectly understandable fury one minute, and then burst out laughing the next. He had compromised his honor to give her a few precious hours of freedom because he, better than anyone, understood how important those hours were. He had reassured her and strengthened her at Goodies; his black eyes had beamed encouragement and support and an absolute faith in her all during her set at the Surrealistic Pillow. Now he had done his level best to protect her from the more unpleasant aspects of his parents' company.

"You are a *very* good man, Duncan Lang," she announced

as their taxi turned left onto East Eighth Street and then made a sharp right onto Broadway.

He glanced down at her, amusement tilting his sensual mouth. "Where did that come from?"

"The truth."

"My parents, I'm afraid, would not agree."

"I guess it comes down to who you want to believe: a couple of ice sculptures or a royal pain in the butt."

He laughed, and she knew the greatest satisfaction that she could give him laughter so soon after leaving that awful house.

"I really am sorry I've caused you so much trouble," she said. "I hadn't really realized that my case was a career breaker for you."

"Oh, it's been more than that. You've been the first real challenge I've had in two long years. That's why I practically tap-danced all the way to the Ritz-Carlton when Boyd first called. Little did I know . . ."

She could feel more than see his eyes gazing at her with a heat that was both intimate and electric, like an Oklahoma thunderstorm converging on a farmhouse. Her heart was racing in her chest. For one wild moment, vertigo nearly tumbled her into his arms, her mouth tilting up for his kiss, but the cab made a sharp right turn, and sanity, blessedly, prevailed.

"What are you going to do now that you've got your whole holiday before you and a Fender Stratocaster in hand?" Duncan asked, just as if he hadn't felt that electric moment too.

"Everything on my itinerary," she replied, turning her head to hide her disappointment, "plus come up with enough material to perform at the Pillow next week."

"You were utterly fantastic tonight, you know."

He'd done it again. He'd engulfed her in his warmth without even touching her. "It was the best time I've ever had on stage," she said quietly, looking up at him. "You were right, I *did* know what to do. But it was more than that. I felt so connected to that audience. These last nine years, I haven't performed anywhere that didn't hold at least five thousand seats. Singing to a couple of hundred people is so much more immediate and satisfying."

"Time to rethink your concert venues."

"Oh yeah."

"Have you realized yet that you're traveling at light speed?"

She stared up at him as the cab screeched to a stop in front of her hotel. "I am?"

His smile crinkled his eyes. "Oh yeah."

Laughing and feeling oddly giddy, Harley slid out of the cab after him.

Duncan took her hand as if it were the most natural thing in the world to do, and led her through the Millenium Hilton's revolving glass door and into the darkly elegant lobby. He pulled her into an elevator chatting about some of his musician friends, just as if he didn't feel their hands fusing together, awakening desire that curled her toes and burned her cheeks.

She didn't know where to look. She didn't know what to say as the elevator doors opened on the thirty-seventh floor and Duncan tugged her down the hall. He stopped and looked at her inquiringly. She suddenly realized that they were standing in front of her door. Feeling like a fool, she handed him her guitar and fumbled through her purse, found her key, and clumsily opened the door. Duncan set her guitar just inside the doorway.

"Well . . ." she said, looking up into black eyes that scorched her soul and burned away every coherent thought, "good night."

His hand reached up. Hot fingertips brushed across her cheek. She drew in a sharp breath.

"Good night," he murmured.

He turned and walked away.

It was a full minute before Harley remembered to blink.

As promised, she walked into Colangco International the next morning at nine o'clock on the dot. She wore sandals and a Hawaiian print midriff shirt and pedal pushers that made her feel light and breezy and confident enough to meet Duncan's dark gaze again. Emma—she assumed it was Emma—was sitting at her desk, a telephone headset on her head. Her long straight black hair was pulled back from her small face by a pair of barrettes. Her gray jacket and skirt were conservative. Her large black eyes were wide as she stared at her computer.

"Emma Teng?"

The young woman jumped and then hurriedly pushed a button on the phone jack. "You must be Miss Miller."

"Call me Harley."

"Okay, Harley. It's only fair to warn you that you've entered Armageddon. I advise you to get out while you can."

"Huh?"

Then she heard the shouting coming from the inner office. Duncan's office. His name was on the door. She recognized the cold fury of Colby Lang's voice even through the walls.

"What's going on?" she whispered.

Emma leaned toward her across the desk. "We were hired to protect some diamonds that were going on display at the Bartlett Museum. They got stolen in transit two hours ago. Duncan was the one who came up with the transportation plan."

Harley swore.

"Exactly," Emma said grimly. "I've been listening in on the intercom. Colby, Brandon, and Duncan Lang are all in there along with two police detectives and our client's New York representative. *All* of them, except Duncan, think that Duncan engineered the heist."

"What? Oh, come on! Duncan Lang is the most honest man I've ever met!"

Emma looked her up and down approvingly. "You know

that and I know that, but unfortunately it looks like that's going to have to be proven, in triplicate, to everyone else."

The door to Duncan's office opened and two men walked out into Emma's office. One was in his late twenties, the other in his early forties. Both were white, both wore two-piece suits, the younger in dark brown, the elder in dark gray. Harley stared at them in amazement. They actually looked like what they were—cops.

"You start the canvas in Chelsea and the Village," the older man said as they walked to the outer door, "to see if his alibi holds up, and I'll start the background check."

"Right," said the younger man as they walked out into the hall.

Meanwhile, the shouting in Duncan's office had escalated. The police detectives had left his door ajar. Harley and Emma glanced at each other. Neither made a move to close the door.

"I assigned this job to you, Brandon. *You!*" Colby bellowed. "What in hell were you thinking of to bring Duncan in?"

"He's my brother," Brandon said defensively, "and I was up to my eyeballs in work. I needed some help."

"You know he can't be trusted!"

"Excuse me—" Duncan began.

"All right, *all right,*" Brandon said, an angry edge to his voice. "It's all my fault. Call the cops back and have me arrested."

"Of all the asinine ideas," Colby exploded. "Transporting a million dollars' worth of diamonds in a limousine. *No* armored car. *No* police escort! We might just as well have advertised them in the *Post.*"

"*Brandon* was in the lead car," Duncan said in a dark, carefully controlled voice Harley had never heard before. "The limo was bulletproof. We had our most trusted people in the limo and around the limo in unmarked cars. Brandon billed and cooed over the transportation plan and *you* signed off on it, Dad. It was a good plan."

"If *you* wanted to steal the diamonds, yes!" Colby yelled.

"I did not steal the diamonds," Duncan stated.

"You don't honestly expect me to believe that, do you?"

Harley stared at the door, appalled that Duncan's father and even, it seemed, his brother, could actually believe him capable of stealing the diamonds. What kind of a family were they? How could they think such awful things of *Duncan*? Her fingernails dug into the palms of her hands. If this was agony for her, what must Duncan be feeling?

"Gentlemen," said a fourth man, speaking with a heavy French accent, "I do not care who stole the diamonds, nor does my employer. Monsieur Giscard cares only that they be returned at once. You will find the diamonds, gentlemen, or the repercussions could be . . . fatal."

The door opened and a man with a comfortable girth clothed in the finest of French silk suits walked out of the office. He tipped his hat at Emma and at Harley and then strolled out into the hall.

Harley stared at Emma in perplexity.

"French mob," Emma whispered.

Harley's eyebrows shot up.

"Damn you to hell, Duncan," Colby roared. "You're fired! I want you packed and out of this office in five minutes."

"You can't fire me without cause," Duncan calmly replied, "and you have no cause because you have no proof that I had anything to do with stealing the diamonds. If you don't want a lawsuit on your hands—a highly publicized lawsuit—then I suggest you stop bellowing at me and find the real thief. I've got work to do."

"The hell you do," Colby sputtered. "I may not be able to fire you yet, but I *can* suspend you. Brandon will take over the Miller case."

"Like hell," Duncan said.

"Duncan, be reasonable," Brandon broke in. "You're going to be so tied up with the police because of those damned diamonds that you won't have a second to think of anything else."

"And I *am* suspending you," Colby added.

"Let me explain the facts of life to you both," Duncan said in his new dark voice. "I did not steal the diamonds, so I have nothing to worry about and Colangco has nothing to worry about. The police are checking my alibi, so they're leaving me alone. I have nothing to occupy my time *but* the Miller case. I sold it, it's my job, and I'm going to finish it. Besides, Miss Miller has stated categorically that she will only work with me, not with you, Brandon, or you, Dad. And remember, the media will be scrutinizing Colangco with a fine-tooth comb until the Giscard diamonds are found. Any change in our routine or our caseload and they'll jump all over us."

"Duncan, you can't possibly work under these conditions," Brandon stated. "It's ridiculous. I won't have it. I'm sure Miss Miller will understand the need to change her case assignment under the new circumstances."

"Brandon, Miss Miller understands that I'm the man she wants investigating her manager," Duncan retorted. "End of story. Besides, aren't you going to be up to your eyeballs trying to solve the Giscard case?"

"Well, sure, but—"

"You'll be busy too, Dad," Duncan rolled on. "That leaves me to handle the Miller case. Now, if you would both get the hell out of my office, I'd like to get started."

Colby stormed from Duncan's office, slamming the door with such fury that Emma and Harley both jumped. Without even glancing at them, he stalked past the two women and out into the hallway. Brandon, far more quietly, walked out of his brother's office. Harley stared at him, dumbstruck.

He was beautiful! He looked like a Greek god carved from golden marble.

"Rough morning," he said to Emma in a voice disturbingly similar to Duncan's.

"So I gathered," she replied.

He raised an inquiring brow.

"This is Miss Harley Jane Miller," Emma explained. "Miss Miller, this is one of Colangco's senior vice presidents, Brandon Lang."

"Hi," Harley managed.

"It's a pleasure to meet you, Miss Miller," Brandon said, taking her hand. She stared at it in surprise. Nothing. She felt nothing. "I'm a big fan," he continued. "I understand you've hired Colangco to help you with a business matter."

"Yes."

"I'm sure we'll give you every satisfaction." Brandon looked back at Emma. "Keep the press away from Duncan."

"Right."

With a smile at Harley, Brandon walked out the door.

"Wow," Harley said when the door had closed behind him.

"The Lang genes are pretty amazing," Emma agreed.

Harley glanced at Duncan's door. "Should we?"

"Yes. He's probably feeling like Custer at the Little Bighorn just now. It might help if he knows he's not entirely surrounded by hostiles."

Harley tapped lightly on the door and the two walked in to find Duncan with his back to them as he stared out his corner office windows at the East River.

"Helluva way to start the day," Harley said lightly.

Duncan turned and, to her complete surprise, smiled. "You only say that because you've never woken up after a nightlong revel of Stingers and sexually rambunctious skiers. I gather you got the gist of my morning meeting?"

"It was kind of hard to miss," Harley said apologetically.

"Much as I hate to say it, Duncan, the robbery had to be an inside job," Emma said quietly as she leaned against the glass conference table. "Someone on our end—"

"Or Giscard's," Duncan pointed out. "But you're right, Em. The problem is, too many people knew how those diamonds were going to be transported from the airport to the museum. There's a lot of suspects to look over. The cops are going to have their hands full."

"You're going to leave your exoneration up to the police?" Harley demanded in disbelief.

"I'm going to let the police find the real thief or thieves, which will in the end exonerate me," Duncan corrected her. "That's their job, after all. Besides, any hand I might take in the case now would only look suspicious."

"Trying to cover your tracks," Emma said, nodding knowledgeably.

"Exactly, my dear Watson. *I* know I'm innocent and I have complete faith in New York's finest, so there's really nothing to worry about. Come on, let's get to work on Boyd Monroe. We can at least do something about *him*."

For the next hour, Harley let Duncan and Emma grill her about her world tour. But all the while she was puzzling over Duncan, wondering how he could be so calm after being betrayed by his family, and after the police had basically accused him of masterminding the robbery, and after having his life threatened by a representative of the French mob. Had he had his nerves surgically removed? Was his skin that tough? Was his heart that hardened?

She finally left Colangco to catch a Grayline bus tour of downtown and midtown Manhattan. Then she planned to buy a theater ticket, have lunch, and head back to her hotel to pick up her guitar. She'd make a quick stop at Manny's Music to buy some blank sheet music, and then spend the rest of the day making music. Dinner at the Rainbow Room, then *The Importance of Being Earnest* at the St. James Theater.

It was a good plan, tight, compact, fitting the maximum amount of tourist and musical activity into the least amount of time. The only problem was, she felt guilty just walking out of the Sentinel Building. Duncan was in trouble, big trouble.

She couldn't just wander off and make like a tourist and pretend nothing was wrong.

He's a grown man, he's a trained professional, Harley reminded herself as she walked toward Eighth Avenue and the Grayline bus terminal. *He can take care of himself.*

She said this to herself several times.

Damn Duncan Lang! She wasn't supposed to be worrying about him, she was supposed to be enjoying her holiday! He had intruded into her plans, her thoughts, and her emotions almost from the first moment she had left the Ritz-Carlton and it just wasn't fair. She was supposed to be alone in Manhattan, the kid herself, enjoying her first adult adventure, and instead she had Duncan Lang, or his ghost, forcing himself onto her awareness, into her days, and through her dreams at night.

This was not the stuff of freedom. It wasn't her concern that his family made ogres look good. There was nothing she could do about the fact that he was suspected of stealing a million dollars' worth of diamonds. It was also sheer stupidity to be attracted to a man who made Errol Flynn look like John-Boy Walton.

To think that she had been mooning over the man—yes, *mooning*—late last night when she could have been writing songs or making music or trying to figure out her future.

She had only known him a little more than two days—okay, two terrific days—but the point was, he shouldn't have crept under her skin like this. She was not some empty-headed, hormone-driven, spine-deficient, tongue-tied, pimply-faced, man-besotted *teenager.* She was a woman. A free and independent woman with a mission to enjoy the next week and a half. She was not about to let some *man* interfere with something she had worked so hard and risked so much to get. It was stupid. It stopped here and now.

She bought her tour ticket and climbed to the top of the red double-decker Grayline bus and made herself be present as the bus drove past Herald Square and the Woolworth

Building and through Soho. By the time it reached verdant
Battery Park, Duncan Lang and his ghost were nowhere to be
found and Harley felt just fine. And proud of herself. She'd
done it. She'd taken the day back for herself.

When the bus finally returned to its terminal, she dropped
a few dollars into the tip bucket, stepped out onto the sidewalk, and headed for the St. James Theater. It was an almost
ten-block walk, but she wanted to stretch her legs and, if she
cut down to Seventh Avenue, she'd have plenty to see. Late
July with its heat and humidity was not supposed to be the
height of tourist season in New York, but someone had failed
to tell the thousands of people crowding the sidewalks. Harley strode happily through the throngs, loving the energy
rising up from the sidewalk, and all the colors and types of
people, and the fast-food joints mixed in with renowned
comedy clubs, hotels, and theaters.

"I love this town," Harley murmured as she swung past
Times Square and a towering billboard of Travis Garnett,
rock and roll's newest superstar. She stuck her tongue out at
Jane Miller's equally towering billboard. Harley was free and
independent and to hell with her alter ego. She turned right
onto West Forty-fourth Street and walked up to the St. James
Theater and the ticket booth just inside the lobby as if she
were an old hand at this sort of thing. "I'd like one orchestra
seat for tonight, please," she informed the ticket seller
through the box window as she opened her purse.

Duncan ducked his head into the window beside her.
"Two seats, actually."

It was a bad shock. Harley jerked back. "What the hell are
you doing here?"

His mask of innocence was far from convincing. "I've
been wanting to see this revival of *The Importance of Being
Earnest* since it opened. I hear Hugh Grant is great. But then,
he always is. Two, please," he said to the ticket seller.

"*One,* please," Harley countered, glaring at Duncan.
"How did you even know I'd be here?"

"You showed me your itinerary the other day."

"And you memorized it?"

Duncan shrugged. "Comes with the job. Two tickets, please."

"You can't see a show tonight," Harley indignantly informed him. "You've been accused of theft and you've been hired to figure out what Boyd is up to."

"An evening at the theater is the perfect way to take my mind off of petty distractions. Even Sherlock Holmes indulged in leisure activities when he was working on a case. Two, please," he said to the ticket seller.

"I only brought enough money for one ticket," Harley stated.

"That's okay. I have enough money for two," Duncan said, handing the ticket seller two hundred-dollar bills. She handed him the tickets and three twenties back. "There we are," he said brightly, tucking the tickets and change into his wallet, "our evening's entertainment is all settled. And now to lunch."

"What lunch?"

"*Our* lunch."

"You are assuming way too much," Harley grimly informed him as they walked back out to the sidewalk.

"Isn't it after twelve?"

"Yes."

"Aren't you hungry?"

"Yes."

"Ergo, lunch."

"But not with you," Harley retorted. "This is *my* holiday, remember? Not yours, not ours, *mine*. It's a solo effort."

"But you're my client. I'm responsible for you."

"I'm a grown woman. I'm responsible for myself."

"As my client—"

"As your *employer*," Harley countered, "I get to tell you what to do and what not to do and I'm telling you now to find some other lunch companion."

"But I need to run something by you."

"Then run it by me here."

"A restaurant would be more comfortable."

But Harley had dug in her heels, liked the feel of it, and was having none of his winsome smiles. "Here or not at all. Your choice."

Duncan sighed heavily and pulled a folded computer printout from his coat pocket. "Here's what we got on your bank records. Does anything seem out of kilter to you?"

Harley scanned what turned out to be a pretty detailed account of her different checking, savings, credit card, IRA, and miscellaneous financial accounts designed to protect her as much as possible from the tax man. "It pretty much jibes with last month's report," she said.

"Including the two very large deposits this month?"

"Proceeds from the tour. Nothing looks the least bit out of kilter."

"Damn. I was hoping Boyd was skimming something off the top. It would have made this job so much easier."

"I thought you longed for challenge in your work."

"I do. There's a lot going on under the Boyd Monroe surface. Financial malfeasance would have been just the tip of the iceberg, but at least it would have been a start, something we still don't have."

"You'll come up with something," Harley said soothingly. "Look how easy it was for you to come up with an excuse to waylay me in the middle of my schedule."

Duncan raised an inquiring black brow.

"You could have asked me about my financial records when I checked in with you at the end of the day," Harley continued. "I've spent too many years being watched over and protected from life like I was some fragile china doll not to recognize the signs now. I can take care of myself, Duncan Lang."

"Who said you couldn't?"

"*Don't* run that number on me! You've scarcely let me out

of your sight since you accosted me at Manny's Music, and today, when you have so much more that should be occupying your thoughts and your time, you drop everything to buy a theater ticket and have lunch with me. I am telling you to stop it."

Duncan sighed heavily. "I thought I was being so subtle."

"Oh, you're light years ahead of Boyd Monroe, but that isn't saying much."

"Ouch!" Duncan said, cringing. "You are a handful, Harley Jane Miller."

"How wonderfully condescending of you to say so."

Duncan cringed again. "You have no idea the opportunity you are blowing. I have never felt protective about anyone in my life. This is a one-time offer only. It'll be something to tell your grandkids."

Harley sighed as a grin crinkled the corners of her mouth. There he went again, shifting her emotional gears in midheartbeat. "Grown-up women do not need protection, and I am growing up remarkably fast." She held up a hand to forestall the argument hovering on his lips. "Courtesy I grant you and I appreciate, but overprotectiveness is just insulting."

Duncan scowled. "Does this mean I don't get to see *The Importance of Being Earnest* tonight?"

It occurred to Harley that she was battling an irresistible force, and losing, and wasn't anywhere near as upset about that as she should be.

"Of course you can come to the play tonight." She held up one hand to stop him before he started. "I'll meet you in the theater lobby at seven forty-five."

At six-thirty that evening, Harley sat alone at a table for two in the Rainbow Room fending off vertigo as she looked through the plate glass windows and down sixty-five stories to the streets below. She hastily looked around the restaurant to recenter herself, loving its art deco elegance and expecting

Fred and Ginger to take to the circular dance floor at any moment. But she wasn't happy.

She was dining alone at a table for two when what she really wanted was Duncan Lang seated across the table from her complaining that debauchery wasn't all it's cracked up to be, or telling some silly story about a man he had met at a Kenyan tea party, or stealing her breath with that look she had seen more and more in his black eyes, a look that boldly declared that he saw a woman he wanted to take to bed . . . repeatedly.

Her hand stilled on her water glass as she realized that she was a woman whose subconscious had been wanting exactly the same thing from the first moment she had crashed into him.

Here she was in the world-famous Rainbow Room, with couples all around her talking quietly or laughing or dancing to the music, and she was feeling sexual again, and like a full-fledged woman for the first time in her life, and she wasn't at all sure she should do anything about it. Lust and longing were not on her itinerary. She was supposed to be spreading her wings, not looking for a holiday fling. Harley frowned. Duncan had made no secret of the fact that he was a man who had enjoyed many a delightful fling over the years, but she didn't want to have a fling with him. She wasn't sure what she wanted from Duncan, but she was certain it wasn't that.

"Ah hell," she muttered. No fling meant no kissing, and she was beginning to obsess on just what it would feel like to be kissed by Duncan Lang. And to kiss him back.

CHAPTER SEVEN

All in all, Duncan thought, it had been a good day. Oh sure, he was now the chief suspect in a million-dollar diamond robbery, his family had turned their backs on him, and he had come up empty after spending nearly eight hours digging through Boyd Monroe's bank records. But still, he hadn't been arrested, his family hadn't thrown him out into the street, he had actually had something interesting to work on all day long, and he was about to sit beside Harley Jane Miller at one of his Top Five favorite plays.

It was a very good day.

He walked into the lobby of the St. James Theater fifteen minutes before curtain time. The ten-deep crowd melted away. He saw Harley, only Harley, as she stood against the far right wall, dressed in a sleeveless midnight blue gown that molded itself all the way down her delectable body to her ankles. Not too thin, not too lush.

"Perfect," he murmured. It was a surprise to find he had to wade through a sea of bodies before he could finally stand before her, loving the shock to every nerve in his body when her turquoise blue eyes met his, feeling her smile as if it were a caress.

When had any woman had this kind of impact on him?

"Hi," she said, almost shyly, it seemed.

"Hello, yourself," he replied. He gave in to temptation and reached out to let his fingers slide through her short brown hair. Oh, how he loved to touch this woman! She was becoming positively addictive. "You look wonderful. Ready to go in?"

"I can't wait," she replied a little breathlessly.

He was feeling pretty breathless himself. He sat beside her in the theater, drinking in her laughter and melding it to his own. She was life—sweet, vibrant, life. Her laughter was infectious. Her gasps at Wilde's brilliant use of language made it seem that much more scintillating. She radiated delight as she sat beside him and he drank it in. He'd been denied delight for too long.

"Oh, that was wonderful!" she exclaimed when the final curtain call had been taken and the house lights had come up. "I want to see it again!"

"Done. But you buy the tickets this time," he said as he took her hand and began to pull her toward the aisle. How he loved holding Harley's hand. These last few days, it had become absolutely necessary to his well-being. "Tired?" he asked as they made it to the aisle and became a part of the slow river of people moving out to the lobby.

She shook her head, short hair silky in the light. "Energized," she retorted. "I want to see every play on Broadway now."

They pushed through the lobby and out into the warm night air and West Forty-fourth Street. They turned right with most of the crowd and began slowly strolling toward Broadway.

"I can't believe you live in New York and hadn't even seen *The Importance of Being Earnest* yet," she said. "What do you do with your nights?" Even in the shadows, he could see her sudden blush. "Sorry! I didn't mean to pry."

It was very hard to stop laughing. "Well, well, well, don't *you* have a vivid imagination," he teased. "Unfortunately, reality falls far short. I've worked late, attended interminable family dinners, made the rounds of Mother's stultifying society parties, and escorted the boring daughters of her even more boring friends to a variety of restaurants, clubs, and charity events."

"Man, and I thought *I* had it rough these last few years."

Duncan laughed again. In just a few days, she had somehow banished two years of hard work and boredom and trouble from his soul. He wondered if he would ever be able to repay her.

"Wow!" They had just walked out onto Broadway and Harley had come to a screeching halt. "Wow!" she said softly again. "It hasn't changed. It's still just like Christmas."

Perhaps it was the night air, perhaps it was because he felt so amazingly alive, or perhaps it was all Oscar Wilde's fault, but when Duncan turned from the happiness that enveloped Harley and looked at Times Square, he saw it with new eyes. It *was* beautiful and exciting, even mesmerizing.

She startled him from his reverie by slipping her arm confidingly through his. "Like it?"

"Love . . . it," he faltered, staring down at her, unable to catch his breath. She was exquisite. And more. In that moment, Duncan finally understood just how dangerous Harley Jane Miller had become. He was amazed. This was impossible. He was incapable . . . and she was . . .

Her arm tightened on his. "I'm glad," she said.

Oh God, she was *incredibly* dangerous. He couldn't take his eyes from her. It was shocking how badly he wanted to kiss her. Some sort of magnetic field was wrapping around them tighter and tighter with each passing minute. His heart was pounding wildly in his chest. He had never wanted anyone as badly as he wanted Harley, here, now, in the middle of this crowded sidewalk.

This was unfamiliar territory. He was used to feeling attracted to a woman and, when she was similarly attracted, taking her to bed.

But what he was feeling for Harley went way beyond attraction to places he hadn't been before and didn't understand and was pretty sure he didn't like. "It's late," he tersely announced. "I'd better get you back to your hotel." He searched the street a little desperately, spotted an empty cab, and summoned it with sheer willpower. Harley was trouble. He had to ditch her fast.

He forcibly entrenched himself in his sane, reasonable, gentleman self on the ride back to the Millenium. He politely chatted with Harley about other Oscar Wilde plays as they rode the hotel elevator to the thirty-seventh floor. He calmly escorted her to her room door. He waited until she had inserted her room card key and had safely opened her door.

"Thank you for a lovely evening," he said, shaking her hand.

He had thought that, at least, would be safe.

He had never been more wrong about anything in his life.

Her fingers, as they trembled against his hand, imparted an electrical jolt that fried his brain and sent all the wrong messages throughout his body. He was standing there, in the Millenium hallway, raising her hand, watching her eyes widen with shock and hunger as he pressed his mouth to the tender center of her palm.

"Duncan!"

It was a whisper. It was a moan. It fulfilled too many of his fantasies.

With a groan, he dragged her against his aching body, one arm encircling her, a hand cupping her head as he lowered his mouth to lips that were parted on a gasp. Glory flooded through him.

She jerked her mouth away, as if she had been burned. She stared up at him with blue eyes that looked as stunned as he felt. *"Stop that!"* she said a little desperately, just before she wrapped her arms behind his neck and kissed him hard, her body eagerly arching into his as her tongue shocked his mouth.

Hunger that had been gnawing at him for years welled up within him now and burst every blood vessel in his brain. She was writhing against him, her mouth hot and eager on his as they exchanged wet, fevered kisses that left every muscle in his body rigid with a need that was torturous in its intensity.

A door banging closed at the end of the hallway jerked them apart. But her heat still infused him, burning through walls to touch places he hadn't even known existed. And didn't want to know existed. He had to stop. He had to stop this runaway train now before it derailed everything he knew about the man he had always been.

"This is trouble," he said, struggling for breath.

"Yes," she said, the fever still in her eyes, tearing at his resolve.

He groaned. "I have always made it a point to avoid trouble."

"So have I."

She was just inches away. He had never wanted anyone this much. He had never felt so badly out of control. "Then we should stop."

"Absolutely."

"Good night, then."

"Good night."

Neither of them moved.

Duncan's head was spinning high above the clouds. It was of no use to him at all. "I don't want this," he said.

"Neither do I," she said, and he saw the same truth and the same helplessness in her eyes that he felt.

Somehow he managed to take a step back. That helped.

He could breathe a little again. "We're both adults. We know how to get the better of our hormones."

"Is that all this is?" she said softly.

"No," he ground out, "that's not all this is."

"I was afraid of that."

"Me too." He stuffed his hands into his jacket pockets. "But Harley, I don't do relationship. I don't do commitment."

"I know."

"I am way more trouble than you can handle."

"That's what I figured. So, what now?"

Let me make love to you. Let me sink into your sweet flesh. Let me burn away this agonizing fever and restake my claim on sanity. "You walk into your room and you shut your door and you lock it."

"Right," she said, taking a step back into her room. "You sure about this?"

He smiled then. "No."

She smiled back with the same mirthless amusement. "Good. Neither am I. Good night, Duncan."

"Good night, Harley."

He took another step back, and so did she. Slowly her door closed. He heard her turn the lock and only then could he make himself turn away and begin walking toward the elevator. A sudden attack of vertigo nearly dropped him to his knees, but he kept walking. Sanity and safety lay far away from Harley Jane Miller's hotel room door.

He hopped a cab, but by the time it reached Charles Street he couldn't take it any longer. It was impossible to sit quietly, so he paid the driver off and walked the more than twenty blocks home, drinking in large lungfuls of the warm, humid night air. It did nothing to steady him. He kept telling himself that he shouldn't be happy.

But it didn't help. He felt joyful! And he had never been more shocked in his life. Who *was* this guy? This Duncan Lang was nobody he recognized. He had just agreed *not* to take the woman of his current sexual fantasies to bed for the next several years of nonstop lovemaking, and here he was brimming over with lust and delirium and *joy*.

How could he be joyful after saying no to what he wanted more than air? How could he be joyful when Harley had said no, too? How could he be joyful when he was going home to an empty apartment and an immediate future that was pretty much covered in black clouds?

Those were stupid questions. This disconcerting joy was courtesy of the passionate and innately joyful Harley Jane Miller who gave everything that she was in her music and in her kisses. She had held nothing back in that hotel hallway, and Duncan had never experienced that kind of generosity before. He had never been touched by another's soul before. He had never been welcomed with such eagerness or felt such a suffusion of emotion before.

She was wholly unique in his experience and increasingly necessary to his happiness.

She was?

His steps slowed. How had he become so different from the man he had always believed himself to be?

Badly unnerved, he turned onto his street and stopped cold. A car he had never seen before was parked in front of his building, along with all of the regular neighborhood cars that he did recognize.

"Holy moly," Duncan muttered, dropping automatically into a crouch behind a seven-year-old Toyota. He peeked around the hatchback and carefully studied the American sedan and the man sitting behind the wheel. He was watching his building. He was looking up at Duncan's third-floor living room windows.

Now would be a very good time to be carrying a gun. Unfortunately, none of the cases Duncan had worked on in the last two years had required anything resembling armed protection. Of course, he could always turn around and disappear into the city before the guy spotted him, but how could he know where to hide if he didn't know whom he was hiding from, and why?

He mentally itemized all the things in his pockets: his wallet, a package of tissues, his keys . . . and his Mont Blanc pen! *Perfect.*

Moving cautiously, he began slowly creeping up the street, crouched beside the parked cars, until he was behind the American sedan. A rental car. He memorized the plates and the rental I.D. tag, then inched his way forward to the driver-side door. His heart was beating uncomfortably in his chest. He snaked his hand up to the door handle.

Then he suddenly stood up and jerked the door open. He pushed his pen hard against the driver's fleshy temple before the man realized he was no longer alone. "Try anything and you're a dead man," Duncan growled. "Put your hands forward on the dashboard where I can see them. Now!"

Sighing heavily, the driver obeyed. Under the dim street-lighting, Duncan could see that he was tall and muscular and dressed in a three-piece suit that almost completely masked the presence of a shoulder holster.

"Who are you and why have you staked out my apartment?" Duncan demanded, still pressing his pen to the driver's temple like a gun.

"You are Monsieur Duncan Lang?" the driver asked. The French accent was a shock.

"I am," Duncan replied.

"*Bonsoir,* monsieur," said a second Frenchman from behind him.

Oh *hell.* He hadn't even suspected the driver had a partner, and now a very real gun was pressed to the back of his head.

"Please be so good as to place your hands on the top of the car . . ." the gunman pleasantly commanded, "after you drop the pen, of course."

This was not good. Duncan dropped the Mont Blanc pen,

put his hands on the car's roof, and tried to think of some way not to die in the next few minutes.

"What's all this about?" he asked, his mouth dry, his heart pounding ferociously against brittle ribs.

"Our employer, Monsieur Giscard, wishes you to return at once the diamonds you have stolen from him," the driver informed him. "We have come to collect them."

Duncan swore silently. This wasn't trouble. This was disaster. "You're wasting your time," he said. "I haven't got the diamonds and I don't know who does."

"Really, monsieur, we had hoped better of you than this," chastised the gunman behind him.

"Gentlemen, I am innocent," Duncan stated, his heart racing. "The New York City police have substantiated my alibi for the time of the robbery. When they find the real thief, they will find the diamonds and return them to your employer. Until then, Monsieur Giscard will just have to be patient."

"Alas, monsieur," the driver replied apologetically, "that is a quality which our employer unfortunately lacks."

"In abundance," the gunman added.

"You have my profound sympathies," Duncan retorted, just before he pounded his heel into the top of the gunman's foot and rammed his elbow into the man's diaphragm. He heard a startled grunt and the gun clatter to the pavement as he threw a hard right against the driver's jaw. Duncan hit the ground rolling and came up with the Frenchman's gun locked in his hands. "Ah-ah-ah," he said to the former gunman, who was preparing to lunge at him, "back against the car."

Sighing heavily, the muscular blond complied.

"Really, monsieur," the driver complained, "this is too bad of you. We wished only to discuss the matter of the diamonds and instead you act with violence upon us."

"This is not the American hospitality I expected," the blond complained.

"Nor I," said the driver.

"Excuse me," Duncan said, feeling wildly off balance, "but I think holding a gun to my head is not exactly the way to promote Franco-American relations!"

"Stealing the diamonds of our employer was not helpful either," the driver pointed out.

"C'est vrai," the blond agreed. "If you return them immediately, then the harmony between our two nations may be preserved."

Duncan had the most awful feeling he was losing his mind. "Look, I'll say it again: *I don't have the diamonds, I did not steal the diamonds, I don't know where they are now.* Tell Giscard he's after the wrong man and ask him to suggest someone else for you to hold up at gunpoint."

"Really, monsieur," the driver said severely, "there is no need to be insulting."

"We wish only to conduct this one matter of business with you," the blond complained.

Duncan now understood why Harley had stood on a sidewalk near Bryant Park and screamed.

"I haven't got the diamonds!"

"Monsieur, we are reasonable men," said the driver.

"We are willing to accommodate you," said the blond.

"We have our orders, monsieur. Return the diamonds or lose your head."

"We would much rather you return the diamonds."

Polite, but deadly. What a lousy combination. "I've got new orders for you," Duncan informed them. *"Leave me alone.* If I see you anywhere near me or my home or my office again, I'll shoot first and ask questions later. Get it?"

"Got it," the two said as one.

"Good. Now you," Duncan said, pointing the handgun at the blond, "get into the back seat, on the floor."

Sighing heavily, the blond thug complied.

"Adieu, messieurs," Duncan said, pointing the gun at the driver.

"Let us say au revoir," the driver countered just before he put the car in gear and headed toward Tenth Avenue.

Duncan didn't even give himself time to start shaking. He shoved the gun into the back waistband of his jeans and started running toward Eighth Avenue. This bore no resemblance to his morning jogs through Chelsea. He ran hard and fast, his heart bursting in his chest. With a decent head start, he might just live long enough to pull a Harley.

CHAPTER EIGHT

*H*arley woke up after a night of shockingly sensual dreams, all of them starring Duncan Lang, and wondered if her blush would die away in this century. A shower and a room service breakfast went a long way toward restoring some of her equilibrium. She decided that she and Duncan had acted like two remarkably mature adults last night when they had agreed not to pursue something that definitely should not be pursued. After all, he had his problems and she had hers. He lived on the East Coast and she lived on the West Coast. He was the Playboy of the Western World and she was the vestal virgin of the pop world.

To allow anything to happen, let alone develop, between them was sheer lunacy. She was glad they had both come to their senses last night. She really was.

And she wouldn't think about him. Not at all.

She'd start not thinking about Duncan by calling her

mother and—for the third time since her holiday began—allay the newest crop of Barbara Miller's fears for her daughter's well-being.

It took Harley ten minutes to convince her mother that she was not abandoning her career, shaving her head, and entering a New Age temple. She spent another five minutes trying to convince Barbara Miller that she really should not watch the evening television news-magazines. She reiterated the one lie she had ever told her mother—that she was staying with some friends safe and sound in a high-security house on Long Island. Her mother wouldn't be able to handle the truth.

She took five minutes more to check on her mother's health and reassure herself that her mother really was taking her high-blood-pressure medicine regularly, and then spent another ten minutes listening to all the bad news from Sweetcreek Barbara Miller had told her on their last phone call: the farmers were convinced the sunny July days meant drought; the adored quarterback of the Sweetcreek High School's varsity squad had broken two of the general store's plate glass windows during a night of drunken revelry; Abby Chandler had died and her eldest girl had run off with a man ten years her senior; the begonias were struggling.

Harley finally bid her mother goodbye and hung up the phone with a gusty sigh of relief. It had taken her almost seventeen years to figure out that her mother was happiest when she was worrying about something, anything. In the intervening nine years, though, she still hadn't been able to reconcile herself to a worldview that saw everything as black, or at most gray, rather than red, or orange, or yellow, or anything remotely resembling a cheerful color. If she had believed Barbara Miller's prophecies about *her* life, she'd be lying hungover in the back of some biker bar beside some unwashed human refuse she had picked up the night before.

She glanced at herself in the mirror—jaunty short brown hair, a sleeveless red spandex minidress (with matching cowboy boots, of course), freckles free of all makeup—and grinned. Parents—particularly stress addicts—weren't always right.

She picked up the phone and called Annie to check in, and then she strode from her room. It was time to get back out into the city and find more lyrics to write for "Nice Girls Don't."

She walked out of the Millenium lobby into an overcast morning and had her plan immediately torpedoed by two very tall, very muscular men in expensive three-piece suits who bore a disturbing resemblance to her former body-guards, except these men weren't bodyguards, they were thugs. She might have been cloistered these last nine years, but she could still tell the difference. She was so relieved they weren't some of Boyd Monroe's minions, that she wasn't even afraid when they grabbed one of her elbows each and guided her to one of the concrete planters that lined the hotel's black glass wall facade.

"*Bonjour,* Mademoiselle Hitchcock," said the burly blond with the limp.

"Won't you sit down?" said the beefy brunette with the colorfully bruised jaw.

"We are two strangers to your fair country," said the burly blond, "in need of your expert assistance."

"We depend upon you, mademoiselle," said the beefy brunette.

"It will take only a minute of your time," said the burly blond.

"Two, at the most," amended the beefy brunette.

"Look," said Harley, jerking her arms free of their massive hands, "what's going on? Who are you guys?"

"Ah, now where are our manners?" cried the burly blond with every appearance of distress. "Your pardon, mademoiselle. I am Desmond Farrar."

"And I," said the beefy brunette, "am Louis Mercer. We are very pleased to make your acquaintance."

She gazed up at this Tweedledum and Tweedledee of the

Thug Set with growing amusement. Leave it to the French to manufacture polite goons. "Charmed, I'm sure," she said with a wry grin. "What do you guys want?"

"It is simplicity itself," Desmond assured her.

"A trifling matter, really," said Louis.

"We want only to know the whereabouts of Monsieur Duncan Lang," said Desmond.

"An address would be most welcome," said Louis.

Warning bells began clanging rhythmically in Harley's head. "But I don't know where he lives."

"You misunderstand us, mademoiselle," Louis said. "We know where he lives."

"We had hoped to have a private conversation with him last night," Desmond said.

"But Monsieur Lang objected," Louis said.

Harley stared at him. Good God, had they been brawling with *Duncan*?

"That is why we have come to you," Louis said.

"We want to know where he is currently staying," Desmond said.

"But I don't know that either," Harley said.

Desmond glanced at Louis. "She professes ignorance."

"It is most disappointing," said Louis.

Desmond sadly regarded Harley. "I fear we must impose ourselves on your company until you do know, mademoiselle."

Harley stared haplessly up at the muscular duo before her. "But I'm telling the truth! I've only known Duncan for a little more than three days. I have no idea who his friends are or where he might stay if he isn't at his apartment. Honest!"

Desmond shook his head. "Such an innocent face to hide so many falsehoods."

"The world is a melancholy place, *mon ami*," Louis said sympathetically.

"Mademoiselle," said Desmond with decision, "you

should know that we know your relationship with Monsieur Lang is far from casual. You kissed him last night."

"And with an ardor we could only envy," Louis added.

Harley blanched. *"You were watching us?"*

"Alas, mademoiselle, it is our job," said Desmond. "Our employer ordered us to find, follow, and seize upon Monsieur Lang. We have failed only in the last."

"Our employer is most displeased," said Louis.

"Okay, I'll bite," Harley said. "Who's your employer?"

"Armand Giscard, of course," Desmond replied.

Harley's eyes widened. "And you all think that Duncan . . . The robbery . . ."

"Ah oui, naturellement," Louis said.

"But Duncan doesn't have the diamonds!"

"He stole them only yesterday and already he has sold them?" Desmond demanded.

"No, no, no! I mean, Duncan didn't steal the diamonds and he hasn't got them now."

Louis regarded her with a look of horror. "Has that *cochon* Lang compounded his crime by lying to so fair and lovely a mademoiselle?"

"There can be no lenience for such a man," Desmond declared.

"But he hasn't lied to me!"

"It grieves me that we should be the ones to reveal the perfidy of a man you have kissed with such abandon," said Louis.

"Men were deceivers ever," Desmond sadly quoted.

Outrage vied with amusement in Harley's breast. "Look guys, I promise you that Duncan is not the goon you want."

"Qu'est-ce que c'est goon?" Desmond asked Louis.

"Le scélérat," Louis explained.

"Ah oui. He is the goon we want, mademoiselle, because he is the goon our employer wants," Desmond explained.

"This is why we have applied to you," said Louis.

"I see," Harley said slowly. What she saw was that she

faced the very real possibility of being joined at the hip for life with Messieurs Desmond and Louis if she didn't find some way to convince them of her ignorance and fast. She also saw that Duncan was in mega-trouble and it was up to her to help him get out. How to resolve the two conflicting interests was the problem. "I'd like to help you, guys, really I would," she said. Inspiration struck. "The Hamptons!"

"Quoi?" said Desmond and Louis as one.

"Duncan told me only the other night that his family has a summer place in the Hamptons! Wouldn't that be the perfect place to hide out until the heat dies down?"

Harley made a mental note to stop watching so many gangster flicks on TV, while Desmond and Louis consulted with each other in undertone French.

"Very well, mademoiselle," Desmond finally said, "it is the hideout we had not considered. Besides, you remind Louis of his sister and naturally he wishes to believe you."

"Marie-Louise would not lie about any matter of importance," Louis avowed.

"I, too, am inclined to think you may have provided the information we seek. Therefore, we shall say au revoir."

"Not adieu?" Harley asked hopefully.

"I fear not," Desmond replied.

"It is possible," said Louis, "that if we do not find him first, Monsieur Lang will seek you out, and in that case . . ."

"You will meet us again," Desmond concluded. "If you should see Monsieur Lang before we do, please give him a message for us."

"Tell him," Louis said, "that if he returns the diamonds to us today, we will let him live."

Harley shivered a little as the two French thugs bowed and set off down Church Street. She watched them go, feeling like she was in a convoluted French avant-garde film without subtitles. What a mess! It was definitely time to call in the cavalry.

She ran back into the hotel and up to her room. The

phone was in her hand before her door had even finished closing.

"Colangco International, Duncan Lang's office," Emma announced.

"Emma! This is Harley Miller. Duncan's in trouble."

"How do you know that?" Emma demanded.

"Because I was just accosted by two French goons who are looking for him."

"Oh my God, are you all right?"

"I'm fine," Harley assured her. "But these two guys . . . they looked like they'd been in a fight. Is *Duncan* all right?"

"They jumped him last night, but he managed to get away. He's fine, except he is not going to be happy that you've been involved in this mess."

"He's not?" Harley said, oddly cheered by this statement.

"No. And neither am I. We'd better bring you in."

"What do you mean by 'bring me in'?" Harley demanded suspiciously.

"We need to hide you until this mess is resolved."

"No way!"

"Harley—"

"I just got out of one prison and I refuse to be put into another. Besides, I'm not in any danger."

"But those two French goons—"

"Like me."

There was a pause on the other end of the line. "And why shouldn't they?" Emma finally said.

"Besides, I sent them off to the Hamptons."

"You sent them to . . . ?"

"The Hamptons. Duncan told me the Langs have a summer house there. Desmond and Louis wanted to look for Duncan and I figured that was just as good a place as any to get them out of his hair for a while."

"You know their names?" Emma said in disbelief.

"They introduced themselves. They're really very sweet for thugs."

Emma was laughing on the other end of the line. "Oh, this'll *kill* Duncan."

"Oh God," Harley cried in sudden agony, "what if he really *has* gone to the Hamptons? I've set him up!"

"He hasn't and you haven't. So take some deep cleansing breaths and relax."

"Deep breaths. Right. Got it."

An authoritative rap distracted her. "Look, Emma, someone's at the door. I've got to go. Are you sure Duncan's all right?"

"As rain. Check in later, in case we find out anything on Boyd Monroe."

"Okay," Harley said. She hung up and stared at the phone for a moment. This was not the holiday she had planned.

Someone knocked on her door again.

"Coming!" she called. She walked across the room and peered through the door's tiny peephole. Nausea filled her mouth. Slowly, reluctantly, she pulled open the door. "Hello, Boyd."

He stood before her in his cowboy boots, slacks, and sports coat, but he seemed shorter than she remembered him, smaller.

"You look like a whore!" he exploded.

"Donna Karan would disagree," Harley retorted, her heart pounding blood through her veins in rapid-fire beats.

His eyes widened. "And you've butchered your hair! Didn't you learn *anything* these last nine years?"

"Actually, I learned a lot," Harley replied, shaking inside. "Do you want to come in, or would you rather stand in the hall and insult me so everyone can hear?"

Surprise and sudden uncertainty lit his steel gray eyes. He stalked past her into the room. Hands trembling, she closed the door behind him. She turned to find him glaring at her.

"It's time to stop this nonsense," he announced. "You're behaving no better than a five-year-old running away from home and playing dress-up. You're destroying your career, I hope you realize that. And what about your mother? She calls me in tears every day. Haven't you even *thought* about what you're doing to her? My God, when she sees you like this, they'll have to sedate her!"

"That's enough, Boyd," Harley stated, anger replacing fear. "One more word and I'll call hotel security to throw you out on your ear."

He started to say something, and then stopped. "You're right. I'm sorry." Harley stared at him in amazement. Those were four words he'd never said to her in all the nine years they'd worked together. "I've just been so damned worried about you," he continued, "that seeing you looking like this is a bit of a shock."

That, Harley was certain, was an understatement.

"Didn't Colby Lang reassure you about my good health and well-being?"

"I'm your manager, Jane. I'm practically your father. I had to see for myself."

"Okay. So now you've seen me and I haven't got any tattoos, pierced my nose, or shacked up with a Hell's Angel. So why don't you just head out to Los Angeles and soak up some sun and relaxation for a few days? I'll join you in a week or so."

"No!" Boyd said sharply. He took a deep breath and forcibly unclenched his hands. "No, I want to be close at hand in case you need me."

"I'm doing just fine on my own, Boyd. That's one of the many things you were wrong about."

He adopted the fake sheepish smile she had always hated on him. "I know. I've been bullheaded and blind and that's really why I'm here, Jane. I want you to come back to the Ritz with me."

"The name is Harley and the answer is no."

He took a step closer and she felt it then—a tension wiring his body that had never been there before. "Look, I promise not to interfere in the rest of this vacation of yours. I'll be strictly hands-off. Go anywhere, do whatever you want. Just give me the peace of mind of having you nearby every night. I've been wrong about a lot of things, J—Harley, but I think you owe me that much at least."

Her heart was hammering in her throat. Where was the harm in staying at the Ritz instead of the Millenium? Boyd was right, she owed him a lot, at the least peace of mind.

But her intestines were twisting in her belly and her mind was screaming, *No! Don't give in. Don't give up your freedom.*

Her heart began bruising her ribs again. "Sorry, Boyd. I can't. I mean, I won't. I'm nearly twenty-seven. It's time to cut the umbilical cord."

"Dammit Jane—I mean, *Harley*—" he growled, his face dark with anger, "all I'm asking you to do is park your suit-cases back where they belong."

"They belong here or at the Motel Six or anywhere *I* choose to take them."

Steel gray eyes bored into her. "This is unacceptable, young woman!"

In the past, that phrase had always killed every plan, every argument, every rebellion. It was shocking to Harley how pitiful and powerless it sounded now.

"It may be unacceptable to you, Boyd," she retorted, "but it's what I want and it's what I choose." She walked to the door and opened it. "Goodbye, Boyd. I'll see you in ten days in Los Angeles."

"Harley—"

"*Get out,* Boyd," she commanded and watched, not even amazed, when he obeyed without another word.

She closed the door after him and let the shaking take over for a moment. Wrapping her arms around herself, she made it to the end of the bed and sat down.

She couldn't quite take it in. Boyd had threatened her, and she had held firm. She had even thrown him out. Where had that kind of strength and determination come from? Were Annie and Duncan right? Had these things always been a part of her? Had it really taken great strength to survive Boyd's rule these last nine years?

She began to think so. She remembered all of the praise Duncan had given her for walking out into Manhattan alone on Sunday night and realized she deserved it. She had escaped Jane Miller, she had fended off Duncan's once-in-a-lifetime protective streak, she had stood up to a couple of French thugs, and now she had taken a stand with the man who had controlled every second of her life . . . and she'd won.

Somehow an alchemy had taken place in the five days since she'd left the Ritz-Carlton. She was a very different woman from that desperate girl. She deserved a personal-growth reward, and a banana split wasn't near good enough.

So she caught a bus to the Metropolitan Museum of Art on Fifth Avenue. But all through the museum, she found herself looking over her shoulder and into corners, expecting to see Boyd or Desmond and Louis watching her. But she saw only tourists and bored kids from a dozen different countries and beautiful artwork she had to force herself to enjoy.

She gave up after an hour and walked down Madison Avenue as she had always dreamed. She strolled past the gray bunker that was the Whitney Museum, sitting with great solemnity and sense of artistic purpose amidst all the bright colors and high-end frivolity of dozens of tiny world-class signature boutiques: Versace, Chanel, Gucci, Yves Saint Laurent. This would be so much more fun if Duncan was at her side making wry comments about the haute dignity of establishments that were, when you came right down to it, just some stores peddling a product and trying to make a buck.

Duncan. He had been attacked last night by two thugs who had not been charming to him. He had been attacked . . . Harley forced herself to breathe. He was fine, he was safe, he was working, and she should not be thinking about him. She most definitely should not be wanting his company. She was supposed to be exploring freedom. She wasn't supposed to be dwelling on the way his eyes had looked as they had stared at each other last night in the hotel hallway. After all, she was averse to holiday flings.

Harley gazed unseeing at one of the displays in the amazing stone Loire Valley mansion that housed the Polo shop on the corner of East Seventy-second and Madison Avenue. She had kissed a goodly number of boys in school, but Duncan had shown her what a difference a man could make. She had *loved* molding herself to his hard body last night in the Millenium's hallway. She had loved the feel of his heart pounding against hers, and the way she had fit so perfectly between his strong legs, and the heat that had shimmered through her body as his mouth moved hungrily against hers.

"Oh, stop it!" she hissed at herself, her hands clenched in fists at her sides. "Stop wanting what you should not have."

Maybe if she'd just pulled Duncan into her room and into her bed last night, she would have gotten him out of her system and wouldn't be obsessing about him now. Except she had the most awful feeling that Duncan wasn't the kind of lover she could get out of her system.

She glanced at her watch. Almost noon. She had promised Emma she'd check in. Now was just as good a time to call as later, and she wasn't making any excuses to talk to Duncan. She wasn't.

She didn't even bother trying to pretend she was convinced. She just pulled his card from her purse and looked around for a pay phone.

"Great timing!" Emma cheerfully greeted her. "Duncan wants to meet with you this afternoon in the office around two o'clock. We need some help."

"*His* office? Isn't that the first place Desmond and Louis will look?"

"It is, they have, and you were right: they *are* kind of sweet. A little peeved about their wild-goose chase to the Hamptons this morning—apparently they don't like helicopters—but nice. More importantly, this is a high-security building and a higher-security office. Duncan will be just fine . . . as long as he stays out of Colby's way. You'd think a father would be happy the police had substantiated his son's alibi."

"So, Duncan's in the clear on the diamond case?"

"Well, I got the impression the police are still suspicious, but they *are* looking elsewhere."

"I wish Desmond and Louis would do the same."

"I dunno. I think I might miss them. They kind of grow on you after a while."

They kept growing on Harley too. After she hung up the phone, she thought she saw them standing before the austere Calvin Klein cathedral, and then she thought she saw them looking at some ghastly paintings of clowns and the ocean and John Wayne an artist had set up on the iron rail fencing along the sidewalk as she turned up East Fifty-ninth Street to walk to Fifth Avenue.

But, of course, it wasn't them.

She stared at the Waldorf Astoria, gold eagles glimmering in the sunlight, feeling unsettled and jumpy and way too close to the Ritz-Carlton—and Boyd—for comfort.

It finally occurred to her that this was her holiday and she could do as she damn well pleased. Where she wanted to be was the Sentinel Building with Duncan and she didn't care if she was two hours early. She began striding down Fifth Avenue, ignoring Bergdorf Goodman and Tiffany's. Her thoughts were elsewhere.

"Hey," she said, walking into Emma's office, a little breathless from her walk.

Emma looked up from a computer screen crammed with numbers. "Hey, yourself. You're early."

"I'm sorry. I don't mind waiting. Who's the cutie?" she asked, leaning against Emma's desk and nodding at the framed picture of a very studious young man.

"My fiancé, Lam Ying."

"You're engaged?"

"Got the ring and everything," Emma smugly replied, flashing a small emerald at Harley.

"When's the wedding?"

"The day after I get my long overdue promotion and raise."

"And when is that?"

"You ever hear the odds on Hell freezing over? I work for Duncan and he's not exactly the favorite son around here."

"So you're tainted."

"Like I had Mad Cow disease."

"That's rough."

"It's not so bad. Duncan makes sticking around worthwhile. Speaking of which, there's no need for you to spend two hours lounging against my desk. The suspect is in, and trust me," Emma said with a grin, "he's not going anywhere any time soon. Make yourself at home."

"Thanks." More than anxious, Harley walked into Duncan's office, closing the door behind her. How did one talk to an object of lust? Boyd had not covered that subject during her tenure in his personal finishing school.

Duncan sat at a desk awash in papers as he studied some sort of report that left him oblivious to everything else. This was a relief, because it gave Harley a chance to regain some of her equilibrium. He was dressed all in black today, black shirtsleeves rolled up past muscular forearms, black slacks draped sensuously against his legs, black hair a bit rumpled, as if he had run his hands through the short curls repeatedly. With his dark tan, he looked like a Latin lover who could give Antonio Banderas a good run for his money.

"So," Harley said into the silence, "with all of this leaping out of harm's way, did you letter in track and field in high school?"

He jumped a little, looked up, and smiled right at her. The effect was dazzling. "Are you kidding? I steadfastly refused to participate in any form of organized sports, just to drive my dad nuts. It worked. Still, I think I must have covered the mile in under four minutes last night."

Harley took a step forward. "*God,* Duncan, are you all right?"

"I'm fine. I promise. But you—"

"I'm fine too. They like me."

He started to say something, stopped, and then visibly relaxed. "Who can blame them? But still, don't you think you should lie low—"

"No."

He sighed. "I understand now. You've been sent by the gods to test me."

Harley wanted to make a quip about what kind of tests he had in mind, but it didn't seem wise considering how acutely aware she was of every centimeter of his body and how much her body was responding to that awareness. She sat down in the green office armchair in front of his desk, crossing her legs and wishing she hadn't decided to wear the red dress. It had felt fun and sexy all day long, but now it made her feel way too vulnerable.

Duncan pulled open a desk drawer. "At least carry this on you," he said, handing her a small cellular phone. "This way, if anything *does* happen, you might actually be able to call for help."

"Okay," Harley said, slipping the phone into her purse. "What exactly happened last night?" She blushed crimson. "I mean, with Desmond and Louis."

"Nothing much," Duncan said with a shrug. "We chatted about the diamonds."

"Uh-huh. Desmond has a limp and Louis's jaw is bruised. That didn't just happen from chatting."

"Well," Duncan said uncomfortably, "they pulled a gun on me and—"

"A *gun?*"

"It's okay! They asked for the diamonds, I said I didn't

have them, they disagreed, and I managed to turn the tables on them."

"How?" Harley demanded grimly.

He grinned at her. *Dazzling.* "Turns out I acquired a few street-fighting tactics from all my years of world travel. Much to my surprise, they actually worked. Now, if it had been broad daylight, I wouldn't have left Desmond and Louis bruised and limping. All I'd have done is sit down."

"Uh-huh."

"No, really. It's the best thing going to protect yourself from street crime. Oh, I know someone like my father would choose to slug it out if he found himself in a precarious situation—not that he ever would, of course—but I prefer using brains over brawn. Sitting down is one of the best street safety tactics in the book. It's unexpected, so it disconcerts your attacker, it's unusual, so it draws attention to you— something your attacker does *not* want—and it makes it hard for your attacker to carry through on any dire threats. Oh, and be sure to raise your voice to attract a crowd, but never with words like 'Help! Police!' They're a surefire method of chasing everyone away except your attacker. Use something innocuous. I once sang 'Buttons and Bows' almost on key in a rather nasty situation and it worked like a charm. So remember that if Desmond and Louis ever accost you again."

"Sit down and sing."

"Right."

"Got it. You didn't mind looking like a fool singing 'Buttons and Bows'?"

"I'd have minded being disemboweled by a jealous husband more. Anyway, the reason I asked you to come in is that Emma and I have dredged up every financial document and account Boyd Monroe has ever touched," Duncan said, leaning back in his chair, "and we've come up empty. Zilch. Nada. Nothing."

"You think whatever Boyd's involved in has to do with

money?" Harley asked, disappointed to have the conversation suddenly take such a professional turn.

"Any time someone is as stressed as Mr. Monroe, it either has to be about money or about a body buried in the basement. I figure your manager for the former."

"Well, that's a relief."

His wry smile made the strings of her heart go *zing!* "I'm glad you think so," he replied, "but it leaves us with a problem. If Boyd is stressed about something, anything, having to do with money, and if the money isn't in his legitimate accounts, then he's got it buried somewhere, probably offshore. Any clues where he might hide his secret bank accounts?"

"Sure, ask me the easy stuff, watch me fall flat on my face."

"Sorry," Duncan said with a grin, "but Emma and I have run out of leads. It's up to you."

"Criminy," Harley said with a sigh. "Mind if I pace?"

"Have at it."

Harley shoved herself out of her chair and began to ramble Duncan's office. Where would Boyd hide ill-gotten gains? And how had he gotten them in the first place? And when was she ever going to learn to ignore Duncan's black gaze burning over her body? "My world tour schedule was no help?"

"Nope. Boyd did not make any secret trips to visit a Swiss bank account, or an Australian bank account for that matter."

"So, he had to have been with me," Harley murmured, studying the carpet pattern as she slowly paced around the floor, "when he made a deposit, or a withdrawal, *if* he made a deposit or withdrawal on the tour." She paced silently for eight more minutes. "Criminy, Bermuda!"

"What?"

"Bermuda," Harley said eagerly, lunging at Duncan's desk and gripping it hard to keep from shaking with excitement. "I've been begging Boyd for a holiday for months now and he

kept insisting that I would get my holiday when we go to Bermuda in October. We *always* go to Bermuda on our holidays. Always. I want to go to France, he says Bermuda. I want to go to Disney World and *he* says Bermuda! He even goes there once or twice a year on his own whenever I go home to visit my mother."

Duncan stood up, clasped her shoulders, and kissed her forehead. "You," he said, "are a genius. Oh, Emma!"

Emma walked in and was quickly briefed, which gave Harley a chance to recover her equilibrium. Her forehead. He had just kissed her *forehead* and her knees were still wobbly.

"Okay," Emma said, "Bermuda's a start. But he'd be a fool to use his real name on the account, and from what we've found so far, Boyd Monroe is nobody's fool."

"An alias," Duncan said, turning back to Harley. "What kind of an alias would he use?"

It took only a moment's thought. Harley began to chuckle. "That's easy," she said. "Travis Garnett."

"The rock star?" Emma said in disbelief.

"The very same."

"But why?" Duncan demanded.

"Because Boyd hates Travis Garnett with a passion. If the offshore money ever got found and was proved to be illegally obtained, Travis would be the one in trouble—at least at first—and that would suit Boyd to a tee."

"Why?" Duncan reiterated.

"Because he discovered Travis singing in a San Antonio bar a few years back and wanted to make him the next Garth Brooks. Travis declined. Country was not where he was at. Nor was micromanagement. Gene Farlow became his manager last year and Travis has already made him a millionaire. Boyd starts kicking furniture whenever he hears Travis Garnett's name."

"Worth a shot," Emma said.

For the next hour, Emma and Duncan huddled over his

computer, tapping into bank after Bermuda bank. Harley sat
back down in her chair and watched them with all the intensity of a rabid Yankees fan watching her team play the seventh game of the World Series.

"Bingo!" Emma chimed.

"I love breaking and entering," Duncan murmured, staring at the computer screen. He nudged Emma aside and
quickly tapped some commands on the keyboard. A low
whistle emanated from his pursed lips. "I love it when I'm
right."

The printer began printing out the screen information.

"What did you find?" Harley demanded, standing up and
leaning over the desk as she strained to read the computer
screen.

"Nearly fifteen million dollars," Duncan replied.

Harley's mouth went dry. "You're kidding."

"Nope."

"It isn't a typo?"

"Nope," Duncan said, pulling several pages from the
printer and handing them to her.

She stared in disbelief at years of deposits, none less than
$200,000 and several over the $1 million mark. "Ho-ly shit,"
she murmured.

"Embezzlement?" Emma inquired, still staring at the bank
information on the computer screen.

Duncan shook his head. "We've gone through Harley's
accounts with a fine-tooth comb. They're fine. Mr. Monroe's
funds are coming from elsewhere. There are a lot of wire
transfers here. See if you can trace them, Em. They're coming
from somewhere and someone."

"Drugs?" Emma asked, typing furiously.

"That's my first thought. Harley's tours would be the perfect cover for a smuggling operation."

"I dunno," Harley said, still a bit stunned. "Boyd has
always been violently anti-drug. He screens everyone who
works for me twice a year."

"Sounds like a good cover to me," Duncan said.

"True," Harley said miserably. If Boyd had tied her into drug trafficking . . . ! She shuddered a little.

"I've got us a Swiss bank account," Emma said with growing excitement.

"Now there's a surprise," Duncan said, leaning over her shoulder.

The computer beeped.

"We've tripped a security program," Emma said in an urgent voice. "They're tracing us!"

"Bail!" Duncan yelled.

Emma's fingers scrambled over the keyboard and the computer went dead.

Duncan heaved a sigh of relief. "That was close. Good work, Emma."

"You're going to buy me a rest cure somewhere warm and peaceful when this job is finished, boss," she informed him.

"Done," he said with a grin. "Try again later, Em. If we can figure out the source of Boyd's ill-gotten gains, we'll—"

His phone rang. All three stared at it. So it rang again. Duncan answered it. "Colangco International, Duncan Lang. Oh, hello, Agent Sullivan. Uh-huh. Uh-huh. Well . . . I see. Well, it's kind of a long story. Oh, you do. Well, I'd be happy to come by in, say, an hour? Oh yes, I know where your office is. Right. Goodbye." He hung up the phone.

"Well?" Emma demanded.

Duncan grimaced. "FBI. They wanted to know why I was trying to access one of Angelo Maurizio's Swiss bank accounts."

The blood drained from Harley's face. "Maurizio? The Mafia leader?"

"The same."

"Sheesh," Emma said. "What's Boyd Monroe doing associating with him?"

"I don't think I want to know," Harley said.

"Sorry," Duncan said. "In for a penny, in for a pound. I

meet with Agent Alan Sullivan, who's heading the FBI's Maurizio family task force, in an hour. In the meantime, I'd better figure out exactly what to tell him. May I?" Duncan asked, turning to Harley.

"Oh, sure," she said numbly, handing him the Bermuda bank printout. Had Boyd tied her to the *mob*?

The office was silent except for the occasional rustle of paper as Duncan turned a page of the bank printout.

She studied him as he studied the account information. He might still think of himself as the Playboy of the Western World, but he was wrong. His focus was almost frightening; the intensity with which he scanned the pages was like a tangible force. He was the furthest thing from fluff.

"Now this is interesting," he murmured.

"What?" Harley and Emma said as one.

His intense gaze was suddenly directed at Harley. She nearly took a step back. "How long has Boyd been going to Bermuda?" he asked.

"Ever since he signed me, nine years ago," she replied.

"This account has been open nearly twelve years. Whatever he's up to, Harley, it didn't start with you."

"Well, that's something, at least."

"He's been making two and three deposits a year, some of them directly in cash, probably at the end of each of your tours. I need you to provide the paper trail, Emma," he said with a glance at his assistant. "Let's be careful to document Boyd Monroe's every breath on this one."

"You got it," she replied.

"So, it's drug smuggling?" Harley said miserably.

"Probably," Duncan replied. "The Maurizios are known for their heroin supply. Or it might be arms. Maybe something else. Whatever it is, he has involved you, and for that alone he should go to jail for life."

Harley looked up and realized that Duncan was angry. It was a very controlled, very lethal anger that made him seem more than dangerous as he stood by his desk.

"I'll get to work," Emma murmured, walking back to her office, closing the door behind her.

The intensity Duncan had focused on Boyd's bank information was now directed at Harley. She couldn't feel the floor beneath her feet. "Sorry about the lousy start to your day," he said.

"It was different," Harley wryly replied. "But I'll take Desmond and Louis over a visit from Boyd any time. He never was a morning person."

"What are you talking about?" Duncan grimly demanded as he walked around the desk. He was standing one foot in front of her.

She held up a hand as if she could actually fend him off. "It's nothing, really. Boyd came to see me at my hotel this morning and—"

"He *what*? How the hell did he know where you're staying?"

"I don't know," Harley said with a shrug. "I just figured your dad told him."

"What did he want?" Duncan demanded.

Harley's smile was wry. "He wanted me to go back to the Ritz with him."

"Why?"

"He said he was worried about me. Naturally, I said no, we had some words, so I pretty much threw my independence in his face and threw him out. End of story."

Duncan raked both hands through his black hair. She could feel the tension radiating from his taut body. "First Giscard's men and now Boyd. You are going to stay in one of the company's safe houses until all this is over."

"No," Harley replied, feeling as if she were standing off to one side, watching and listening to them both. "I won't be caged again."

"And I won't have you endangered by Giscard's men *or* your loving manager! He's connected to *Angelo Maurizio*, Harley. You're going into a safe house and that's final."

"Like hell it is," she retorted. "You have no right to tell me what to do."

"You are my *client.* I am responsible for your safety. I—"

"The only thing you are responsible for, Duncan Lang, is finding out what Boyd is up to. That's it."

"Dammit, Harley," Duncan said as he grabbed her, "this isn't a Hitchcock film. This is real life and these men are *dangerous.*"

"What you have failed to take in," Harley retorted, jerking herself free, "is that I handled all three men just fine today. I don't need your help or your protection. I am fully capable of taking care of myself."

Duncan swore and turned away from her to pace in a small circle. He stopped and glared at her. "At least let me assign some bodyguards to look after you."

"*No.*"

Duncan uttered a sound that was halfway between a groan and a strangled roar of fury. "You are the most stubborn, unreasonable, infuriating woman I have ever met in my life!"

"Thank you."

With a groan, Duncan reached out to cup her face with both hands. "Don't you understand that you're special and precious and I don't want anything to happen to you?"

He'd done it again. He'd shifted her emotional gears, catching her completely by surprise. "Thank you," she whispered, feeling as if she were shining with happiness. He must feel it too, this hunger that knew no mercy, this connection that throbbed between them and in them.

Duncan's hands fell from her face as if they'd suddenly been burned. He turned abruptly away from her. "This is all my fault," he muttered. "I should have found out what Boyd is up to long before this. Then he wouldn't be a threat. And Giscard's men wouldn't be accosting you, because they wouldn't have seen you in my company, because you wouldn't have *been* in my company."

"Duncan," she said quietly, "Desmond and Louis have

been perfect gentlemen with me. They won't do anything to hurt or even scare me, I promise."

"Harley," Duncan said as he swung around to face her, his black gaze stormy, "would you *please* give me some excuse to start avoiding you?"

Her breath caught on a little gasp. "Why?"

He stood, hands clenched in fists at his sides, face taut. "Because if I stop seeing you, then maybe, just maybe, I can stop thinking about you every damn minute of the day!"

"Oh," she said, happiness surging through her.

Duncan groaned as he reached for her. His kiss was hungry and sweet at the same time. *Oh, yes!* She wrapped her arms around him and returned the kiss, her own hunger and a joy she had never thought possible arching her against him.

"God," Duncan gasped when he finally ended their kiss. But his arms held her tight against him. Her cheek rested against his broad chest. She could hear the galloping beat of his heart. She closed her eyes, hoping to stay like this forever. "This has never happened to me before," he said, a hint of wonder in his voice. "You are absolutely dangerous to every belief I've ever had about myself. I don't know what to do."

"This works for me," Harley murmured, her body drinking in his warmth and strength. "All *I've* been doing is thinking about you, when I'm on a bus, or in a museum, or looking at a bad painting of John Wayne."

His chuckle tickled her ear. Then he pulled far enough away from her so they could regard each other within the circle of each other's arms. "We barely know each other," he pointed out.

"I'm not so sure about that," Harley countered, gazing up into his black eyes. "We may not know ourselves very well, but I think we know each other."

"You *are* dangerous," Duncan murmured. His thumb began to slowly caress her mouth. "But you've got to remember, Harley, that I'm trouble like you've never seen before."

"I know."

"Forgetting for the moment that the only word to describe every relationship I've ever had is 'casual'—"

"And I'm not forgetting that."

"Okay. Good. You should also remember that I've got the police *and* the French mob after me."

"Sounds like you need a friend right now."

His eyes darkened, stealing her breath. "What if I want a lover?"

Harley trembled a little in his arms. There were so many different answers she wanted to give. "What if I'm a distraction you can't afford right now?"

His fingers brushed across her cheek and slid through her hair. Oh, she loved the way this man touched her!

"We've already established that I think about you every minute of the day, whether you're with me or not. You *are* a distraction and my life is pretty much of a mess right now, but Harley, not having you in my days is becoming intolerable."

"Duncan—"

Something resembling a foghorn bellowed from the desk phone. "What the hell was that?" she demanded as Duncan shoved her down into her chair.

"A warning system Emma set up for me," he tersely informed her before sitting himself on the corner of the desk before her. "Dad's coming."

His office door slammed open and Colby Lang stalked into the room. He checked himself when he saw Harley. "Good afternoon, Miss Miller."

"Hello, Mr. Lang. It's good to see you again," Harley calmly replied as if a moment before she hadn't been in his son's arms.

"You've been discussing your case, no doubt."

"Yes. Things are moving very quickly. Duncan is a remarkable investigator. You must be very proud of him."

Duncan turned a bland face to his father and waited expectantly. It took years of training for Harley to hold back her grin.

"I believe my son has some . . . potential," Colby Lang replied. "Duncan, when you have a moment, I'd like a word with you." He stalked back out of the office, closing the door far more quietly than he had opened it.

Harley looked up at Duncan staring at that closed door. "The diamond case?" she asked.

He turned and gave her a rueful smile. "I'm afraid so. It looks like I'm going to have to take a hand in solving it after all. The police and my family I can handle, but when the French mob wants to wring a million dollars' worth of diamonds out of me that I don't have, and when they start accosting *you* to get to *me,* it behooves me to find the real thief, and fast."

Harley nodded. "Time to chart your own destiny."

Black eyes narrowed at her. "I don't do commitment, Harley."

"No, no, of course not," she murmured.

"Look," he said, looking harried and off balance, "I am trying to be noble here. I am trying to tell you that I am dangerous to your holiday and your independence and even possibly your heart if you become so foolish as to actually care for me. You should get out of this, Harley. You should get out now."

Harley knew she was grinning like an idiot, but she couldn't stop. And she knew she shouldn't be this happy. Duncan's history of love 'em and leave 'em gave her nothing to hang her hat on. He was not the father figure Boyd had been. Far from it. He was neither steady nor safe. He *was* trouble, not because of French henchmen, but because of the new emotions he had stirred within her and the chances he made her want to take. Physical chances. Heart chances. "Life is to be enjoyed, and chances are there to be taken," she quoted softly.

Duncan's eyes widened. He slid off the desk. "Harley?"

"Have dinner with me tonight. Seven o'clock. Your hideout, wherever that is."

Duncan was staring at her. "The penthouse apartment upstairs. I'll get you cleared through my security people. . . . Harley, are you sure?"

"Of course I'm sure!" she blithely replied as she stood up and began walking to the door, fighting the desire coiling through her veins every step of the way. "I'm sure you're a great cook, and if you're not, we can always do takeout. Good luck with the diamonds and Boyd and Agent Sullivan."

"Harley," he said, catching her arm.

She glared up at him. "Duncan, if you don't let me go right now, I'm going to demonstrate how dangerous *I* really am."

Black eyes blinked at her. His hand slowly released her arm. "Seven o'clock is what? Six hours away?"

"A little more than five."

"Okay. I'll try to make it till then."

Somehow she was out of his office, the door closed firmly behind her. She began to breathe again.

"You're hyperventilating," Emma commented.

Harley made herself focus on Duncan's assistant. "Am I?"

"Yep." Emma looked her up and down in open amusement. "Must be that fast track you're on."

Harley regarded her with interest. Emma Teng was a fascinating and perceptive young woman. "Think I should get off?"

"I'll wring your neck if you do."

That was a surprise. "Why?"

"Because I've worked with Duncan for a little more than two years now and this is the first time I've ever seen him happy."

Harley walked over to Emma's desk and held out her hand. "Will you be my best friend?"

Emma grinned and shook her hand. "You're stuck with me for life."

CHAPTER NINE

*I*t was nearly four o'clock when Duncan looked up from the police report on the Giscard diamond robbery to find Emma standing in his office doorway. "Why are you smiling like that?"

"How am I smiling?" she asked, walking into his office and dropping a folder on his desk.

"It's sort of a seraphic, I-know-something-you-don't-know kind of smile."

"Oh, that. Well, I do. There are my interviews of the people we had guarding the diamonds during transport," she said, tapping the folder.

"I never thought you'd succumb to the stereotypical Asian inscrutability, Em," Duncan complained.

"I'm a firm believer in using whatever works. I've already talked to most of Giscard's people who were involved with bringing the diamonds into the country. Nothing yet."

She walked serenely back out of his office. Disgruntled, Duncan tossed aside the police report he'd already read seven times and picked up the folder of interviews. The middle finger of his right hand rapidly tapped his desk for the next hour, slowing only when Harley entered his mind, which was every other sentence of the transcripts. He swore now and then, but kept pushing on. He would not think about Harley's delectable body lounging in the chair opposite him in a red minidress that did shocking things to his sanity. He would not think about her hot mouth returning his kiss. He would certainly not think about dinner tonight.

Or whether he should serve a Pinot Grigio or an Orvieto with the linguini and clam sauce he had planned to serve. He should probably factor in the Italian salad dressing. And then there was the question of what coffee to make after dinner. He didn't know if Harley liked plain coffee or cappuccino or espresso or . . .

Duncan caught himself. "Damn!" he said aloud, and then made himself reread from the top Emma's interview with Mike Gonzales, the driver of the diamond limousine. But the moment he had read the last line on the last page, his mind claimed Harley for its own, marveling again that she could want him enough to take him on with no guarantees. It was oddly disconcerting. He *had* been noble, he *had* warned her off, and she had chosen to pursue whatever this was between them anyway. All sense of responsibility should be ended. He should be thinking only of pleasure. Instead, he thought of the risk she was taking, and he wondered if he had the right to pursue this. She was probably a virgin, which meant this would be her first affair, and he was not the kind of man a beginner should tackle. But then, she was not the kind of woman *he* should even be considering tackling, because she *was* dangerous. She stirred depths of desire he'd never felt before. She touched his heart in ways he'd never thought possible.

He frowned as he added the Gonzales interview to the

growing stack of papers on his right. Emma poked her head
into his office. "Five-thirty, boss. I'm heading out. You need
anything?"

Five-thirty! Ninety minutes away from seeing Harley,
touching Harley, hearing her voice . . . "A straitjacket
would be helpful," he muttered.

"What?"

"Go home to your daily dose of CNN. I'll see you in the
morning."

"You're in bad shape, boss," Emma said with a grin.

Duncan groaned. "I know it. Get out of here before I ask
you to go buy me some illegal pharmacological help."

"I'm gone," Emma retorted, and she was.

With a sigh, Duncan stood up, stretched, and did his level
best to walk at a steady, normal pace to the secured penthouse elevator off of his father's office. He didn't have to
worry about running into Colby again. Fortunately, his father
prided himself on leaving the office punctually at five o'clock
every day he was in it.

He started to pass by his brother's office when Brandon
called him in. Reluctantly, he turned into the blue office. He
and his brother had said very little to each other since the
robbery. He had writhed under the knowledge that his perfect brother—the man he had resented and worshiped his
entire life—believed he was guilty. Brandon sat at his desk
looking like the *Town and Country* poster boy in his immaculate Brioni suit, not a blond hair out of place, his manicured
nails gleaming against his pen as he stopped in the middle of
signing some contracts.

"I hear you're looking into the Giscard case," he said,
setting the pen down and leaning back in his chair.

"I'm the only one who seems interested in proving my
innocence, so it made sense for me to take a hand."

"It's my case, Brother, and I resent your interference."

Duncan's black brows arched up. "Afraid I'll steal some of
your thunder by finding the real thief?"

"No," Brandon snapped. "I'm afraid you'll infuriate Dad *and* bring even more suspicion down around your neck."

"Your concern is duly noted, Brother."

"Dammit, Duncan, this isn't a game! You're in a lot of trouble. Why do you insist on making it worse?"

"I just figured that if we come at the case from different angles, we'll catch the real thief between us."

Brandon sadly regarded him. "Can't you even be honest with *me*?"

Duncan stiffened. "You know, it amazes me that someone I've only known four days believes I'm innocent, while my entire family is ready to serve as judge, jury, and executioner."

"If you just had some kind of proof you could offer—"

"My word is not enough?" Duncan coldly demanded as he died inside.

"Duncan, you've got to understand that with your past, even a brother needs a little something more to go on."

"And an alibi substantiated by the police isn't enough?"

"You could have had someone working with you."

"Ah yes, the accomplice angle the police harassed me with for over two hours this morning. Well, great minds clearly think alike. Good night, Brother."

"At least get that Miller woman out of your hair. She's a distraction you don't need right now. Send her back to Boyd Monroe where she belongs."

"*No.*"

"Dammit, Duncan, you need to be concentrating on your problems, not hers! She's trouble."

Duncan's smile was mirthless. "I know."

"Then get rid of her."

"Not . . . yet."

"Duncan—"

"Brandon, I am going to the penthouse. I've got a date and a lot to do to get ready."

"A *date*?" Brandon sputtered. "When your entire future is in question?"

"I know my future. Nothing questionable about it. I told you, I've got a date tonight. See you, Brandon. And try to cheer up. If I *am* arrested and convicted of the robbery, at least peace will finally return to the office when I'm gone."

He walked away from his brother feeling battered and bruised and wondering once again what it was Harley saw in him that his family did not that made her repeatedly take him at his word, even when the evidence—like his past—was against him.

Emma believed him too. He would have said it was a woman thing, except his mother had recently passed on the ardent hope that he would turn himself in to the police before the company and their family suffered any more harm.

He continued puzzling over it, trying to ignore the ache in his heart, and stopped himself just in the nick of time from barreling into the uniformed guard standing duty by the penthouse elevator.

"Hi, Pete," Duncan said, distractedly punching in the security code on the elevator call pad. "Anything happening?"

"It's been pretty quiet," the former Army sergeant replied. "Gwen spotted those two French guys down in the garage this afternoon, but they cleared out without causing any trouble. No one has seen them since."

"Great," Duncan said as the elevator doors slid open. "They may be hovering around Miss Miller when she arrives later tonight. Tell everyone to keep their eyes open."

"You got it."

The doors slid closed. The elevator swooped up one floor to the penthouse and opened on another security guard.

"Evening, Mr. Lang," said the at-attention recruit from the police academy.

"You have got to learn to call me Duncan, Tom, or I'm going to get a complex."

The twenty-three-year-old flushed. "Sorry . . . Duncan. Training's hard to break."

"No problem," Duncan said, inserting his security card into the lock pad at the penthouse door. "See you later, Tom."

Once the door was securely closed, locked, and alarmed behind him, Duncan gave up all pretense of being cool, calm, and collected. He legged it for his shower, stripping off clothes as he ran.

Twenty minutes later, he was clean, dry, and agonizing over what to wear . . . which made him laugh at himself. He was *far* gone. Then he heard the front door buzzer.

He glanced at the small bathroom clock. It was only six. Damn! It could be his father come to harass him some more, or Tom reporting some trouble. And he only had an hour left to dress and make dinner.

Sighing, Duncan haphazardly pulled on the pair of jeans he'd been considering and strode barefoot to the front door. He turned on the security monitor and found himself staring at Harley Miller, looking tense. He jerked open the door.

"Harley! What is it? What's wrong?"

She was wearing That Red Dress. Her eyes widened as she stared at him standing half naked before her. "I'm sorry," she said, walking stiffly past him into the apartment. "I know I'm an hour early. I tried. I really did. But I just couldn't wait any longer."

She pushed the door closed. Then she knocked the air out of him by shoving him hard up against a wall, her hands grasping his head, her body pressing him flat into the wall as her mouth claimed his with a desperation that was just this side of violence.

Joy such as he had never known surged through his veins, knocking out all the pain and grief and worry. With a hoarse cry, he wrapped his arms around her, pulling her against every square inch of his body he could manage, and then his hands were all over her. He cupped her taut buttocks and hauled her hard against his own desperate hunger. Her soft cry melded with his groan as her mouth found his ear. His arms tightened around her. She was teething his earlobe, sending excruciating sparks up and down his body. Then her wet tongue began tracing his ear, stirring frenzy within him.

He ripped down the zipper at the back of her dress and let his hands spread across warm, silky flesh.

She gasped into his ear as he gasped. She wasn't wearing a bra. His hands could slide unimpeded from the nape of her neck all the way down to a brief pair of panties that were no impediment at all. His fingers slid eagerly inside silk to mold her flesh as she whispered his name over and over again, her voice urgent and strained, inflaming him. That he could do this to her . . . That his hands could stir such delicious agitation. . . . She pulled his mouth back to hers, her tongue sinking into him, ravishing him.

She shocked him again when he felt her hands at the front of his jeans, opening them, shoving them down over his hips. Then they were stroking and kneading his buttocks before sliding hungrily up across his back and then down again.

Harley's hands—her beautiful hands—were caressing him, tantalizing him, galvanizing him.

He reached down and began to pull the red dress up her body as she bit and sucked at his arched throat.

"Oh *yes!*" she breathed when her naked breasts first met his naked, heaving chest. "God, Duncan, where the *hell* is your bedroom?"

That made him laugh as he pulled her dress and her pendant up and over her head and tossed them to the floor. His tongue laved one painfully erect nipple. He continued down over ribs and soft belly, loving her moan. It was almost more than he could bear, this combination of piquant femininity and scorching flesh. He felt like a virgin all over again. He suckled at the concave flesh of her hip, her body jerking with surprise and pleasure as his fingers slowly tugged the scrap of red silk panties down.

"Much better," he murmured against strawberry blond curls, bewitched and unsure because he'd never felt like this before. He slid his body slowly back up hers. *"Oh sweet Jesus,"* he moaned. Nothing in his life had prepared him for how good Harley felt. Or for the blaze in her turquoise blue eyes.

"I hope you have lots of condoms in this place," she said in a husky voice that nearly undid him.

He sought relief by sinking his mouth against the side of her now-arched throat. He began to suckle. "The one valuable thing the Boy Scouts passed on to me," he murmured against her hot skin, wanting to drink in her creamy flesh and absorb it into his own, "was to be prepared."

"I am. I swear. Oh God, Duncan!" she cried out as his self-control went up in flames and his fingers sank into hot, wet—incredibly wet—flesh.

He knew with a sense of exultation that he could take her here, now, in this entryway, with Tom on the other side of the soundproof door, and she would revel in it . . . but his condoms were miles away in a box in the bedroom and this was Harley in his arms. Intoxicating, glorious, blessed Harley. She deserved every possible protection, and he wanted uninterrupted hours of feasting on her. A tiled entryway was not the best place to start.

"You realize, don't you," he said in a low voice in her ear, "that restraint is not my forté?"

"Thank God!" she fervently replied.

He smiled, his fingers slowly swirling through honeyed flesh. "But Colangco's background check on you suggests this could be your first time. You could be having second thoughts. You could be nervous."

"Do I *feel* nervous?" she demanded, one leg wrapping around his to give his fingers easier access.

"You feel . . . incredible," Duncan groaned, lifting her up. She kicked off her red cowboy boots, and then wrapped her legs around his waist, their strength a heady aphrodisiac as he carried her in to the apartment.

Her mouth suckled and laved his ear with restraint-shredding intensity as he carried her through the bedroom doorway. Only the greatest self-control kept him from throwing her to the floor and taking her then and there. Somehow he managed to stay on his feet until he bumped into the bed. Then he lunged forward, following her down and down to the satin-covered comforter.

Harley lying naked against silver satin, turquoise blue eyes burning up at him, was the most erotic thing he'd ever seen in his life.

Shaking badly, he claimed her mouth with a desperate hunger, sucking at her, holding her prisoner with the sheer force of this need that was thrilling and terrifying and would not be denied. Her body undulated beneath him, tumultuous and wanton, as if he was already in her.

Never before had he been consumed by this almost violent need to give every pleasure a woman's body could withstand. Harley's gasps and cries and moans as he gorged himself on her outweighed any mere physical pleasure he might claim. This was Harley writhing beneath him—because of him—nothing could match this.

Her breasts were soft creamy flesh his mouth tried again and again to drink in, her fingers locked in his hair, her head restless against the comforter.

He licked and suckled and nibbled his way down her rib cage, relishing all the variations she created from the single word "Oh!" Her hip bones, he found, were as sensitive as his ears. For one quivering moment, he thought she might even come as he sucked at them, hard and then soft, before closing over the lovely curve of bone and skin.

Her stark cry almost made him come.

He slid farther down the bed, pressing kisses to her soft inner thighs as his fingers separated tender folds of hot flesh. He felt drunk on her scent and her heat and her saturated sex. Groaning, he sank his tongue against the locus of her hunger and shuddered as her primitive cry enveloped him.

She was swearing. She was pleading. She was gasping on half words and animal cries that were almost words.

He loved that he could make her incoherent.

He loved that he could feel the heat of her rising passion shimmer into his blood as his tongue probed and stroked. He loved the vibrant bond pulsing between them that helped him understand her every choked word and strained gasp, telling him when to push her farther and when to pull back into gentle, soothing caresses until neither of them could stand it any longer and he drew that hard, exuberant bud into his eager mouth.

He lost himself in her luscious flesh, in her frantic struggle toward a fulfillment she had never known, and there was a glory in that *he* had never known. That he could give her what she craved was more satisfying to him and more exhilarating than any other moment in his life.

"Oh, my darling," he moaned against her succulent flesh.

He slid two fingers into honeyed heat and she came with a strangled wail. He shuddered against her, rocked to his soul as she began climbing to another climax.

"I can't . . ." she whimpered. "Oh, please . . . *Duncan*!" she screamed as he sucked hard. She seemed to shatter, the million tiny shards of her coming showering over the room.

And over him. Shaking badly, he slowly made his way up Harley's taut body, understanding that tension and her urgent fingers as they slid over him, welcoming him, pleading with him. Dragging himself away from her in a fumbling search for his box of condoms was the hardest thing he'd ever done in his life.

He was on his knees, his back to her as his trembling hands rolled on the slick latex. Then he felt her soft body mold itself to his back and taut thighs, her arms wrapping around him, her fingers slowly stroking across his chest and his own hard nipples.

"It's about time," she murmured in his ear.

Laughing, he turned, only to be engulfed in her stormy gaze. "I got carried away," he said, dragging her sweet mouth to his and sucking her into him as she had drawn him into her.

"Oh," she said, her voice shaking, "is *that* what that was?" She slid back down onto the bed and pulled him down on her. Provocative blue eyes boldly met his. "Any variations on the theme?"

He stared down at her, mouth lush from his kisses, hair a silky tangle, her expressive face revealing a depth of passion no woman had ever given him.

Thank God, he thought. Thank God Boyd Monroe and Barbara Miller and the Princess of Pop had failed in their brutal attempts to murder this passion that blazed up at him, because now it was hers to give. Because now he could lose himself in it and in her.

"I know dozens of variations," he ground out, burying his mouth against her creamy throat. "We're not leaving this bed until we've tried all of them."

Her sharp cry as his teeth sank into her was a mixture of laughter and relief and unexpected pleasure.

How in hell had he managed to keep himself from her for so long?

"Dammit, Duncan," she said, heart pulsing against him, "*do* something about this ache that just keeps growing every time you touch me."

Hands cupping her face, he watched her eyes as he slowly slid into the other half of his soul. He knew the most piercing joy as blue eyes stared back, shocked as pain and passion moved as one through her.

"Ohhh!" she said on a long sigh, her body shifting subtly to accept all of him—skin, bones, breath—into her. "Do that again."

Mesmerized by blue eyes that took him all the way through into her heart without question or reserve, he began to move slowly, reveling in the woman who welcomed him with growing eagerness, awed by every changing expression on her face as she learned this new pleasure and then doubled it by finding how to match her own movements to his.

He had never been with a woman who gave all of herself in her lovemaking as Harley did. It was both blissful and haunting, lyrical and ravaging. He had never wanted to give all of himself to anyone as he wanted to give himself to Harley now, to thank her somehow for this gift he could not name.

An alchemy had occurred, turning every physical pleasure he had enjoyed many times before into something deeper and truer, something terrifying and perfect at the same time.

"Yes," he whispered both to Harley and to this agonizing alchemy. "Oh, my darling!" he cried out as she wrapped her legs around him, pulling him into the very center of her being.

She arched her body into him, gasping as he thrust into her, hard now, fighting past fear and newness and a life that had never prepared him for this moment to claim something he couldn't even name or visualize but had to have. Had to have now, and now, and now.

She was sobbing his name, her fingers digging into his back with a delicious pain. Their bodies were fusing together and their hearts, and their souls. He had never known such rapture. It was sorcery. It was Harley. It was holy.

"Yes," he said to all of it and to her. "Harley," he said and her legs tightened around him, wringing a low cry from his throat. "Harley," he groaned, "look at me. Look at me!"

Her head shifted, her eyes slowly opened, and he just simply lost it.

He drove into her hard, fast, feeling her climax, and roaring through it, taking her with him, stoking the inferno that blazed against him and in him and through him. He felt the coming frenzy building higher and higher within her as she cupped his head in her surprisingly strong hands, blue eyes staring deep into him, down all the way through to the truth, her face taut, hands urgent as they clasped him, as she moved with him, feeling the final thin barrier shred between them.

"Give me *more*," she said, wrapping herself around him, drawing everything he was out of him and into her warm soft body as it erupted into his.

It was several minutes before consciousness, let alone sanity, returned to Duncan. It came in small, delicious waves, Harley's scent on every breath, Harley's heat in every awakening centimeter of his body. He slid his tongue slowly over his lips, savoring the taste of her.

It was hard to open his eyes, but glorious to see her curled against him, still asleep. Without moving, he let his gaze slowly trail down her enchanting body and then back up to her face, quiet and lovely before him.

Clarity came suddenly and without warning. He stared at her in wonder. She had just taught him the difference between sex and lovemaking.

He had enjoyed too many hours of sexual play and pleasure and occasionally dissatisfaction not to recognize now that this stunning moment in time bore no relation to those women or those other moments in time.

He had never made love before, because he had never loved before. But he loved now. He loved Harley. He loved her and it was a shock because he had convinced himself long ago that he was incapable of deep emotion, let alone loving a woman with a depth and an exhilaration he could scarcely fathom now.

He loved her.

He loved a woman just tasting the first delirious joys of freedom and independence. He loved a woman who had lost years of her life to an artificial cloister.

He loved a woman who had just entered into her first affair and was too passionate not to want more.

He loved a woman he could not hold.

CHAPTER TEN

*H*arley woke to the delirious sensation of Duncan Lang feasting on her hip. Her hands slid down to find him hard and hot enough to almost burn her fingers through the new condom.

He'd planned ahead. How considerate.

She raised her head to nibble at his oh-so-sensitive ear, her tongue slipping in to caress and lick. "Come here," she whispered, her breath making him shudder. He moaned her name as she guided him to the ache that was doubling with every heartbeat.

"Is this what you want?" he asked, sliding into her only an inch.

"Yes," she said, her breath catching.

"And this?" he murmured, sliding in a little deeper.

"Yes."

"And this?" He thrust hard and deep.

"Oh, yes!" she cried, bucking, taking him fully, shocked again at how perfect this was, this union of his hot flesh with hers.

She had wanted to discover during her holiday how she liked to feel, and now she knew. She liked to feel like *this*. She loved the heat of Duncan's skin. She loved his low groan as she wrapped her legs around his strong hips. She loved that she couldn't catch her breath.

She loved meeting his unspoken demand to go farther, risk everything, bungee-jump with him off Mount Everest into a firestorm that burned away all of the world, his cry raw and triumphant as it merged with her own stunning climax. She loved that they ended safe in each other's arms, murmuring each other's names, like talismans.

The world slowly settled back into place around them and with it the knowledge that Duncan had lost himself in that firestorm. In her.

She hadn't known life held such satisfaction.

She hadn't known how good it felt to be held in strong arms against warm male flesh—both hard and soft at the same time.

She hadn't known that sex had a scent, that it was slippery and sweaty and tangled and utterly consuming. She hadn't known that you could laugh during sex and weep and curse. She hadn't known she could feel so much and live.

Duncan stirred against her, turning slightly as he removed the condom.

"Next," she murmured against his naked chest.

His low, rumbling chuckle tickled her lips. "If you turn out to be sex crazed . . ." he began.

"Yes?"

"I'll die a happy man."

Now it was Harley who chuckled as she rolled on top of him and grinned down into his beautiful shining black eyes. "I'm so ashamed of myself."

"Why's that?" he asked as his hands slid through her hair.

"Because I'm not at all shocked at myself."

"Should you be?"

"A virgin? A delicate flower of Oklahoma *throwing* herself at a man and practically forcing him at gunpoint to ravish her? *Someone* should be shocked," Harley pronounced.

Duncan laughed as he wrapped his strong arms around her. "Just out of idle curiosity—and let me assure you I'm more than grateful—but why exactly was it that you threw yourself at me an hour early?"

She grinned down at him. "It's entirely your fault."

"Tell me what I did so I can do it again real soon."

Harley burst out laughing. "You kissed me—and you're a great kisser, by the way—you held me and you feel great—and then you said you wanted a lover and my mind and my libido went into overdrive imagining what that would be like until I found myself writing the *most* erotic songs in my hotel room, trying to combat major lust for the first time in my life, and failing miserably. By the time five-thirty rolled around, I had enough sexual energy burning through me to power Las Vegas into the twenty-second millennium. I had to direct it *somewhere*."

"And you chose me. How thoughtful. I'm grateful. Truly I am."

"I'm just glad you were home and not averse to a woman making the first move."

Duncan laughed, his hands reaching up to trace her cheekbones, her jaw, her throat. "Oh sweet darling, that wasn't a move, that was a full frontal assault!"

"Did you mind?" Harley asked, sinking toward him.

"Do I look like I mind?" he demanded.

"You look . . . delicious," she murmured, lowering her mouth to his.

There it was again, that stunning fusion of energy as his lips met hers and he sucked hungrily at her, binding her to him like a tractor beam. She couldn't break away. She never wanted to break away.

It was a moment before Harley realized her body was thrusting against his, and that he was hardening again, his heart pounding against hers with the same rising fury. "We are not normal," she declared.

"Normalcy's no fun," he retorted. "Trust me." He stared up into her eyes with a hunger that was mesmerizing. "Take me."

Heat flooded through her. Variations on the theme. And she wanted him *now*.

"Soon," she said as she slowly slid down his body, loving his moan of pleasure.

His hips, she found, were as sensitive as her own. But something else quickly claimed all her fascination. One article she had read in one of the more forthright women's magazines recommended treating it like a lollipop. Another had recommended the popsicle technique. She decided to try both.

His tormented cries assured her she had made the right decision.

It was several hours before they finally slid under the covers, and several hours after that before they finally agreed that, since neither of them could move so much as a toe, they really ought to get a few hours' sleep.

Harley had never shared a bed before, had never slept with anyone before. It surprised her how easy it was, how perfectly they fit together, how natural and right it was to lie in Duncan's arms. It had nothing to do with sex and everything to do with a man who had once suggested they were kindred spirits and now seemed to be proved right. She wished she was butter so she could just melt into Duncan's warm skin. She settled for sliding a leg between his thighs, snuggling even closer, her head resting on his smooth chest, his arms wrapped around her as if he would never let her go.

She hadn't known there were so many different kinds of perfection.

She woke up a few hours later because sunlight was beam-

ing against her eyes. The curtains had claimed the least of
their attention the night before. She turned her head from the
double glass doors and the terrace beyond to find that she
and Duncan had moved scarcely at all while they had slept.
She smiled against his warm skin.

Even her life-changing set at the Surrealistic Pillow hadn't
generated this vast happiness that filled her and engulfed her,
surrounding her like some wonderful golden cloud.

It had never occurred to her that taking a holiday would
bring her to this delicious moment. It would have surpassed
even her wildest fantasies. But then, she hadn't met Duncan
when she had made her escape plans. She'd never met any
man who had inspired the overpowering desire to throw him
against a wall and have her way with him.

Harley shivered. Thank God Duncan hadn't laughed at
her, or looked at her like he thought she was crazy, or asked
her very politely what the hell she thought she was doing.

Thank God, somehow, for reasons she could not fathom,
the Playboy of the Western World had wanted her as badly as
she had wanted him. As she still wanted him.

That was a shock, to find, after a night of lovemaking in all
its variations, that the hunger and the desire still burned as
brightly in her as ever. She had thought that, once satiated,
they would fade away. She had thought that, once giving
herself all that she wanted, that need would disappear.

It seemed she was wrong. Very wrong.

She woke Duncan up and told him so and found—to her
astonishment—that he felt exactly the same way.

Two hours later he left the king-size bed, despite her pro-
tests. He returned a few minutes later and surprised her by
lifting her up into his arms and carrying her into the bathroom, which turned out to be a mini-spa complete with a
sunken whirlpool tub which he had filled. Carefully, he carried her into the hot water, smiling at her gasp before setting
her on the curved marble bench. The water reached her chin.

"Trust me," he said, settling beside her, "you need this."

She had already figured that out herself. In the last fourteen hours, she had used—energetically—muscles she hadn't known existed. The hot bubbling water slowly soothed away a myriad of aches and the stiffness that had threatened to take over several key parts of her body.

She realized, sitting beside Duncan, thigh to thigh, almost shoulder to shoulder, that any reasonable former virgin would not, should not, be feeling so completely comfortable outside of bed and still naked with her first lover.

But Harley had never felt so comfortable in her life. Did the man have magical powers, or had five days wrought so strong a connection?

She clasped Duncan's hand under the hot water and rested it on her thigh as she leaned against him. "Is it always this good?"

His silence made her look up. She found herself staring into eyes that drew her into the vortex of the galaxy. "No," he said softly. "Never."

Her chest ached. "But I'm so new at this."

"That," he said in a low voice, "has nothing to do with it."

Staring up into those fathomless black eyes, she believed him, because it was her truth too. Duncan was an incredibly skilled lover, but the power of their lovemaking had come from the emotion within it and behind it and between them. She didn't want to ask about that emotion, or even explore it. It was too new and she was a little too frightened of what she might find within this fullness in her heart.

The power of the phrase "one day at a time" finally became clear to her. She would not go borrowing trouble, let alone insight, just yet. There was now, this moment in time, with this man who was teaching her to see aspects of herself she hadn't even known existed. And there was this feeling surging within her, akin to power, that gave her boldness and freedom in this moment, and she liked that very much.

Her free hand slid between his thighs and brought him quickly to life.

"Harley!"

She smiled as she shifted and settled herself between his knees, standing waist high in the water, still stroking him, her other hand still locked in his. "As you pointed out . . . oh . . . six or seven hours ago, there are times when condoms are not necessary."

"What you do to me," he groaned. The fingers of his free hand slid into her, his thumb remaining behind to stroke and push and tease until their moans filled the marble room. Water splashed out of the tub in waves as they thrashed together, their voices rising in desperation until finally, with what little strength remained to them, all they could do was hold each other up to keep from drowning.

Finally they left the now much shallower tub, stepping through puddles on the marble floor to towels and robes.

Harley's stomach growled audibly and at length, which made Duncan laugh.

"As if you have the right!" she gasped in outrage, throwing a towel at him, which he ducked. "You promised me dinner last night and completely reneged."

"You feasted on other delicacies," he smirked, which brought one of her first blushes of the morning.

"You owe me dinner," she stated.

"I'll make up for it tonight, I promise."

Her body warmed with relief. She turned to studiously hang up some damp towels so he wouldn't see it in her eyes: this was more for him too, not just one night of pleasure, and now she knew it for sure. "You can start by feeding me this morning," she said lightly.

"You may have anything and everything that's in the fridge," he vowed. "What's mine is yours."

Harley took him at his word. Dressed in one of his blue T-shirts that only reached her mid-thigh, she pulled a large pineapple, two melons, and a basket of strawberries from the well-stocked refrigerator, and followed that up with butter, a loaf of bread, and the discovery of a wide variety of muffins.

"What are you having?" she asked as she popped two slices of bread into the toaster.

"Leftovers?"

She grinned at his hopeful tone. "I'll save you a scrap or two."

It was the loveliest breakfast Harley had ever had, not because of the food, which was great, but because of Duncan who kept her feeling completely at ease on this morning after by telling her silly stories of some of his failed amorous escapades in foreign climes.

By the end of breakfast, her foot was sliding up and down his leg. His terry cloth robe was no impediment at all.

"Stop that!" he primly commanded.

"Why?" she asked with a grin. "You liked it last night."

He managed to maintain his prim expression. "That was last night and this is this morning."

"So?"

"So, I have to go to work and you have to go touristing and making music."

"I don't mind waiting a day," she said with her newly minted lecherous smile.

He blinked and hurriedly scooted off his kitchen stool. "Well, I do. I'm working on two very important cases right now, if you'll recall, and I really should get at them."

"But this is Saturday. The weekend."

"I don't think Boyd or Giscard's men care."

"Oh, you're no fun at all," Harley pouted.

She suddenly found herself enveloped in Duncan's arms, his mouth tender and seductive against hers. "Aren't I?" he murmured.

"Well," she said dazedly, "I meant in that particular moment."

Chuckling, he pulled away from her. "I am going to get dressed, I am going to go to work, and then I am going to cook you dinner. You can do anything your heart desires, as long as it doesn't involve other men."

Harley felt her eyebrows arch up at that. "Are you saying . . ." It was hard to get the blood back into her face and to get her vocal cords to resonate properly. "Are you saying that you want me under exclusive contract?"

The expression in his black eyes stole all of her breath away. "That's exactly what I'm saying."

"Oh." There were no words for the joy surging through her.

He turned away suddenly and started putting the leftover muffins away. "At least until you get a better offer."

That threw her. They had just become lovers and he was already talking about her moving on to someone else? "I don't see how that's possible," she said softly.

He froze for just a moment, and then continued wrapping up the muffins. "It's early days yet," he said lightly. He glanced over his shoulder at her. "Aren't you supposed to be getting dressed?"

There were currents and depths of emotion and thought swirling through this kitchen that Harley couldn't grasp, couldn't understand. It was the first time she had ever hated Boyd, because for the last nine years he had denied her the life experience she desperately needed now to understand what was really going on. She was afraid to say anything, for fear it would be the wrong thing, and she didn't even know what that wrong thing was.

"My red dress is going to be a dead giveaway when I walk out of here, you know," she said at last.

He turned, his eyes searching her, seeking something she didn't understand. "Do you mind?"

"No. I pretty much feel like shouting it from the rooftops. Do you mind?"

The force of his dark gaze practically lifted her off her feet. *"Never,"* he said.

Oh *God,* how could anyone be this happy and live? "Even though this is just another reason for your father to be furious with you?"

Duncan smiled. "Dad would shrivel up and die if he couldn't be outraged by at least two things I do a day. Now, remove temptation from this kitchen and go get dressed."

"You think I'm tempting?"

"Very."

Harley shook her head at the wonder of it all. "Wow."

She dressed quickly and alone, which was a disappointment. She wanted to watch Duncan pull on socks and briefs, jeans and a shirt. She wanted to watch him brush his now dry hair and see if he ever admired himself in the mirror. But she dressed alone and walked back into the living room just as he walked out of the kitchen.

"Amazing," he said, looking her up and down with a warmth that did lovely things to her own temperature.

"What?" she asked, a little breathlessly.

"That dress has lost none of its impact."

That made her grin. "Oh?" she said innocently, turning in a circle before him. "You like it?"

His arms swept around her. "I like who's just barely in it more." He kissed her, long and slow and soft until her knees were no use at all.

"I like *that*," she said with a happy sigh when she finally rested her cheek against his chest and heard the rapid thumping of his heart.

His fingers sifted through her hair. "I told you we were kindred spirits."

"Yes, you did. Are you sure you have to work today?"

"Positive."

"For a man who's so sure of himself, you're holding me awfully tight."

His low chuckle rumbled against her ear. "Just because I'm certain doesn't mean it isn't hard letting you go."

"You really say the most wonderful things."

"And all of them true," he said, a touch of wonder in his voice.

She looked up at him. Oh, how many places could he

touch her heart? "You've never lied to me, have you? Even when it would have been so much more convenient. I've never met anyone so honest before."

The corners of his mouth lifted in a wry smile. "That's because you've only had a small pool to fish from. There's greater variety in the big pond of life."

She grimaced. "Ye gods, he's getting philosophical. I'd better leave."

"Absolutely," he agreed, still holding her tight.

"I have music to make."

"Yes," he said, his warm mouth pressing a kiss to the top of her head.

"You have work to do."

"Lots," he agreed, kissing her ear.

The ache began to grow inside her once again. "Duncan?"

"Hmm?" He was nuzzling her neck.

"Duncan, I'm going to have to throw you to the floor and ravish you if you keep this up."

"You always say the nicest things."

That made her laugh and freed her neck from his erotic assault. She grinned up at laughing black eyes. "Hold that thought until dinner. *After* dinner. I'd actually like to get a meal this time before dessert."

"I'll try to curb my . . . appetite."

A blush began creeping into her cheeks. "You do that," she said hastily as she pulled herself from his arms and began to walk toward the front door. *That* Front Door where he'd stood last night, broad naked chest and muscular arms meeting her shocked gaze and roasting every doubt and second thought and worry she'd had that he didn't want her.

And this was the result: she was standing in front of That Front Door remembering the feel of his body against hers as she had pressed him into the wall and she really needed to do that again. Right now.

"Duncan," she said.

He groaned from behind her, wrapping his arms around

her and pulling her back against him. "One of us has got to exercise some self-control."

"Why?"

There was silence. "Give me a moment, I'm thinking."

That made her laugh again. She turned in his arms and kissed the tip of his nose. "I'll see you at six tonight."

"Not seven?"

"I didn't make it to seven last night, what makes you think I can make it to seven tonight?"

"Six, then," he said smiling down at her, his eyes full of happiness.

Oh, he was trouble, all right. She reluctantly pulled herself from his arms and started once again for That Front Door.

"Harley."

She turned with renewed hope. "Yes?" she said eagerly.

"Now that both Giscard's men *and* Boyd know where you're staying, you'd better change hotels again this morning."

"Oh," Harley said, hiding her disappointment. Business was no fun on a Saturday morning after. "Right. Sure."

"Don't tell anyone but me where you're staying. Emma's got your cell phone number if she needs to get ahold of you."

"Right. Well, see you at six." Harley walked out of the apartment to the small hall in front of the elevator and the Colangco guard standing watch. A different one from last night. But that didn't matter. She was leaving his boss's penthouse apartment just before nine o'clock in the morning. The inference was clear.

She had never felt more self-conscious in her life.

"Hi, John," Duncan said from behind her. "This is Miss Miller . . . I mean Smith . . . I mean Hitchcock . . ."

"Miller is just fine," Harley said hurriedly, her blush crimson now.

"Whatever she's calling herself nowadays," Duncan said, laughter in his voice, "she's got carte blanche, John."

"Yes, sir," John replied as the elevator doors opened.

Harley stepped into the elevator, not daring to look at John or at Duncan. She stabbed the Lobby button and prayed for the doors to close. They didn't.

"This isn't what you think, John," Duncan gravely continued.

"No, sir, of course not," John replied with equal gravity.

Harley raised her gaze from the toes of her red cowboy boots to glare at Duncan. He was glowing with suppressed laughter. "We play *checkers* tonight," she informed him just before the elevator doors closed.

Her blush had just barely died away by the time her cab dropped her off in front of her hotel. She walked through the revolving glass door into the cherry wood Millenium lobby and promptly felt masculine hands grab her. She was hustled over to a seating area to the right of the entrance before she could even catch her breath.

She looked up. Way up.

"*Bonjour,* Mademoiselle Hitchcock," said Desmond.

"Won't you sit down?" Louis asked, his bruised jaw looking lurid under the low-key lighting.

"No thanks," Harley said through a dry throat. "How are you guys doing?"

"Monsieur Lang was not in the Hamptons," Desmond sternly informed her.

"No?" Harley said in a small voice.

"*No.*"

"Mademoiselle, how could you use us so?" Louis demanded.

"What did we ever do to you?" said Desmond, much aggrieved.

Harley was awash in guilt. "I'm sorry guys, really I am. I don't know what came over me."

"It must be *l'instinct d'amour,*" Louis said with a sigh.

"We French, we understand such things," Desmond said. "But why must it appear *maintenant* when our employer is so insistent upon the return of what rightfully belongs to him?"

"Hey, I'm all for getting Mr. Giscard's diamonds back to him," Harley said. "Really I am."

"Then," said Louis, "having recently spent so much time in Monsieur Lang's company, perhaps you would be so good as to tell us now where to find the diamonds."

"Duncan's working on it, guys. Honest."

"If Monsieur Lang is truly investigating the matter, why has he not produced what we seek?" Desmond demanded.

"Well, he's working on this other case too, and these things take time."

"Monsieur Giscard informed us just an hour ago that we do not have *le temps,*" Desmond informed her.

"Our employer lacks patience," Louis explained.

"In abundance," Desmond added.

"Retaliatory measures will have to be taken if the diamonds are not returned to us by tomorrow morning, mademoiselle," Louis said.

"Be so good as to tell Monsieur Lang this," Desmond said.

"I'll tell him," Harley said, her heart bumping in her chest.

"Bon," said Louis.

"Adieu," said Desmond.

And they were gone.

They really knew how to remove the stars from a girl's eyes. Harley headed for the elevator. She'd better pass on their message to Duncan.

She walked into her room and saw her Stratocaster lying on the bed where she had left it. Her fingers brushed across the gleaming black surface. Ah, sweet sanity.

She called Duncan's office and got Emma. "Do all of you work on Saturdays?" she asked.

"Only when the company's reputation is on the line," Emma replied. "Those hellacious diamonds seem to have disappeared into thin air."

"Speaking of which . . ." Harley relayed the French threat. "Tell Duncan not to worry. I'll find a new hotel fast. Are we still on for lunch?"

"You bet. You can meet me here."

Harley hung up and looked around her hotel room. Lovely as it was, Duncan was right. It was time and past time to move.

But Duncan's scent was still on her skin, the taste of him was still on her mouth. She'd never get anything accomplished today like this. Besides, her brunette wash was beginning to fade and disguise was still important. Yes, Colby Lang and Boyd Monroe had given a press conference the other day to announce that Jane Miller was safe and sound and simply on a short holiday to help recover from the rigors of her world tour, but that didn't mean she wouldn't be mobbed if people recognized her.

So she showered and put a second brunette rinse in her hair, then dressed in jeans and sneakers and a flaming red knit top. The way she was feeling, she'd be wearing red every day for the rest of her life. She glanced at her itinerary notebook and smiled. It didn't matter anymore. Her priorities had changed. She had changed.

It took only half an hour to check out of the Millenium and into the Loews New York on Lexington Avenue.

She sat down on her new bed with her Stratocaster and went back to work on the songs she had started yesterday. The problem was, they were as erotic as she'd reported to Duncan and that focused her thoughts on their gorgeous muse.

She hugged the Stratocaster and finally let herself take stock of how new she felt and different and lighter. She couldn't remember ever being so aware of every inch of her body from her little toes all the way up to the ends of her darker brown hair.

All those romance writers had gotten it right after all. Sexual experience did make you look different, because it was making her feel different about her body and her heart and herself and that had to be reflected outward.

She was still amazed that Duncan had wanted her last

night and this morning with a hunger and a passion that had matched her own. She was not voluptuous. She was not beautiful. She had caused him untold amounts of trouble.

And she could still hear his moans of pleasure and need as she had touched him, caressed him, licked him . . .

Heat was burning her cheeks and other parts of her anatomy once again. It was no good wanting what she could not have, and she could not have Duncan until six o'clock tonight. Until then, she'd better put the heat into her music.

Still, just after twelve that afternoon, she looked hopefully at his closed door as she walked into Emma's office.

"He's on the phone with one of his contacts in Monaco," Emma informed her as she stood up and pulled her purse from a desk drawer. "I've been given major do-not-disturb orders."

"It's probably for the best," Harley said with a sigh. "Any trouble getting here?"

"Cab to door, perfectly safe."

"Good. Let's go. I'm starved and you're buying."

"I am?" Harley said in surprise.

"You're rich and I've got the information you want, don't I?"

Harley ruefully regarded the slender woman before her. "I intend to pump you mercilessly."

"Exactly. You're buying. I made reservations at the Manhattan Ocean Club."

"You don't believe in half-measures, do you?"

"Harley, the man walked into the office glowing this morning. *Glowing.* *You're* the one who apparently doesn't believe in half-measures."

The damn blush was back again. "He's . . . um . . . inspirational."

Emma guffawed and then hooked her arm through Harley's. "Let's get going. I've got a diary waiting for a lengthy report tonight."

When Harley finally returned to the Loews, no one leapt

out from behind the bushes or the doorman to try to grab her. She spent the rest of the afternoon writing a song that was slow and sexy and might never be heard in public. She didn't care. She'd sing it to Duncan and maybe it would ignite that hot glow in his eyes that turned her muscles to mush. She certainly hoped so.

CHAPTER ELEVEN

*H*arley woke slowly from the drugging pleasure of sleeping in Duncan's arms, his warm body curved around hers beneath the comforter. There was no way that life could get any better than this.

Turning up last night in jeans and a plain old knit top had done nothing to curb Duncan's libido. He had jerked her into the apartment, slamming the door behind her, and then pushed her hard against the entryway wall as he devoured her with hungry kisses that had sent the world spiraling away. Only the loud buzzer from a kitchen timer had pulled them apart and reminded him of his vow that he really would feed her this time.

And he had. Harley had never realized it before, but there was something both nurturing and erotic about having a man cook for you. The fact that he was a surprisingly good cook had only added to the pleasure. It had been lovely to sit across the table from him and talk about his work and her music and the plays they both wanted to see once Desmond and Louis had returned to France. It had been friendly and comfortable and satisfying, as it had been with Emma, only different because underneath the conversation with Duncan had been a deep river of desire they had silently and mutually agreed not to tap just yet. But it had given everything a lovely glow, like the candles Duncan had lit. It had made her aware of the different levels they had created together and in such a short time.

She saw in his moments of surprise and delight and uncertainty that this was new for him. He was a virgin when it came to intimacy and connection, much more so even than she. And she liked that. She liked that she was his first true lover, and he was hers. Kindred spirits. Parallel lives. What magnetic field had finally shifted to bring them together, as she was certain they should be together?

How could they not? Here they lay, his skin flowing into hers, as his life had flowed into hers. They were connected, she and Duncan Lang. The question she had fended off for nearly two days now rose up: how long? How long would they be bound together? He had used no words to tell her what he felt for her, but she knew that it was more than physical desire. His kisses told her that, the way he touched her when they made love or sat across a table from each other told her that. But he had gone scrupulously out of his way to remind her that he had never committed to any woman in his life.

Whatever their relationship could be called, it had no guarantees. Her mother would be horrified. But then, her mother had had the guarantee of a marriage solemnized by a church and wedding guests and vows, and all of that had ended up meaning nothing. She was alone. Her mother had been alone for twenty-four of Harley's twenty-six years and had been too afraid to let another love into her life in all that time.

With Duncan's warm body molded against her, Harley understood some of that fear now. To have love and joy suddenly stolen away was a frightful thought. To open yourself to possibly letting that happen again could be terrifying. But Harley was not her mother. She had spent most of her life trying to be very different from her mother, because Barbara Miller's fear of life was more frightening to her than any leap into the emotional depths.

Her thoughts tried to avoid that phrase, not because it frightened her, but because what it implied frightened her. It implied love, growing love, and she hadn't wanted to acknowledge that to herself, let alone him. He was so skittish about relationship and commitment anyway that she didn't know how he'd take it. She was so skittish about something so new in her life that she wasn't sure how she would take it.

Duncan stretched a little against her and murmured something in his sleep that sounded wonderfully like her name. Her whole body was glowing. Hmm. She seemed to be taking this whole love thing remarkably well.

A large warm hand slid across her breast, cupping it, as thumb and forefinger began to stroke one rapidly hardening nipple.

"Good morning," she gasped, eagerly leaping into the emotional depths.

Just after seven o'clock, she sat attentively on a kitchen stool while Duncan instructed her in the proper way to make a perfect omelette. She had quickly grown addicted to watching Duncan cook. She loved the flair he used to chop vegetables, the sensual way he swirled a hot omelette pan and the melting butter within it, the deft way he cracked open eggs and tossed away the empty shells.

"You are as passionate about cooking as you are about your work," she informed him as he zestfully beat a bowl of raw eggs to froth.

He missed a beat as he looked up at her in surprise. "I am not passionate about my work."

"Oh, of course you are," she retorted. "You're passionate about *life,* Duncan, didn't you know that?"

He begged to differ . . . at length.

"I give up, I give up!" she said, holding up both hands in defeat and stopping him in the middle of his reasoned denial that he had a passionate bone in his body. "The fact that you forget to eat when you're working on a case—Emma told me—and that your whole being is focused on the tiniest minutia of a case, and that you are fiercely determined to find and prove the truth in a case no matter the cost, and that you think about your work even when you're brushing your teeth, means nothing. Just like the exuberance that radiates from you whenever you cook means nothing. I've got it now. You are not a passionate man."

"Exactly," he replied as he slid a perfect omelette onto a plate and handed it to her. She swiveled around to the kitchen counter and breathed deeply. Marvelous! She'd hire the man as her personal chef if he wasn't already passionately committed to his own work.

Duncan sprang his plan on her as he sat down beside her. "I have an idea," he said after taking a sip of fresh-squeezed orange juice.

"Yes?" Harley said hopefully.

"About *Boyd,*" he said dampeningly.

"Oh." Harley sighed. "Okay, what about Boyd?"

Duncan cut into his own perfect omelette. "Boyd's been sticking very close to the Ritz-Carlton. No visitors except Brandon, who apparently is trying to keep him placated so he doesn't say nasty things about Colangco to the press. What *is* telling is that Boyd goes out once a day to make a one-minute phone call from a public pay phone, a different one each time. We haven't been able to trace the calls. And we can't catch him with his hand in the Maurizio cookie jar if he just sits around the Ritz all day long. I'm convinced from those phone calls and his frayed nerves that he's missed an important deadline. I think if we push just the right buttons, he'll go running to his contact within the Maurizio organization and *that* should tell us how Boyd has earned his fifteen million clams."

She silently regarded him until he finally set down his fork and knife and looked at her questioningly. "You're very good at this, you know."

"I always liked playing Clue," he said. "I could even beat Brandon."

"No," Harley said, her hand cupping his cheek, making his eyes meet hers. *"You are very good at your job, Duncan Lang"*—she felt the tremor in his heart as if it were her own—*"and you love doing it."*

She heard his breath catch. "Thank you." He almost believed her. She saw it in his eyes.

She kissed him, gently, tenderly, and then pulled back with a smile. "You're welcome. Just out of idle curiosity, in all those boring jobs you worked on for Colangco these last two years, did you ever screw one up?"

"No," he said, looking puzzled.

"Any complaints from clients on the company customer satisfaction surveys?"

"No," he said, puzzlement turning to wariness.

"And did Emma tell me the truth when she said more than three-quarters of your clients asked for you by name when they called Colangco to do more work for them?"

"Harley," he said, looking grim, "what are you up to?"

"I know I don't have a degree from Columbia," she said modestly, "but it seems to me you've more than amply demonstrated your ability to do your job and do it well."

"So?"

"So," she said with a bright smile, "you once told me that you had something to prove to your family and I think you're wrong. *I* think the only one you have to prove anything to is yourself."

He scowled at her. "Eat your omelette."

Her smile brightened. "What's the matter, Mr. Lang? Can't take a home truth now and then?"

"We were talking about *Boyd*."

"So we were," Harley demurely replied.

"Anyway," Duncan said, glaring at her, "I intend to make Boyd run to his contact. That will set off the chain of events we want to finally close this case."

"I'll buy that. How are you going to do it?"

Duncan smiled with malicious pleasure. "I'm going to tell him the truth. I'm going to tell him that you've hired me to find out what he's up to. I'm going to casually mention his Bermuda bank account. I'll drop a hint about your tour schedule. I'll allude to Colangco's warm relationship with national and international police forces. And then I'll send him on his way."

"Wow," Harley said. "He'll *freak*."

"Exactly," Duncan said with a satisfied smile. "We can double the impact if you're there with me. Sort of drive home the point that you're onto him and the jig is up."

"Gee," Harley murmured. "I wonder what I should wear to a shakedown?"

It turned out that a black knit dress that almost reached her knees was the best choice to drive home how far she had already moved away from Boyd and to give his meeting with Duncan an ominous tone. Bare legs and black pumps completed the ensemble.

She walked into Emma's office ten minutes early to find Duncan's door closed.

Emma's whistle was low and impressed. "You will kill him."

"Who?" Harley asked.

"*Both* of them."

"Good," Harley said with a smirk as she sat down in the chair beside Emma's desk. "What's Duncan up to now?"

"Studying the videos we've got on the Giscard diamonds for the zillionth time."

"Videos?"

"We tape everything we do, for backup in case anything goes wrong, and to protect ourselves from any wrongful claims of illegal activity."

"Hacking into bank computers is not illegal?"

"We don't tape that."

"Of course not," Harley said with a grin. "Has Duncan found any leads on the robbery yet?"

"No," Emma said with a sigh. "He's come up bone dry. So have the police. They were in here again this morning, grilling him."

Harley's hands were rigid. "They can't arrest him just on suspicion, right?"

"Right."

Emma's office door was suddenly thrown open. Boyd Monroe walked in, stopped, and stared in disgust at Harley.

She stood up slowly, to give him the full effect and to collect her suddenly disordered emotions.

He wore his usual nondescript clothes, but Harley had never seen him like this. Somehow his Marine-short brown hair had more gray in it. His trim, compact body was so tensed he looked as if he would shatter if you touched him. Boyd *was* running scared, just as Duncan had said. She had never seen Boyd scared.

"Still dressing like a slut, I see," he sneered, walking up to her.

"Still thinking you can bully me into caving, I see," she retorted.

"Don't play word games with me, little girl. I taught you everything you know. I hope you're proud of yourself. Your mother went into hysterics when I told her that you're running around New York all by yourself."

"You *told* her . . . ?" Harley gasped.

"Someone had to."

"You had no right!"

"I have *every* right!" he seethed, grabbing her by her upper arms in a painful grip. "I have spent the last nine years protecting you from the users and the abusers in the music industry. I've kept you safe from the druggies and from the men who only want you for your money or your fame. I've given you that fame, and the money, and the adulation of millions. You have nothing to complain about."

"Take your hands off me, Boyd," Harley said in a low, authoritative voice she had never heard before.

"Don't use that tone with me, little girl," he snapped, squeezing her arms tighter. "Are you forgetting who taught you everything you know? Are you forgetting that I am the one who got you the recording contracts and the concert dates and the TV performances that put your name on the world map? You—"

"This is your last chance, Boyd."

"Are you threatening *me*?" he demanded in amusement. "Don't forget, *Jane,* that you need me to walk into a recording studio. You need me to walk out on a stage. Without me, you are just a timid little hick from the Dust Bowl. You're nobody."

"Boyd," Harley said quietly, amazed she could hear herself above the banging of her heart in her ears, "you're fired."

He took a shocked step back, freeing her arms. But he made a quick recovery. "Is it that time of month again?" he sneered.

She felt as if she were standing in the middle of an isolation booth. All of his usual weapons failed to touch her. "I'll have my accountant mail you your percentage of the tour proceeds. You'll get your ususal percentage from the next album, of course, and we're done."

"There is no way in hell you can cut your next album without me, little girl," Boyd grimly informed her.

"Yes, I can," Harley retorted, her throat dry. She hadn't planned this. She hadn't even let herself fantasize this. But it was happening. She was making it happen. And she was right. The calm in the midst of so much emotion within her told her she was right. "You've taught me well, Boyd, and I'm grateful for that. You made me a star, and I'm even grateful for that. In return, you've become rich and you've become famous in your own right. You won't have any trouble finding other singers willing to put their lives in your hands."

He grabbed her shoulders with both hands. *"You can't do this, Jane."*

She wouldn't let herself wince beneath his death grip. "My name is Harley, and yes I can. Emma," she said to the young woman sitting so still and quiet at the desk beside her, "would you be an angel and type me up a brief severance letter for Boyd? It won't take more than two sentences."

"My pleasure," Emma replied, turning to her computer.

"You'll regret this to the day you die," Boyd seethed, gray eyes drilling into her.

"Boyd," Harley said softly, "I plan to celebrate the anniversary of this day with pink champagne to the day I die."

Duncan's office door opened. "Mr. Monroe," Duncan said in a tight voice. Harley could hear the anger behind it. "I'm glad you could make it. Won't you come in?"

Boyd glared at her for another moment, then suddenly released her and stalked into Duncan's office. Black eyes met hers.

"Are you okay?" Duncan demanded in a low voice.

She could breathe again. She hadn't realized she had stopped until just now. "I'm fine," she said as she walked up to him. "Never better. Honest. Come on, let's scare the hell out of him."

It only took five minutes. Duncan was merciless behind the friendly, even jovial tone he adopted. Harley had never seen Boyd sweat before. Perspiration beaded his forehead. She had never seen him give himself away before. But his hands were clenched on the arms of his chair, white and bloodless as he held on for dear life. His voice sounded strangled. His body seemed to shrink in the chair. He made a halfhearted attempt at a comeback when Duncan finished, threatening a libel suit, threatening to smear Colangco's name in the press, but Duncan was unimpressed and he showed it.

He slowly enunciated every numeral of the Bermuda bank account number. "Perhaps that means something to you?"

Boyd literally burst out of the claustrophobic confines of his chair and moved with awkward, jerky steps to the office door. "You can both go to hell!" he bellowed before throwing the door open and escaping.

She stared after him, amazed at the pity welling within her. He truly had done so much for her. It hurt to see him reduced to such misery and fear, and to know that she had helped cause that.

"That went well," Duncan said brightly.

Harley smiled then. "You're a lethal man, Duncan Lang."

"It's amazing the skills you can pick up in the fast lane."

"Won't Boyd just go and move his fifteen million to another bank?"

"He can't. I've frozen his Bermuda account."

"Wow," Harley said, staring at him. "You *are* lethal. Shouldn't you be following Boyd to see what he does next?"

"Already taken care of." Duncan pressed a button in a desk pad beside his phone. The paneling behind his desk slid up to reveal three video monitors all in a row. "I've got our people watching him and taping him every minute of the day. We'll get him, Harley, and soon. I promise. Once we know what he's up to for sure, we'll alert the Feds and they can step in and do their thing."

"Jeez, Duncan," she said, staring at the monitors, "you could crack an international arms deal wide open and never leave your office!"

"I like my office. Legwork," he explained with a grin, "is anathema to me."

"Gee, and you pursued me anyway."

"I did not pursue you," he retorted with mock hauteur. "I was working on a case that necessitated leaving my office now and then."

She smiled and kissed him. "Of course." She started to slide off his desk, but his hand caught her wrist and held her still. She looked down at him curiously. He seemed almost nervous!

"I was thinking," he began, not quite meeting her eyes, "that it might make sense for you to just . . . move all of your things into the penthouse. It would be more convenient," he hurriedly added, "and . . . um . . . reduce our concerns about Desmond and Louis accosting you again. Of course, if you'd rather keep the privacy of a hotel room, I'd perfectly understand."

She couldn't stop him rambling on because her throat was too constricted. No words of her own would come out. The Playboy of the Western World wanted her to move in with him!

"I mean," he said, "you're just really starting to spread your wings and explore being independent and . . . um . . . moving into the penthouse—"

"With you," Harley managed.

"Yes . . . uh . . . with me. It might not be what you need right now."

Harley blinked back the tears welling in her eyes. "Haven't you figured it out yet?" she said softly as she slid onto his lap and twined her arms around his neck. "I want to spend every possible moment of the day and night with you. I could happily live out my life on a desert island with you. There is *nothing* I want more than to check out of my hotel and into the penthouse."

She proved it by kissing him, hard. For a moment he was utterly still. Then his arms enveloped her, squeezing her with a ferocity that matched his kiss, his body hardening beneath her, flooding her own body with the most delicious heat.

"I promise not to leave you any room in the closet for your own things," she gasped, her head arching back as he sucked at the frantic pulse at the base of her throat.

"Thanks," he moaned, dragging her mouth back to his.

"What in blue blazes do you think you're doing?" Colby Lang bellowed from the doorway.

Harley looked dazedly across the room. Duncan's father stood there, staring at them, purple with rage.

"Kissing my client," Duncan calmly answered him.

"No, no, no," Harley said with equal calm, though she was desperately fending off laughter. "I kissed him first," she explained to Colby, "then he kissed me back, then I kissed him, and he kissed me. I think that's the correct sequence of events."

"That certainly was my recollection," Duncan murmured.

Colby slammed the door closed behind him as he stalked into the office. "Miss Miller," he seethed, "this company has rules, *ethics,* which must not be breached *by anyone,* particularly my own son!"

"Well," Harley said brightly, "Duncan really didn't have any choice. I kind of insisted."

Colby gargled incoherently.

"It was a mutual choice," Duncan corrected, his arms still wrapped around her waist as she continued to sit on his lap.

"This is something I *can* fire you for, young man!" Colby threatened.

"But you won't," Harley informed him, "or I'll be forced to take my business elsewhere and say very unkind things about Colangco to the press."

"And you won't because it will cause a maelstrom of public suspicion, coming as it does on the heels of the Giscard diamond robbery," Duncan added. "The last thing you want, Dad, is public speculation about one of your own sons stealing from a company client. Our reputation will be besmirched. Our revenues will go down. It's a bad decision any way you look at it."

"I will not be blackmailed by my own son!" Colby bellowed.

"Let's call it extortion, then," Duncan amiably replied.

Colby Lang erupted into a vituperative ten-minute tirade

that slandered his younger son with every crime known to man. Then he stormed out of the office, slamming the door behind him.

"That poor door has really taken a beating lately," Duncan remarked.

"What a horrible man," Harley said. Sitting on Duncan's lap, her eyes were on a level with his. Her fingers brushed across his tense face. "If you believe any of that poison he just spewed all over you, then he wins." His black eyes met her steady gaze. There, deep down where no one else would see it, was the pain he had hidden for years.

"His basic thesis is correct, though," he said in a tight voice. "I am not a good man. I've done things—"

"Many things," Harley corrected him, her fingers pressed against his mouth to silence him, "and none of them done to deliberately hurt another human being. Your father can't say that about himself. He has gone out of his way to hurt you at every opportunity."

"Harley—"

"I'm not without some experience in these matters, Duncan Lang. There's a lot wrong with my mother, but she was always clear and I was always clear that she loved me and loves me still. The things she has said that have hurt me were said without conscious intent to cause pain. Colby *and* your mother, on the other hand, made you believe the most awful lie. They made you believe you're not a good man. I can't convince you otherwise. No one can. You'll have to prove them wrong yourself *to* yourself. Please try, Duncan," she whispered, her fingers brushing through his black curly hair. "You don't deserve this agony."

"It's not so bad."

"Yes, it is."

He was stiff and silent for a moment. "How do you see so much?"

"Because you show me so much."

He looked into her eyes. "You're just as dangerous as I

thought." He pressed a kiss to the palm of her hand. "What on earth made you barrel into my life?"

"You step onto a new path and it's amazing the places it will take you," Harley replied, just before pulling him into a bone-melting kiss that lasted a very long time.

"I'll send John and Emma along to help you move out of the hotel," Duncan said as his lips caressed her jaw, "just to make sure Giscard's men don't try to waylay you."

"Emma?"

She felt his smile against her throat. "She's got an eighth-degree black belt in karate and she's the best shot in the company. She could handle our French goons with both hands tied behind her back."

"Wow," Harley murmured, loving his warm hands caressing her body. "I had no idea I had such a dangerous new best friend."

"Wait till you meet her fiancé. He makes Jackie Chan look like he's moving in slow motion."

"Sounds like they'd make a helluva double date."

Duncan chuckled and playfully nipped at her chin with his teeth. "I'll see when they're free."

There was a light rap on his office door. "Are you decent?" Emma inquired.

"Yes," Duncan called, feigning exasperation.

Harley grinned at him. "You really do have the most awful reputation."

"This is not news," Duncan said as Emma walked into the room.

She didn't even blink at seeing Harley seated on Duncan's lap. "Agent Sullivan sent over this FBI summary of Angelo Maurizio's recent activities. I thought you'd want to have it right away," she said, dropping the folder on his desk.

"Thanks, Em," Duncan said. He saw that she was wavering between staying and leaving. "What's wrong?"

"Nothing, really," Emma said, taking a backwards step toward the door.

"Emma."

"Well," she said grimacing, "it's just a few little things that . . . bother me."

"Like what?"

"Like why is it, if we're the only two Colangco employees working on the Boyd Monroe case, that someone else downloaded the entire computer file?"

"It's probably just Dad snooping. You know how he worries. Besides, he promised Harley he'd provide oversight."

"Fine, but his computer didn't download the file. In fact, from what I can tell, *no* Colangco computer downloaded that file."

Harley felt Duncan stiffen beneath her. "That's odd."

"That's what I thought," Emma said, folding her arms against her chest. "You want to know something even odder? Even though Harley's case has been closed for days now, our same Computer Sneak downloaded her file too."

"When?" Duncan demanded, his face taut.

"Yesterday, when Harley and I were having lunch together."

"Damn!"

"It might just be Colby working from a new computer, of course . . ."

"And then again, it might not," Duncan grimly concluded. "I pretty much hate this."

"Then it's a good thing I'm moving," Harley interceded.

"Good plan," Emma said approvingly. "Where to now? A Colangco safe house?"

"You might say that," Harley said with a grin.

"Emma," Duncan said with grim amusement, "I need a favor."

Before she moved out of her hotel, Harley made use of Colangco's public relations department to issue a press release as Jane Miller, stating that she and her manager had made an amiable parting of the ways. Boyd could say whatever he wanted to when the press ambushed him, she didn't care. She'd covered the basics. Her fans and the industry would do what they wanted with them.

Then, with Emma and John's help, she moved her things from the Loews New York and into the Colangco International penthouse apartment, thinking with malicious pleasure that Colby Lang would bust a gut when he found out.

The minute Emma and John walked back out the door, she called her mother to try to repair some of the damage Boyd had caused, but it was an uphill struggle. Her mother was always happier when she could think the worst. Harley hung up the phone with a gusty sigh of relief, shrugged Sweetcreek off her shoulders, and called Annie Maguire, whom Boyd had fired, to rehire her and bring her up to date.

Then she got to work.

Once she had unpacked, relegating Duncan's clothes to a single square foot in the double closet, she sat down cross-legged on the king-size bed and tried to work with her Stratocaster. The music wouldn't come, but the lyrics did. It was unusual for her. The music almost always inspired the lyrics. Still, Harley had written too many songs over the years not to know she should go with whatever creative flow chose to present itself. The right melody for "No Guarantees" would come if she was patient.

So she sat cross-legged on the bed and worked on the lyrics for "No Guarantees" and then for "Life in the Deep End." She had meant to return the favor and cook dinner for Duncan tonight, but as so often happened when songs were moving easily through her, she lost all track of time and had no idea Duncan had even walked into the apartment until he coughed politely at her from the foot of the bed.

She jumped, which made him laugh.

"Hi, honey, I'm home," he crooned.

She made up for her previous distraction by rising onto her knees and dragging him into a major, and deeply satisfying, clinch that ended half an hour later, her music sheets scattered all over the floor, along with their clothes, as they lay naked in each other's arms, striving to catch their breaths.

"I'll have to try that line again," Duncan said, which made Harley laugh.

"I'm afraid I'm not very domestic," she confessed. "I forgot to make dinner."

"That's okay. You have other redeeming qualities. Besides, I've made plans to go out tonight."

"Out?" Harley said in surprise, rising up on one elbow to stare down at him with the utmost consternation. "With Louis and Desmond gunning for you?"

"I've arranged a diversion for our two French shadows. We'll be fine."

An hour later she forgot all about Louis and Desmond when she stepped into Duncan's arms on Goodies' dance floor. She found that dancing with Duncan when well embarked on a sexual relationship was very different from dancing with Duncan preintimacy. It was more sensual, more exhilarating, more silly and free than the first time they had come to Goodies. There was a lot to be said for this new path she had stepped on.

"Hot band," Harley said when they finally claimed a booth. The black bass guitarist, in dreadlocks, was the only woman. The rest of the Rockin' Robins were white guys in their late twenties and early thirties, except for the Hispanic drummer. Their affection for each other was obvious, their love of the music clear in every note they played and sang.

"I thought you'd like them. So do a couple of record companies. They're on their way up." Duncan gazed at her for a moment. "Was it hard being elevated to Pop Royalty so suddenly?"

Harley thought about the seventeen-year-old girl she had been. "It was amazing, and awful, and unreal. For the first two or three years, the world was tilted off its axis and by the time it righted itself . . . I was this person I didn't know anymore."

"I don't think you lost yourself as much as you believe," he said, reaching across the table to hold her hand in his. "I know you like to put her persona down, but I've been listening to the Jane Miller recordings these last few days and they really are quite strong, even with the overblown string section. You wouldn't have been raised on high—and stayed there for nine long years—if they'd been anything less than superb. Your audiences are not stupid, Harley. They know quality when they hear it. Rock star, pop star, or whatever, you'll stay on top."

"You know, it's funny," she said, frowning, "ever since I bought my Stratocaster, I haven't worried about staying on top of the musical heap. I've just worried about disappointing my fans. They've been so great, Duncan, you don't know, and here I am planning to switch gears on them. Joni Mitchell's fans broke out into open rebellion when she made a blues album. A lot of Neil Diamond's fans burned him in effigy when he came out with a country album. Hell, even Bob Dylan was booed off the stage when he switched from acoustic to electric guitar back in the sixties."

"You can't worry about how other people are going to react. You have no control over any of it. All you can do is write and sing the music you care about."

"It takes a little getting used to," she said wonderingly.

"What?"

"Being with a man who cares so deeply about my happiness and satisfaction rather than his own agenda."

The band had completed their set and were on a break, which explained how their lead singer and guitarist could now be standing at their table, gleefully ruffling Duncan's black curls.

"Hi, Duncan. Good to see you again."

Harley looked up at the affable musician and decided he was cuter close up. His hazel eyes were warm and friendly, his retro wardrobe of bell-bottom jeans, red paisley shirt, and leather vest with two-foot-long leather fringe revealed a lean body that was more sinew than muscle. His shoulder-length golden brown hair was held back by a leather headband. The man had to have groupies at least five feet deep at any given performance. And somehow he knew Duncan. *Very* interesting.

"Mark!" Duncan said happily, removing his friend's hand from his hair. "It's great to see you again too. You were terrific up there."

"Really good," Harley added sincerely. "I liked your cover of 'Let's Go' much more than the original by Ritchie Valens."

"Thank you," Mark said with a charming smile. "You must be Harley. Duncan mentioned on the phone that you're a bit of a performer yourself."

She cast a startled glance at Duncan and then looked back up at Mark. "A bit," she conceded.

"Would you like to sit in with the band on the next set?"

"What?" Harley said, more than surprised.

"Go ahead," Duncan urged. "It'll be fun."

Harley stared at him. He had set her up! "I don't have my guitar."

"You mean this?" Mark said, pulling her black Fender Stratocaster from behind his back.

She looked from Mark to Duncan. "How on earth did you pull this off?"

His smile was downright smug. "I have connections."

"*Why* did you pull this off?"

"Purely selfish motives," he assured her. "I've never seen any human being as happy as you were on the Surrealistic Pillow's stage and I needed another fix."

"Come on, Harley," Mark said, taking her elbow and beginning to pull her from the booth, "Susan needs the company."

"If I make a fool of myself, I get to blame you," Harley informed Duncan as she stood up.

"You won't," he replied. "Make a fool of yourself, I mean."

Time stopped for a crystalline moment as their eyes met. She felt the bond between them that seemed to have existed before they had met and that had grown steadily stronger ever since.

Then someone jostled her and the spell was broken. Time returned to its steady progression as Mark led her into the crowd of people.

"You must really trust that man to take me on sight unseen like this," Harley said to Mark after a minute of struggling toward the stage.

"I do," he replied, forging ahead.

"How come?"

"He's never lied to me before. He says you're one of the best and I believe him."

"Duncan thinks I'm one of the best?" Harley reiterated, thrilled and blushing at the same time.

"Yep," Mark replied, pulling her up a small set of stairs to the stage.

"That man never ceases to amaze me."

"Me either."

Harley glanced at him curiously and Mark grinned back at her. "I've known Duncan since our raucous years at Columbia. He's never wanted me to meet his girlfriends before. Never. That makes you very different and very special and me more than curious. So, let's see what you can do. You can plug into the amps here," he said, handing her a black cord.

Bemused, Harley plugged her Stratocaster into the amps and then Mark introduced her to the rest of the band.

"It's about time," Susan said in a lovely Jamaican accent, shaking her hand firmly. "I've been telling these guys for years that there's just too damn much testosterone in this band."

"I'll do what I can to help you out," Harley said. She quickly tuned her guitar as Mark went up to the microphone, introduced the band once again, and then introduced her. The crowd was perfectly willing to take her at face value. Apparently whatever Mark did was fine by them.

"We'll start with a little something by the Beach Boys to get you all in the right mood," Mark announced. Then he leaned toward Harley where she stood on the small stage beside the microphone she shared with Susan. "You join in on backup, Harley."

"Right," she said, just as if anxiety weren't tickling up and down her spine. She had sung lead for so many years that she was afraid she was about to embarrass Mrs. Shepherd, her high school chorus teacher. The fact that she had never jammed with a band before was not a confidence booster. Her face felt bloodless. "What exactly is it we're starting with?"

" 'Dance, Dance, Dance,' of course," Mark replied with a grin.

"Silly me," Harley said to Susan as Mark, at center stage front, began the guitar intro.

She hung back through "Dance, Dance, Dance" and the Rascals' "Good Lovin'," finding her way musically through Mark's lead guitar work, Susan's bass, and the acoustic guitar, blending her voice with Susan's to play it safe. By the time they began "Twist and Shout," though, she was actually feeling comfortable and let herself insert a few guitar riffs here and there while she and Susan played around with the backup vocals. When the band swung into "This Is Dedicated to the One I Love," she knew for the first time in nine years the thrill of creating harmony, amazed at how well she and Susan worked together.

"Let's get our guest artist up front," Mark said into the microphone, reaching over and grabbing Harley's elbow, "and have her take the next song. Your choice," he told her as he traded places with her.

She felt Duncan's steady gaze from the audience and her confidence held. "Let's do the Jefferson Airplane's 'Somebody to Love,' " she told the band in an undertone. Mark's eyebrows shot up—wearing a turquoise blue 1950s Dior gown, she did not exactly look like a hard-ass rock-and-roll babe—but he didn't stop her.

Harley took a deep breath . . . and swung into the song . . . and was having the time of her life by the end of the first verse. It was great to feel a part of a band, their musicianship and energy feeding her own. She wanted to hurl herself into Duncan's arms and thank him for this joy with several million kisses, but she had a song and a set to finish.

The applause was rapturous as it washed over her. It felt almost—but not quite—as good as making love with Duncan. Grinning, she headed back to Susan and became aware that the rest of the band was applauding her too. It was so unexpected that she stopped dead and stared at them as if they were nuts.

"Let's have another from Harley Smith," Mark called out through the microphone he shared with Susan. "Any other surprises for us?" he asked Harley.

"That was surprising?" she said, puzzled.

"Grace Slick wouldn't dare cover that song again if she heard you, Miss Miller."

"Wow!" Harley said, blushing. Then it hit her. He'd said Miller. "Ah, shit!" she blurted out and then frantically covered her mouth with her hand. "How did you know?" she whispered miserably.

"Good guitar work is like a fingerprint—instantly recognizable. You combine that with that amazing color of blue eyes you've got, and it's just a tad obvious, especially when an old college friend clues you in," Mark replied with a grin.

"Ah-ha." She turned back to the center mike and took a deep breath. "Okay, gang," she announced, "this next song goes out to the loose-lipped senior rep from Colangco International sitting in our audience tonight. This one's for you, my little chatterbox." She began the guitar intro to "Secret Agent Man" and heard Mark burst out laughing.

She spent the rest of the set working with Susan, finding ways to use her Stratocaster to build off her bass work, exploring harmonies with her, loving that she could share her voice to create something even better. When Mark looked right at her and launched the band into "Devil with a Blue Dress," she laughed herself silly through the entire number. When he pulled her forward for one last song, she looked right at Duncan Lang and sang "Desperado," hoping he'd take its advice to heart and let her love him.

When the song was over, she asked the band to play something for her, left the stage, grabbed Duncan, and pulled him onto the dance floor. She molded herself against him, loving his heat and the strong beat of his heart as Mark began to sing Jim Croce's "Time in a Bottle."

"Thank you," she whispered as Duncan held her tight.

CHAPTER TWELVE

*E*ven with the shower going full blast, Duncan heard Harley scream. Soaking wet, he leapt from the shower, snatched a handgun he had stashed in the cupboard under the sink, and burst into the sunlit bedroom, ready for anything. Except what he found.

Harley—wearing only panties and one of his green T-shirts—had her back pressed up against the wall. She was staring at the bed—at the guitar lying in the middle of the bed—with a look of horror.

"What is it? What's wrong?" he demanded.

She pointed a shaking finger at the black guitar. "It was country. My new music was coming out *country*!"

He would have laughed if he hadn't still been recovering from nightmare fantasies of Harley being kidnapped, Harley being electrocuted, Harley being poisoned by a blow dart.

"Is that all?" he said, lowering the gun as he sagged against the doorjamb.

"Is that all?" she exploded. "You don't seem to understand. *I was creating the music I've rebelled against my entire life!"*

"And this surprises you?"

Harley uttered a strangled scream of frustration.

"This surprises you," Duncan conceded. He made sure the safety was on, leaned into the bathroom, and set his Browning automatic pistol on the counter. Then he walked over to Harley, led her to the overstuffed peach armchair by the terrace's double glass doors, and made her sit down. "Let's talk about arrested development," he said as he sat down on the matching overstuffed footstool in front of her.

"I'm gonna belt you, Duncan Lang," she retorted, shaking an angry fist at him.

He couldn't hold back a grin. She was definitely the most fun he'd ever had. "I think it's time for you to sit back and hear a few home truths."

She folded her arms mulishly across her chest. "I've got a couple for you: you're naked and you're getting the footstool wet."

"It's drip dry and so am I. Home Truth Number One: you're from Sweetcreek, Oklahoma, and your musical roots are country and rockabilly. Ah-ah-ah," he said, holding up a finger to halt the arguments waiting to burst out of her open mouth, "it's true and you know it. Home Truth Number Two: every teenager rebels against something in the status quo. With your musical soul, it was only natural that you rebelled musically and turned to hard-core rock and roll. Home Truth Number Three: Boyd Monroe arrested your musical growth by browbeating you into becoming and remaining the monodimensional and colorless Princess of Pop for nine excruciating years . . . and you are *not* sweet little Miss Jane Miller . . . and thank all the gods for that. Home Truth Number Four: nor are you Patti Smith, Grace Slick,

Chrissie Hynde, or even Pat Benatar. Home Truth Number Five: Sweetcreek has been creeping back into your vocals more and more with every song you've sung these last seven days."

"It has?" she said in a small voice as she sat hunched in the huge chair.

"Yep. The way you sashayed through 'That'll Be the Day' last night was better than gazing into a crystal ball, Miss Harley Jane Miller. Home Truth Number Six: this holiday is helping you reclaim your true self, which means it's no surprise to me that you're also getting back to your country and rockabilly musical roots, which brings us full circle back to Home Truth Number One. Very neat, if I do say so myself."

She scowled at him. "You're still naked and you're still wet."

He stood up, leaned over, and kissed the tip of her slightly freckled nose. "I'm also right, and you know it."

"Yeah," she muttered, scrunching farther down in the chair, "but I don't have to like it."

Stubborn to the end. No wonder he loved her so much.

When he left the apartment a half hour later, Harley was still seated in the bedroom chair, arms folded across her chest, scowling. It was a good thing they each had work to do, or he'd be spending a very unpleasant Monday right about now. As it was, he had the pleasures of searching the Giscard Lear jet with a fine-tooth comb to look forward to. It meant distracting Louis and Desmond, again, but the team he had assigned to follow the French henchmen's every step was beginning to enjoy the challenge. It also meant putting up with his own company tail, which he had assigned to watch his back whenever he was out in public until the Giscard case was solved. He disliked feeling self-conscious all day long, but he disliked any violence enacted on his body even more.

"It's bad enough working over the weekend," Emma complained as they walked up the narrow steps to the Giscard jet's side door, "but why do we have to be out here before eight?"

"The early bird catches the worm," Duncan said, stepping into the jet.

"The early bird catches hell from her fiancé."

"Your devotion to duty is admirable, truly."

"My devotion to duty is making Lam Ying devoted to cold showers!" Emma exploded.

"Oh dear," Duncan said, looking at Emma with honest concern. "Does your family know you're a fallen woman?"

Emma shook her head in disgust. "You are the most infuriating man, Sherlock."

"I have heard that song before, Watson. You start up in the cockpit, I'll start back at the tail, and we'll work our way to the middle."

"Holmes," Emma said, sighing heavily, "the police have been over this plane with everything from X-rays and fluoroscopes to the K-9 patrol. If there was something here, they'd have found it."

"But they didn't," Duncan said as he slid a stick of cinnamon gum into his mouth.

"Because there was nothing here for them to find!"

"Emma, the diamonds were safe and sound when Giscard's courier boarded this plane in Paris. They were gone when the diamond case was opened at the Bartlett Museum. That means they were either taken from the case while on this plane or they were taken somehow in the limousine on the drive to the museum, and I've already searched the limo and come up empty."

"You're going to come up empty today too," Emma sourly retorted.

"Look, if this *is* the scene of the crime, there's a good chance it will spark some brilliant deductive reasoning on my part that *will* lead us to the clues we need."

Emma sighed again as she headed for the cockpit. "You

read far too many Sherlock Holmes stories in your impressionable youth."

An hour later, they had worked themselves to within seven feet of each other.

"Damn!" Duncan said, on his back as he investigated the bottom of a plush captain's chair.

"What is it?" Emma asked.

"Harley was right: I *do* love this job." He had found his life's work these last few days, even though it had been staring him in the face from the day he was born. Loving the family business. Knowing just the niche he wanted to carve for himself. It was the stuff of fantasy. It was unbelievable.

And it was true.

Amazing. It turned out he really did have a dream: to be the best private investigator going . . . and to share his life with Harley. The hell of it was, one was in jeopardy and the other impossible. She'd be leaving New York soon. And she wouldn't be coming back. He tried to distract himself from a sudden stab of pain by reexamining the bottom of the chair. "I wonder if I can convince Dad to open up a full-scale criminal investigations division in the company, and let me run it."

"On the day Glinda the Good Witch appears before you, swirls her magic wand, and tells you to tap your heels together three times, take me with you."

Duncan lifted his head and grinned at Emma. "Done."

Thirty minutes later he stood at the top of the passenger stairs staring out at the surrounding tarmac, the other private jets, and the hangars beyond. He and Emma had found nothing. Worse, he had not been struck by a brilliant stroke of deductive reasoning. He had come up more than empty. Four days ago his brother had stood on this very step and had taken possession of Giscard's black leather case. Was it empty then? Did the diamonds somehow vanish into thin air in the back of the Colangco limousine? Or was Giscard playing with their minds? Had he decided to use the Bartlett

Museum's jewelry exhibit as a front for an insurance scam by sending his courier onto this plane in Paris with an already empty case?

"Um, Duncan?" Emma said from behind him. "There's an office with our names on it that's waiting for us."

"Sorry, Em." Duncan headed down the stairs, rerunning the surveillance videos he had studied over and over in his mind. Brandon had taken the case, walked down these stairs, taken three steps, and handed the case into the limo and to the two Colangco men waiting to guard it in the back seat. The guards and the driver were longtime Colangco employees and completely trustworthy. Duncan had handpicked them himself. Besides, Emma had investigated them under a microscope.

Brandon had walked back to his car and led the mini-caravan into the city. On the drive to the Bartlett Museum, the limo had been caught in some stop-and-go traffic, but no one had approached the car, no one had left the car. The limo hadn't even been stopped over a manhole cover for more than a few seconds.

"You're thinking too much, Holmes," Emma said as they walked through the small terminal. "Stop worrying at it like a dog with a meaty bone. Let your mind rest. That's usually when you get the answer you need. It worked for Albert Einstein—he preferred the shower method—and it can work for you."

"What do *you* think happened to the diamonds?" Duncan said, holding the glass door open for her.

"Every hypothesis I even half formed has been shot to hell by our surveillance tapes," Emma said, walking out to the taxi stand. "I'm beginning to believe it was either a case of astral projection or a sudden flux in the space-time continuum."

"That's a whole lot better than I've been able to come up with," Duncan said as he followed her into the back seat of a yellow cab. "I thought maybe the Tooth Fairy was a little tipsy on Thursday morning and got confused on her pick-up route."

Emma snorted. "So, do you still love this job?"

Duncan sighed and rested his head on the back of the bench seat. "Yeah. Turns out my parents were right all along. I *am* psychotic."

"Whatever works, Holmes."

He chuckled and squeezed her hand for a moment. "I'm going to get you that promotion if it kills me."

The cab dropped them off at the Sentinel Building. Duncan walked into his office, grabbed the Giscard diamond surveillance tapes once again, popped the first one into the center video monitor, sat down in his chair, and settled in for the long haul. He was missing something. He knew it. He felt it in his marrow.

But what the hell was it?

Harley had been scowling at her guitar for the last two hours, trying to blame it, trying to blame Duncan, trying to avoid some inevitable conclusions, and failing. With a groan, she pushed herself from the peach armchair and headed for the kitchen. Like her mama had always said: when in doubt, *bake.*

But even as she was punching and kneading the yeasty dough, she knew it wasn't enough. She had to be *moving*—all of her—if she was ever going to find any peace and reconciliation between who she had been, who she had wanted to be, and who she was, as a woman and as a musician. She waited until she had pulled the two loaves of bread safely from the oven, then she headed back to the bedroom to change out of Duncan's floured T-shirt and into her own blue T-shirt and jeans. Next she walked into the bathroom and grabbed for her hairbrush, but it was out of place. Just like she was feeling. She looked down at the counter, found her brush, ran it twice through her hair, and then headed out of the apartment. She took the elevator down to the lobby, walked out of the Sentinel Building, turned left onto Fifth Avenue, and kept going.

She didn't glance across the street at the Henri Bendel shop. She failed to note the irony of the towering gothic spires of St. Patrick's Cathedral set right beside that tower of consumerism, Saks Fifth Avenue. She was wrestling with home truths and thinking only how grateful she was to be moving, striding down the sidewalk, oblivious to the other people around her, her arms swinging, storefronts melting into each other as she passed, her soul trying to whisper some long-suppressed facts of life.

The whisperings came to a screeching halt when two men—two men who were not Desmond and Louis—grabbed her arms.

"Holiday's over, Miss Miller," said the refugee from a bad *Godfather* knockoff on her right.

They knew who she was!

"In you go," said the man on her left as they dragged her toward a brown American sedan.

Harley freaked. "Let me go!" she yelled, kicking and biting and surprising the men completely. They let go of her just long enough for her knees to buckle. She sat down with a thump on the sidewalk, her heart thundering in her breast, and began singing "When the Saints Go Marching In" at the top of her lungs.

It was the only song she could think of.

The two men stared at her—and at the dozens of people up and down the sidewalk staring at them—in horror. Then they bolted into the car and it rocketed away down Fifth Avenue.

Harley kept singing. She was a pro. Pros always finished a song when they had an audience. Vaguely she recognized that she wasn't thinking clearly, that reaction was setting in, that she was shaking.

She finished the song, stumbled to her feet, bowed, because the people around her were applauding, and numbly pulled the cellular phone from her purse. She had no idea that she had memorized Duncan's number until she heard the phone ringing and Emma's brisk voice answering.

"Colangco International, Duncan Lang's office."

"Emma," Harley said, her voice sounding strange in her ears. "Two men just tried to . . . Well . . . I guess you could say they tried to kidnap me."

"Oh dear God! Are you okay?"

"Scared to death, but unharmed and I think . . . safe."

"Where are you?" Emma's voice was tense, urgent.

"Um . . ." Harley looked around her, really for the first time. "I'm on Fifth Avenue, almost at Forty-third Street."

"Stay put. Keep a lot of people around you. I'll be right there."

But five minutes later, it was Duncan who leapt from the cab that had screeched to a stop before her at the curb. It was Duncan who grabbed her. Duncan who held her. He was shaking.

"Oh my God, Harley. Are you all right? Did they hurt you?"

Five minutes had given her enough time to get her nerves back in order. She cupped his taut face in her hands. "I'm fine, Duncan. I promise."

"God," Duncan said, wrapping himself around her and holding her tight, "I should never have left you alone. I should have been with you—"

"But you were, Duncan, you were," Harley said. "You were in my blood. I sat down and started singing and those two men bolted, just like you said they would."

He stared down at her. She could see the struggle he was waging to calm himself. "You sang?"

" 'When the Saints Go Marching In.' I got a very nice round of applause from the bystanders too."

"Hey," Duncan said, hugging her again, but with less desperation, "talent stands out—or sits out—wherever you are.

Mind if I assign some bodyguards to follow you around until this damn case is solved?"

"I'd like a phalanx of bodyguards, thank you very much."

That made him smile. "You've got it. I never thought Louis and Desmond would pull something like this on you."

"But it wasn't them, Duncan."

"What? Are you sure?"

"Positive."

Duncan considered a moment. "They may have brought in specialized muscle for the retaliatory measures they promised." His smile was chilling. "They're dead men when I find them." He kissed her hard, then rested his forehead against her forehead. "Come back to Colangco, Miss Miller, give Emma a description of those men, and then *stay put*."

"Willingly."

Leaving Harley in Emma's office to start creating computer-generated composite sketches of her two attackers while he walked back into his own office as if nothing had happened was the hardest thing Duncan had ever done. But now the stakes were much higher. *Harley* . . . He had to find Giscard's diamonds and he had to find them now. He turned the center video monitor back on and watched the Colangco cavalcade drive up to Giscard's Lear jet once again. The tapes were hiding the answer to this case and he was going to find it.

It was the lights flashing into life all around him that finally dragged his gaze from the monitor. "What the . . . ?" He looked around. The day had turned to night outside his office windows . . . and Harley was standing in the doorway.

"Hi, there," she said amiably. She opened up her dark blue raincoat. She was wearing a black corset . . . and nothing else. "Dinner's ready. And dessert."

The video monitor went black as Duncan lunged out of his chair. "You could put the alarm clock industry out of business," he said as he followed her out the door.

"Thanks," she said, leading him toward the penthouse elevator.

"Are you okay?"

"I'm doing really well, Duncan. Honest. Everyone's been terrific."

"What were you doing out of the penthouse this morning anyway?"

"Trying to think." She stopped at the penthouse elevator. "If I'm not Jane Miller and I'm not Patti Smith, how about country harlot?"

"Works for me."

He held her close on the brief ride up to the penthouse, grateful that he *could* hold her. It seemed Harley had been right about this too. He *was* a passionate man, at least when it came to his work and to her. *Kindred spirits,* Duncan murmured to himself. Each of them bumping the other up against preconceived, and apparently fallacious, notions of who they were and what they wanted.

He was touched to find that after everything that had happened today, Harley had actually made dinner for him. She hadn't even sent out for Chinese. A large bowl filled with Caesar salad and slices of grilled chicken, with bread on the side, was waiting in the middle of the dining table. He stared at the crusty baguette for a moment.

"You baked?"

"I had to do something to keep from going nutso," she said, the raincoat decorously closed as she sat down at the table.

"Those men—"

"No, no, no," she said with a sweet smile.

He made himself relax. "Then what?"

"*You,* of course. Home truths are a pain in the butt, Duncan."

He grinned at her. How he loved that soft Sweetcreek twang. "Sorry."

"No, you were right," she said, stabbing her fork into her

salad. "It's just that I've had such a strong belief system about who I am that it was a little shocking to find that rock and roll is actually more of an avocation now and I've moved on to become something else."

"How did you arrive at country harlot?"

"Well, I just took my country roots, mixed them up with a little teenage rebellion and Princess sweetness, and voilà! It's not going to work, of course," she glumly concluded.

"It's not?" This was disappointing. He liked the corset.

Harley sighed heavily and leaned back in her chair. "Nope. Turns out I've got a base core of morality that doesn't believe in promoting a promiscuous bad-girl image on the impressionable minds of my younger fans."

"That's tough."

"Yeah."

"So, who are you going to be?"

Harley sighed again and returned to stabbing at her salad. "My country-rockabilly self, once I figure out exactly who that is and what it all means."

Oh God, he wasn't going to be around for any of that. Duncan forced himself to take a breath. "What does this do to the last album you owe Sony on your contract?"

"I don't know." She stared into space a moment, shook her head, and returned to her salad. "If worse comes to worse, I can produce a greatest hits compilation. They'll be satisfied."

"Will you?"

She looked up, blue eyes puzzled, not so much by the question, Duncan thought, as by him, as if she still didn't understand that her happiness and satisfaction were as necessary to him as air. "No," she said, "but then, I don't know about anything that satisfies me anymore . . . except you, of course."

"Thank you," Duncan said, surprised at how happy she'd just made him.

"I have managed to adequately convey that to you these last few days, haven't I?"

Memories of Harley arching beneath him flooded his body. "Oh yeah," he said.

She smiled sunnily at him and returned to her salad. "Good. How did your day go?"

He had meant to only provide a brief sketch of his activities, but Harley kept interrupting with questions, which led to further elaborations and the rather startling realization, halfway through the conversation, that she was sincerely interested in what he did and thought and felt about all of that. He had never let that realization sink in before this. It was too disconcerting. It made him think he might not be the man he had believed himself to be most of his life, because Harley Jane Miller wouldn't have been interested in that man, and she was clearly interested now. And the realization hurt too much, because acknowledging her interest made him hope that she would stay when her holiday ended, and that wasn't going to happen.

She was moving at light speed away from the prison she and Boyd had manufactured these last nine years, and here he was cramping her broadening wings. She needed to be independent and taste freedom fully, and instead he had pulled her into his life, into an increasingly dangerous case, into his bed, and into his temporary home.

Where was the freedom in that?

He gazed across the table at Harley, candlelight shimmering on her raincoat. She had to fly free and he wouldn't stop her, couldn't stop her, because he had lived too long not knowing himself to deny Harley her own flight of self-discovery.

His gaze blurred. Duncan blinked back sudden tears, amazed that he could care so much in so little time. Amazed that he was so determined to let go of what his soul wanted so much.

Still, he had tonight, and the certainty of waking up beside

Harley tomorrow morning. He would hold on to that. And he would try to find a way to steel himself for the end. Somehow he would have to prepare himself for what couldn't be withstood. But there was tonight. He had tonight to drink her in fully and give as deeply to her in return. He would find his courage tomorrow. Right now, need and desire were twisting inside him.

He stood up and walked around the table to where Harley sat. "Ready for dessert?"

She gazed up at him, turquoise blue eyes knocking the wind out of him. "Yes, please."

Without another word, he picked her up and carried her into the bedroom.

Somewhere, far, far away, a phone was ringing. With a groan, Duncan dredged open his eyelids and stared blearily at the bedside clock. Three-twenty. He and Harley had been asleep for less than an hour.

"Tell it to go away," she complained from deep within the cocoon he had made around her.

His hand fumbled across the bedside table and finally collided with the phone. "This had better be good," he mumbled into the handset.

"I guess it depends on your point of view," a man's voice replied.

Duncan was suddenly wide awake. "Carmine?"

"You told me to call the minute I found something," the bookie said by way of apology.

"I meant it. You got something on Boyd Monroe?" He felt Harley come awake.

"No, nothing on him," Carmine Bellini replied. "But something just surfaced and I thought you'd better know."

Duncan had never heard this note of anxiety in his old friend's voice before. "I appreciate that, Carmine. What have you got?"

"It's about your brother."

Duncan sat bolt upright, unaware of Harley, or the tangled covers, or even the bed. *"Brandon?"*

"I'm afraid so, *amico*. There's no good way to do this, so I'll just say it right out: Brandon owes the Maurizio family a little more than eight hundred grand."

The taste of cold metal soured Duncan's mouth. "Why?" he managed.

"Gambling debts."

He was trembling inside. "That's impossible. There must be some mistake. Brandon doesn't gamble."

"Yes, my friend, he does. Big time. In fact, he's one very high roller. It turns out to be one of the best-kept secrets in town. But I've got it from Dante Maurizio himself, Duncan, and you know he manages all of the Maurizio gambling interests. Your brother has been dealing directly with the Maurizios for years. That's why they let him run up such a big tab. But *Angelo's* called it due. They're very confident about getting payment in full, Duncan."

Awful ideas were burning in Duncan's brain even as his heart screamed and screamed that they weren't possible. "The Maurizios are playing hardball?"

"Si, molto hardball."

"God," Duncan said with a shudder.

"If I hear anything else, I'll let you know."

"Grazie," Duncan said from somewhere outside his body.

"I'm sorry about this, *amico.*"

"No, I'm in your debt, Carmine."

Duncan watched himself hang up the phone. He couldn't think. He could scarcely move. *Brandon?*

"Duncan, what's wrong?" Harley asked. She was kneeling on the bed, pressed against his thigh and ribs and shoulder. But he couldn't feel her.

Jagged shards of thought were piercing his brain. If it was Brandon, if he had really . . . No, it was impossible. He couldn't have. It would drive a stake into their parents' hearts

and then twist it for greater effect. It wasn't in Brandon to do
that. It wasn't. And there was the company to think of. His
birthright. He was next in succession. Brandon wouldn't do
anything to endanger Colangco. It was insane to even think it.
And disloyal and cruel and ugly.

"Duncan," Harley said, her voice urgent, her arms around
him holding him tight, "is Brandon in trouble?"

The metallic taste in his mouth jeered at his desperation.
Eight hundred thousand dollars. Eight hundred . . . thousand . . . dollars. Brandon would put the barrel of a gun in
his mouth before he'd let their father find out. Or would he?
After all, Brandon had never accustomed himself to self-
sacrifice. It really wasn't even in his vocabulary.

Duncan pulled free from Harley's arms and slid from the
bed.

"Duncan?"

"I have to go to the office," he said, pulling on the jeans
Harley had peeled off him only a few hours ago. "There's
some work I need to do."

"Tell me what's wrong," she said.

He wouldn't let himself look at her. He wouldn't let himself seek, let alone take in, the comfort and support he knew
were just inches away. It was no good leaning on them now
when they would be gone so soon. "It may be nothing," he
said, pulling on his shirt. "It may be everything. I have to go."

He slid his bare feet into his loafers and walked out of the
bedroom. Alone. More alone than he'd ever felt in his life.
Hating himself more than he had ever hated anyone in his
life.

He refused to let himself think as he rode the penthouse
elevator down to the office, walked down the hall past his
father's and Brandon's offices, and into his dark office. He
stood there for a moment, staring at the partially lit skyscrap-
ers outside his windows. God, he really was going to do this.
He threw on his office lights and sat down at his desk.

He turned on his computer, numb through and through

except for a tiny pocket of terror shaking inside his heart. Then he swiveled his chair around, turned on a video monitor, and popped the airport surveillance tape into the VCR. He fast-forwarded through the Lear jet's landing and taxiing to the private hangar, then stopped just before Brandon got out of his black Aston Martin parked in front of the Colangco limousine.

Duncan watched, as he had watched nearly two dozen times before, as Brandon—his tall, golden, beautiful brother—walked across the few feet of tarmac between the car and the Lear jet's narrow staircase. He watched Brandon walk up the steps, greet the Giscard courier, identify himself, and take the black briefcase from the courier's hand. He watched Brandon thank the courier, turn around, walk back down the steps and across the few feet of tarmac to the limo. He watched Brandon hand the briefcase to the two guards waiting in the back seat. He watched Brandon get back into his Aston Martin and lead the limousine out of the private airport.

Duncan stopped the tape and rewound it to the moment just before Brandon first got out of his car. Brandon walked across the tarmac, up the steps, greeted the courier, identified himself, took the briefcase—

Duncan froze the tape. His brother held the briefcase by its handle, but in front of him, not at his side. It wasn't visible on the tape. Brandon could have planned it that way. Hand shaking, Duncan advanced the tape in slow motion. "No!" he whispered.

The courier had turned away first, back into the jet, before Brandon turned and started back down the narrow stairs.

"Brandon, no," Duncan pleaded.

A terrible memory assaulted his brain. Stiff and nauseous, Duncan turned to his computer and brought up the Giscard case report. He scrolled through the report quickly, knowing exactly what he would find.

There. Brandon had contacted Giscard. Brandon had convinced Giscard to loan the diamonds to the Bartlett Museum, even though Giscard had been turning down the museum's requests for nearly a year now. And Brandon had convinced him that Colangco was the right company to protect those diamonds.

He had even given Giscard the security briefcase to hold the diamonds during transport.

Numb, Duncan turned back to the video monitor and rewound the tape in slow motion to the moment when Brandon stood at the top of the stairs, briefcase before him, and the courier turned away back into the jet. Then he ran the tape in real time, stopping it as Brandon completed his turn to start back down the stairs.

Three seconds. Plenty of time for a talented amateur magician like Brandon when he had the right tool in hand.

He had just lost his brother and with him a world and a self Duncan thought he had known all of his life.

Mingled horror and fury constricted Duncan's throat. His brother . . . The good son . . . The Golden Boy . . . The Paragon he had both rebelled against and tried to emulate . . . His brother had stolen a million dollars' worth of diamonds to pay off his gambling debts, threatening his family's honor, Colangco's reputation, and—by asking him to come up with the transport plan—setting Duncan up to take the fall for him.

He had deliberately betrayed his own family.

It took a moment for Duncan to realize that tears were sliding down his face. He hastily brushed them away, still not quite able to take it all in. Brandon . . . *His brother* had not only stolen the Giscard diamonds, he had calmly held Duncan out to their parents, the French mob, and the New York police as the most likely suspect for the robbery.

Duncan surged out of his chair, pain and anger and despair rioting within him. He wanted to hit someone, throw something, do *anything* to relieve this pressure cooker boiling within his soul. He spun around . . . and saw Harley seated quietly in a guest chair in front of his desk. She was looking up at him, quiet and still.

He gasped from the sudden shift in emotion within him. "How long have you been here?"

"I got here about a minute after you did," she said softly. "Did Brandon steal the Giscard diamonds, Duncan?"

The question left him bloodless. The rage drained out of him. There was only pain. "Yes," he said, that one word stark and ugly in the room.

"And he set you up to take the fall for him?"

"Yes."

"And he's not the man you've always believed him to be."

"No."

Harley stood up, walked around the desk, and took his hand in hers. "Come here." She led him over to the green leather sofa. He sat down sideways on the couch, knees drawn up, numb with shock and disbelief and certainty. She surprised him by insinuating herself between his knees, sitting cross-legged, her arms around him. "Tell me."

The words poured out of him. It felt like the Hoover Dam had suddenly been blasted wide open. He told her how Brandon had stolen the diamonds and why Brandon had stolen the diamonds. He told her other things too. He told her about being five and worshiping his seven-year-old brother as he watched him play with his second-grade classmates on the private school playground. He told her about being fourteen and jealous as all the prep school girls swarmed around his golden brother.

He told her about turning sixteen and being stunned and thrilled when Brandon gifted him with *his* very first sexual experience: a high-priced and talented call girl Brandon had found in the little black book he had lifted off of one of their father's best friends. He told her about graduating from prep school convinced he could never match Brandon's brilliance and success. He told her about returning home after nearly five years determined to try once again to mold himself in his brother's image.

When Duncan finished, the world outside his office windows was gray, not black, and the pain had been reduced to a dull throbbing in his heart.

"What will you do now?" Harley asked into the quiet.

Oh, her sweet expressive face. He could gaze at it forever. Let the world drop away, let him have this—her—peace. He gave himself the pleasure of sifting his fingers through her soft hair. "I'm going to prove that my brother is a thief," he replied, shuddering a little. He sighed as her hand cupped his cheek in concern. He pressed a kiss to the center of her palm and then held her hand in his. "The tape proves nothing. It doesn't matter what I know, I have to come up with the evidence to prove it to Giscard, to the police . . . and to my parents."

"It sounds impossible."

"No," he said with a sad smile. "I know how to do it."

"Duncan?" she said tentatively. It puzzled him.

"Yes?"

"Something's been nagging at me."

"What is it?"

"Well," she said, looking anxious, "it's the whole Giscard case. The diamond robbery has always bothered me because it seemed a little too pat, a little too convenient. I mean, look at the timing: it happened right after you were hired to find me and then switched to working for me. At first I thought I was just being egocentric—you know, the-world-revolves-around-*me* sort of thing—but now I'm not so sure."

"Harley, Brandon *stole* the diamonds. I can prove it."

"I know. But what if the diamonds are a blind?"

Duncan stared at her.

"What if the diamond robbery wasn't about money?" she persisted. "What if it was about distracting you from my case?"

"But why?" he demanded.

Harley stopped. "I don't know."

But he didn't hear her. Shock was rippling through him. He stared intently at a spot on the wall over her right shoulder. Brandon and Maurizio. Boyd and Maurizio. And Harley. He looked at her. "What if you aren't egocentric?" he said. "What if you've been the link from the very beginning?"

"Yeah, but how?"

"Money," he said, surging to his feet and beginning to pace. "With Boyd and Brandon, it's all about money. Go back to the beginning, Harley. When you walked out of the Ritz-Carlton, Boyd was upset because *he couldn't get to Los Angeles on time.* Ergo, he had a rendezvous, probably with one of Maurizio's West Coast operatives. He had a rendezvous to deliver whatever he'd brought into the country from your world tour." Duncan stopped. He stared at Harley as if seeing her for the first time. "You know," he said slowly, "I don't think I grasped before the full implications of Boyd's continued stay at the Ritz. You walked out on him and Boyd didn't make his Los Angeles rendezvous. Ergo, *he couldn't make the rendezvous because you took with you what he was supposed to deliver to Maurizio's people.* That's why he was so desperate to get you back. To get his delivery back, *he had to get you back!*"

Harley was very white. "But I didn't take anything of his when I left!"

"Yes, you did. You just didn't know it. Come on," he said, dragging her out of his office.

Minutes later, they stood in the master bedroom of the Colangco penthouse apartment staring at the meager items Harley had placed on the king-size bed: Annie Maguire's dark blue raincoat, hat, one-size-too-big pumps, and Visa card; the beige sack dress and underwear she had worn that Sunday night; and even the pins she had used to hold the dress up above the hem of the raincoat. Her blue toothbrush and her hairbrush-and-comb set completed the gleanings.

"It's not much," Harley said.

"The answer is here, I know it is," Duncan said. "Let's get started."

They slowly and methodically ripped Annie's raincoat, hat, and shoes to shreds, scanning every centimeter of material for anything the least out of place. They came up empty. They did the same to Harley's dress and underwear. Nothing. They used magnifying glasses to pore over Harley's toothbrush, hairbrush, and comb. Failure stared back at them.

They started all over again. And then again. They found nothing.

"Are you sure this is all you took?" Duncan asked as they sat together, tired and dispirited, on the side of the bed. "No bobby pins? No toothpaste?"

"This is all I had with me. I swear," she said.

He turned his head to her to say something. Then he stopped, and stared. "No, it's not," he said hoarsely. His hand reached out and grabbed the gold musical note pendant that hung from her throat. "You had this!"

He nearly strangled her pulling the gold chain from around her neck. His fingers were trembling as he studied first the chain and then the pendant through his magnifying glass. "Ah-ah-ah," he murmured, "what have we here?"

The pendant split in two on hidden hinges and revealed a small inner compartment.

Duncan breathed out. "I love it when I'm right."

"What is that?" Harley demanded.

"A computer chip," he said excitedly. "It could have government secrets or high-tech secrets, something like that. Whatever is on it, it's enough to make Boyd sweat and more than enough to make Maurizio very angry that it's not already in the possession of his West Coast operation."

"And that's why Boyd tried to get me to go back with him to the Ritz," Harley said, staring at the chip. "It was the only chance he had of getting his hands on this. How did you open the pendant?" she demanded.

Using his thumbnail, Duncan showed her the tiny hidden catch on the back of the pendant near the right side edge.

"But that wasn't there when I bought this," she said.

"Then Boyd had a duplicate pendant made and switched them."

"But why take such a chance on having *me* be his mule?"

"He knew that you always wear the pendant, and he figured it was the perfect way to smuggle secrets. At least the compact ones. The band instruments and stage paraphernalia could have hidden anything larger. You really were the perfect front for his operations."

"I think I'm going to be sick," Harley said, looking shaky.

"Not now, my country harlot," Duncan said, pulling her to her feet. "Let's go see what's on this thing."

It only took a few minutes to install the chip. Duncan turned his computer back on. They stared at a screen full of gibberish.

"What happened?" Harley asked.

Duncan leaned back in his chair, frustrated almost past bearing. Then it hit him. "It takes two to tango."

Harley studied him a moment. "Sort of like Siamese twin computer chips?"

"Exactly. One can't work without the other."

"So, we've got one. Where's the . . ." Harley's eyes widened. "Duncan! Could Brandon have the other chip?"

"It's more than likely," he said, fighting the nausea. All of the pieces of the puzzle were cascading into place in his brain. "Two chips, two ports of entry, two couriers. That's the thinking man's delivery system." He burst out of his chair and started pacing the office. He couldn't hold still. He didn't think he'd ever be still again. "Here's the scenario: Brandon is struck by a major case of gambling fever and ends up owing the Maurizio family big time. Naturally, they tell him to pay up or else. Brandon says he doesn't have that kind of cash, they lean hard, Brandon gets desperate. Then *Angelo* Maurizio steps forward and offers him a way out. All Brandon has to do is a small job for him in Florida and the debt will be wiped clean."

"*Florida?*"

"Yeah, I think so. That Miami case always bothered me. It was a real simple, by-the-book project. Normally, it would have gone to one of the junior staff, or to *me,* but Brandon insisted on taking it."

Harley sat down in his chair and swiveled it around to face him as he paced. "Okay, Brandon picks up the second chip. Now what?"

Cold perspiration was soaking through Duncan's T-shirt. "I think . . . I think he was supposed to fly to Los Angeles, act as Boyd's contact, and deliver the chips. He had a lot more freedom to move around than Boyd, because Boyd was micromanaging your life."

"It seems like centuries ago," Harley said quietly.

"Yeah," Duncan said, staring out his office windows at the pale world beyond.

"So, Boyd has his chip, and Brandon has his chip, and everything's fine. Until I walk out of the Ritz-Carlton."

"Boyd panics and I don't blame him," Duncan said, shaking his head. "No one messes with the Maurizio family. He must have known by then that Brandon was his contact, so he does the most natural thing in the world. He calls Colangco, expecting that he'll get Brandon to help him find you. I remember how badly surprised Boyd was when I met him for our first interview. He said flat out he wanted my brother, that he was expecting my brother. Jesus, how blind can I get?"

"As I understand it, that was the normal reaction of *any-one* meeting you for the first time," Harley commented.

He almost smiled. "So, I'm a bad shock to Boyd, but I may work out. I may find you. But Boyd's taking no chances. He either finds a way to contact Brandon, or has Maurizio contact Brandon. My money's on Maurizio. All he had to do was call Brandon, say he's got a problem, issue the usual sort of threats, order him to fix the problem, and *voilà!* Big Brother's back in town bright and early Tuesday morning and he finds trouble waiting for him. I'm not doing what he and Boyd need me to do: I'm not returning you and your pendant to Boyd. I might still pull it off, but just to be safe, Brandon decides on a backup plan." This couldn't be happening. Brandon couldn't have been manipulating all of them from the very beginning. It was insane. "Brandon will take over Boyd's case, find you, and get you back to Boyd safe and sound. That means getting me off the case." Duncan swore softly. Not a day had gone by in the last week that Brandon hadn't tried to talk him off the case or try to convince him to return Harley to Boyd.

"What I don't get is why he chose the Giscard diamonds for a diversion," Harley said. "I mean, wasn't that a little extreme?"

Duncan shrugged against the walls closing in on him. "Not really. I think Brandon chose that job because it was closest to hand. Any complex case would have done, but the Giscard diamonds had a lot of advantages. First, stealing them brought in both the police and Giscard, so I'd really be preoccupied and it would seem the most natural thing in the world for Brandon to step in and take over your case. Second, Dad was certain to fire me or at least suspend me when the diamonds disappeared, again putting Brandon on your case. But I think . . . I hope that the most important factor was that Brandon could wait until the very last minute before deciding to go ahead with the theft. If I had returned you to Boyd any time before Thursday morning, I don't think Brandon would have stolen the diamonds. But I didn't, so he did."

"Only it was worse than that," Harley said softly, as she uncurled herself from the chair and began to walk toward him. "Wednesday night, we arranged with your father *not* to send me back to Boyd, *and* Colby agreed to let you investigate Boyd. Colby probably even called Brandon that night to tell him. The last thing Brandon wanted was to have anyone investigating Boyd. He had to stop you, Duncan."

"Oh," Duncan said, stuffing his shaking hands into the back pockets of his jeans.

She brushed her fingertips across his frozen face. "So Brandon steals the diamonds and the police and Giscard's men descend on you, just as planned. His problem should be solved. Only it wasn't, because your brother never expected you to fight your dad to hold on to my case, and he certainly didn't expect you to win. And I'll bet he didn't think you could come up with a decent alibi the police could substantiate."

"No," Duncan said from somewhere within a ten-thousand-foot-deep glacier, "with what he knew of the way I used to live my life, he would have counted on my not having any reliable witnesses who could testify to my whereabouts at the time of the robbery."

"So nothing is working," Harley said, her blue gaze warm and steady. "You're still investigating Boyd and I'm still running free."

"And Maurizio had to be leaning hard on both Boyd and Brandon by last Friday." Duncan heard himself laugh. It sounded ugly. "Brandon has been a daily visitor, Boyd's *only* visitor, at the Ritz these last several days. I just assumed Dad had sent him to keep Boyd tractable. But of course they were meeting, working together, trying to find some way out of this mess."

Harley swallowed. "Yeah. Things are going from bad to worse. You actually tell Boyd what you're up to, *and* I fire him, and Brandon can't get rid of you. That would make them both desperate, and I think," she said slowly, "that it might have pushed Brandon out of hiding. What if *he* was the one who downloaded your case files on Saturday afternoon, Duncan? He needed to find me, grab the pendant, and get rid of Boyd, but I wasn't at the Millenium anymore. I'd moved to the Loews on Saturday morning."

"Oh, there's no doubt that was Brandon's handiwork," Duncan said bitterly.

Harley began gnawing on her lower lip. "And what if he searched the Colangco penthouse?"

"There's no way—"

"He knows every minute detail of the Colangco security system," Harley ruthlessly countered, "and besides, things felt out of place to me the morning after you lured me into performing with the Rockin' Robins at Goodies. Little things, like my hairbrush, were all just a little bit . . . off."

"All right," Duncan barked, and then hurriedly softened his voice. "It's possible." But it was already certain in his mind.

The blood drained from Harley's face. "Duncan! Do you think . . . We've assumed it was Giscard's men who tried to grab me yesterday. But what if they were *Brandon's* hirelings sent to drag me back to Boyd?"

The horror of it, the likelihood of it, was twisting in Duncan's bowels. "Not hirelings, Harley," he ground out, "muscle, probably Maurizio muscle." Rage knotted his veins, blinding him, strangling him. When he thought of what might have happened to her . . . In that moment, he wanted to vivisect his brother with his bare hands.

"Duncan. Duncan!"

He forcibly pulled himself back from that murderous chasm. Harley was standing before him, her hands on his shoulders. He couldn't feel her.

"I don't think they were sent to hurt me," she said, holding his eyes with her steady blue gaze. "They said, 'Holiday's over.' I think they were sent to return me to status quo, to Boyd, *and that's all.*

Duncan made himself breathe.

"It's ironic, isn't it?" she said softly. "If I hadn't made a break for freedom, Brandon and Boyd could have delivered the computer chips and no one would have been the wiser. You, at least, wouldn't have been suspected of the diamond robbery, because there wouldn't have *been* a diamond robbery." Warm blue eyes burned into the ice around his soul. "But here we are."

Duncan took a deep breath and slowly released it. "Here we are." So, this was Hell. "I know how to prove Brandon stole the diamonds. I know how to connect Maurizio to Boyd and to Brandon. All I've got to do now is produce sufficient evidence to connect Boyd and Brandon to each other. I'll need your help, Harley."

"Anything," she said, kissing his hot, dry eyes. "What do we do first?"

"I have to talk to the FBI. They've been trying to hang a life sentence on Angelo Maurizio for years. They'll need to be brought up to speed on all this."

"But Brandon—!"

Brandon. Oh dear God, Brandon. He made himself look into her anxious blue eyes. "I'm going to tell them everything."

CHAPTER THIRTEEN

She couldn't stand it anymore. It had been hours, and not a word. Harley walked down the long corridor, through Emma's empty office, and into Duncan's office. He sat in front of his computer, oblivious to the world. But she could see his pain in the taut lines of his face and the rigid way he held himself in his chair.

"You've been at this since dawn, haven't you?" she said.

"What?" He glanced at her. "Oh, hi, Harley. Yeah, I guess so."

"Have you eaten?"

"What?" Duncan said distractedly, his fingers flying over the keyboard.

"Food. You know, nourishment."

"It's not lunchtime, is it?"

"Duncan," Harley said gently, "it's after two o'clock. I'll

order something up and you will eat it, if I have to chew it for you myself."

He stopped and turned to her in happy surprise. "I like being fussed over!"

Harley wanted to laugh and weep at the same time. How had he survived a lifetime's famine of simple, human consideration? "Good," she said with forced lightness, "because I like fussing over you. How goes it with Brandon?"

Duncan sighed and leaned back in his chair, half facing her. "Emma located the manufacturer of the diamond security briefcase. It's a little shop in Brussels that caters to the particular whims of certain high-class criminal types." Duncan paused. "Funny, that's the first time I've called my brother a criminal."

Hours of worrying exploded in Harley. "Ah hell, Duncan! Why don't you just chain him to a wall and drive a couple of Mack trucks into him a few times? It would be so much more *satisfying*."

"But messy," Duncan replied, turning back to the computer. "My parents value discretion above all else."

"Ah hell," Harley muttered. He wouldn't play, he wouldn't vent, he wouldn't weep. He wouldn't even eat. She could at least do something about *that*. She used the conference table phone and ordered a large pizza and soft drinks.

When their late lunch arrived, Harley physically dragged Duncan to the glass conference table, shoved him down into a chair, ordered him to eat, and stood over him to make sure he did so. His desk phone rang just as he was finishing the last of his root beer. He grabbed the handset on the second ring. "Lang."

He hung up the phone ten seconds later. He looked like death warmed over.

"What's wrong?" she asked.

"Nothing," he said, turning to her, affecting nonchalance. "That was Emma. The FBI just installed the necessary surveillance equipment in Boyd's suite while he was out making his daily call to Maurizio. Are you ready for this?"

"Oh yeah."

"We'll be setting up Boyd for the fall of his life," Duncan warned her.

"Good. At the least, he's used me. At the worst, he's betrayed his own country with the secrets he's sold over the years. I want to help put him in jail."

"And you called *me* lethal."

"It's not nice to fool with the Princess of Pop," Harley said darkly, hiding her delight at his answering grin. She hadn't been certain she'd ever see him smile again. Her fingernails dug into the palms of her hands. Oh, how she wanted to rip Brandon to shreds for what he'd done to his brother!

But first, there was Boyd to get through.

Half an hour later, Harley walked into the Ritz-Carlton, Duncan's large, warm hand holding her hand in silent support. She didn't notice the marble lobby. She scarcely realized an elevator was carrying her back to the twenty-third floor and the start of this amazing tableau. She could only think about Boyd.

It surprised her how easy it was to set up the man who had micromanaged her life for nine long years and had helped make her a star along the way. It surprised her that all of the pity she had felt for him on Sunday when she had fired him had been burned away by the anger she felt now at being so badly used and for such a terrible cause. What other secrets had she carried around her neck for him? How many people had suffered, maybe even died, because of what her good luck charm had hidden?

She felt as if the gold chain were burning through her skin, like acid, while she and Duncan were slowly and methodically searched by the four bodyguards posted outside of Boyd's hotel suite. As if they could protect him from Maurizio. Once assured that they weren't armed and that Boyd was indeed expecting them, the guards unlocked the door to the suite and let them pass.

The resemblance to the suite she had escaped just nine days ago felt like bad déjà vu. She and Duncan walked across marble floors to the pale green carpeted living room. The curtains for the windows and glass terrace doors overlooking south Central Park were drawn. The suite was shadowy and stale from days of fear. Boyd stood at the small wet bar, pouring himself a whiskey. He never took a drink during business hours. The full whiskey tumbler shocked Harley almost as much as his gray face did. He looked like death.

"Did you decide to come crawling back, *Jane,* or do you just want to add another charge to my libel suit?" he demanded as he turned to face them. The whiskey glass wobbled precariously between his fingers. He was staring at her pendant. She had worn a black scoop-necked shirt with her black jeans so that he wouldn't miss it.

"Neither," she answered advancing into the room, feeling Duncan's strength supporting her as he stayed one foot behind her. "We've been through a lot together, Boyd. I don't want us to end badly. I'm going home to Sweetcreek tomorrow and I want to say goodbye properly, with no ugliness between us."

Boyd considered the amber liquid in his glass. "That's good of you, Jane . . . I mean, Harley. You've practically been a daughter to me. I'd hate to part as enemies."

"Thank you," Harley said, making herself walk closer to him even though she was afraid to smell him, to feel the taut energy of his compact body, to touch him. "I was wondering if I could have one of your famous gold pens. You know, as sort of a keepsake, a memento of our time together and all the contracts you've signed on my behalf."

"Sure," he said, his steel gray eyes burning a hole into her pendant as he reached into an inside coat pocket and pulled out a gold pen. He held it out to her, then pulled it back when she reached for it. "How about a trade?" he said, his tongue darting out nervously over dry lips.

"A trade?"

"Keepsake for keepsake."

"Sure, Boyd. Anything you want."

"Well, whenever I think of you, I always see you wearing that pendant. How about giving me that?"

"My pendant?" Harley said doubtfully, though eagerness was singing in her breast. "I don't know, Boyd. It means a lot to me."

"You bought it when you signed with me; it only makes sense to give it away now that we've . . . parted company."

"You're right," Harley said, slipping the pendant over her head and holding it out to him. "Take it with my blessing."

She saw what an effort it was for him not to snatch it from her fingers. But he held himself back. He gave her the pen; he took the pendant. It was all very civilized.

His thumb stroked feverishly across the back of the gold note.

"I hope your future brings you everything you deserve, Boyd," she said quietly.

"Thank you . . . Harley. Keep in touch," he said.

"Sure."

Somehow she made it back out of the suite. Duncan held her hand, his strength infusing her as they stepped onto the elevator.

"How does revenge feel?" he asked.

"Awful," she whispered.

"I think Agent Sullivan is right," he said, giving her a reassuring squeeze as the elevator doors closed. "You won't have to testify against Boyd in court. The Feds will play him off against Maurizio. He's bound to make a formal confession."

"It doesn't matter. He really was like a father to me, Duncan."

She hadn't expected to cry. But then, she had never been

betrayed in her life . . . until now. Until Boyd. It was the ugliest feeling in the world. Duncan wrapped her in his arms and held her, absorbing her pain as she had done for him this morning.

The elevator doors slid open. They stepped into the small, elegant Ritz-Carlton lobby, and Duncan's cellular phone rang. He pulled it from his pocket. "Hello." He listened for a moment and then hung up, his face expressionless. "Brandon's on his way. We've got to get out of here."

She raised her free hand and brushed his cheek. "Duncan, I'm so sorry."

His smile was forced. "It's all right, Harley."

They took a cab back to the Sentinel Building. Neither of them felt like talking. To get Boyd out of her life by firing him was one thing; to know he'd probably be spending the rest of his life in a federal penitentiary was a whole other ball of wax. It felt horribly permanent. She stared at her life and saw a huge chasm where Boyd had been. She glanced up at Duncan, wondering what he saw. But his stony expression revealed nothing.

It was a shock when he refused to go back to the penthouse with her.

"I have to finish my report on this case," he informed her as they stood beneath the domed gold-leaf ceiling of the Sentinel Building's lobby.

"But it's after six," Harley argued. "Surely the report can wait until tomorrow. You need a break."

"It can't wait until tomorrow. Your part of the case isn't closed until I write the final report, and I want this case closed. It shouldn't take more than two hours. I'll take my break then. We'll have dinner. Send out for whatever you like."

Harley stared up at him, trying to understand this wall that had slammed down between them. "What's going on, Duncan?"

"Nothing," he replied, stepping into the express elevator.

"I'm just doing my job. You know, the one I'm so passionate about."

The doors closed on him and he was gone.

Slowly she turned to the penthouse elevator and the uniformed guard standing beside it.

"Evening, Miss Miller."

"Hi, John," Harley responded, though she barely saw him and wasn't even really conscious of stepping onto the elevator. Duncan was shutting her out when he needed her most, and she didn't know why. Brandon was walking into a noose tonight and that had to be like acid burning Duncan's soul. Why wasn't he letting her give him the comfort he needed? Why was he making the pain worse by fending her off?

"Why are you doing this?" she demanded hours later as Duncan rose from a dinner neither of them had eaten and shrugged back into his dark blue jacket.

"Because I have to," he replied.

She stood before him, holding him, pleading with her whole body. "You don't have to put yourself through so much misery. The FBI will handle Brandon and Maurizio, you don't have to be there."

"He's my brother, Harley," Duncan said, gently breaking free of her arms. "I have to see him do this thing myself or I'll never really believe it. Besides, I promised Giscard I'd personally take the diamonds in hand and make sure Louis and Desmond get them to the Bartlett Museum safely."

"Then at least let me come with you."

"No."

"Duncan, don't make yourself walk through this alone. Please."

"I won't be alone, I'll be with Agent Sullivan."

"You know what I mean!" Harley said, the anger a sudden frenzy in her breast. He was locking her out. He was deliberately locking her out of his life.

"I'll be fine."

"You'll be in hell. Duncan, let me help."

"I said no," he retorted. He even started to walk toward the front door.

Harley swore virulently and at length, which got his attention. "What the hell is this?" she finally demanded. "Latent macho tendencies rearing their ugly head? You don't think real men lean on the women in their lives now and then?"

"Not at all. I just choose not to lean on something that won't be around tomorrow."

"Yes, I will."

"I was speaking metaphorically."

"Dammit, Duncan, let me in!"

"This is a family matter, Princess," he said in a cold, irritated voice, "and I intend to keep it strictly within the family."

She felt as if he had just slapped her. She lost her breath for a moment from the shock of it. "And what am I?" she demanded in a low, urgent voice.

He turned, but didn't quite look at her. "My current lover. There's a difference. But you know that, Princess."

She forced herself to fend off the pain. She forced herself to think logically, reasonably. "You have never deliberately hurt another person in your life, Duncan Lang. Why are you doing this to me now?"

He looked at her then, dark eyes bleak. "Because I have to."

He walked out the front door, closing it quietly behind him.

The cab dropped Duncan in front of his parents' immaculate five-story red brick town house. He stared up at it thinking that it was ironic, really. All he had ever wanted from his parents was love and respect. They had never given them to him, and now he was about to ensure that they never would. He was about to pull their world down around their ears and he hated himself for that, because he knew what it felt like and he would visit that pain on no one.

He walked up the brick pathway and knocked on the front door. His father had the locks changed every six months. When Duncan had left for prep school at the age of fourteen, Colby had stopped giving him a key to the house. He'd been knocking ever since.

Johnson opened the door and greeted him with austere surprise. The butler's inference was clear: behold the Prodigal Son come twice to his parents' door in only a week. The Apocalypse must be close at hand.

"I realize this is Tuesday night, Johnson," Duncan said as he walked into the checkerboard-tiled reception hall, "but I believe my parents are here nonetheless."

"They are, Master Duncan," the butler replied in his cool English accent.

"In the library?"

"Yes, sir."

"I'll announce myself," Duncan said, starting up the stairs. He liked the reassuring feel of the smooth mahogany handrail against the palm of his hand. It almost allayed the chill that pervaded the house and seeped through his jacket and his shirt, raising goosebumps on his arms.

Harley, he thought with sudden agony and then pushed her image from his mind with ruthless force. He had reached the third floor. He walked slowly down the landing to the library doors.

He entered the rose and white room quietly, without his usual flourish. There was nothing to defy or celebrate tonight. He walked across the oak parquet floor to the couple seated opposite each other on matching neo-Federal chairs. Elise Lang wore a rose peignoir. Colby wore a paisley silk dressing gown. Both were reading and oblivious to him. He had never wanted to maintain that status quo so much in his life.

"Good evening, Mother. Good evening, Father," Duncan said.

They looked up from their respective books, his mother's expression one of surprise, his father's expression one of loathing.

"You're half dressed, Duncan," Colby sneered. "Where's the habitual woman on your arm?"

"I felt this should be a private matter between us," Duncan calmly replied. "I've solved the Giscard diamond robbery, Father."

Colby stared up at him in disbelief.

"You were right," Duncan said, walking over to the cream-colored armoire and opening the top doors to reveal a large-screen TV and VCR, "it *was* an inside job. You just picked the wrong son for the thief."

Shock shimmered behind him.

"Duncan Lang, I will not have you stand there and slander your brother!" Elise Lang declared in a frigid, shaking voice.

"I understand, Mother," Duncan replied, pushing the videocassette into the VCR. "That's why I thought it best that Brandon explain things himself."

Both Colby and Elise Lang began protesting and berating him at once. Then the tape began to play and they saw their eldest son shake hands with Angelo Maurizio. Their sudden silence made the bile rise in Duncan's throat. How in God's name was he supposed to survive this? He stepped to the side of the white video cabinet and watched, not the tape, but his parents. He saw their disbelief, their conviction that this must be some awful fabrication. He understood. He'd felt like a victim of *The Twilight Zone* himself as he had watched his brother remove a contact lens case from his pocket, open it, and drop the two computer chips into Angelo Maurizio's hand.

"Delivery as promised," Brandon said.

"If a little late and on the wrong coast," Maurizio said as he studied the chips. He sat sleek and regal behind a huge mahogany desk, while his golden brother stood before him like a serf.

"Look," Brandon said, "I can't help it if Boyd Monroe screwed this deal up. I told you I'd bring you the chips and I have. Does this cover the eight hundred grand I owe you or not?"

"Of course it does," Maurizio said smoothly. "A deal is a deal, after all."

"Good. Then here's a little something on account."

Brandon pulled a velvet pouch from the pocket of his Armani suit and poured the Giscard diamonds into Angelo Maurizio's hands. "They're valued at one million dollars," he said. "You can have any expert you want authenticate them. You'll see I'm telling you the truth."

"They are magnificent," Angelo agreed, holding up one of the largest to examine it with honest appreciation. "These, I take it, are the Giscard diamonds which disappeared on their way to the Bartlett Museum last week?"

"You don't have a problem receiving a rival's goods, I hope?" Brandon said.

"Not at all," Angelo expansively replied. "It is a pleasure to hold something of such value to Armand Giscard. Tell me, how did you do it? The police and Giscard's own men are certain that your brother stole them."

Brandon shrugged. "That's how I planned it. Duncan's past made him the most likely suspect. It was easy to pin the job on him. I used an old magician's trick to make it seem like the diamonds had disappeared when, in fact, they were hidden in a secret compartment in the courier's briefcase all the time. I figured everyone would panic when the briefcase was opened and the diamonds weren't there, and they did. It only took a second to empty the secret compartment's stash into my pocket."

"You are an impressive young man, Mr. Lang," Angelo murmured from beneath lowered eyes. "I look forward to continuing our mutually beneficial association."

Brandon grinned like a kid on Christmas morning. "You'll

tell your bookies I can start placing my bets with them again?"

Maurizio smiled. "I'll tell them you've got a million-dollar limit. They should welcome you with open arms."

Duncan stopped the tape and hit the rewind button. The horror on his parents' faces had turned to numb acceptance. Denial, for once, would avail them nothing. He stood before them, hands clasped tightly behind his back. Quietly, he began explaining the whole convoluted Boyd-Brandon scheme, sparing his brother nothing. "This is only part of the surveillance tape the FBI made today," he concluded. "It will be used in court to convict Maurizio of a long list of crimes."

"Oh my God," Elise Lang croaked.

"In exchange for the evidence I had gathered on Monroe and the computer chips, as well as Brandon's testimony against Maurizio and Boyd Monroe, the FBI has agreed to grant Brandon immunity. Fortunately, he really was no more than Maurizio's glorified errand boy on a single job. The FBI has further agreed to tell the media that Brandon, at the solicitation of the FBI, had agreed to act as a double agent to finally get the evidence the Feds needed to put Maurizio away for life. They're taking Brandon's statement now."

"Oh my God," Elise whispered.

"It's okay, Mother. Brandon's going to come out of this looking like a hero." Duncan couldn't keep his mouth from twisting into a smile. "Why should this job be any different? I gave the diamonds to Giscard's henchmen and they, in turn, delivered them to the Bartlett Museum an hour ago. I've spoken with Giscard and he has spoken with the New York police. The cops have agreed to drop their investigation. I have arranged with Carmine Bellini, an . . . acquaintance of mine, to pay off Brandon's debt to the Maurizio family so we won't have that connection haunting us."

"You used Colangco funds without my authorization?" Colby erupted.

"No, I used my funds from Grandfather's trust."

"You don't seriously expect me to believe that you didn't run through your trust the day you turned twenty-five, do you?"

"Check the bank records, Father." Duncan forced himself to smile. "You'll see I'm actually a very good money manager."

Colby was silent a moment. "You'll be repaid, of course."

"No." Duncan forced himself to speak calmly, even pleasantly. "I don't want your money, Father, and I don't want to hurt Colangco by denuding its accounts. I think my money was well spent for the lesson learned. So," he pushed on, before Colby could start grandstanding, "only one question remains: what are we going to do about Brandon?"

"He's safe from the police and that awful mobster," Elise Lang said in a weak voice. "We don't have to *do* anything with Brandon. We may go on as we've always done."

"Wrong," Duncan said flatly. "Brandon is a compulsive gambler. He has a big problem that he refuses to acknowledge. Left to himself, he'll get in debt again and use one of Colangco's clients to dig himself back out again. He's a loose cannon. He's got to be plugged."

Elise hysterically berated him for a full five minutes, flying at Duncan like a mother hen protecting her prized chick. He had expected nothing less. Brandon was her Beloved Boy. She had never tried to hide her preference. Even after having the truth forced on her, even after accepting it, she could not tolerate anything that impugned her son's character.

"Are you willing to risk Colangco's reputation, even its very existence, on Brandon's ability to choose a winning basketball team, Father?" Duncan inquired as his mother burst into tears and retreated to her chair.

"No," Colby said, his voice cracking. He cleared his throat. "No," he said in a firmer voice. "Brandon will have to be sent away."

Elise rose like a towering Fury to lambast her husband for

betraying their son, for even thinking of tearing him from her arms.

Colby's hard gaze silenced her in mid-sentence. "It's got to be done, Elise, and it will be done at once. If Duncan hadn't stepped in, Brandon's actions could have destroyed Colangco and the Lang name. We might even have seen Brandon arrested, tried, and convicted. Think of the headlines, Elise. Think of the gossip."

Elise Lang sat down suddenly in her chair, white and trembling.

"He mustn't be given another chance to ruin us," Colby stated. He had aged ten years in the last few minutes. "He won't be given another chance. I'll send him off to Australia, ostensibly to open a branch office of the company. We'll give him an allowance. I'll have people watching him to make sure he doesn't get into any further trouble. In a year, we'll formally announce his departure from the firm. By then, no one will remember Maurizio or the Giscard diamonds. No one will think his removal from Colangco is at all suspicious."

"That's pretty much the plan I came up with," Duncan said.

Colby gave him a long, hard look. "It seems to me you've been pretty busy lately."

"It's been a full day."

"I may have . . . misjudged you."

"It's possible," Duncan conceded.

"But what will Brandon *do*?" Elise wailed.

"Maybe he'll finally become the internationally famous magician you wouldn't let him be," Duncan retorted. "He might even earn enough to keep his bookies' accounts current."

"I won't have you being hateful to Brandon!" Elise cried. "I won't."

"Sometimes the truth *is* hateful, Mother."

"I suppose," Colby said, unable to mask the loathing in

his pale blue eyes, "that you want to take over Brandon's position in the firm now."

"No," Duncan replied, surprising his father. Even now, he loved it when he could do that. "You will agree, I think, that I've pretty much rescued Colangco from disaster. I could always spill the beans to the press, of course, but unlike my brother, I find that I actually do believe in loyalty and honor. But that's not to say I don't deserve something in return for all my hard work and silence."

"What do you want?" Colby grimly demanded.

Absolution? Peace of mind? What do I want? His father had never asked him that before. "I want to head a new Colangco division devoted to criminal investigations," Duncan said calmly. "I want Emma Teng promoted to full investigator, made my partner, and fully and equitably compensated for her new position. I want a free hand in running the division, hiring and firing, and choosing what cases I take on. You can groom whoever you want to take Brandon's place, except, of course, that I must agree to your choice, and your selection understands up front that this is a salary-and-commission deal only, without hope of any kind of company ownership, because Colangco is *mine,* Father. *My* birthright, my future. Mine. I want you to change your will and the necessary Colangco paperwork so that I inherit the company upon your death or retirement."

"Is that all?"

Duncan met his father's deadly gaze. "That's all."

Colby's eyes faltered for a moment. Clearly, he had expected much more unreasonable and lengthy demands. "Very well, I agree. I'll make all the arrangements tomorrow after I . . . talk to Brandon." His cold expression crumbled for just a moment.

Duncan looked quickly away. He knew how devastating this was for his father. He didn't need to see it too. "I'll be around to sign whatever papers you need me to sign," he said. "Good night, Mother. Good night, Father."

He walked out of the library, and down the stairs, and out the front door of his parents' house. He made it to the sidewalk before his legs gave out. He sat down heavily on the curb, staring at the well-lit, quiet street. Life as he had known it had just come to an end.

CHAPTER FOURTEEN

*F*or the next few days, when Harley wasn't making music, she was making love with Duncan. She woke up in the morning to make love. Duncan went to work and she worked on her music. Duncan came to her on his lunch hour and they made love. Duncan went back to work and she went back to her music. After dinner they made love all night long.

Her days were almost perfect, except there was a quality in Duncan's lovemaking, as if he were savoring one last sip of wine before the bottle was empty. She didn't understand. His need for her was as voracious as hers for him. His satisfaction as deep and full as her own. And over that, and through it, and beneath it, was this feeling . . . almost of despair.

Like her pendant, he had a hidden compartment locked deep inside of him, locking her out. Ever since the night Duncan had told his parents the truth about Brandon, that hidden compartment had been lodged between them. She could not open it. She could not move it. He would not discuss it. And that was the greater worry. He would not talk to her, not about Brandon, not even small talk. No matter how hard she threw herself against those walls, they would not come down. He would drug her instead with his kisses and his hands and then take her to bed. But even in the throes of ecstasy, she wanted to cry out at the pain of this new exclusion. Even as he taught her worlds of pleasure she had not even fantasized existed, he would not let her heart touch him with the same depth, the same intimacy, as he touched her.

He gave all of himself to her and would not let her give everything in return. That tiny hidden door within him remained shut and locked and silent.

It frightened her and angered her and confused her all at the same time. He knew a secret, and it seemed to be about her, and he wasn't telling.

The only balm was the strong feeling of union that pervaded every moment they were together or apart. They were connected, she and Duncan, not merely physically, but on every level. His silence could not change that. And in that connection there was hope. In that connection there was trust and support that she felt even as she walked onto the small Surrealistic Pillow stage on Friday night more than a little scared, because she would be performing some new material. She looked out at the audience and saw among the crowd every single member of the Rockin' Robins. Whoa. No pressure there. Then she felt Duncan's gaze warming her skin. She looked into the audience and found him easily. He smiled at her with utter confidence. Then he winked.

Bless the man! She laughed and opened her set with "Nice Girls Don't." She could hear the Sweetcreek in her voice now. It was also coming through stronger and stronger with each new song she wrote. So she had been a little unsure of how this rock-and-roll crowd would react. They were her test audience, her musical guinea pigs. If she could pull off the new material with this audience, she might stand a chance with her old fans and whatever new ones were lurking out there in the wide wide world of music.

She threw in some of her favorite old rock songs, like Elvis's, "I Can't Help Falling in Love with You" and Carole King's "I Feel the Earth Move," because she loved them and she knew the audience did, too, and because she wanted to sing them to Duncan. She even dragged Mark on stage to sing the Marvin Gaye–Tammy Tyrell duet "Ain't No Mountain High Enough," flirting outrageously with him through the song and grinning when he flirted right back.

The audience went nuts and stayed nuts. Hmm. Maybe she *could* publicly shift musical gears and still maintain her career.

After her set, Mark and Susan and the rest of the Rockin' Robins crowded around the table she shared with Duncan, everyone talking at once, except for Duncan. He just sat back in his chair, silently watching them all, laughing at their jokes, and . . . glowing. There was no other word for it. His eyes met hers and she gasped, because she realized in that moment of connection that *he* was happy because *she* was fully immersed in her brave new world of new friends and new music and new ideas that had nothing to do with what Boyd had demanded from her or her mother wanted.

Tears filled her eyes for a moment and she hastily looked away. How many ways could she find to love this man? And how could she ever break through the new wall to convince him of her love without frightening him off?

On the cab ride back to the Colangco penthouse apartment that Friday night, his hands and his mouth were all over her, igniting a fever in her blood that burned all night long. So she sang Peggy Lee's "Fever" to him the next night at the Surrealistic Pillow, his gaze burning into her heart from thirty feet away. When they walked out of the club later that night, she found the Colangco limousine waiting for them. She understood why when, with the door closed behind them and the limo pulling away from the curb, Duncan grabbed her and took her on the back leather seat, the privacy screen between them and the driver shielding her cries and her writhing body as Duncan gave her no chance to think or speak or do anything but feel him in every inch of her body and her heart.

On Sunday night, she walked out of the Surrealistic Pillow higher than she'd ever been in nine years of performing on stage. It was she who grabbed Duncan in the back seat of the limo, her hands taking him with a swiftness that drew a strangled groan from his throat. It was she who pushed him down onto the leather seat and took him with all of the energy the club's audience had just pumped into her.

When the limo stopped in front of the Sentinel Building and the driver opened the back door, they stepped out onto the sidewalk looking like any other well-groomed couple enjoying a night on the town. Except, of course, that her ripped panties were shoved into Duncan's jacket pocket and he was holding that same jacket in front of him to keep from advertising to the passersby on the sidewalk that she had deliberately aroused him again just before the limo had pulled to a stop.

"You'll pay for this," he had warned as the driver opened the back door.

"I hope so," she had sunnily replied.

The moment the Sentinel's elevator doors closed behind them, he shoved her against the back wall of the elevator, his mouth sucking at her throat, his hands ripping open her sleeveless leather vest, buttons scattering on the floor. His hands roughly cupped her breasts for his mouth as he drank in one and then the other, Harley's hands clawing frantically at his back as they sped past the fifteenth floor.

His hands slid up under her short leather skirt. "Duncan," she pleaded, her heart shuddering in her breast. "Duncan!"

Dark, flaming eyes scorched her. "Payment in full, sweetheart." He grasped her naked flesh and suddenly lifted her up off her feet. Her gasp became a sob as he thrust into her, shock and pleasure melting her across his shoulders. He thrust again and she wrapped her legs around him, saying *yes* to this stark taking unlike any they had shared. He pressed her hard into the elevator wall, driving rhythmically into her, her naked breasts rubbing against his silk shirt, her teeth scoring his ear, his groans filling her as the elevator doors slid open.

They were alone. With Louis and Desmond back in France, there was no longer a need to post guards around the apartment.

Still buried deep within her hot flesh, Duncan carried Harley out of the elevator, impressing her further by managing to input the proper security code on the keypad and open the door, despite the obvious distractions. He carried her two feet into the apartment and got no farther. With one hand, Harley shoved the front door closed while her eager mouth claimed him, her tongue thrusting deep into his heat.

She was vaguely aware that he had crushed her against the entryway wall. His rapid thrusts blotted out every sensation but his rough possession, his fingers digging into her, her body opening to him more and more as her desire arced into the sun.

His skin through his shirt was burning her hands and her engorged nipples. His voice was guttural as he spoke wicked words of encouragement into her ear. His breath took on a staccato beat. He was coming and carrying her with him. Coming and burying himself deep inside her, as if he would never leave. Coming and shouting her name as she shattered in his arms.

He leaned against her for support, crushing her into the wall, his breathing as harsh as her own, his muscles as weak as hers as her legs slid helplessly down him, her feet meeting the floor.

"God, Duncan," she said at last, "where the *hell* is your bedroom?"

Chuckling, he took her to bed.

All of the ferocity seemed to have been burned out of him, but none of the fire. He made love to her for hours with a tenderness that pierced her soul as he brought her to one leisurely climax after another, different from any she had known. They built slowly, almost dreamily, their sudden violent conclusion easing away into another slow, steady buildup of pleasure that seemed to have no end. She began to drift in and out of consciousness, sharp pleasure rousing her, gentle hands soothing her once again. She felt his mouth pressing a gentle kiss to the palm of her hand before sleep finally claimed her.

She woke the next morning just as slowly. She could still feel the smile on her mouth. But she couldn't feel Duncan beside her.

She woke up with a vengeance, looking wildly around the room, and finding it empty.

"Duncan?" she called, afraid and not knowing why.

He walked into the bedroom through the living room door. He wore black jeans and a black T-shirt. He was barefoot. His black hair was askew. His black eyes were shuttered. "Awake so soon?" he asked.

He had stopped in the doorway. His face was taut and expressionless. A mask. He was not coming to her to touch her, to hold her, to kiss her good morning. Ice sheeted her skin. "What's wrong?" she whispered, holding the silver comforter against her breasts.

"It's been two weeks, Harley. Holiday's over."

She realized she was shaking. For a moment she couldn't breathe. "The holiday's over," she repeated. It must be some sort of code.

"Time for you to pack up and get on with your life," he said quietly.

"Oh," she said in a small voice. So this was why he'd been pushing her away these last few days. "I always knew there'd come a day when you got tired of me, I just didn't think it would be this soon." It was hard to make her jaws move properly for the words. "But then, I'm no Comtesse Pichaud. Or is it that we've just run out of variations on the theme and it's time for you to move on? No, don't answer that. It was stupid of me. You just don't want me anymore and that's all there is to it."

"Harley—"

"It's all right, I expected this," she said, dying inside. "I won't make a scene. I won't even make a fool of myself. I can't make you want me again if the connection is gone."

"Harley, will you shut up?" Duncan barked at her. She jumped a little in the bed, staring at him in confusion. He seemed so angry! "This has nothing to do with wanting you or not wanting you," he informed her. "It's simply that you planned a two-week holiday and the two weeks are up. Time for you to fly back to Los Angeles and make an album."

Her teeth felt as if she had just tried to bite through a rock. "You've decided this?"

"It was always your plan, Harley. I'm just helping you keep to your schedule."

Her gaze never leaving Duncan's masked face, Harley slid out of bed, picked up her green robe from the armchair in the nearby corner, and pulled it on. She was shaking like she had malaria. "I didn't know there was a schedule for us too."

"A summer fling is, by definition, short and sweet."

She felt as if he had just sucker punched her. "Is that what I am to you?"

"No. That's what I am to *you.*"

She blinked. Then she got mad. "And who the hell told you that?" she demanded.

"I'm a detective. I deduced. It's what I do."

"Well, you deduced wrong. How *dare* you walk around deciding what I feel and what I need? You act like God on high dictating what I will and will not do and I'm not having it, Duncan. I'm not!"

"Harley," he said in that maddeningly calm voice, "you

lived for nine long years without romance and adventure. You finally break free and what do you do? You take a lover. Your first. You start a new life and a new career. It doesn't take a very big stretch of the imagination to realize you're going to want new lovers in that new life."

"You know," Harley said, stalking toward him, "there are times when I really just want to belt you one."

"That's only because I'm right and you know it."

"I don't and you're not!" she yelled, hands clenched in fists at her sides. "Man, when you go off on a wrong tangent you really go whole hog. You are not and have never been a *fling,* Duncan Lang! You are my love. You are my other half. You are the man I want to sing to for the rest of my life. Don't you get it, you flaming moron? *I love you.*"

The mask slipped badly for a moment, but a quick breath put it firmly back in place. Still, that brief glimpse had told Harley everything. This was no by-the-book brush-off. He was in agony.

"Duncan," she said softly, her fingertips caressing the planes of his beautiful face, "how could you think I'd make love to you without loving you?"

He took a quick step back to escape her hand. "A first love affair is always highly emotionally charged," he stated. "The passion and the feelings are real, but they burn out, Harley. They burn out much too fast."

"You've had a lot of experience with affairs—first and otherwise—I know that, Duncan. But what we have is different. I'm not like those other women. I'm your kindred spirit."

His hand reached up, as if he would touch her. Then it suddenly dropped to his side. "And I'm just your first of many lovers."

She wanted to scream! "Look, I didn't come to you as an innocent. Being a virgin and being innocent aren't the same thing! I had lots of boyfriends in high school. I know what lust feels like and what infatuation feels like. I've had summer loves. Boyd may have scared off potential lovers, but I've met

hundreds of men in the last nine years and none of them—
none of them, Duncan—moved me or touched me or connected with me the way you do. None of them drew me the
way I was drawn to you the first momemt our eyes met. I
knew almost from the beginning that you are the love of my
life and that conviction has only grown stronger every day
since."

"Harley, I'm all wrong for you."

"Bullshit."

He seemed to be holding on to the wall between them
with his fingernails. "You need someone stable and secure,
someone you can lean on and trust, not a man who goes
through women like tissues and has never had a relationship
that lasted beyond a long weekend."

"Look, you blockhead, haven't you figured it out yet? You
partied your way through life in a desperate search for happiness. You don't need to do that anymore because you found
me and *I* make you happy. Emma says so. *I* say so."

"It doesn't matter." His hands were shaking. He put them
behind his back so she wouldn't see them. "Harley, you were
absolutely right when you ran away from Boyd and that
prison he and the Princess of Pop crammed you in. You were
absolutely right to fire Boyd, to break with him for good. And
you were absolutely right when you stepped onto that new
path you're on and started to chart your life's course for
yourself. You've had the merest sip of freedom and independence. Your heart and soul need more, you know that. I
know that. You need to start fresh on the world, with no one
to protect you or guide you or do anything that keeps you
from making your own decisions. Annie Maguire was right.
You need a lifetime of freedom and I don't want to get in
your way. That's why you're packing up and leaving me today."

For the first time, Harley began to fear that she wasn't
going to be able to talk him around, get him to see reason, to
stop this insanity. She turned in a quick circle and then

stopped and glared up at him. *Damn* the man! "You are, right at this very moment, keeping me from making my own decision about where I will live, how I will live, and with *whom* I will live. Will you, just for one damn moment, stop playing God long enough to hear that I love you, and to believe that I love you, and to accept that where I want to be while I embark on this new life of mine is at your side?"

He managed a crooked smile. "And how independent do you think you'd feel fending off my God complex day in and day out?"

She opened her mouth, and then closed it again.

"How can you fly free," he softly continued, "if you stay at my side?"

"Damn you," she said bitterly.

"That's already been done."

She stared up at him fully, deeply, and what she saw stole her breath away. That tiny locked compartment in his soul had cracked open. Fear was there and the lack of hope he had hidden from her for so long. He truly believed he couldn't have her in his life.

"You bastard!" she gasped. "You love me, don't you? *Don't you?*"

"Harley—"

"My God," she said in amazement, "all this time I thought that you couldn't love me, or you wouldn't love me, or I'd have to somehow find a way to trick you into staying with me one day at a time until we'd piled up a life together, and here you've loved me all along!"

"I never said—" he stiffly began.

"Oh yes you did," Harley said, glowing inside with the wonder of this discovery. "You've said it every time we made love and every time you touched me outside of this bedroom, and every time you looked at me. You've said it every time you gave me your support so I could take another risk. You're saying it now. Only a man who truly loved would send away the woman he loves for her own good."

"You deserve the chance to make your own life," he said helplessly. "You told me when we first met that the reason you took your holiday was to find out if you could make it in the real world all on your own. Well, it's time, Harley, for you to chart your new career, to date other men, to travel and perform and experience all of life, and prove to yourself that you *can* make it on your own."

Oh God, how many ways could she find to love the man? "I never imagined I could be filled with so much happiness and so much misery at the same time."

"Happiness?" he said, dumbfounded.

She smiled tenderly up at him, her fingers brushing his cheek. "Of course. Because you love me."

He was very still before her. "And misery?"

Her heart was pounding in her chest. She couldn't believe she was doing this. "Because you're right and I am going to pack up my bags and go out into the world to make my own life."

"Oh," he said.

Sadness welled up within her as she brushed a few black curls off his forehead. "You're not God, Duncan, but you are right. Well, mostly right. I guess I do need to prove some things to myself. I need to fully find my true voice and chart a new musical career. I need to make it living on my own in the world without Boyd's protection. And I need to prove to you that you really are the love of my life. How long is that going to take? How long do I have to stay away from you and live my life and love you before you believe that I love you?"

She saw it in his eyes. He didn't believe she'd come back once she'd flown away. "Six months," he said.

"Oh, give me a break. One month."

"Give *me* a break. You won't even have gotten your feet wet. Five months."

"Two."

"Four."

She considered that. She could get a lot accomplished in four months and just barely manage to survive without Duncan in her days. "Deal," she said, holding out her hand.

He gazed suspiciously at it a moment, and then slowly clasped it in his own. There it was again, that heady magnetic field that flowed between them whenever they touched. He tried to pull away, but she held him fast. "Now, the other half of this agreement," she said sternly, "is that when I walk up to you four long months from now, you are going to have to believe me when I tell you I love you, and you are going to have to do something about it."

"Whatever you say, Princess."

Harley sighed and released his hand. "You really are the most irritating, tenacious, bullheaded man I've ever met."

"That's undoubtedly one of the many reasons you love me."

"Uh-uh. Want me to tell you why I love you?"

"No!" he yelped, looking ludicrously frightened.

A low, silky laugh she had never heard before bubbled out of her throat. "Home truths are never easy, are they? That's okay, I'll keep quiet . . . for now. On one condition."

"And that is?" he demanded suspiciously.

"That right here and right now you *tell* me that you love me."

"Harley—"

"I need something to hold on to these next four months, Duncan."

She saw it in his eyes: if he said it out loud, it became real, and that would make the pain of goodbye that much worse. Because he didn't believe she was coming back.

"It's okay," she said softly, fingertips brushing against his hard mouth, "you don't have to say the words. I know you do. That's all that matters. I'll start packing."

"Harley—" His hand caught her arm as she turned toward the closet.

She looked back at him, puzzled by the wild light in his eyes. "Yes?"

"Harley, I do love you." He released her arm and began to walk stiff-backed toward the kitchen. "I'll make you some breakfast while you pack."

CHAPTER FIFTEEN

JANE MILLER ABDUCTED BY ALIENS!

PRINCESS OF POP IN TORRID AFFAIR WITH PRINCE OF WALES!

HARLEY JANE MILLER ADMITTED TO SANITORIUM—CASE HOPELESS, DOCTORS SAY.

HARLEY CARRYING GARTH BROOKS'S LOVE CHILD.

"I don't know why you hold on to these horrible gossip articles," Barbara Miller said as she sat with Harley on the living room floor of Harley's midtown apartment and helped her sort through her clipping file.

"Because they make me laugh," Harley said with a grin. "That last home pregnancy test *did* convince you I'm not carrying anybody's love child, didn't it?"

"Oh Harley," Barbara Miller said, blushing, "how could you even *think* I'd believe such a trashy story?"

"Mama, you called me at three A.M. last week in hysterics, sobbing that you were too young to become a grandmother."

"Well, I am."

"I know," Harley said with a grin as she leaned over and kissed her mother on the cheek. "And I'm just a wee bit too preoccupied right now to deal with diapers and midnight feedings."

"I do wish you'd slow down. You're always so *busy*. Concerts and benefits and recording sessions. And all those dozens of men you've been dating—"

"Not dozens, Mama," Harley murmured wickedly. "Only twenty-six . . . so far."

"But *why*, baby?" Barbara Miller demanded. "You were never this wild back home in Sweetcreek."

"Well," Harley said, trying to hide her grin, "I had a point to make."

"To *whom*? Nymphomaniacs Anonymous?"

Harley burst out laughing just as Annie Maguire—now her official Personal Assistant—walked into the room, wireless phone in hand.

"Carol Fielding's on the line," she announced. "She's got David Letterman's booking agent on hold. Travis Garnett had to cancel out of today's show—he's just been diagnosed with strep. Want to take his place?"

"Sure," Harley readily replied. "Dave's cool. He likes the new me."

"That means you'll have to be at the Ed Sullivan Theater in less than three hours," Annie warned.

"No problem. Mama and I can postpone the Circle Line cruise around Manhattan to another day, can't we, Mama?"

"Of course we can, baby," Barbara Miller replied.

"Thanks," Harley said with a fond smile. She looked back up at Annie. "Start scheduling."

"Right," said Annie as she walked back into her office, phone glued to her ear.

"Your secretary is such an *efficient* woman," Barbara Miller said uneasily.

"Assistant, Mama, not secretary, and yes she is."

"All these new people in your life," Mrs. Miller fretted. "Carol Fielding is your . . . agent?"

"Right. And Dale Hampton is my new manager, and Iris McCraig is my new publicist."

"I'll never get them all straight."

"It's okay, Mama," Harley said, hugging her. "I'm the only one who has to."

"Do you *really* know David Letterman?"

"Mama, I've been on his show three times in the last four months. Of course I know him. The man has adored me ever since I sat on his desk and sang 'Redneck Blues' on his show. Haven't you been watching?"

"Of course I've been watching," Barbara Miller retorted. "It's just that you seem so casual about it, that's all."

"He's just someone with a job, making a buck, like me."

"I'll bet he doesn't work half as hard as you, though. *No one* works as hard as you do. I'm worried, baby. I'll swear you haven't slept more than four hours a night in the week I've been here."

"Now, Mama—" Harley had tried gallons of hot cocoa, dozens of relaxation tapes, and working herself to exhaustion. Nothing helped. Her head hit the pillow and there was Duncan in her thoughts, in her heart, her body remembering the feel of every inch of him, her arms craving him, her mouth aching for his kiss as she lay alone and sleepless.

"And it was the same," Barbara Miller persisted, "the last time I visited too. You remember, when I came for that Chinese wedding in September."

"I remember, Mama, and I'm fine."

She had been a bridesmaid at Emma's huge September wedding. She had sung at her wedding. She had tried not to look for Duncan, tried not to feel his gaze occasionally flick across her skin, tried not to let her eyes meet his. Apparently, he'd been trying too. Their gazes never quite met. They never stood closer than fifteen feet from each other. They never spoke, not a word, not even hello.

She and her mother continued sorting through all of the newspaper and magazine stories about her life these last four months. Somehow, though, the substance of her days was missing. She had known such joy as she had finally, fully, spread her wings and soared into freedom and independence and personal responsibility. She had known so much pain as she went to bed night after night alone. She had never felt such exhilaration as when she began performing as herself, as Harley Jane Miller, singing the new music that was herself and having her audiences receive it, enjoy it, and sing it back to her with applause. She had never felt such sharp grief as when she looked out into her audience night after night and failed to find a pair of black eyes warmly smiling back at her.

And even though a week didn't go by that Harley's face wasn't plastered on some newspaper or magazine's front page, she had gone out into Manhattan by herself to window-shop down Madison Avenue or to stroll through Central Park or to wander through a record store. She had gone out without disguise, as herself, telltale strawberry blond hair and blue eyes and all, and she found that Boyd had been wrong about something else. She wasn't mobbed. Oh sure, people came up to her, some even asked for autographs. But most of them just wanted to tell her how much they enjoyed her music, and that was lovely. It angered her that Boyd had denied her such pleasure for so long.

It angered her that he had denied her a life for so long.

Well, she had her life now, with a vengeance. She had done everything she had dreamed about and everything she was supposed to do. But it wasn't enough.

And it was finally time to do something about that.

"Mama," she said slowly, "there's someone I want you to meet."

•   •   •

"Package just arrived for you, partner."

Duncan looked up from the report on the Kramer arson case as Emma placed a large box on his desk. "Where's Diane?"

"Your assistant is currently browbeating Interpol into giving up what it has on Hans Hubert for the Dietrich case."

"So what is this?" he demanded, jabbing a finger at the box wrapped in birthday paper.

"You want my personal opinion?"

Duncan warily regarded his partner. "Give me your best shot."

"Elementary, my dear Holmes. It's a time bomb," she announced and then sauntered out of his sunlit corner office, closing the door behind her.

Duncan opened the box, looked inside, and heartily agreed with her assessment. Gingerly, as if it might explode at any moment, he lifted a huge scrapbook out from its cocoon of red tissue paper. On the cover had been pasted a picture of a huge birthday cake, candles blazing. Terrific. A gag gift. Just what he needed on his thirtieth birthday. He turned to the first page of the scrapbook. JANE MILLER IN MIDNIGHT TRYST WITH ROCK STAR screamed the headline. Duncan groaned aloud. He knew the story by heart.

Slowly flipping through the pages, he found he knew every story by heart. He knew the name of every man Harley had dated these last four months. Twenty-six men by his last count, all of them rich, all of them successful in their chosen fields, all of them good looking. He hated all of them. He knew what clubs they had danced at, what premieres they had attended, what restaurants they had dined at. He knew the men's faces, and ages, and fortunes. He knew what they had told reporters about Harley: how funny she was, what a great kisser she was, how she liked taking them on midnight drives out into the country, her foot pressed against the accelerator as they raced beneath the stars.

She had taken to lovers like a hungry bear just coming out of hibernation takes to salmon. Duncan hated it when he was right.

He also knew all the stories tracking the 180-degree turn she'd made in her career. He had memorized the profiles of her new management team. He had already worn through his CDs of her two newest albums: *No Guarantees,* the live recording of a benefit concert for the Breast Cancer Foundation at Bryant Park she had used to finish out her Sony contract, and *This Is Dedicated to the One I Love* from her new record company—Lyon Records—with the Rockin' Robins providing backup on the title cut. Two albums in four months. He didn't care if both albums continued to sit at the top of the *Billboard* charts. The woman was insane.

His hand faltered when he came to the page with Emma's wedding program pasted on it. Knowing Harley was in the same temple and then the same ballroom with him had been agony. Hearing her sassy voice serenading the newly married couple had been excruciating. Knowing that he could gaze at her fully, and dared not; knowing that he could touch her, and would not; knowing that he could say something, anything, and she would answer and he would hear that sweet Oklahoma twang again, had all been more than his heart could bear.

He had driven to Atlantic City that very night and gotten roaring drunk and stayed roaring drunk the entire weekend he was there.

It hadn't helped.

Nothing had helped these last four months. He had buried himself in his new job, working nights and weekends at Colangco and loving it. But in the end, he always went home to his dark Chelsea flat and lay down in his empty bed and felt the stabbing absence of Harley in his life.

Knowing that she was living in Manhattan was maddening, because he found himself searching every face during his morning run through Chelsea and Greenwich Village, thinking he might catch a glimpse of her, perhaps in the Times Square crowd when he went to buy a theater ticket, or as he prowled through Central Park.

He was a fool, as Emma continually reminded him, and he was a fool to keep looking through this damn scrapbook. Whoever had made it and sent it to him was clearly into mental abuse. Maybe it was from one of the many women he had spurned in the last four months, or from one of the suspects he had recently helped put behind bars.

He turned to the last page. The shock of it stole his breath. "Happy Birthday!" blared the greeting in bright red ink, "How's the God complex coming along? I've loved you for nearly five months now. I've come a long way, baby. Ready to make good on our agreement?"

It was signed, in lavish, exuberant, handwriting, "The Princess Bride."

"Like it?"

Ashen, Duncan looked up to find Harley Jane Miller leaning against his closed office door. Her strawberry blond hair was a surprise, even after all the pictures he'd seen of her since she'd left him. Her turquoise blue eyes were wide and innocent. She was wearing That Red Dress.

Damn his heart for pounding wildly in his chest! He pointed an accusing finger. "You," he pronounced, "are a sadist."

"Nah, I'm just thorough," she said, pushing herself off the door and walking toward him. "I had a job to do and I wanted to do it well."

"*And* rub my nose in it."

"Duncan, Duncan, Duncan," she said with maddening calm as she insinuated herself on top of his desk, crossing one nearly naked leg over the other, "you're a brilliant detective. Your deductive reasoning is based on facts, a plethora of facts, in black and white, and in triplicate. You wanted proof of dating and traveling and performing and charting my new career and experiencing all of life all by myself, as we agreed upon four months ago, and here it is."

"I am fully aware of the wide swath you have cut through life *and* the eligible bachelors in this and several other towns."

"You kept tabs on me," she said with a little pout of her lower lip, "how sweet."

He could gladly have murdered her with his bare hands. "I told you once that you'd take other lovers. Good of you to prove me right," he said bitterly.

"Duncan," she said, sliding her right arm over his shoulder, "dating a man is not the same thing as having an affair."

"No?" he said coldly, forcing himself not to be petulant and knock her arm away.

"No. I give you my word of honor as a true daughter of Oklahoma that I didn't take one of those men to bed. Not one. I've been as celibate as you've been these last four months and, if you were in your right mind—and I'm kind of surprised at how glad I am that you're not—you'd know that."

"Oh," he said and for a moment couldn't think of anything else to say. "How do you know *I've* been celibate?"

"I know because you love me and you believe in faithfulness and honor."

"I do?"

"Yep. Besides, Emma told me."

She had startled him into a smile when he was depending on righteous anger to protect him from the gut-wrenching pleasure of seeing her, smelling her, hearing her again. "Why are you here?" he demanded. "And what in hell made you send me this . . . this monstrosity?"

Harley smiled. "Man, you just will not remove a single brick from that wall of yours, will you? Look, Duncan, don't you get it? I dedicated my last album to you. I wrote and recorded love songs to you. I told you four months ago that I would prove to you that I love you and want to spend the rest of my life with you and," she said, tapping the scrapbook, "I think I've gone out of my way to make good on that promise. I have given myself plenty of time to get over you," she said, slowly leaning toward him. "I have dated lots of other men, I even kissed some of them. I charted my new career and my new life all on my own," she said, her other arm sliding around his neck, "and now you're going to have to make good on our agreement and believe me when I tell you that I love you." Her lips were a breath from his. "And I do love you, Duncan Lang. Are you going to do anything about it?"

He stared into turquoise blue eyes and felt her love pour into him. He felt it down to his marrow. With a gasp, he *knew* that Harley Jane Miller loved him, that she was back, that she meant to stay, that he truly could have all of his dream for the taking. All he had to do was say . . .

"Yes!" as he claimed her lush mouth, his arms crushing her to him as he'd fantasized every night these last horrendous four months. Life poured back into his veins as she arched into him, feverishly returning his kiss, her tongue meeting his in an urgent dance that drove sanity right out of his brain.

He covered her face in kisses, his hands frantically roving over her delectable body to reassure himself that she really was here, in his arms, writhing in his embrace, loving him, dragging his mouth back to hers to sink her tongue deep into him, igniting something primal in his soul.

He tore his mouth from hers and drew in a harsh breath. "I'll tell you what I'm going to do about it," he growled. "I'm going to marry you, tonight, in Paris, whether you like it or not!"

Harley burst out laughing and the sunlight returned to his soul. "Oh, you are going to be *such* a trial," she said, shaking her head at him. "Loving me, planning my fantasy wedding, kissing me until my bones melt. I don't know how I'll stand it."

Grinning, he pulled her off his desk and onto his lap as he sat back down in his chair. "We've never discussed any of the practical particulars."

"Such as?" she asked nuzzling his ear.

He gasped. "Such as . . . um . . . children."

"Yes."

She was sucking at his earlobe. "How many?" he managed.

"Let's start in a couple of years with three and take it from there."

She shifted on his lap to pay similar attention to his other ear. "Okay," he said. "Where . . . Harley! . . . Where will we live?"

"Manhattan, of course."

"Y-Y-Your apartment or mine?"

She suddenly straddled him and began pressing kisses to his eyes, his cheeks. "Let's find something that's *ours*."

"Fine by me," he groaned.

"There is just one thing," she said breathlessly.

He looked into passion-lit blue eyes. *"Anything,"* he assured her.

She grinned at him and his heart just simply imploded with happiness. "You are going to have to meet my mother."

He grinned at her, feeling free and gloriously alive and in love and loving all of it. "Whatever it takes, Princess."

The office door banged open, completely failing to dislodge them.

"Dammit, Duncan, have you no understanding of decorum?"

They turned their heads at the same time to find Colby Lang glowering at them from the doorway.

"Not when your future daughter-in-law is sitting on my lap," Duncan replied.

For the first time in his life, Colby Lang was rendered speechless.

About the Author

MICHELLE MARTIN is the author of seven other novels. She lives and writes in Albuquerque, New Mexico.

If you enjoyed *Stolen Moments,*
be sure to watch for Michelle Martin's
next charmer of a romance,
set in Virginia's elegant horse-breeding country. . . .

"Michelle Martin writes fresh, funny, fast-paced
contemporary romance with a delicious hint of suspense."
—TERESA MEDEIROS, NATIONALLY BESTSELLING
AUTHOR OF *TOUCH OF ENCHANTMENT*

Available from Bantam Books in early summer 1998

DON'T MISS THESE FABULOUS
BANTAM WOMEN'S FICTION TITLES

DON'T MISS ANY OF THESE
EXTRAORDINARY BANTAM NOVELS

On Sale in December

THE PERFECT HUSBAND
by LISA GARDNER

A terrifying paperback debut about a woman who
put her husband behind bars, became his next target
when he broke out, and had to learn to fight back
to save her own life—this un-put-down-able
novel is a non-stop thrill ride!

____ 57680-1 $6.50/$8.99 in Canada

STARCATCHER
by PATRICIA POTTER

A powerful story in which war and
feuding families conspire to keep apart two lovers
who have been betrothed for twelve years.
But, like Romeo and Juliet, they are determined
to honor a love meant to be.

____ 57507-4 $5.99/$7.99 in Canada

Bantam Books by

Michelle Martin

Stolen Moments

____57649-6 $5.50/$7.50 Canada

Stolen Hearts

____57648-8 $5.50/$7.50 Canada

Ask for these books at your local bookstore or use this page to order.

Please send me the books I have checked above. I am enclosing $____ (add $2.50 to cover postage and handling). Send check or money order, no cash or C.O.D.'s, please.

Name _____

Address _____

City/State/Zip _____

Send order to: Bantam Books, Dept. FN 65, 2451 S. Wolf Rd., Des Plaines, IL 60018
Allow four to six weeks for delivery.

Prices and availability subject to change without notice.   FN 65 12/97